T0197297

LIEGEMEN

LIEGEMEN

K. W. GARSON

LIEGEMEN

iUniverse books may be ordered through booksellers or by contacting:

iUniverse
1663 Liberty Drive
Bloomington, IN 47403
www.iuniverse.com
1-800-Authors (1-800-288-4677)

ISBN: 978-1-5320-5922-3 (sc)
ISBN: 978-1-5320-5923-0 (e)

Print information available on the last page.

iUniverse rev. date: 01/23/2019

To my beloved, my wife and friend

Jeanette …

She doesn't nag,
She doesn't scold,
She's the woman with whom
I want to grow old.

ACKNOWLEDGMENTS

To the Teachers Who Took an Interest…

Paul Jorett

Sharon Wagner

Art Jacobs

&

… to Robert Rabinowitz for his insights

… and to Lenny Gerwitz for Great Music

PREFACE

The evil deeds related here,
By little boys are often done;
And little girls, too, I fear,
Love mischief even more than fun.

But be assured, my little friends,
That those who follow evil ways
Will find that sin in sorrow ends,
And makes us wretched all our days.

Let fun and frolic be your aim, —
Laugh, romp, and sing, while you're
at play;
But evil deeds and wickedness,
Oh, children! put them far away.

—from *Evil Deeds and Evil Consequences*

1

Tom D'Arcangelo paused outside *Ristorante Catania,* under its dim green, white, and red neon sign, made slightly brighter by Christmas lights. He looked into a brown and gray broth of winter sky, its snow sifting through the streetlights, then shut his eyes to feel the snowflakes on his face.

Snow always brought memories of his father. Even as that remembrance grew dimmer, Tom recalled the man's delight seeing snow, his smile when just hearing a wintry forecast. He called snowfall the 'ghost of the old man.'

That winter, the City of Brotherly Love's first snow fell on the Saturday before Christmas, and Tom thought once again of his father. But only for a few moments. Then the weight of the evening intruded.

His uncle, Vince Sarzano, had told Tom to join him for a holiday dinner. For most a holiday celebration given by one's employer is welcome. Office parties are opportunities to cut loose on the company dime, to overindulge in food and spirits, to inebriation or requited sex—to be given the liberty to make an ass of oneself or be lionized or subjected to workplace abuse the following week.

But Jimmy Cardinello was not one's customary employer. In the Philly news media he was referred to as 'reputed crime family head', 'suspected South Philly crime boss' or 'alleged organized crime kingpin'. To the police and the local bureau of the FBI, he was a head of racketeering, loan sharking, gambling, prostitution and narcotics.

Cardinello was also a legitimate owner of *Catania* as well as another upscale South Philly restaurant, six pizzerias, two taverns, three hoagie shops, a cheese shop, a men's clothing store, an automobile repair shop, a gentleman's club and a funeral parlor. He gave money to the local Catholic church, donated to South Philly food banks, and supported the athletic programs of the Archdiocesan schools. When someone in the neighborhood parish lost his or her job, had their utilities shut off or had otherwise fallen on hard times, Cardinello would make a few phone calls to the appropriate person or send money to alleviate the suffering.

In South Philadelphia Jimmy Cardinello was respected, a stalwart supporter of the community. To most he was a local hero. Many were willing to overlook his criminal activities.

It was for the criminal enterprise that Tom's uncle Vince was employed. And it was for him that Tom had been asked to join that night.

After Tom's father died, both his brother Matt and he, fifteen and seventeen years old—with the help of their uncle Vince—were hired to work at several of the Cardinello businesses. They ran errands, unloaded trucks, stocked shelves or cleaned up. When older, they made deliveries, bussed tables, did prep work in the kitchens, and eventually graduated to waiting on tables.

Two middle-aged couples exited the restaurant, one man holding its heavy wooden door for the others. Nat Cole's *Christmas Song* floated out through the restaurant's foyer. As they trudged off down the street, each couple arm-in-arm, another man and woman passed Tom and entered the restaurant. He could hear the husky, sultry greeting of buxom Gina Salvatore at the door and knew he would have to brave her brazen flirting. Unless she was away from the door showing someone else a table, there was no way to avoid the embarrassment. He waited for several minutes to savor the chill and sparkle of snow before entering.

"Look who it is! Hello, Gorgeous! Where *have* you been? Long time, no see! Long time, no hugs, Sweetheart!" She took ample arms and squeezed him. Tom put his arm around her waist in return and, leaning sideways, pecked her cheek.

"No copping a feel in public, Gina. You'll embarrass me," he pleaded. "I usually work on the nights you're not here. I miss the hugs, I do."

"Lisa, come here! Tommy, my dark angel, is here to light up my life. My guy! Don't he look fine? Umm-hmmm!" Gina swung him to her side with her arm around his waist. "Isn't Tommy D'Arcangelo the spitting image of George Clooney before he went gray, when he was in *ER*—the *young* George Clooney, I mean. Isn't he, Lisa? The young George, before he went and done all them crappy political movies."

Lisa nodded. She smiled with a knowing gleam in her eyes; she had worked with Gina for some time.

With a hand up to shield his face from Gina, Tom whispered to Lisa in a theatrical aside: "Tell her she's crazy." He gave an exaggerated roll of his eyes. "Lisa, tell Gina she's delusional, deranged."

Gina ignored him. She was on her roll. "Lisa, this man is taken, I'm told. But she doesn't have the ring yet, so there's still a chance for us—you're next in line after me, sugar!" she said to Lisa.

"The ring is on the way, Gina. This Christmas Santa could visit my lady," Tom said. This was a bold-face lie. He, wisely, had never gotten Carla a ring. He had begun to see the cracks in their relationship and was procrastinating breaking up until after the holidays. He'd say anything to call Gina off. On one slow night at the restaurant she had embraced him in the coat check room and whispered that he was 'making her panties wet'. Since then D'Arcangelo avoided being alone with her.

Gina thrust a mock pout. "Then I guess we'll have to wait until you get bored, Sweetie! Right, Lis'? In a few years they get tired of even the most beautiful babe and go out prowling. I know men." She winked at her co-worker.

"I'm offended at that stereotype of my gender," Tom huffed. "Darling, where is my Uncle Vince tonight, may I ask?"

She looked at him, eyes wide with surprise. "Meeting with the big boys tonight, are ya? They're in the Botticelli Room upstairs in the back."

He nodded. "Vince asked me to join them tonight."

"I know, he told me. Well, earlier he was on the third floor with Mr. Cardinello, but the others are in the Botticelli Room having dinner."

"Thanks, Sweetheart." Tom removed his overcoat, shook the now melted snowflakes from it and slung it over his arm. "What would I do without you?"

She smiled, puckered her lips and winked at him. "Honey, I'm tellin' ya, ya don't know what you're missing."

OUTSIDE THE BOTTICELLI ROOM door stood a young, fit man, dressed in a restaurant's busboy's white jacket, with his hands crossed at the waist. Tom noticed the coat was suitably large to allow a shoulder holster. The guard stepped forward to block Tom's way. Tom had seen him before but did not know him.

"I'm Tom D'Arcangelo. Vince Sarzano invited me."

The sentry nodded. "Yeah, I know, but I need to pat you down. You know how it is."

"Sure." Tom held up his arms and awaited the search. The sentry squeezed the overcoat over his arm, then ran his hands over his entire body, nodded and stepped aside.

Tom opened the door into a cloud of laughter, clattering glasses and cigar smoke. The room was a large banquet room that could seat ten times the number there. Tonight it was lit only in the center for a gathering of men who worked for his uncle. Two long tables were placed end-to-end in the middle of the room. Other tables disappeared into the darkness.

In the near darkness two men stood talking, their backs to the seated men. One had his arm around the other's shoulder, their heads disappearing into the shadows.

"Hey-y-y, it's Tommy D'Arcangelo! Vince was asking about you!" shouted Lou Spagnolo, who commanded the floor at his end of the table where he stood telling jokes. "I think you know everyone here? Do I need to make introductions?" He laughed.

Tom looked around at the seven men at the tables placed end to end to form one long table. The men held their glasses or cigars up to him and greetings erupted loudly, scattering clouds of tobacco and fumes of alcohol:

"*Bongiorno*, Tommy!"

"Welcome! 'Eyyy!"

"Tommy D, star centerfielder!"

"Hey, it's our ballhawk! All-Star! How ya doin'?"

"Hey, how's things?"

"Yeah, he knows us."

"Hey, Tommy, welcome to the show!"

Tom knew them all from one event or another, fund raisers, funerals, weddings, ball games. He realized how often they had been at the restaurants where he had worked, and he had heard uncle Vince talk about them so often that he felt he knew them as if they were friends and family.

"Good to see you, guys. This'll be a treat for me. I'm usually on the serving side of the restaurant, rather than eating with any of you," he said.

Lou coughed, then rasped out: "Yeah, what a fuckin' treat that is! I don't know what's worse, having to feed these guys or sitting with them and watching them eat. Hey, did those two cheap pricks"—he waved his hand at the Maranelli twins—"ever tip more than fifteen percent?"

"Don'tcha mean," someone chimed in, "did they ever leave a tip? Fuckin' cheap bastards!"

Phil and Chris Maranelli were the youngest of Vince's crew. Tom had played softball with them and knew them better than most of the others on the restaurant teams. They were great athletes who played flag football, softball, shot darts, and bowled on teams and leagues in South Philly. The twins grew up in New York and were the most sarcastic, and insulting people Tom had ever met. They enjoyed pummeling a person's ego, rendering the cutting remark into an art form.

"I'm real glad that fucking Tommy's not waiting on me tonight. The food will be here a lot sooner. I'd like to eat before morning," Chris Maranelli said.

"We might get our food while it's still warm," agreed his brother. "And this way we'll get a waiter who hasn't had his fingers in the snatch

5

of every waitress in the place. Hey, somebody smell his fingers. Do they smell like tuna?"

Ray Del Greco sat next to the twins. Ray was a former boxer who was quiet and reserved. After winning his first five pro bouts locally he was nicknamed "The Smokin' Italian". He retired undefeated after his mother had fainted at the sight of his battered blue-black face. He promised her never to fight again, although he still trained at the local gym. His mother said she'd live until Ray could no longer fight, just to keep her eyes on him. He once told D'Arcangelo: "Mom said she'd beat me to death if I ever fought again and I believe her."

On occasion D'Arcangelo had worked out with Ray at the local gym, getting boxing and conditioning tips. He was wise enough never to spar with Del Greco and glad Ray had never asked him.

Joe Difeo was the old guard. He had been with Jimmy Cardinello from the early days. A stub of a man, Joey had three children he doted on, even now that they were grown. His youngest was born with Down's Syndrome and still lived with him and his wife. Difeo was fiercely protective of his son and worried about him daily. It was understood that no one ever spoke of Donnie DiFeo as anything but a totally functioning normal person.

"Joey is a one-man crusade for Down Syndrome people," Vince had once told Tom. "Don't ever let him hear you call Donnie a retard!" After hearing that, Tom swore he saw the protective father continually surveying to see if anyone was looking askance at or talking about his Donnie.

Carmen Malzone was shaven and bullet-headed with a dark goatee. His forearms were immense, his biceps like thighs, his neck like a buffalo. He hoisted the heaviest weights in the gym and went every day except Sunday when, unless he was at work, he dutifully went to Mass at St. Madeleine's with his wife and three girls. Tom's family went to each girl's confirmation and Carmen always expressed the wish that one of them would enter the convent.

Domenic DiSanto was balding, with a thinly trimmed moustache, his build now a lump of butter, his clothes in need of a tailor. DiSanto paraded a perpetual sad and concerned look, like that of a seeing-eye dog. I know he lived alone with his sister, who didn't work—in fact, had never worked—and was supported by him. He and his brother had inherited DiSanto & Sons' funeral business when their father died. Dom helped out with the business but let his kid brother and wife run it almost entirely. On more than one occasion, his uncle Vince had told him with a smile the DiSanto crematory was useful for the Cardinello business.

Tom noted that Frankie Cannizarro, usually around for these occasions and never far from Uncle Vince's crew, was absent.

"Hey, Ray," he asked, "where's Frankie? I thought he'd be here for sure. I know he loves to eat."

"Oh, you haven't heard? He's in Italy. His father's dying."

"No, I hadn't. Sorry to hear it."

"When Frankie returns, we're going to have a service at St. Madeleine's for his old man," Ray said. "Jimmy wants to do the right thing by him, y'know."

UPSTAIRS ON THE TOP FLOOR Jimmy Cardinello had called a brief meeting with a few of his crew members. Although 'business' was to be discussed with his chiefs, this was Cardinello's annual holiday office party "for Vince and Lou and my boys." Most of his crew called him Boss, Mr. Cardinello, Mr. C. or, to his close friends, Jim. But for some reason the newspapers referred to him as Jimmy.

Cardinello did not look the part of the mobster in charge of a crime family. He resembled instead a partner in a prestigious accounting firm, dressing conservatively. To add to his dapper appearance, he had all of his shirts, pants, and suits fitted by a personal tailor, a bespectacled old Neapolitan named Ottavio who spoke little English. Jimmy had only recently replaced horn-rimmed glasses with a pair less obtrusive, rimless and modern. Jimmy Cardinello looked like a bottle of expensive Scotch.

Two hours earlier, three members of Sarzano's crew turned the meeting room inside-out and upside-down looking for bugging devices. Still, they spoke in code about the family enterprises that were criminal. 'Groceries' were drugs; 'video' was prostitution; 'sporting goods' was gambling; 'banking' covered loansharking. These were interspersed with talk of Cardinello's legitimate businesses.

"How's the sporting goods business? Everything okay there? No problems? Do we have enough football equipment?" Cardinello asked Vince.

"Good, very good there," he reported. "Everyone is okay. Nothing major. Playoffs are coming and the end of the football season brings in a lot more business."

"What's this I hear about that dentist? What's his name? He still owe us?"

"His name is Schonfeld. He seems to have left for places unknown. We can't find him."

"So Dr. Schonfeld is missing. How much does the prick owe us for his toothbrushes?"

Vince exhaled. "Thirty-two grand."

As Cardinello sipped and savored his coffee, his eyes widened. He wiped his mouth with a cloth napkin. "That's a lot of dough for dental supplies."

"When we find that kike, he'll need dental implants," Vince vowed.

Jimmy Cardinello put down his coffee. "Watch the ethnic slurs here. Lots of my friends—*our* friends—are Jewish. Ya know what I mean? Jake Rosenkranz, to name one. You don't like anyone calling Italians dagos or greaseballs. I want to extend the same respect to those we do business with." He smiled. "It's not like he's a some fuckin' moolignon, you understand."

Vince shrugged. "Sure, Boss. I know what you mean. I didn't mean anything by it, you know. I know a lot of good Jewish people. But hey, this guy's takin' off for parts unknown is giving me *agita*. And around Christmas and all."

"Did you send Frankie to inquire after him?"

"Frankie and I looked for him, but no fuckin' luck. Like I said, he's vanished."

Frankie Cannizarro, known to friends as "the Hammer," collected gambling debts not promptly paid. A former steelworker and iron rigger, he resembled a refrigerator. Frankie visited those who failed to pay.

"I come as a representative for Mr. Cardinello," he would explain. "I understand that you owe him some money. Please either pay me now or get that money to him as soon as possible."

Despite the nickname, Cannizarro had never used a hammer. He preferred brass knuckles, leather sap gloves or, his favorite, a blackjack. "A metal hammer? Fuckin' ridiculous. Too much blood and stuff," he said. "Goes right through the head. Used a rubber mallet once. On someone's knee."

If Frankie had to visit a second time, he broke a few fingers or facial bones. Losing gamblers then paid up, even if they had to sell their wife's jewelry, or they departed the Delaware Valley quickly. A third visit with payment not forthcoming and Frankie could show up with a waste removal crew.

In past collection duties Cannizarro had been stabbed, slashed, bludgeoned with a bat and crowbar, even shot, but had always gotten the job done. His prominent forehead had a jagged indentation on it and a scar crossed from his left cheek across his mouth to his lower right chin. His face alone gained the attention of his debtors. None of the South Philly crew had enough nerve to call him Frankenstein to his face, although everyone had at one time or other thought it.

"You and Frankie been to his home, I suppose? Is this dentist married?"

"Yeah, he is," replied Sarzano.

"Have you talked to his wife?"

"Yeah. We got some leads talking to her though."

"'Leads'? What are we? Fucking detectives? Did Frankie *talk* to her?"

Vince fought the urge to squirm. He didn't like to see a family brought into the collection of gambling debts of one member. The fewer people involved, the better, Sarzano reasoned.

"No, Jimmy. I thought that I'd try something a little less intimidating, you know what I mean? You know how you're always saying that we need to consider some new ways of doing business."

Vince didn't like getting Cannizarro involved with his crew's collection and used him only as a last resort. Cardinello shot Vince a steely look as he sipped his espresso, then smiled, nodded and laughed.

"Yeah, yeah, I did say that, didn't I? My words come back to haunt me." He shrugged and smiled. "So what did you do and what did you find out?"

"You know, Anthony's son, Tommy?"

"Anthony? Anthony who? Vince, I must know forty Anthony's, for chrissakes."

"My sister's husband, Anthony D'Arcangelo, the cabinetmaker, the one who played the mandolin?" said Vince, adding "—God rest his soul."

Anthony D'Arcangelo had died suddenly of a heart attack while shopping at the Italian market one Saturday morning. "My nephew and godson, Tommy."

Jimmy nodded. "Yeah, yeah, sure. Your nephew. His father played at my daughter's confirmation. He was an artist with that thing. What about his son? The football star of the Catholic League?"

Vince shook his head. "No, Tommy is his brother, Anthony's youngest. The older brother was the football player. Tommy's been doing some business for us for some time, making some money while he was going to college. He's a smart kid, smooth, too. He works at the restaurant part-time. You've seen him.

"Yeah, I know who you mean. Skinny kid. Likes books."

Vince didn't know how the Boss knew that, but just charged ahead.

"Tommy suggested that he go to the house and he posed as an insurance and claims adjuster for Schonfeld's dental practice—I told you that he's a smooth operator. He spoke to the wife and Tommy finds out that she has no idea where her husband is, and that she's fucking pissed off. She's divorcing the guy as we speak."

"Did you check his place of employment? He's a medical doctor, for chrissakes. They usually don't just vanish. If they get into trouble, they get a loan. They have equity. They can usually lay their hands on thirty grand, no sweat."

"Oh, yeah. I went to his office, and they seem pissed, too. They say that 'he will be away indefinitely.' Tommy D'Arcangelo chatted up the dental assistant over lunch and found out that he's vamoosed from the dental practice and they don't know where."

Jimmy Cardinello finished his espresso, placed the cup in its saucer and slid it away.

"So this dentist owes us thirty two grand, disappears from his job and wife, and we don't know where he is at the moment?"

Vince shrugged. "That's about it, Boss."

"This character could be in the islands or South America by now, for all we know. Maybe he intended to retire anyway, ditch his wife. Maybe she's in on it and will meet him later. Who knows? Tuscany is popular these days. Wouldn't that be fucking ironic? He's in Italy!"

"I thought of that. We are going to find out if he has a second house somewhere, Mexico, Florida, Venezuela, the islands. Maybe he's hiding out there."

Jimmy rubbed his chin. "Was this guy well off? I mean thirty grand is a lot of money, but not beyond what these guys make, ya know? Did he have some other debts, too? Find out more and get back to me about this fucker."

"Sure, Boss."

"Is this smooth Mr. D'Arcangelo downstairs with your crew?"

Vince nodded. "Yeah. He's having dinner with the fellas in the back room. Like usual, ya know."

"Tell him I'd like to see him—now. Also, have them bring some more coffee. Some chocolate biscotti up, will ya?"

ANDREA BOCELLI's *"AVE MARIA"* filled the dining room as Vince came downstairs. He met the waiter assigned on his way to the back room, gave him Jimmy's request for more coffee, then stuck his head in the room. Ten guys were drinking and smoking while listening to Phil Aiello's Niagara of jokes.

"What sex act do nine out of ten people like?" Phil asked the group. He gave them a few seconds for serious consideration, then barked: "A gang bang!"

Tom D'Arcangelo turned to Phil, jerked his head toward the two men standing in the dim light, and continued over the laughter. "Hey, Phil, who are the guys over there? Never seen them before.

Maranelli looked at them, then leaned close to Tom's ear. "That's Freddy Panzera up from Delaware and Joey Avellone from up around Scranton. They were talking to the Boss earlier. Guess they got somethin' goin' on with us now."

Phil continued after the laughter. "Guy walks into his bedroom. He's carrying a goat under his arm. His wife is in bed. The guy says 'I'm gonna fuck this pig!' The wife points at the goat and says 'That's no pig. That's a goat.' Then the guy says 'I was talking to the goat!'"

The room howls. Tom stood up to place his jacket on the back of the chair and saw the two men hunched together in the shadows. He tuned to the conversation on his left. Joey DiFeo and Dom DeSanto were discussing an enterprise. Tom listened to what they were saying while still facing Lou Spagnola's geyser of humor.

"Ya know how the mob is all the rage now? Ya know, *The Godfather*, *The Sopranos*, *Donnie Brasco*? I see these shirts with the Bada Bing logo. All that shit? I heard somebody on the radio call it 'Gangster Chic'," Joey said. "Well, I have an idea. We run off some tee shirts and bumper stickers, maybe some windshield things—?"

DeSanto nodded. "You mean decals? Hmm-hmm yeah?"

DiFeo continued. "We sell them down at the market. Maybe we can even get a website and sell them—how do they call it? On line on the internet? There's money to be made, I tell ya. We just put our heads together and come up with some catchy ideas. I thought of a few already."

"Yeah, like what?"

"How about tee shirts and shit that say 'What Would Don Corleone Do?' Ya like that?"

Dom nodded in consideration. "Could we do that? Don't we have to pay for rights to use that shit?"

"Fuck no! How about this? Bumper stickers with mob wisdom on it? Like one that has a gun on it and says: 'Three in the Head, You Know They're Dead.' Catchy, huh? I love it."

"Three? I thought it was two?" Dom deadpanned.

D'Arcangelo decided to direct his attention back to the joke-telling at the other end of the table. The room roared then turned as Vince, who had come striding into the room like a general into his war room. Uncle Vince even looked like a tank squadron commander: thick, manicured steel-gray hair, with eyes to match, square jaw, refrigerator shoulders, with an intense walk and bearing.

"Tommy, the Boss wants to see you upstairs."

The room went silent.

"Me?" Tom asked in surprise. He shot up from the table, slipped on his jacket, straightened his tie and buttoned it.

"Better you than me," Phil Maranelli said with a laugh.

His brother Chris chimed in: "I told Cardinello you're a shitty waiter. He's going to fire your lame ass."

"Watch your back, Tommy," Carmen Malzone warned. "Remember Luca Braza. Don't put your hand on his desk."

Laughter all around.

"Don't fuck this up, Tommy," Lou Spagnolo ordered, then broke out in a loud coughing laugh, grinning at the others as if he'd just delivered a joke's punch-line.

Vince stopped his nephew, placed his arm around him, and commanded the room.

"Everybody!" he announced. "Tommy is going to be joining us in the future."

"Hell, I told you he's a crappy waiter, Vince."

"Not as a waiter, asshole. I mean, he'll be joining the business as a partner. I'd like all of you to express your best wishes in his new endeavors. *Capische?*"

The smoky room got silent. Vince stood next to his nephew expectantly.

One by one, the men at the table stood and lined up to approach D'Arcangelo with a handshake and a welcoming hug. They filed around the table and back into their seats.

Before the drinking and eating began Spagnolo pointed to the ceiling. "Don't forget you have to kiss the Boss's ring, like the Pope."

The room erupted in laughter, then went back to chatting and drinking as Vince led his nephew upstairs.

As TOM ASCENDED the stairs he thought about the only real conversation he'd had with Jimmy Cardinello. They had on a few occasions nodded to each other and gave cursory salutations at the restaurants. But only on one occasion had he spoken to the big boss.

D'Arcangelo was having lunch with a girl who was in a college play with him. After rehearsal they had gone out the night before, had dinner and drinks and ended up at his house. There they had smoked grass and had wild sex, after which she had burst into sobs accompanied by showers of tears. He realized that night actresses were in the same category as dancers in neurotic traits. The next morning he took her to brunch at a local dining spot near his house.

Tom looked over from their table to see Jimmy Cardinello seated nearby. Tom saw two of his bodyguards sitting at an adjacent table, reading the newspapers. Cardinello had several library books piled on the table next to him, with one propped open as he waited for his breakfast. Cardinello looked over and recognized Tom. Tom didn't know if he should acknowledge him by going to his table or not, so he just waved. Jimmy smiled and nodded in return.

"Do you know that man?" Teresa, the play's Lady Macbeth asked.

"Uh huh, I do. He's a friend of the family."

"Looks like he likes to read. Is he a professor?" she asked.

Tom grinned at the idea. "Not really. He's in the local restaurant business. My uncle works for him."

"I see."

"He's helped my family out quite a bit. I work at his restaurants, waiting tables and doing odd jobs. He helped pay my way through college. My brother and I needed the money after our Dad died … when we were younger."

Teresa smiled in understanding. "Maybe you want to go over and say hello to him then? Go ahead if you need to. Don't let me stop you," she said.

"That's okay."

"Go ahead," she urged. "Be polite, Tommy."

"I'll wait until he's ready to leave," Tom said, then changed the subject. "Isn't the food here really good?"

After Tom's second coffee he excused himself to use the men's room. Jimmy Cardinello entered and took the adjacent urinal.

Jimmy unzipped his fly. "Hey, how's it going?"

Tom was surprised he spoke to him. "Okay, Mr. Cardinello. Good."

"Nice looking girl, kid. I approve."

"Thanks. Yeah, she is, isn't she? Smart, too."

Tom looked straight ahead at the tiled wall. "I see you have some books. What are you reading?"

"Catching up on the education I never got. Went to the library. Wonderful place, the public library. Reading *Moby Dick*. I read the classic comic book when I was a kid. Saw the movie with Gregory Peck. There was a remake of it on TV a week ago I liked—with that guy from *Star Trek*—so I decided to read it."

"It's tough going, as I remember."

"Yeah, Melville's a whole lot more cerebral than Hemingway. *The Old Man and the Sea* was a lot easier, ya know?"

"Mm-hmm," Tom agreed, hiding his surprise. *Jimmy Cardinello just used the word 'cerebral'. The reputed South Philly crime boss read Hemingway!*

They stood there listening to the draining of urine. Suddenly Jimmy laughed.

"Ever wonder how many times you have stood at one of these things? When you're in the restaurant business for as many years as I have been, you piss in one a lot. More than home."

Tom agreed. "I know I've been here often."

They zipped up and washed their hands at marble basins.

"Operas," Cardinello said.

"Operas?"

"The other books? They're on operas. One tells the stories of the operas, the other has some great pictures and stories about the singers."

"I didn't know you were an opera lover, Mr. Cardinello."

Jimmy dried his hands and then took out a comb and ran it through his thick, steely hair. "Let's say, I know my Italian operas ... they're the best. That German stuff is crap. I mean, Beethoven, Mozart, they're great musicians—don't get me wrong. For opera? Puccini, Verdi, Donizetti, they're the greats. Italian is the language of music for a fucking reason. Makes me proud to be Italian, ya know what I mean?"

"Uh-huh. Sure. You're preaching to the choir, Mr. Cardinello. Nice talking to you," Tom said and returned to his school friend.

Tom was always amused at the Italian-centric pride of many of his Italian friends. He didn't want to ask Cardinello how Benito Mussolini made him feel.

INSIDE THE ROOM Tom nodded, bowing slightly, to Jimmy, the way someone would greet His Eminence, the Archbishop.

"Hello, Mr. Cardinello. How ya doin'?"

Jimmy smiled. "Fine, Thomas, fine." He looked at Tom up and down and nodded.

He turned to Vince. "I like that, you know? Nice suit, nice tie, leather shoes, looks sharp. Everybody looks like they're going to a fuckin' gym these days. What do they call it? 'Dressing down'? Didn't I see two of your crew downstairs with fucking sweatsuits on? This is a nice place, for chrissakes, and it's near Christmas, ya know?"

"Yeah, Boss. You're right. I agree."

Vince had spoken to his crew about warm-up suit wearers. "The Boss said only niggers and people from fuckin' Kensington wear shit like you guys are wearing." But his talk had little effect on their behavior.

"Have a seat, Thomas."

"It's actually Tommaso, sir. My father gave us the Italian names. My brother is Matteo, too, instead of Mathew. But everyone calls me Tom or Tommy."

"I like that, Tommy. You know I liked your father. He had *style*— he was a craftsman as a cabinet maker and, man, could he play that mandolin! That brother of yours was a hell of a football player and athlete. Didn't he wrestle, too. What's he doing now?"

"Matt's a gunnery sergeant in the Marine Corps, sir. Looks like he's making a career of it. Served in Iraq—shot it out with ragheads in Fallujah—but he's in Afghanistan now."

"A goddam real patriot, eh? When he gets done putting his boots on those fucking maggots, he'll always have a job here—with us, with the business. You tell him that. He'll learn some real good skills in the service. You play football, like your brother?"

"No, sir. I played baseball. Ran cross-country. My brother got the muscles and most of the athletic ability in the family. He's built like our dad. I'm built like my mom—skinny, wiry."

MATT WAS INDEED the tougher of the D'Arcangelo boys, without any doubt. Any grit Tom had acquired he attributed to his brother. Like most brothers they had their share of tussles. But a sure sign he was tougher was *not* beating up his younger brother. At fifteen Matt once had his lip split and tooth loosened in a fight with a boy *four* years older. The next time Matt saw that high school senior he went right back at him. Matt returned home with a broken nose and black eye. What impressed Tom was that his brother never once cried.

Their mother, upset at his appearance, applied ice to his face.

"If you keep this up, you're gonna get killed," she predicted. "Who is this kid beating you up?"

At this moment their father came into the kitchen, saw the scene, but said nothing.

"Joey Mariani," Matt growled.

"You mean the grocery market guy's kid? That Mariani? He's a whole lot older than you."

"I'm gonna get bigger!" Matt warned.

Mom turned to my father. "Tony, would you say something to Mariani? Tell him to say something to his kid. I mean, look at your son's face, for pete's sake?"

Tom's father nodded. Mrs. D'Arcangelo scowled at her husband, disapproving of his level of enthusiasm.

"If you don't, I'll ask Vincent to say something to him."

She disapproved of her brother's ties to the Cardinello family and often said so, but she was not above asking a favor if it meant protecting her family.

"I'll say something to Mariani," Dad said. "I promise. But you—," he pointed a thick finger at Matt "—stay away from that kid before you need surgery."

"Either of you play that mandolin?"

Tom shook his head. "No, sir. Neither of us have Dad's musical ear, I guess."

"Tommaso, you look good. Real good. I hear that you're a smooth talker. Vince says you are. Are you?"

Tom shrugged and said nothing.

"Modest, eh? If Vince says you're smooth, I believe him."

Vince pointed with his fork at Tom. "He was in theater at his college, Jimmy, right? That improvisin' stuff actors do—helps him with the bullshit." Vince beamed at his nephew and godson.

"Really? In theater? Acting? You're an actor? What?"

"Yeah, at St. Joe's I was in the theater group. Did a little bit of acting."

His uncle stopped forking rum cake into his mouth. "He's being modest again. He was a fucking *star*! A fuckin' leading man."

Jimmy placed his elbows on the table and folded his hands over his coffee. "No shit? What were you in?"

"In my junior year and senior year I acted in two Shakespeare plays. I played Banquo in *Macbeth* and my big part, Iago in *Othello*. Later senior year I played Gus in a Pinter play, *The Dumb Waiter*—it's modern. Some other bit parts, too, early on in college."

Even though Jimmy read *Moby-Dick* and Hemingway, Tom doubted that he had ever heard of Harold Pinter and couldn't come near understanding the irony of Tom's part in that play.

"You get good reviews?"

Tom shrugged. "Yeah, okay reviews."

Vince interrupted. "My goddaughter showed me the school paper. It said he was fantastic. The kid's real modest. That acting helps him with the con and the bullshit, trust me. He probably gets a busload of pussy, too," Vince snickered. "Look at him—a good-looking guy like him, he's probably banging your waitresses every which way, right?"

Vince made a back of the fist pounding gesture toward the table. "Look at him. He looks like a young Robert Mitchum, don't he, Boss?"

Jimmy nodded, thrusting his lower lip out in agreement. "Lots of quim?" he asked.

"Nah. I got a steady girl. We've been dating for a couple years now. I like her a lot. She's really nice, smart, real sweet."

Jimmy pointed his fork at Tom. "That's good. So tell me, Leading Man, Pacino or DeNiro? Who d'ya like?"

Tom didn't have to ponder this question. He had thought of this before. "I'd have to pick Pacino. He's got greater range, I think—he's done Shakespeare, *Richard the III.*"

Vince spiked a forkful of cannoli and waved it around in the air. "I'm a Michael Corleone Pacino guy, but not a Serpico Pacino guy, you know what I mean?" He and Jimmy both laughed.

The door opened and a waiter brought in a tray of Sambuca and coffee. Jimmy changed the subject. "Your mother passed away not that long ago, eh? I knew your mother. She was a good woman. Cancer. Awful. Your father passed away when you were in high school, if I remember right—your mother a few years ago? Just you and your brother now. You still live in the old home around the corner?"

"Yeah, still there. Property values are going up. I remodeled a bit after Mom died. Helped get rid of some of the memories. Made it my own, you know? Half of it is my brother's anyway. He doesn't want to sell right yet. When he's home he stays here."

"Good idea. These days everybody wants to move to fuckin' Jersey! Nothin' wrong with South Philly. Except maybe for all the Spicks and Vietnamese."

"Well, if I were married, maybe I'd move. But not now. I like it here."

"I liked your mother. Great woman, great wife, great mother. Never forget your mother, Tommaso. After all these years I still place flowers on my mother's grave."

Cardinello placed his open hand over his heart. "Never, *never* ever forget your mother. You'd be a bad guy if you did."

Tom nodded. "I visit Mom's grave on her birthday, when she died, and holidays. She loved Christmas. I always put a wreath and some roses there for her. Thanks again for the flowers when she was in the hospital. You sent roses, her favorite flower. Damn, she loved roses … of all colors."

His mother had loved the flowers, but she never cared for Cardinello. "Too bad it came from *him*!" she had said, D'Arcangelo remembered, Cardinello's name spoken as if he were Satan. Tom had half expected her to spit and make the sign of the evil eye.

Cardinello stirred his coffee. "Good boy. Sure, you're welcome, Tommy."

The waiter finished serving the coffee and deserts and left.

"What do you think about this deadbeat dentist? He still around?"

Tom was taken aback. Cardinello was asking for his opinion on 'business' matters. Tom took a deep, thoughtful breath, then exhaled. "Not sure really. But he does have a house in Cape May. He could be hiding out there. It's worth a look. But he won't be there long. His wife is divorcing him and she wants her half."

"You sure of that?"

"Yeah. I shortstopped some of their mail. Lots of correspondence with a law firm, specializing in divorce cases. I talked to her … and her daughter, too. Said I was an insurance agent from his dental practice. I think the whole family's pissed at him. The wife thinks he's got some young poontang he's running off with."

Jimmy turned to Vince. "Let's resolve this matter. Find out if he's down the shore. Check his house there. Ask around."

"Shall I take Frankie with me?"

Cannizarro was away in Italy. Vince knew his absence would delay going to Jersey to find the dentist until after the New Year at least. Vince hoped to avoid the search until the New Year.

"No, no sense in doing that if the dentist's not there. Besides, Frankie's in Italy. Handle it yourself. Get Frankie involved later if our man is there. Take one of your crew, Spags or Ray … or take Tommaso here"—Jimmy smiled at him—"if he's not headed for Broadway. I want the money the doctor owes us. If he's not there, get back to me. Tommy, I need to talk to Vince in private, okay? Good talking to you."

"Sure, Mr. Cardinello." Tom stood up to leave the room.

"Tommy, call me Jimmy or Boss. All the others do. Okay?"

"Sure, Boss."

As soon as he said the word, he regretted the sound and wished he had chosen Jimmy. Tom buttoned his jacket and left the room.

Cardinello waved Vince close. "If we can't find this guy, maybe Frankie can visit the house and talk to his wife or daughter—just to scare them—and get this guy to pay us. Just to scare them. Know what I mean? Tell him I said no rough stuff with any of the women. Oh and, Vince, I think you should touch base with the other families in South Jersey, Gennaro and Carmone. Just to let them know what we're up to ahead of time? You know, so they don't think we're muscling in on their territory? It's a courtesy to those families, ya know what I mean?"

"Good idea, Boss. Shall I contact the Irish family, too?"

"Let me call them. I wanted to speak to Old Man Donnelley about something else anyway."

"How about those Russkis?" Vince added, knowing quite well how Jimmy Cardinello felt about them. The South Philly Italian families never spoke to the Russians.

"Fuck no. But let's not get in *their* way over there. You know, I'm sorry the Iron Curtain fell. They should all be deported back to that fuckin' hell-hole. They're some really crazy motherfuckers, and they're all over here now."

TOM REJOINED THE BANTER of Cardinello's crew downstairs. Dinner was being served but the Lou Spagnolo comedy improv continued as the waiter served him a plate of veal scallopini.

"Hey, what does a gynecologist and a pizza delivery boy have in common?"

"What, Lou?"

"You better tell me before my food gets here, Lou," said Chris Maranelli.

"Glad I'm not getting pizza," said Sugar Ray.

Lou delivered the punchline loudly: "They can both smell it, but they can't eat it!"

Lou stood up at the table. "Before we say grace, I got one last one: What should you do if your girlfriend starts smoking?"

There were some groans and laughs.

"What, Lou? Tell us."

"Use a lubricant!"

"Last one, Lou," someone begged. "I can't eat while I'm laughing."

"Where's he get this stuff?" someone asked.

"It's the vig from some *Saturday Night Live* writers that lost bets with him. They pay him with material."

"Lou, I read that 'bunga-bunga' one on the internet. But you *can* bring a joke to life," said Phil Maranelli.

"How does Lou remember them all? Fuck if I can."

Joe Difeo snorted. "He doesn't fill his head with his wife or kids' birthdays."

"One more, guys," Lou continued the routine. "Man comes home to find his wife sitting in the middle of the living room floor naked from the waist up. He sees she's rubbing her tits with newspapers. 'What're you doing? Why're you rubbing your tits with newspapers?' he asks her. 'I heard that rubbing one's breasts with papers will make 'em bigger— it's a lot cheaper than breast implants!' she replies. The husband thinks a moment then says: 'Why not use toilet paper? It's softer and it sure has worked on your ass!'"

The room erupted with gruff howls.

"Hey Lou, enough already! Somebody give him the hook, will ya? Our food's gonna get cold!" Ray del Greco yelled.

"Last one, guys! A young kid goes to his dad and asks him: 'Dad, can you tell me the difference between a pussy and a cunt?' The father replies: 'Sure, son.' He takes down a Playboy magazine and opens it to the centerfold. He takes a felt-tip pen and circles the Playmate's quim. 'That's this girl's pussy,' he tells his son.

'Okay, but where is the cunt?' the boy asks. The dad answers: 'It's everything *outside* the circle!'"

Laughter exploded again from the table. Spagnolo sat down and lit a cigar, chuckling between his teeth.

"Oh, I can't wait to tell my wife that one, Lou!" announced Malzone, who then turned to Del Greco and said *sotto voce*, "Val would fucking stab me if I did."

"Shit, my wife works in a pharmacy. If I told her that joke, I'd not be able to eat anything for fear of her poisoning me."

Dinner talk ranged from in-laws' eccentricities, to first Philly, then national, politics, to the psychology and physiology of the female, the best CSI programs, to a competition between the Maranelli twins on who could best add to the lexicon of slang for semen—"ball bisque, baby batter, spunk, nut butter, trouser gravy, man chowder, penis butter, XXX custard"—to true crime offerings on cable television, and finally to the Philly sports scene.

"The Phils will never have a great pitching staff in that fucking ballpark!"

"When the fuck are we ever gonna win a Super Bowl?"

"The Iggles will never win with that fuckin' *moolignon* at QB!"

"Are the Flyers ever going to get another goalie like Bernie Parent?"

"The Sixers? They fucking blow! College ball is so much better in this city. I'd rather watch high school ball for chrissakes."

"Jeezus, can't our teams win anything?"

Food was now flowing from the kitchen, and the banter settled down to family matters. Tom ate and listened—laughing occasionally—and spoke only if spoken to.

AFTER COFFEE AND DESSERT, the table was cleared and decks of cards and chips were pulled out. It was time for some serious poker-playing.

"Just give me your money now and you'll save some valuable time," Chris Maranelli suggested to all in the room.

"Fuck you, douchebag!" Carmen said. "Open a fresh deck. Let Dom look it over and cut it. Not Phil. You two twin fucks might be in cahoots. I read somewhere twins can read each other's minds. I've been suspicious of you fuckin' guys for some time now. You might have an advantage over us when we play cards."

"If he's reading his brother's mind, we got nothin' to fear," Joey said, pointing to the side of his head and giving his best facial expression of a mentally deficient person.

Tom D'Arcangelo had heard about these card games. They went until five or six in the morning, with several thousands of dollars crossing hands. He got up and started to say his goodbyes. He suspected he'd get shit from them and they didn't disappoint.

"Ain't you stayin', Tommy?" Chris Maranelli loved to fatten the pots with fresh blood. "I thought you were joining the team? Don't pussy out on us now."

Tom headed to get his coat. "Not tonight, thanks. Maybe some other time. These games are too rich for my blood. Plus, I'm a terrible card player. I'd be a lamb to the slaughter. Besides, I have to pick my girl up at school."

The other Maranelli heard the exchange as he opened a deck and oversaw the chips being used. "Is this faggot pussy-whipped or what? C'mon, kid! Play an hour or so," Phil urged.

"Sorry guys. Some other time. Not tonight, gentlemen," Tom said and smiled. "Merry Christmas."

As he was leaving the room, Tom heard Phil Maranelli yell out to the room: "Hey, how do you stop five spooks from raping a white girl? Throw 'em a basketball!"

Tom closed the door on the Cardinello crew's laughter. He shook his head at their unabashed bigotry and misogyny. For a moment he had that feeling of shame when one contributes to prejudice by failing to say anything against it.

DOWNSTAIRS TOM EVADED a parting shot of a hug and kiss and possible discomforting remark from Gina and made for the exit. Lisa stood at the door smiling at him.

"Gina's in the kitchen," she said, "so you're safe."

"Lisa sweetheart, would you tell Gina I said 'Merry Christmas' and to have a happy and safe holiday? And the same to you?"

At the door Tom pulled his gloves on and exited *Catania*. The steady snow had ceased. Only a few powdery wind-blown flakes circled streetlights. He stood there a moment and thought about the men he had just left. Tom knew that some of them had beaten or murdered someone. A few of them in that room had done terms in prison. Despite that, he liked them; he couldn't help it; they were just ordinary guys, with families, children, and worries like everyone else.

Then he thought of his mother and what she had said to him several times in the days leading up to her death: "I told your father; I told your brother, too. Now I'm telling you. If you get involved with those men, with what they do, you will regret it."

Tom looked up one final time at the night sky. It seemed darker now, starless, like crows' wings. The snowflakes had ceased falling and now only an icy wind razored his cheek.

2

D'ARCANGELO DROVE to the university library to pick up his girlfriend. Carla was researching her dissertation, its proposal due at the end of the next academic year, and typically, she was not procrastinating. He parked outside the library, called her cell phone. Whirling snowflakes crossed the light beyond an overhang of the large windows that ran from the ground to high ceiling, and he paced back and forth in their glow. So close to Christmas and finals completed, the library was empty of all but serious graduate students.

After a few minutes Carla exited the building hefting a backpack filled with books over one shoulder. As soon as Tom saw her he jumped into the car, reached over and pushed the car door open. She slung the backpack onto her lap and slammed the door as he turned the ignition.

"Bastard! Fucking creep!"

Surprised at her entrance, he laughed. Her uncharacteristic profanity amused him—she seldom spoke like that and disliked it when Tom did. "What'd I do now? Those librarians again?"

"No-o-o, not you, Sweetie. Some bastard in the library came up, sat beside me, put his arm around me and grabbed my tits—motherfucker! Let's get the fuck out of here."

"Grabbed your tits? He *touched* you? A fucking student? Who? What happened?"

"There are not a lot of people around, and I was gathering up things after you called to say you were here. This asshole walked by me once, then came back, sat next to me as I was getting up to leave, and started to fucking grab me."

"Did you report him? Tell security or something?"

"Of course. I yelled and shoved him away, grabbed my pencil and pointed it at him and broke away. He scared me *and* I was pissed! If he touched me again, FI was going to stab him in his fucking eye."

"What'd he do then?"

"He took off into the stacks."

Tom stopped the car, reversed into the parking spot and switched the ignition off. "Let's go look for this motherfucker."

"Tommy, let's forget about it, okay? We could spend hours looking for the guy and not find him. The library's enormous."

He looked at her in disbelief. "You're kidding?"

"No, Tommy. I'm just as pissed as you are, but it's not worth it."

He started the engine again. "Okay, but if you read he raped someone in the women's bathroom, think how you'll feel."

"You're right," Carla agreed. "But I reported it to security. It's their ballgame now. Hey, he could have raped someone before he got to me."

She always made excellent sense. It was something he had come to expect from her. Carla was in so many ways just more logical than he. Period. Was that a reason why he recently felt himself questioning his relationship with her? He didn't think so. He liked, indeed preferred, intelligent women, but he did feel a nagging doubt about moving to the next step with her. He had not yet figured it out. That was the one reason he had persisted with her for this his third holiday season. He adored her mother and father, in essence Carla's family. But he had never felt quite comfortable with her alone. He wasn't sure why, but it was difficult not to trust his gut. Tom knew it was better to come clean before he got in too far. And he wasn't that obtuse not to see a parallel with his breaking away from the Cardinello family.

"All right. But the next time you come here, I stake you out. If that prick shows up again, I beat the shit out of him."

"Tommy! What good would that do? You'll get caught. You'll end up with an arrest record. And then no law school. That perv will get caught sooner or later and put in jail. Leave it to for police."

She composed herself and kissed him on the cheek. "Thanks for picking me up. You know I don't mind taking the subway home."

"At this hour? After what you just told me? Not on your life. Why do you think I'm taking karate classes? The city's a fucking jungle. Remind me to carry my gun next time I'm up here in north Philly."

Tom started the ignition again. "Get much work done?"

"Yeah, I did. Really, things are coming together on this paper. I did all the research, got the books, copied all of the journal articles and downloaded the ones from the computer, and skimmed them.

"How about you? Have a good time with the boys?" She turned an intent, purposeful eye at him.

Tom pulled off into and down the street. "Yeah. I had the *rolantini melanzane.*"

Carla was silent. "Did you talk to your uncle Vince? About what we spoke about the other night?"

Oh shit. Here it comes, he thought. He was hoping to avoid any discussion about his uncle and the evening.

"No ... I didn't ... not tonight. Didn't really have an opportunity to talk alone, you know what I mean? It was a party, for chrissakes. But I *will*. Soon. I promise."

Carla looked away out the window, seeming to wish herself far away. They rode down 12th Street through north Philly into center city in silence. He was just about to remark: "Did you notice that it got really cold in here?" when Carla broke her icy silence.

"Look, Tom. You've been out of college for over a year now. Since we met you've told me you're going to get away from those guys, that you know that they do bad things, and you want no parts of them that you don't want to get any more involved with them. When is that going to happen, Tom? When am I going to hear that you broke this off. *When?*"

"Carla, look. I meant what I said. But this evening was not the night for this. Trust me on this, OK?"

They drove in silence for the remainder of the trip to her family's house in South Philly. Tom pulled up in front of her family's house and Carla whisked out without a word. He began to wish her goodnight, but his farewell was lost in the car door's slam. Carla crossed in front of the car and came around to the driver's window. He rolled it down.

"Tommy, listen to me. I do trust you. But you know me—behavior is more important than words. I hear what you've said, and I believe you will do it. But I need to see you follow up with action."

She took a 3x5 card out of her pocket and handed it to him. Tom flipped on the car's map light to read her handwriting.

"What's this? Dr. Howard Horowitz? A psychologist? Huh?"

"He's a clinical psychologist. He comes highly recommended. Two friends of mine said that he got them over their blocking on their Ph.D. work. He's in Philly, nearby in Mt. Airy. He might help you get over this block you have. I'd like you to talk with him."

"A *shrink*? Ahh-h-h, Jesus! Who am I, Woody fucking Allen? I didn't even know I was 'blocked', for chrissakes."

"Tommy, listen to me. He might help you sort things out. Please. Do it for me."

"Carla—," Tom began.

She cut him off. "Tom, listen to me. I said this before to you. I am going to say it just *one* more time and this will be the last time. I don't want to be a nag or to scold you. Remember when we watched *The Godfather*? At the end—when Diane Keaton saw Michael as the new don—I turned to say to you that I didn't want to be that Diane Keaton character? Do you remember that night?"

He nodded. "Sure, I remember that night."

Tom recalled Carla's drama had dampened the afterglow of a great film and had killed his buzz for the performance of Pacino and Coppola.

"I won't associate with those guys and with what they do. What they want in life is not what I want, Tommy. I don't think it's really what you want either. I meant it then; I mean it now. I can't be with someone who is like them."

"Carla—"

"Give Dr. Horowitz a call. Go see him. Get your head on straight." There was a knife edge to those final imperative statements.

She reached in the window of the car and stroked his cheek tenderly, demonstrably, and then leaned in and kissed him, and whispered: "Make a decision, Sweetie."

WAKING EARLY, TOM slipped into his running gear, knit cap, and heaviest sweat suit and, after some orange juice and a banana, hit the now frigid streets of South Philly. Monday was a three-mile day and he was glad to put his cardio workout behind him early in the morning. He ran the three miles quicker than usual, knowing he had a lot to do that day and raced home to shower and shave while coffee was brewing.

Tom returned home to see a message on his home phone. He punched the tape: it was Carla.

"Hi, Sweetie. Guess you're out running. I didn't mean to be bossy last night. But please, call Dr. Horowitz. It can be your Christmas gift to me, okay? As usual, I'll be making cookies with Mom for the next few days. Stop over and sample some, if you like. You know she thinks you're too skinny. Ciao."

He hit the delete button.

"Fuck," Tom growled and fished the card out of his wallet. On the phone he tapped out the number of the psychologist, expecting and praying for a taped message.

Surprised that the phone was picked up and the doctor's soft voice greeted him, Tom introduced himself haltingly, then asked if an appointment was possible.

"I can see you this morning at 10:30. How's that for you?"

Today? Right away? How good can this guy be? Aren't these guys booked months in advance! Tom had hoped to wait until someone either ran out of money, got their neuroses together, committed suicide, or just decided that shrinks are bullshit.

D'Arcangelo would much rather wait until the New Year. But with this sudden pressure of Carla, the soft, almost hypnotic voice of the psychologist, and his ever growing feeling of becoming more involved with the family business, of crossing a threshold from which it would be even more difficult to retreat, he agreed.

"Uh, sure." Tom said. "See you later today then.

The psychologist gave brief directions and asked him to ring at the side door of his large house.

TOM HAD SHOWERED and shaved and dressed when his cellphone jangled. It was his Uncle Vince.

"Tommy! You awake yet? How ya doin'? Remember, Jimmy wants us to travel down the shore to check in on our deadbeat dentist— see if he's there. Pack an overnight. We should be back later tomorrow. I don't want to spend too much time on this. And I don't expect to find him either. It's Christmas after all. I need to do some shopping for my godson and goddaughters. But there's no sense in waiting to find this guy until next year. I'll be over around eleven. Okay?"

"Eleven? Vince, look, I've got a dentist's appointment then. Can't we leave early in the afternoon? One o'clock maybe? We can be there by three, four and look around a bit, have dinner there. We'll have tomorrow and be back in the afternoon. I need to get this tooth worked on. It's hard to get a dentist's appointment these days."

It always surprised him that lies could just roll out of his mouth, as casual as breezes on a summer day. But not without the glimmer of guilt. He knew what he was doing and it seldom pleased him.

"Okay, sure. Call me when you get back from the dentist. Don't make any bets with this guy!" Vince laughed at his joke. "I'll pick you up at your place. Don't forget to bring that address of his summer home there. Did you say you had a lead on this guy's boat?"

"I saw a framed picture at his wife's house. He was standing in front of his boat with his daughter. Remember her name? Rachel. He named the boat after her: *Faithful Rachel*. We might be able to find out where that boat is— and he might be on it."

"Good thinking, Tommy, but there's a lot of boats in Cape May, if he's still there. Call me when you're back at your place. Oh, by the way, I saw the forecast on the Weather Channel. Just our luck—it's going to be bitter fucking cold. Better dress for it."

TOM DROVE FROM SOUTH PHILLY north through center city around Logan Circle along the Parkway to Kelly Drive. Then through East Falls past the Falls bridge and then on to Lincoln Drive the few miles to Mt. Airy for his appointment with the psychologist Carla recommended.

The sky was gray, the sun wrestling through the clouds only for brief minutes. Brisk winds sent crisp leaves from the Wissahickon scurrying through the air and across streets. As instructed, Tom rang the buzzer at the doctor's small office, tidily attached to the large colonial home's garage, detached from the house. The house was adjacent to a large park where people hunched over coffee in travel mugs, talking while their dogs cavorted and chased each other.

Tom announced himself to a small Radio Shack intercom. "It's Tom D'Arcangelo."

"Come in, please," between scratchy clicks from an intercom.

Tom turned the doorknob. The doctor came to the door to meet him as he entered the foyer. Horowitz was a clean-shaven, trim man in his mid-sixties, bald on top, with frizzed mostly white hair around his ears. He wore a navy blue cardigan sweater with a shawl collar over a white Oxford shirt with its collar unbuttoned, tan slacks, and running shoes. The doctor extended his hand. "I'm Howard Horowitz. Nice to meet you. Come in, have a seat and I'll be right with you. Would you like some coffee or tea? Water?"

I could use some Jack Daniels, Tom thought. *I bet that comment will not go over in an introductory moment.*

"Coffee would be great. Black for me."

The doctor disappeared for a few minutes.

Tom examined the room. Wood-paneled, dark, and covered with art, Native American and Inuit prints, and African masks. Books on shelves by various psychologists and doctors, but the greater number on literature and philosophy.

Horowitz soon returned, handed over a mug of coffee, sat down cradling his cup, saying nothing. Tom looked around the room. He took a sip and pointed to the masks. "Why do all the shrinks have aboriginal masks on their walls? Is there some significance to that?"

The doctor shrugged, unsmiling. "No significance. I just like them." He then paused. "Have you seen that many shrinks?"

"No, not really. I mean, no, none at all. But in the movies they usually have wood-paneled offices with African masks on them."

"In the movies?"

"Yeah, I've seen several movies where shrinks have them."

"Those shrinks were probably Jungians," the doctor said stone-faced.

"Say again?"

"Jungians. Followers of the school of analysis founded by Carl Jung. Analytical psychology?"

The doctor saw that his humor was missed.

Sensing that he'd missed something and not wanting to look like an ignoramus, Tom nervously blurted out all of his knowledge on the subject: "Yes, I've heard of him. Archetypes, collective unconscious, stuff like that. Swiss guy. Are you a Jungian then? Or Freudian? What school are you from? I mean what school of psychology do you follow?"

"I don't adhere to any particular 'school' actually."

That stopped Tom. He began to feel apprehensive about Carla's choice of shrinks. He didn't know what to say next.

"I just figured since so many movies had shrinks' offices with masks on the walls that this was a common practice, and when I come here I see masks. I thought they must have some significance. You know what I mean? For psychologists." Tom knew he sounded more and more nervous.

"I just like masks."

"Oh. Okay, sure." Tom sipped the coffee again. He sat looking around the room. Horowitz just looked back at him.

No particular school of psychology? "Don't you guys usually have some diplomas in your offices? You know, where you went to school? Where you got your doctorate?"

Horowitz smiled. "You mean, maybe from the University of Vienna? I don't have mine framed. I'm sure I can find them in my files somewhere, if you'd like. Next time I will look them up and put them out. Would that make you feel more secure?"

"No, I guess you've gone to school for this kind of thing." Tom's statement sounded almost like a question.

"Yes, I have," Horowitz nodded. "University of Washington for my undergraduate degree, the University of Chicago for my masters, NYU for my doctorate. Would you like to know more about *me*? Subject of my dissertation?"

Tom stammered an assent. "Uh, yeah. Sure." *Is this fucker making fun of me?* he wondered.

"I grew up in Boston. I have two children, boys, now grown, and have been married twice. My first wife passed away. I was in the army and loathed every minute of it. I played baseball growing up. Now I do some running, cycling, and play tennis. I like reading, literature mostly. I subscribe to *The New Yorker*. I listen to classical music, I seldom watch television, although I do enjoy going out to an occasional movie. I'm politically active when it's called for and have been arrested several times for that. I suppose one could call me a liberal with progressive socialist leanings. I'm suspicious of governments generally. Is that enough about me?"

Tom nodded. He looked around stalling for time.

"Aren't you going to take notes or something? Am I being taped?"

"No, no notes at this time. I would tell you if you were being taped. I seldom use a tape recorder. Unless you begin to speak in tongues."

Tom didn't comment on that reply.

Another joke that missed its mark, thought Horowitz.

Tom put his cup down on the table opposite Horowitz. "Did you ever see *The Sopranos*? Tony Soprano, the gangster, goes to a shrink because he's having anxiety attacks—sort of a mobster's midlife crisis?"

"No, no, I haven't seen it, but I have heard about the show."

"Isn't a shrink, like sworn to secrecy by some medical ethics, not to disclose what he hears from his patients?"

Horowitz nodded. "There are certain doctor-client confidentiality rights, but they are not unlimited."

"Oh? How so?"

"For instance, if I or my family were to feel threatened, or I perceived that someone could be injured by a patient, I would need to report it to the authorities. If you were to admit to molesting a child, I'd be bound by law to report it. But, generally speaking, what you say here will stay here."

"So it's like Vegas," Tom tried to interject a bit of humor that the psychologist either missed or chose to ignore. Horowitz sat in silence for a minute, then extended an open hand toward him, gesturing Tom's turn to speak. "My girlfriend wanted me to come to see you talk about a problem I'm having …."

Horowitz nodded. "So you're here because your girlfriend wanted you to see me? Do *you* object to coming here?"

Tom shook his head. "It's fine with me. If I didn't want to be here, I'd have told her so. It's not that. But I feel like I'm at a point in my life when I need to make some choices, and … let's say, uh, I'm having difficulty making those choices."

Horowitz said nothing. He stared back at the patient and sipped his coffee.

"Do you want the short story," Tom asked, "or the long one? There are two, I think."

"Tell me the one you feel is most important."

Tom leaned forward and spoke softly. "I grew up in a house where my uncle was—is—employed by … shall we say? … people in questionably legal businesses. We all knew about it, too. My family, I mean. My mother, father, my brother and I, all of our family. My mother even suggested that my grandfather was involved at one time. My father died suddenly of a heart attack when I was fifteen. My brother was seventeen then. My uncle—my mother's brother—and his 'business partners' looked after my mother and my brother and me until we could get on our feet. My brother Matt eventually joined the service—he's making a career of it, he says—he's been in the Marines for eight years now.

"Every month my mother got an envelope, just like social security but in cash, from my uncle. I got offered some work at some of the businesses—all legitimate stuff, bussing or waiting on tables, that kind of thing— and at twenty I started to go to college, part-time and working half-time. To make some extra money I started running some gambling at the university. Poker and cards, you know, and some side betting, mostly on football and basketball games. That expanded to providing strippers and the occasional hooker to fraternities for parties. Sold some students some marijuana, LSD, and X—ecstasy— on occasion. Gen X, Millennial designer drug shit—you know what I mean? It became a sideline while I attended classes full-time. I did quite well. Paid my tuition. In my senior year I even expanded to a few other schools in the area."

"Did you ever get your degree, by any chance?"

"Yes sir, I did. I wasn't Phi Beta Kappa, but I had a 3.8 GPA."

"3.8? That's not bad—quite good actually."

"Now that I've graduated, I am thinking about my future, what I want to do with the rest of my life, as you might imagine. I have a girlfriend I like, I think. I thought I'd maybe go to law school."

"Does your girlfriend know about your life of crime?"

The phrase stung Tom. *Life of crime.* "Wait, 'my life of crime'? That's a bit harsh. Aren't you being a bit dramatic?"

Horowitz shrugged. "Illegal gambling, procuring prostitutes for college students, narcotics—these are criminal enterprises. Cardinal Rigali might forgive you at your next confession, but the police and the judicial system might like to see you do graduate work in Graterford. I understand some criminals become jailhouse lawyers."

"Yes, Carla knows about what I did in college. I told her, but if I didn't, she would have figured it out sooner or later. She's smart."

"And so your girlfriend doesn't want to be a 'mob wife'?"

Tom shook his head. "That's for sure."

"Well, do you love your girlfriend? Is it a serious relationship? It must be one to make drastic life changes, go to law school, things like that."

Tom shifted in his seat. "I'm not so sure how much I love her or want to settle down with her really."

There! D'Arcangelo had said it finally to someone other than himself.

"Oh, I see," Horowitz said. "I believe you said you 'have a girlfriend you like, you think'. Seems fairly equivocal to consider going to law school for a person you just like. And that was 'maybe go to law school, wasn't it? That sounds a bit noncommittal and uncertain, too."

"I guess that sums it up," Tom replied. "I'm not even sure I want to attend law school, really.

"So what decision are you finding hard to make? Is it your mob friends and a lucrative but possibly dangerous illegal career as opposed to passing the bar and marrying your girlfriend having children and coaching little league? It wouldn't be unusual to find a conflict between something exciting and adrenaline-producing and more mundane and possibly hum-drum routines of marriage."

"You're assuming that my girlfriend and I are destined for much of a future."

"Are you destined for a future?"

"I don't think so. It's always difficult to break up with someone. I'd always want them to break up with me."

The psychologist shrugged. "People uncouple in many ways. Seldom do they just break it off with a showdown of their real feelings. Usually people are reluctant to hurt another person. Often they do things to be given the boot. Be grumpy, distant, find fault with the other person, unfaithful sexually. That kind of thing."

"That's sounds right. I don't want to hurt Carla. She's a good person."

"I'm not going to tell you how to break up with your girl. You need to find that for yourself. What would you like to have happen to you if the shoe were on the other foot?"

"I guess I'd like the person to be square with me. Tell me right off. Right up front. In ninth grade I tried out in for the varsity baseball team. I thought I was hot shit. The high school varsity coach cut me. He said to me, "You're not ready. Want to play JV? I appreciated that."

"Well, there's your answer. If you want to break it off with your girl, just tell her."

Tom shook his head. "You're way off base. Two years ago now, my mother died of cancer. The day before she passed on I was with her in the hospital. She made me promise that I'd not get involved in, as you put it, a life of crime. She saw my brother join the Marines to avoid the mob, and she wanted me to escape it, too. But when war broke out, she was worried sick about him. I thought about joining, too, but she made me *promise* not to enlist. She had all these IVs hooked up to her and when she was dying she begged me to promise her I would stay away from the mob.

"What did you say to her?"

"I told her that I would, of course."

"Did you mean it? Do you *want* to do as you promised her? Or were you just saying that because she was dying?"

"Yes, yes, of course. I meant it. She's my mother. I loved her. And she was right. A life of crime is not a good life."

"Why do you think you have put off fulfilling this promise to your mother? Do you really *want* to quit your association with these guys?"

"Yes, I do. But you probably can't imagine—it's not easy."

The psychologist smiled. "I think I *might* be able to imagine this. But tell me, why is it so hard for you to keep this promise to your mother?"

Tom was silent. He couldn't answer. He didn't know. He shrugged. "I was hoping you could tell me that."

"I can offer you some possible reasons, as I see them. But only you can *know* the real reason. Or reasons."

TOM RETURNED home, packed a small overnight bag, ate a bowl of cereal with a banana and a slice of wheat toast. He was sitting at the kitchen table over a second cup of coffee looking over the LSAT exam book when the doorbell rang. He went to the door and peered through the curtain. As expected, it was his uncle, who stood on the top step, holding a bowling ball bag.

"Uncle Vince! Hey, so we're still going down the shore?" he asked. Tom had actually hoped the plans had been changed and they weren't going.

"Jimmy wants us to take a trip down the shore to Cape May for a couple days. Look for the deadbeat dentist. I'll drive. Pack a few things. We'll probably stay overnight. One night max. OK?"

"What's with the bag? Were you bowling? Do they have lanes down there?"

"I'll show you after you pack."

"I'm packed already and ready to go."

Vince placed his bag on the sofa and unzipped it, took out the ball and shoes and placed them on a cushion. Then he reached and pulled out a false bottom and took out a small revolver, wrapped in a cloth. "Nice clean piece. And well hidden."

"Mind if I look at it?" Tom asked.

"Careful—it's loaded."

Tom took the black .38 snub-nosed revolver. Its hammer was filed off, and the grip and trigger wrapped in a cloth tennis racquet grip. He opened the action to see if it was loaded, then clicked it shut.

"Wanted to be sure the equipment is OK." He handed it back to his uncle.

"You're thorough, Tommy. I like that about you," Vince said.

I'm guess he's not thinking about getting into a gunfight, Tom thought. *It took him five minutes to get the gun out of the bag.*

But taking a gun along on this trip made Tom suddenly uneasy. He was glad it was buried at the bottom of the bag and his uncle wasn't carrying it—or, worse, had asked him to.

"You ready to go?" Vince asked. "Let's get this over with. I gotta get back and get some shopping done."

"I know what you mean. My bag's packed upstairs. Let me get it and we're on our way," Tom said and went to retrieve it.

When he returned his uncle was sitting in the living room. Vince had picked up one of Tom's books on the end table, *The Complete Poems and Plays of T.S. Eliot.* He held the volume in his hands on his lap, hunched over it like a monk. Tom stood there with his bag over his shoulder waiting for his uncle to look up.

Vince seemed to be reading the same lines over and over, then he turned to Tom.

"What does this mean?" his uncle asked. He read:

> *Time present and time past*
> *Are both perhaps present in time future,*
> *And time future contained in time past.*
> *If all time is eternally present*
> *All time is unredeemable.*

Vince paused for a long moment, his face screwed up as if in pain. "What the fuck does that mean? Is this guy nuts or what? They teach you this shit in college?"

Tom laughed. "Well, that guy is considered one of the great poets of the twentieth century. I wasn't reading his poetry though. I'm reading the plays. I am going to see one performed in the spring. What do those lines mean? Well, poetry isn't like mathematics. There's not usually one correct answer. It can mean different things to different people. There's room for doubt, questioning, ambiguity. Poetry is … subject to interpretation."

Vince shut the book and placed it where he found it. "Oh," he said. "Okay. Right."

THEY DROVE OFF in his uncle's gunmetal grey Town Car. Vince crossed the Walt Whitman Bridge on to the Atlantic City Expressway to route 55 toward Cape May. First Sinatra and then Dino floated out of the CD player.

"You don't mind old school, do you?"

"Sure, Sinatra's fine. Just no smoking while we're driving, okay? I'm in training," Tom said. He knew Vince had been trying to stop smoking for a decade, and although he had only a few smokes a day, his uncle had failed to quit completely. Tom wanted to discourage his uncle and avoid ruining his own lungs.

"Does this car smell like smoke? No fuckin' way."

They drove without speaking except for the music, which was unusual—Vince loved to talk. Soon the uncle broke the silence.

"Training? Training for what? You look fine to me. You playing softball again this summer?"

"Martial arts. I've been taking classes out in West Philly."

"Ah, Bruce Lee. Kung fu man, eh?"

"No, it's karate actually. Japanese. Shotokan. Kung fu is Chinese."

Vince nodded. "Could always come in handy. I bet it keeps you in shape, too."

"It's a helluva workout."

They drove in silence for a few miles.

"Hey, you're a college man"—Tom's uncle must have used that phrase to preface a sentence several times a month addressing his nephew—"I rented this video the other night. The box said it was 'existential'. What does that mean? 'Existential'? I don't get that word there, you know what I mean? I mean, aren't most movies dealing with some kind of existence? Except maybe cartoons?"

Vince thought about what he'd said for a moment, then added: "Well, except maybe for *The Lion King*."

Oh, this conversation should be interesting, Tom thought.

"I wasn't a philosophy or religion major or anything, so I'm not an expert, but it refers to a philosophy, a modern philosophy. I had a course in it and we studied it, among others. Existentialism became popular after the Second World War."

"Philosophy? The movie didn't discuss any philosophy. None I can see."

Tom ignored him and went on. "Existentialism was prominent in Europe, particularly France. Jean-Paul Sartre and Albert Camus, writers mostly, focused on it. It deals with, I understand, an emphasis on individual responsibility. It says that we're in a purposeless universe, there's no God, and that we make meaning in life in what we do. What movie you talking about?"

"It was recommended by a girl I been seeing."

"You seeing a new girl?"

"Yeah. She's a Jersey girl, but smart. The movie had an odd title—*Woman in the Dunes*."

Tom knew his uncle's taste in movies. It seldom included reading subtitles. He looked at Vince in disbelief.

"A Japanese film? I saw it. Did you like it?"

Tom had seen it in college in a film course. He couldn't believe his uncle had watched it, nor that he was actually dating a woman who recommended it. Tom could more easily understand cosmology and quantum physics than Vince watching that film. Bruce Willis movies were his style. His uncle once confided his favorite movie was *Heaven Knows, Mr. Allison*.

"Yeah."

"Really? You liked it?"

"It was an old Japanese movie. She said she liked it, so I told her I'd like to see it. This existentialism stuff ... does the Church believe in it? Ya know, I can't see a priest would—"

"Hell no. Existentialists are—*Watch out!*" Tom pointed to the road and braced himself with hands on the dashboard. *"Deer!"*

A deer with white tail raised had suddenly scrambled from the woods across the highway and dashed to the wooded center divider. Vince slowed and swerved into the right hand lane as the deer danced on to the dense wooded divider between the highways.

"Damn, that was close!" he exclaimed, looking in the rear view mirror. "Fucking Rudolph! When is hunting season, for chrissakes?"

"A deer would make a nasty dent in your grillwork," Tom said. "Let's keep our eyes open wide. There might be others."

"Maybe that's a good omen," Vince laughed. "Santa's workshop and all that."

But the rest of their trip was uneventful. The pair crossed the canal bridge to Cape May past the marinas just after four o'clock, and although still early, it was already twilight rapidly dimming into night. Tom craned to look over at the boats and made a mental note to check them out tomorrow.

Vince noted the boats and saw Tom looking over his shoulder at them. "You think his boat is there? He'll be on it?"

"Maybe. Dunno today," Tom said. "There are other slips and marinas, too. We'll check some out tomorrow."

"It's a long shot that he'll be here," Vince groused. "This is a fuckin' wasted trip. Don't tell Jimmy I said that! At Christmas time, too."

VINCE AND TOM CHECKED into the hotel along Beach Drive and took rooms on the top floor. Vince's room was down the hall from his nephew.

While Tom was unpacking Vince knocked on his door. "Tommy, I'm heading up to AC. Gotta talk to someone there. I'll be back later, okay? Entertain yourself here for a while, I'll be back in two, three hours. Is that okay with you?"

Tom hid his surprise at this sudden unannounced side trip.

"Sure, Vince. I'm a big boy. But I'll wait until you get back. We'll get a drink and dinner. Unless you're going to eat there? I might take a walk over to the mall to stretch my legs and then come back and read for a while."

"If you can wait that long for dinner, great, but if you can't, eat without me," Vince said. "I won't be offended. See you later."

Once he was settled, Tom took off for the six-block walk to the mall. The temperature was now in the low twenties. Furious gusts of wind dropped thermometers to the low 'teens. He was immediately sorry he had ventured outside and thought he should have hunkered down at the hotel bar. But he wanted to get some exercise before tomorrow, thinking a brisk walk might help him sleep. Because of the wind he stayed on the back streets away from the beach and ocean and, once there, stayed on the periphery of the three-block mall that provided shopping and restaurants for the Cape May residents and tourists.

Washington Mall was deserted. A biting wind forced him to tuck his chin into his scarf and collar, hunch his shoulders, and hold his cap on. Tom turned in to a pub named *The Ugly Mug* and ordered an Irish coffee to warm himself before the trip back to the hotel. He was hungry but wanted to get back to the hotel to see if his uncle had returned. Tom knew Vince didn't like to eat alone and would want to have dinner with someone.

Our Lady Star of the Sea, the Roman Catholic Church, stood at the north end of the mall. Its stained glass windows were illuminated and, through its doors, the lights seemed to be on in the chapel. Tom walked over and hiked the steps to see if he could enter. To his surprise the door was unlocked. He entered a vestibule and was careful to pull the door shut behind him. Tom entered the sanctum and stopped at the holy water font, took some, bowed to the altar, and crossed himself before entering. Though no longer a believer, he knew he did these things for his mother, as if she were looking down from heaven at him.

An organist was practicing for the Sunday's services while a priest busied himself to the side of the sanctuary near the altar.

Tom went halfway up the nave and slid into a seat near the aisle. The organist played the weekend's hymns and then what Tom recognized as a famous Bach work, the Passacaglia and Fugue in C Minor.

He sat in the pew and looked around at the stain glass windows with its depictions of characters and scenes from the Bible, of the infant Jesus, the young and older Jesus, Mary, Joseph, angels, and heavenly lights. The music added to the spirit of the building and the time of the year for me. It was far better than the last time he was in a Catholic Church for a christening of Carla's nephew, where he was one among a scrum of wailing babes. Tom couldn't help thinking of the climactic scene from *The Godfather* when Michael Corleone eliminates the heads of the crime families. ("Do you renounce Satan and all his works and all his pomps?")

Tom looked around the church, at the priest tending to the vestry area, at how the Stations of the Cross were rendered, at its stained glass windows. On the few occasions that he came to be in church, he always thought of his mother who attended regularly. She admitted to him that she went for its peacefulness and its music, the choir and the organ. Tom's father had bought his mother a small organ; she had taken a few lessons and taught herself to play, mostly show tunes and pop standards and played often, although she claimed she had great anxiety when she had to play with people around.

The organ's mournful pipes cued memories of his mother and her death that night in the hospital. Tom had gone to visit her that evening after morning classes and work, and when he entered her new room, where she had been moved close to the nurse's station. Her doctor turned to him and motioned him outside while the nurses busied themselves with new IVs. Tom had spoken to her oncologist often and felt as if he knew him. Tom respected him, although he was often suspicious of doctors generally and even disliked the few he had come to meet.

"Tom, if you have family you want to see and who might want to be with your mother, you need to call them right away. There's a great possibility that she'll not make it through the night," the doctor had told him.

Tom called his mother's sister and family and even tried to call her brother Vince away in Florida on a fishing trip. His aunt lived at the Jersey shore, and she and her husband jumped in their car to race to Philly.

His mother's oncologist had explained that she had been put on a morphine drip to palliate her suffering and that she could ask to have it increased as she wished.

Doctor Heller could see the question in the son's face, the question his patients' loved ones couldn't ask.

"I'm afraid that we've done all we can do, Tom. We're just able to make her comfortable for a while. I'm sorry."

Tom's mother awoke just once to acknowledge him. He sat at her side, and when she stirred, stood over her.

"Hi, Mom. Is there something you want? You need? Water?"

"Yes, that would be nice—," she said. "Water."

He got her a plastic cup and poured water from a pitcher. She sipped it carefully, then handed it to him.

"Tommy? Would you read to me?"

"Read? Sure. What would you like?" He looked around. There was a book of popular fiction, a Bible, and a newspaper on the table near her bed. Tom gave her the choice.

"The paper. Read me the paper."

He took up the newspaper, chose an article and began to read softly. After several minutes, they were interrupted by a nurse who came in to take vital signs.

"Are you in pain, Mrs. D'Arcangelo?" the nurse inquired. "We can increase the pain medication, if you like."

"No, not just now."

The nurse looked at her chart and checked the IV one last time, then turned to Tom. "Call me if she's in pain or if anything is needed." The nurse gave Tom a weak smile departed.

"Tommy?" His mother summoned him and grabbed his hand with cold fingers.

"Yeah, Mom."

"Remember what I said about your future?"

"Yeah, Mom, I remember."

"Those men—your uncle's friends—are not *your* friends. They're bad. Remember that. *They are evil.*"

"Yeah, Mom. I know."

"Keep reading to me, would you?"

"Sure, Mom." He went back to the story in the paper. Those were the last words his mother ever spoke to anyone.

She slipped into a deeper sleep. Tom continued reading and talking to her until the nurse returned once again to take vital signs.

"I think she's stopped breathing," he said. "Is she still alive?"

The nurse placed a stethoscope on her neck and chest. She shook her head. "Her heart is still beating."

She checked the IV line and increased the morphine dosage. "That should help her with any pain she might feel."

He knew what the nurse was doing.

"Thank you," he said.

THE ORGAN'S LAST MEASURES of the Passacaglia and Fugue vanished into the air. Lost in thought about the past and his mother's death, Tom was approached by the priest.

"May I help you in some way?" he asked softly.

"You already did, Father. I'm glad the Church was open and I could listen to the music."

Then for some reason, Tom elaborated: "I was thinking about my mother who passed away. Something made me come here to remember her. She came to church a lot."

"Do you want to talk about her with someone, my son? I can spend some time with you, if you'd like."

"No. Thank you, Father. As I said, you've already helped me."

"If you're not in great need then, I am going to lock up the Church for the evening. You're welcome to come back at any time. Please, come to a service sometime."

TOM RETURNED to his room at the hotel, tuned in the radio and searched for a classical music station. He showered and shaved then flopped in a chair to read *Go Down, Moses,* the one book he brought along. The radio was playing a string quartet of Debussy. Tom tuned it louder to block out the wind howling around the eaves of the hotel.

He had read an entire chapter when there was a knock at the door. Tom thought it had to be Vince, but he went to the door and looked through the peephole. A tall blond woman in her mid-twenties stood in the hallway.

He opened the door. The woman's long dark overcoat was open, revealing a white blouse, a short, tight black skirt, over black tights and calf high black boots. She wore a large green beret and a thick red scarf.

"Are you Tommy D'Arcangelo?" she stepped confidently into the doorway. "Hi, I'm Nina. Vince said you might need some company for the evening."

Tom looked at her then scowled. "Uh … Hello, Nina. Where's Vince now?" he asked. "I think I need to talk to him."

Tom leaned his head out of the door peering around the woman. She parted to the other side of the doorway. Her perfume wrapped him in a sudden aroma of allure.

"He's with Sherry right now. Vince met us in Atlantic City at the Puss in Boots Club. We work there."

"Uh huh. I want to talk to him, I think."

Tom thought back to Vince's first attempt to set him up with a woman. It was his nephew's twenty-first birthday and he intended to initiate him into the mysteries of adulthood. He took Tom to some gentlemen's clubs on Delaware Avenue where Vince picked up the tab and where, with the room swirling from too many Manhattans, an exotic half Asian half-African American woman named Cinnamon 'picked him up'. Tom later found out Vince had paid her to come on to him. Cinnamon revealed herself to be the craziest woman D'Arcangelo had ever met. And although only twenty-one, he had slept with both an actress and a ballet dancer who—Tom thought—registered 9.0 on the Freak Scale. Cinnamon was off the charts wild. When finally sober, Tom ordered his uncle to never again set him up with anyone. Ever.

Nina stood in the doorway, then leaned closer. "I think they're busy. He might not like being disturbed, you know?"

She smiled warmly. "Could I come in? It's freezing outside and I'd love to warm up a bit."

She pulled her scarf from around her throat, revealing a red velvet cloth choker with a gold pin on the front pulled around her long, sculpted neck and the white blouse with tasteful but not overly obvious cleavage. She removed the beret and her blond hair fell to her neck in waves that circled her face.

"The Puss in Boots Club?" D'Arcangelo asked.

"We're dancers there."

"Really? Dancers at The Puss in Boots Club. What a surprise."

"That we're dancers? Don't I look like one?"

"That's not what I meant. Look, I didn't know I was going to have company tonight. I've settled down for a *quiet* evening."

She dropped her scarf and stepped forward and dangled a set of keys in his face.

"Vince wanted you take these. He said you might want to get an early start in the morning and need his wheels. He said to call him later or early in the morning. He also said to tell you 'the bowling ball was in the car'?" She shrugged expressing her lack of understanding of this last statement.

As Tom reached for the keys, she moved closer to him. Her perfume coiled round him as he looked into exquisite iceberg blue eyes.

"I'm OK with quiet," she said softly, leaning ever closer to him. He thought he heard purring. Tom pulled away from her as he felt hormones rising to take the bait of her beauty and availability.

"I meant quiet as in *alone*, you know what I mean?"

She raised an eyebrow in disbelief, then frowned. "Oh? Don't you like me? Maybe I'm not your type? I know you're not gay." She slid closer still; Tom edged away. "I'm disappointed."

He shook his head. "No, of course not. You're really good-looking. Stunning actually. You look like that girl in the Bond film—*From Russia With Love*—the KGB agent."

She shook her head slowly, deliberately. "Never saw that one."

She moved closer. "Did she have one of those Bond girl names? You know, like Pussy Galore or Holly Goodhead?" She smiled.

"No, she had a typical Russian name, one that's escaping me at the moment—for some not-so-odd reason."

He stepped away from her perfume; despite the cold that had wafted in from the hallway Tom thought he could feel the heat of her body. "Well, you look a lot like her. Take my word for it," he said.

"Well, if she was a Bond girl, she must have been *very* beautiful." She stepped close again for her aroma assault.

He retreated again.

She looked away for a moment, lost in thought, then came back: "Look, Tom, Vince paid me already. And"—she emphasized slowly—"*I need the money*. If you kick me out and he finds out I'm not your escort, he's gonna want the money back—and rightly so. I could go back and see if he wants me to join the two of them for the evening, I suppose. But I *really* don't like that kind of thing, you know what I mean," she dropped her hands holding her hat in one hand and scarf in the other to her sides, "You know what I mean? C'mon, Tom," she began to plead. "Please?"

"Wait one minute. Okay? Be right back," Tom said and zipped down the corridor to Vince's room. He stood outside, leaning close to the door, preparing to knock quietly. That close to the door he heard a woman's loud groaning, muffled screaming and an earthquake on the bed.

He returned to the room. Nina stood in the doorway, unmoved from when he whisked past her. She said nothing, but gave him a knowing look.

"Please, Tom," she said.

Tom considered her predicament for a moment, then against better judgment he agreed. "All right. Shut the door. Come on in. There are two beds. Pick one, it's yours."

He pointed to the one in front of the television. "Why not that one? You can watch TV—just keep it low."

"Thanks. That's great." She smiled and closed the door. She took off her coat and threw it on the easy chair. The coat only hid elegant curves and feminine appeal. Tom didn't want to stare too hard at her. He tried but found it difficult to think of Carla.

"Look, I'm starving," Tom said. "I have been waiting for Vince to come back to have dinner with him, but"—he shrugged—"he obviously has other plans. I'm going to get a bite to eat and a drink before I hit the sack. There's a restaurant and a bar downstairs. I'd like to grab something there, then come back here to read a bit before turning in. If you want to join me, that'd be nice. You hungry?"

Nina nodded vigorously. "Famished. Are you sure you don't want to order room service?"

"Good," Tom said. "No, no room service. I don't like lying to Vince though. I won't tell him we got it on. You don't have to say anything, just hang on my arm and he'll think we did the nasty. Okay?"

"Well, I don't like lying either—and that still is lying—but we'll agree to a sin of omission then."

"'Sin of omission'? Were you a fuckin' nun before you became a dancer?"

"You know what a 'sin of omission' is then?"

"Certainly. Twelve years of Catholic school, Sweetheart."

THEY LEFT THE ROOM and went down to the hotel's restaurant and bar. Both ordered a glass of red wine and silently studied the menus.

"A salad and the scallops and linguine sound real good to me," she said. "How about you?"

"Salad and the lobster tail dinner with baked potato looks good." Tom closed the menu. "So you work at The Puss in Boots Club?"

"Uh-huh," she nodded sipping her wine.

He said nothing in reply. He sipped his wine and stared off around the restaurant, his mind wandering, He began to think about their mission the next day to find the dentist and collect on the gambling debt. The gun in the bowling ball bag weighed on him. Tom disliked that Vince had brought a gun along. He thought back to what his father had said about guns. He had told his sons that when guns were around and there was a "problem," the guns were likely to be used. He told them that if you have a gun, you feel the need to use it, and people get killed. "What do they say? 'When you have only a hammer as a tool, everything looks like a nail',," their father told them. "Guns should only be around if you need one for self-defense."

Their father would look directly into his sons' eyes, wink with his right eye and hold it closed for just a moment, then used one of his favorite phrases: "I *know* what I'm talking about."

With Tom's knowledge of the gun and their mission to find Schonfeld to recover the gambling debt, he began to feel as if he were standing in a marsh.

Nina took another sip of her wine as the waitress took their orders and then vanished to the kitchen. The dancer interrupted Tom's musing. "You seem like the morose type."

"I seem like the 'morose type'? Morose? Really? 'Morose?'"

Her use of the word, and that an exotic dancer had labelled him with it, amused him. He smiled. "Maybe I'm just quiet."

"Why didn't you come with Vince to the club to check out the dancers?" she asked. "You might have seen someone else you'd rather be with. Someone more attractive?"

Tom doubted he would ever see someone as knockout beautiful as she. He thought about what to say in reply and decided to evade saying anything meaningful. He tugged on an ear lobe and replied, "I didn't go there because I'm chorophobic."

She looked at him, smiled, took a sip of wine, placed the glass down and snorted in obvious disbelief. "You're *afraid* of *dancing*?"

Ohh. Two points for vocabulary! Tom was surprised.

"Umm, all those dancers up there flailing around scares me, makes me real nervous," he said straight-faced. "Lap dances make me break out in a cold sweat. I'd need to rush outside for air to avoid an anxiety attack."

She arched an unbelieving eyebrow. "You're bullshitting me. Or really fucking weird."

"How long you been dancing at the club?"

"Been working there since I graduated."

"Since high school? Is that legal?" Tom scrutinized her to determine her age. She looked young, but in her early twenties.

She wrinkled her nose and shook her head. "No, college. I graduated a year and half ago now."

"Really? You graduated from college? What did you major in?"

He knew there was no degree in erotic dancing.

"Linguistics and phys ed."

"What? Now *you're* fucking with *me*. You're kidding me, right? Linguistics? And phys ed?"

"No. Why would I kid about that? I was a real jock in junior high and high school and later in college. I carried two majors. I loved being on teams and competing."

"How about the linguistics? How'd that happen?"

"I was an English major and I really got interested in linguistics—that's the study of language and languages—not necessarily specific languages, like French or Russian, and I went from there."

"English major? Me, too." Tom fought the urge to test her knowledge of linguistic theory.

"Now I'm catching up on some science courses that I missed in undergrad. Chem, bio, some math. Don't laugh—I want to be an EMT for a while, then get into nursing. It's a good career."

"Why would I laugh? Nursing's a great profession. You're helping people. That's not funny at all."

Tom mentioned his mother in her last days. "Those nurses kept my mother alive. The fucking doctors get all the respect and all the money. They stop in, check the charts, and collect ten times as much money as the nurses. Doctors are hardly ever even there."

Nina raised her glass to take another sip of wine. "Let me guess. You guys think all of the girls who dance at the clubs are either dumb cunts or sluts. Am I right?"

Tom considered her to be on target. He had met many erotic dancers—he had in fact supplied them to frat parties.

"Not all of us think that," he said. "You're generalizing. I imagine that some of the dancers are one or the other, maybe some are both. There must be some who are neither."

The waitress arrived with their salads and they began to eat. After a few minutes D'Arcangelo broke the silence.

"So Vince went to your club, picked up two girls, one for him and you for me, and paid you to fuck me? How much, may I ask?"

She frowned. "When he came to the club, he didn't ask for a hooker. Vince knew Sherry already. He didn't want you to feel like a third wheel. He asked for someone to keep a good-looking, college-educated guy—an intellectual and nice guy, he said—*company* for an evening. As I said, I really need the money. He paid well."

"May I ask for *what* in particular? Shoes, makeup, car insurance, that kind of thing?" Tom know a lot of hookers were drug users. He examined her face for a sign that would show she was lying.

She ignored his prying question. "He paid me to be an escort for you—not to fuck you, all right? I'm not a hooker. Hookers don't have dinner with their johns. Are you wearing a priest's collar?" Her eyes flashed. He had touched a nerve.

"Easy. Chill out, all right, I got the picture, OK? Have you done this 'escort work' before?"

"On occasion, and I can tell you straight that I don't make the beast with two backs with all of these clients."

Tom smiled at her Shakespeare. His eyes must have opened wide. "But you have with some?"

"My, aren't we voyeuristic? Yes, I did, with *one* of them. But most of the time an escort is just window-dressing. Sometimes gay guys not out of the closet or someone who wants to parade a nice babe around at a concert with his work colleagues. Maybe some asshole who wants to look like a big shot with his clients."

D'Arcangelo nodded understanding.

"I went out with one guy, a professor with two doctorates, whose wife had recently died. He just took me out, we had dinner and went dancing and he talked the night away. Told me about his wife. He never even tried to get into my knickers. He was sweet really. I made a thousand dollars that night."

"Sounds lucrative. Think maybe I could get into something like that? An escort? For women, of course." Tom stroked thick black hair over his ear. He chuckled, just thinking how Carla would react to the idea.

"Maybe. You're good-looking enough. Did anyone ever tell you that you look like an actor my mother adores?" She thought a moment. "Something Granger?"

"Stewart Granger?"

"He was in *Strangers on a Train*. Hitchcock film, I think. She watches it over and over.

"That would be Farley Granger. I look like him?"

"Yeah, I think so. But for escort work you need the right personality. Gotta be able to talk and make the people enjoy themselves, make them relax, see that they have a good time. You get better tips that way. You can't be a gloomy Gus."

"I'll work on that. Try not to be so morose."

"And no, I don't need the money for me. I need it for my brother—and now my mother."

Tom sensed he was in for some bullshit. "Oh? They out of work or something?"

"My younger brother has cerebral palsy. He lives at home with my mother. She's looked after him, with our help—my father's died some time back. A year ago my mother started acting strangely. We had her tested and she has been diagnosed with early stage Alzheimer's. My older brother and I are working to make enough money for her doctors and medications."

"I'm sorry to hear about that. Sounds pretty grim."

"She's taking some medicines that seem to help her. But they're fucking expensive."

Tom leaned forward over the table and lowered his voice. "Can I give you some advice? Vince means well. You can use the money, I understand. But getting involved with—let's call them 'these guys', you know what I mean—could get you into trouble. I can tell you right now some of the guys Vince knows wouldn't take 'no fucking' too kindly. They might not be as understanding as I am if you turn down their advances—unless of course you need the money that bad, you'll screw for it."

"'These guys'? You mean *mob* guys?"

"In a nutshell, yeah. Mob guys."

"You're not telling me something I don't know. My father was … well, shall we say—'involved'—with the Jersey mob. He went missing. He disappeared. Know what I mean?"

D'Arcangelo nodded and looked away. "I think I do."

"Oh, I realize that there's some danger. But I need to take some chances for that kind of money, at least for a little while longer. Then I'm out of it."

Tom looked away. The room suddenly seemed darker, as if they had dimmed the lights. He looked at her and said, "I understand. Let's hope you don't regret what you're doing. I wouldn't play the game too long. The odds catch up to you."

Nina and Tom finished their salads in silence. The waitress brought the entrees and asked if they wanted more wine.

"Have another, if you want," he said. "This is on me."

"Sure," Nina assented. "Another red wine. But two's my limit."

"Give me a Glenfiddich. Up. Make it a double."

AFTER A DINNER in which they exchanged college experiences, they returned to the room. Tom locked the door and took up the phone and gestured to the bathroom.

"Why don't you take a shower, get ready for bed. I need to call Vince before we sack out."

He began dialing. Nina stripped to her panties and bra and, as she vanished into the bathroom, Tom noted her lovely dancer's body, alluring sacral dimples and, most-appealing, lack of tattoos.

Tom hoped that they were taking a break from screwing.

Vince picked up the phone. "Yeah."

"Hey, Vince. How you doin'?"

"Waitin' for room service. How are you?"

"Just got back from dinner downstairs with Nina."

"How's the food here? I'm fuckin' starved."

"Food's good, Vince. I got the car keys and we can take off early tomorrow to scope out the boat and his house."

"Look, Tommy. I will probably not be with you, so be careful. Take the bowling ball with you. Know what I mean?"

"I don't think I need that, Vin. Really."

"It's a tool, Tommy. Do what I say. Take it with you, just in case. Better to have and not use it, than need it and not have it. Trust me, you *won't* have to use it. But take it—for protection."

"Yeah yeah, okay."

"Now here's something else. You're on a recon mission, right? Just recon, know what I mean? Survey the territory. Don't talk to this guy, even let him know we're around. If you spot him, come back, get me, and we'll both talk to him, okay? Got that."

"Sure, Vince." Tom fought the urge to ask why he would need that gun.

"Remember what I said. Recon. Get back to me if you find him, and we'll both go after him to get our dough. But I seriously doubt he'll be here."

"Okay, gotcha. Have a good night, Vince."

"Tommy, what do you think of Nina? Sharp, huh?"

"Shows you Uncle Vince was thinking of his nephew." Vince added a salacious laugh to that last remark.

"She's smart. Real nice, too. I like that."

"I thought you'd like someone who wasn't just a skirt. I know you, kid."

Tom imagined Carla delivering a swift, hard kick to his uncle's testicles. "Yeah thanks, Vin. Have a good night. See you in the morning after I look for Schonfeld."

Tom hung up. He heard Nina in the bathroom showering. He got his pajamas together and checked the heat in the room. The outside temperatures had dropped to a polar blast and the curtains billowed slightly from the now gusting howling winds. Though one of the best hotels in Cape May, its rooms were not insulated for frigid winter weather at atypical arctic temperatures.

He checked the thermostat at the door and put the heat on a higher temp and its fan at maximum.

Look at the brighter side of things, he thought. *This chill will make that girl's nipples stand up.* It was an image he thought he might enjoy.

Nina appeared from the bathroom, shutting the door, with a towel wrapped around her head, a towel hanging over her shoulders covering her breasts, and one wrapped around her hips. She began to towel her head briskly and noted the temperature of the room. She began to—literally—steam.

"Isn't the heat working? Jesus, it's freezing in here."

"You've noticed. I have it turned to the max, but this hotel's not designed for arctic blasts. The shore is not usually this cold. In fact, it's often even five to ten degrees warmer than Philly."

She looked at him in disbelief. "What are you, an apologist for hotel management? Shit, you're paying them for hospitality. Heat is a part of that." She then laughed at his timidity. "I didn't realize I was dining with someone from The Weather Channel."

Tom ignored her. "Do you have a robe or pajamas? You might want this." He tossed her a heavy flannel shirt from his suitcase. "Turn the TV on if you want. I'm going to read."

"That bathroom is steaming and warm. Better take advantage of it. I'm getting under the covers!"

Tom gathered his pajamas and headed for the shower, consciously trying *not* to look at the unabashed Nina taking off her towels and getting into his flannel shirt.

He shaved, brushed his teeth, and took his time in the hot shower, before venturing out into the frigid bedroom again. Nina was under the covers. Instead of watching the television, she was reading a textbook on anatomy and physiology.

Tom made sure the door was double locked and slid into bed with his novel. He realized the sheets and blankets were not heavy winter weave and slid from bed and searched the closet and drawers for extra blankets, but found only pillows.

Nina looked at what he was doing. "No extra blankets? Want to call the front desk?"

"They'll tell me to come down to get them or send someone up after we've fallen asleep. Have you noticed that staff are few and far between? I don't feel like getting dressed. Want to flip a coin to see who goes?"

"Unh-unh. Not me, honey. This girl's in for the night."

"Sleep tight then. Turn the light out when you're done reading."

"I'm turning it out now. It's too late and too cold to memorize the anatomy of the nervous system. Good night, Tom."

"Good night."

She turned her end table's light out and said: "And thanks again for not kicking me out."

"Sure, yeah," he replied, flipping the novel open.

Tom awoke within two hours. The wind gusts were alternately moaning, howling, whistling around the eaves of the hotel's roof; its wrought iron balconies performed like the woodwind sections of numerous orchestras. The room was frigid and the heat had not improved on its performance. He went to the bathroom to piss out the alcohol of the evening.

"Hey!" Nina's voice rose from her side of the room as he returned to his bed.

"Yeah?"

"I'm freezing here. Aren't you?"

"Me, too."

"Can we combine blankets and covers in one bed. That way I'll get some sleep. I can't sleep when I'm this fucking cold."

Tom didn't think this was a good idea but agreed. He wasn't as suspicious of an ulterior motive as he was of his own weakness.

"Yeah, sure. That makes sense. Let's do that."

She grabbed the coverings from her bed, draped them over Tom's bed and quickly slid in next to him. The extra cover and blanket with the added body heat warmed the two of them immediately. She turned facing away from him and backed a taut butt against his. Tom felt an immediate, uncontrolled arousal and was glad he faced away from her.

The unacknowledged tension between Carla and him had diminished their sex life of late.

"Much, *much* better," she sighed. "G' night."

Tom grunted a "good night" to her and felt the growing warmth of her body and after some few minutes began to relax and sink into sleep.

He lay there thinking about the beautiful woman next to him, finding it hard to fall asleep.

Maybe I should see if Nina means that about not fucking her escorts. What the hell? If I'm going to feel guilty, I might as well commit the sin. Tom thought.

This brought him to thinking about his relationship with Carla. He felt that their time together was limited. It was all over except for the final curtain. But he felt he didn't want to ease out of his relationship with her with infidelity. She deserved better and he wanted to take the moral high ground.

Before he slipped into unconsciousness, he had the guilt-ridden fantasy of Carla knocking on the door and discovering him with another woman. Tom knew that Carla would never resort to a scene or any kind of violence. She would knock, size up what was going on and just leave, except for perhaps an epithet and a slammed door. And he would never see her again.

3

IT WAS NOT YET TWILIGHT when Tom awoke. He slid into his clothes, questioning why he was leaving the warmth of a bed with one of the most beautiful women he'd ever seen to go out into arctic cold and darkness. Why not just tell his uncle that he wasn't up to it? That he was enjoying himself too much. Vince had, after all, brought this exotic dancer to him.

He started and warmed his uncle's Lincoln and drove past the Coast Guard Training station toward Cape May's eastern-most causeway. Radio weather forecasts promised no sun, overcast, bitter winds and arctic cold that day.

At a large convenience store located before the small bridge to the marina and its fishing boats and slips, Tom picked up a Danish, large coffee and orange juice, then drove less than two hundred yards to a parking lot adjacent to the nearest marina, waiting for dawn. He downed the juice then sipped the coffee slowly. The lights of a small breakfast luncheonette began to shine through the darkness of the marina as the staff readied for the eventual morning traffic.

When twilight came and there was enough light, he raised his binoculars to scan along the nearest slips, expecting nothing but sail- and motorized boats painted with clever or personal names tossing and creaking in the wind.

"*Motherfucker! This is impossible!* I don't fucking believe this!" Tom announced. "There it is!"

He climbed out of the car and stood staring at the boat as if it were a nuclear submarine. It was the 40-foot sailboat he had seen in the photo, *Sweet Rachel* painted on the prow and stern. Tom cautioned himself not to leap to conclusions.

Maybe this is someone else's boat with the same name. Fortune is sure smiling on me. Or maybe something else, he thought.

He went to the trunk of the car, opened the bowling ball bag. After looking around to see if anyone was about, he removed the waistband holster and revolver from the false bottom. He clipped it inside his belt at his back under his sweater, then went back to the car to finish his coffee and wait for a decent light to approach the boat.

Why don't I just tell Vince that I couldn't find the guy and get the hell out of here? Tom asked himself.

That seemed to be a great idea. And the more he thought about that, the better he liked it. Then came the counter-argument:

But what if Vince wants to stop here later and sees the boat? It's right here in plain sight from the dock. He'll know I fucked up, Tom thought, *or didn't want to do the job. Fuck!*

He feared his uncle's withering glare and suspicion of Tom's faint-heartedness and lack of thoroughness. Or worse, of deception.

Tom walked along the pier toward the *Sweet Rachel* in its slip. Frost had iced up on it and he skated-walked across it carefully.

When he got to what he thought was the dentist's boat he stopped for a minute to look around, then crossed the gangplank.

"Hello? Anyone aboard?" he yelled. Tom slid a few steps more toward what he thought was the main hatch.

"Anyone aboard?" he shouted once again. He hoped no one would answer and did not expect anyone to reply. Of course no one could or would hear him, he told himself.

The hatch suddenly slid open with a thud. The head of a man with a graying close-cropped moustache wearing a black knit watch cap popped out. He spied Tom immediately. "Who are you? What do you want?"

Tom was taken aback for a brief second. Despite the cap, from his picture he recognized the pointed face with a pronounced cleft chin.

It was Schonfeld. All Tom had to do was ask if he was someone else—make up a name, apologize and retreat and then tell his uncle that they had found their man. Let Vince do the rest.

The dentist climbed a few more steps. He was holding a newspaper folded in one hand.

"Are you Leon Schonfeld?"

"Yeah, what do you want?"

Tom slid forward gingerly and from eight feet away held out his wallet with the fake private investigator ID, one of several he had a friend from the media lab at college create.

"My name is John D'Angelo. I'm a private investigator. I'd like to talk to you."

"Private investigator? I don't want to—don't have to!—talk to you. Get the hell off my boat! Now!"

"Dr. Schonfeld, I was hired by the law firm that will represent your wife in the upcoming divorce hearing. I was sent to see if you were here. I'd like to talk to you—"

"Get off my boat! Now!" The dentist's voice had risen, his tone quavering between hysterical and hostile.

"Dr. Schonfeld, look, I'm *not*"—Tom emphasized the 'not'—"serving you any papers or anything like that. You might want to know what I have to say."

"Get the *hell* off my boat! Now!"

"Dr. Schonfeld, don't you want to know what your wife is up to? Concerning yourself and your estate?"

"That bitch is going to get as much as she can, I'm sure!"

Tom looked up at the nickel gray sky. "Look, Dr. Schonfeld, it's freezing here. I feel like an Eskimo on an ice flow. Let's talk down below or—hey, there's that breakfast place back there at the end of the marina"—he pointed to it—"they're open now. Let's have a cup of coffee there and talk. Just for *fifteen* minutes. I give you my word: I promise you I'm *not* here to serve you any papers."

Schonfeld eyed him suspiciously but said nothing. Tom saw the dentist's hesitation and pressed the attack.

"I have no subpoenas to serve, you have my word. I *will* have to report that I found you here in Cape May. But by then you can be in another slip, in Bermuda, or wherever this thing can take you. But I think you might like to know what your daughter said."

"My daughter? You spoke to her? To Cheryl? She asked for me?"

"Cheryl? Do you have two daughters? I spoke to Rachel," D'Arcangelo said, unable to conceal his puzzlement.

The dentist nodded. "Yes, Rachel. Just testing you. Why don't you come below? I just brewed some coffee and you can fill me in on what that bitch-wife intends to do to me." The dentist retreated down the hatch. "Pull the hatch shut behind you, would you?"

Tom lowered himself backwards down the ladder, slid the hatch closed, stepped down a few more steps and turned around in the boat's ill-lit galley. The dentist had dropped the newspaper to reveal a small black automatic in his other hand pointing at him.

Tom slowly raised his hands. He stared at the gun barrel like some fakir at a weaving cobra. Now he really regretted not just leaving after finding the dentist's boat.

"Whoa! Dr. Schonfeld, that's *not* a good idea. Let's just put the gun away. I'll forget I saw it and we can begin again, OK? I'm *not* armed. You can pat me down if you like. Go ahead, pat me down," Tom said. He held up his arms higher inviting a pat down. "I'm not carrying a gun. Your life is complicated enough, isn't it, without getting firearms involved?"

Tom didn't think the dentist would take him up on his offer. But D'Arcangelo knew he'd have to jump him if he got that close. Luckily, Schonfeld believed him.

"Sorry. I didn't mean to point it at you, really. I just carry it sometimes … for protection."

Schonfeld slid the gun into his jacket pocket. "Take a seat and I'll get some coffee. I just brewed some. Cream or sugar?"

"Black, if it's not too strong, thanks. As long as it's hot. Cold as a polar bear's balls out there—not what I associate the Jersey shore with, I must admit. I only come down here in the summer. Is it always like this in winter?"

"It's cold but not this cold. This is a real cold snap," Schonfeld said. "I've never felt it like this before. I'm running the heater and it still feels like I'm in Greenland."

Tom slid into the table's booth bench as Schonfeld placed a cup in front of him and poured two steaming cups of coffee. Tom looked around the galley. A short barreled 20-gauge Mossberg pump shotgun hung fastened on the wall within arm's reach of the dentist.

The dentist sat down.

"That's the 007 gun, isn't it? Walther PPK, like in the Bond movies?"

"No, it's a Sig-Sauer. Swiss made, I think? I'm not much for guns."

Tom was glad to hear of that. But his heart was still beating faster than normal. "Me neither. That's why I don't carry one. In my experience they usually get people into trouble."

Tom pointed to a chess set on the boat's galley table. "You play chess?"

"Did at one time. Played in tournaments for years. I reached an expert rating … got too caught up with work and family, so I gave up studying it. Thought I would make it to master level, but—," he shrugged. "I do go over *The Times* chess columns though."

The dentist poured coffee from a carafe into two wide-bottom mugs.

Tom put the cup of coffee to his mouth and took a sip. Because he had been on the high school chess team he fought the urge to ask Schonfeld if he wanted a game, just to see how good he really was. Tom didn't want to blow his intentions there—he had already ignored his uncle's orders—and the unexpected array of firepower at the doctor's disposal made him nervous.

"I'd like to play a game, but you'd probably beat me in twenty moves. I'm not that good. Played a little on the chess club in high school. I was sixth board—that's the last—against other schools."

Schonfeld nodded. "Not many people play chess any more. It's all video games. So tell me, what is my adoring wife up to?"

"Your wife is divorcing you. Plain and simple. Better get a good lawyer or you'll lose everything. She's real pissed off. And a friendly word from someone who's been divorced—the law firm I am working has two types of lawyers: sharks and barracudas."

"What love! How does she know that I didn't kill myself? She assumes I just ran off. I might be floating in the river for all she'd care."

An interesting and not inappropriate image, Tom thought. *No need to dwell on the irony of his statement.*

"She's pretty pissed, I can vouch for that." Tom took another sip of coffee and pointed toward the shotgun in its rack. That firepower within the dentist's reach made Tom uneasy. "Is that for duck hunting? Or pirates?"

The doctor slid into the bench across the table from me. "Not a fisherman, I see. Lots of boats have them—to shoot sharks."

Tom nodded, raising the mug to his mouth.

"What about my daughter? What does Rachel say?"

"I spoke with her, trying to find you. She seems to feel differently than your wife. She's more forgiving. She's genuinely worried about you, in fact."

"She's not like her mother, that's for sure. Her mother is a bitch with a capital B—I think she's hated me for years. I wished she'd have run off with some other man! My daughter loves me, I believe. She saw through my wife's trying to poison her against me."

"Yes, you're right about that. Rachel said she doesn't want to lose touch with you—she's worried about that. She spoke well of you, Dr. Schonfeld. She thinks you're going through a mid-life crisis of some sort. Said something about a Brazilian woman you met—?"

He looked down into his coffee, resigned but markedly shamefaced. "Hmm. She knows about Sonja then. I do miss my daughter, Rachel."

"Dr. Schonfeld, I know you might think I'm young and not wise in these affairs, but I am divorced and, in this line of work, see lots of people splitting up. Can I give you some advice? You might want to think about getting in contact with your wife and working something out. Divorces can get very bitter when things fester. It can become a battle of wills. War. Sometimes it's just best to pay off the problem. Handle it like any business deal. Like selling a house in a bad market. It's a procedural thing. Bite the bullet and do it."

Tom wanted to add that Schonfeld might also want to think about paying off his gambling debts before Frankie Cannizarro comes to visit.

It would be rather difficult to put a cap on someone's tooth with one hand in a cast, Tom thought. And impossible if rigor mortis had set in.

"I don't have enough money to pay my wife off. Never will. She needed to marry Bill Gates or the richest surgeon listed in Philly *Magazine's* 'Top Docs.'"

"You know her better than I," Tom said. "I just wanted to pass on what your daughter said to me and to give you a heads-up. Take it for what it's worth. Rachel seems like a nice person."

The thought suddenly wormed its way into his conscious mind. *Maybe I haven't fooled this guy at all. Suppose this guy shoots me right here. Says I was trespassing, trying to rob him him, in self-defense? And with this gun I'm carrying. Who would know? Jesus Christ, have I been stupid!*

D'Arcangelo measured the distance between the dentist and himself. The automatic was in the doctor's pocket, the shotgun on the post to his right. The cabin was not small and the table was in his way. He sized up Schonfeld: in his mid-fifties—twice Tom's age—but slender and appearing fit. Looked like he worked out a bit, maybe played tennis or squash. He still might have good reflexes.

Tom thought that if he had to, he could just pull the pistol tucked in his waistband and save himself. But he didn't want to murder anyone, not even in self-defense. It was best to get off this boat immediately and back to the hotel.

I gotta get the fuck outta here—and now! Tom thought. *Time to make an exit, as soon as possible, without arousing suspicion as to my real mission. I had imparted my information; I am nearly finished with my coffee. It was time to leave.*

"I need to take a leak. Is that the john?" Tom asked.

"Yes, that's the head." Schonfeld pointed to the door just behind Tom.

D'Arcangelo slid from the bench trying casually to keep his eyes on the dentist, who was staring pensively into his coffee mug, as if calculating a move over a chess board. Tom opened the door to the boat's head a mere ten feet from the table. He took one last surreptitious look at Schonfeld, who appeared lost in thought, then closed the door slowly.

In the head, Tom finished, zipped up and flushed. His mind spun over what to do next. He would finish his coffee in casual talk, then disengage himself from the dentist as gracefully and quickly as he could. Tom pulled the revolver from its holster and jammed it in the right pocket of his coat in case he needed it. He took a slow, long breath to calm himself.

D'Arcangelo opened the door expecting to see the doctor sitting where he left him. Schonfeld wasn't there.

Tom opened the door wider and then saw the doctor standing at the bottom of the step ladder looking upwards at the boat's hatch. Then Schonfeld grunted unintelligibly, groaned loudly and staggered backwards, jerking the gun from his robe pocket. Three shots from above tore into the dentist's chest. He spun around and away, a final round into his back. The shots were muffled by a silencer. Schonfeld fell backwards over the back of the seat where Tom had sat. He knocked over his cup of coffee and sent chess pieces flying.

Tom pulled the door shut ever so gently and silently. He wanted to lock the door, but thought that doing it would be heard. *Better not lock it,* he thought. If whoever shot Schonfeld found the door locked, he might just fire through the door. Tom flattened himself against the wall as much as possible. He backed along the head wall and drew the gun from his coat pocket.

Suddenly, what Vince had said about having the gun made a whole lot of sense.

The blood rushed through his head, a thundering pulse drowning everything. He was unable to hear anything on the other side of the door.

Then the handle to the door turned ever so slightly. Tom tried not to move. He knew if the door opened, he had a split-second to decide to shoot. If he delayed, he would be joining Schonfeld in the obituaries.

Tom waited, both hands with a vise-like grip on the .38 pointing at the door.

Then the door suddenly swung open.

A man wearing a black leather coat and knit cap, black jeans and running shoes stood in the doorway. The man, startled at seeing a gun facing him, swung his automatic with silencer toward Tom, slamming it into the door jamb with a *thwap!*

This gave Tom just a split-second to shoot first. He fired rapidly, wanting to put up a protective shield of lead blocking any rounds firing toward him. The revolver roared, once, twice, three, four, five deafening shots into the man now spinning in the doorway. The man staggered backwards, two rounds in his chest, two in mid-section, and one, as he was falling, through his neck. The neck wound brought a loud gurgle and the body hurtled noisily to the deck.

He leapt clumsily from the john and stood over the body. Blood roiled out of a few wounds. The man had fallen, the automatic weapon dropping now on the deck. His feet had tangled and his legs twisted one over the other.

Tom had never seen anyone shot before. Now there was a man at his feet gushing blood, dying. And Tom had caused it.

His hearing hummed with the shots in the confined area, and the smell of the gunpowder burned his nose and eyes. Tom staggered back away from the body and leaned against the head's doorframe. He realized he was still pointing the pistol at the body for another round if needed.

"Holy fuck! Holy fuck!" was all Tom could sputter. "Jeezus fucking Christ! Oh, fuck fuck, FUCK!"

D'Arcangelo had killed someone. Someone he didn't know. That he had never seen until that instant. He felt the sudden desire to rush to the man's aid, to help him live, to stop the bleeding.

Tom thought, *Wait! Suppose there's another guy with him? A backup? Why had I fired all those shots? Two would have been enough!*

He realized he had only one round remaining. He crouched moving forward and pointed the gun at the hatchway. He looked around for the dentist's gun in case he needed it. Suddenly, he felt dizzy, nauseous, confused. The slight movement of the boat in the water seemed exaggerated and sickening.

Breathe! he told himself. *Breathe!* He once experienced a week-long acting workshop in college, where the instructor had lectured about controlling the body and breathing He had spent the first day solely on autogenic and yoga training, so much so that the class wondered if they were in an acting seminar at all. "Acting is *breathing*. Your breath is your control. Breathe to prepare for what to do next; breathe to relax yourselves; breathe so you can *move*," he admonished. "Breathe to think."

D'Arcangelo stopped focusing on the body on the deck, his mind spiraling, and he began to take several deep breaths. After what seemed like hours but in reality was minutes, he centered and calmed himself.

The explosions had receded into silence and the boat's creaking, the water lapping the hull. Tom listened for anyone or anything. Nothing. He slid to the ladder and took a few steps up to the hatch. He listened, but all that he heard was the wind through the rigging and tapping of ropes and pulleys. He listened for a while, for a siren, footsteps, a cry of someone to another. Nothing.

Tom climbed the ladder steps and poked his head out of the hatch and peered around. Nothing. No one. Just the slicing razor wind and cold that now felt gloriously revitalizing. He stood there inhaling the air for a full minute, then left the hatch slightly ajar, just to hear anything from the outside better and returned to the hold.

Tom looked at Schonfeld. The dentist lay twisted where he fell after the three shots ripped through his chest. The automatic was just barely in his hand, his finger looped through the trigger guard.

Tom stood over him to see if he was breathing, then reached to put his fingers on the carotid artery. He saw no movement of his chest and felt nothing in his neck. Even in the dim light of the boat the dentist's face seemed inordinately pale. Tom stepped around his body and returned to Schonfeld's assailant. He seemed dead too; there was no motion from his chest and his eyes were half open under heavy lids. The man's legs were twisted and his arms extended as if he were being crucified.

D'Arcangelo had killed a man. A wave of guilt showered over him, followed by paralyzing anxiety and fear.

He listened once again for anyone coming to check on the boat, but still heard nothing. He stood there for several moments, taking deep diaphragmal breaths to gather his thoughts.

Then a plan came to his mind. He turned back toward Schonfeld, removed the gun from the dentist's fingers, and jammed it into his pocket. Tom then reached into the head and grabbed some paper towels, moistened them, and wiped the revolver he had used to clean off his prints. He then put it in the dentist's hand, and pressed Schonfeld's fingers on the trigger and the barrel. Tom rubbed residue from the barrel of the revolver onto the dentist's cuff, fingers and hand. He took his opposite hand and used it for print identification on the barrel and stock. D'Arcangelo twisted the assassin's body ever so slightly to face Schonfeld. Finally, he wiped the prints from the boat's head. He took that cup he had drunk from, put it to the man's lips and placed it in the hand of the man in the knit cap and then returned it to the table, being careful to wipe his prints off the cup and table.

Tom wiped the door handle of the head and the toilet and threw all of the paper in the toilet and flushed it. After listening again for anyone coming, he slipped on his gloves and went to the prow of the boat, and opened some drawers, looking for he knew not what. Tom opened a door under the sleeping area, and saw two large athletic bags and a small gym satchel. He pulled out the satchel and opened it to find some three paperbacks of John Updike and Gabriel Garcia Marquez novels, and then pulled out one of the large cargo bags and opened it.

Inside were stacks of cash wrapped in bank denomination bands, more money in bills than he had ever seen before.

"Holy fuck! Holy fuck!" Tom repeated over and over as he rummaged in the cargo bag pulling out stacks of one hundred, fifty and twenty dollar bills. As soon as he saw the bag was full of cash, he cinched it closed. He grabbed the second bag and found it full of the same: cash of large denominations neatly wrapped.

"Wait until Vince sees—," Tom said, then stopped. It hit him. They had come for Jimmy's money, thirty-two grand. He stopped rustling the money in the cargo bag and listened.

Was that someone coming? Tom stood there for almost a minute, listening to the wind in the rigging and the gentle rocking of the boat. Nothing.

In that oppressive moment of silence the idea came to him.

Breathe! he thought and took several long and deep breaths.

He counted out fifty thousand dollars in hundreds out of the one cargo bag and placed it in the gym bag. He left the books in it.

"That's for Jimmy," Tom whispered.

He cinched the two cargo bags, then looked around. He wanted to step carefully around the bodies and the blood running across the deck.

Once Tom skirted the oozing bodies, he returned to the hatch, slid it open, and poked his head out. Cold air hit him, but he felt it without it penetrating his bones. Adrenaline was stoking him. The slashing wind felt refreshing.

Although now later in the morning, the sun was barely visible, a mashed nickel on aluminum foil. Tom still saw no one. He put on his gloves, and after one look around, decided to risk it. With a cargo bag over each shoulder and the gym bag in his left hand, he popped open the hatch, looked around one more time. He tried to appear nonchalant in returning to the car. The weight of the bags helped him skate across the boat deck.

At the car, Tom fought the urge to rush in opening the trunk. He put the gym bag in the trunk with the bowling ball bag, and the cargo bags on the other side. "That's why Uncle Vince likes Lincolns—the big trunk."

He drove off. While he knew he had not yet crossed the Rubicon, Tom had entered Italy with his legions. Like Caesar, he was about to cross that river. He began to search for a place to stash the cargo bags full of money.

Tom looked at his watch; Vince would be wondering what happened to him. Tom drove from the marina, but instead of taking the jug handle to Cape May, continued over the causeway away from the marina, watching carefully neither to speed nor drive so slowly as to draw a trooper's attention.

Tom knew that there were two major roads leading back to the Cape, over causeways that crossed the canal. World War Two had divided the cape into an island, and, once over the canal, he wanted the least traveled, most rural roads. He remembered there was one that went to West Cape May, along the farmland, less developed western side of the island.

After Tom crossed the causeway once again, he looked for a route that took him to another access road. Once over the bridge and into the farming area, he looked to the right and left for someplace to hide the money.

He drove slowly to the first road that promised a route away from housing toward forested areas. Tom saw a sign for Rea's Farm, a large still-working farm that—he'd once read in the Cape May newspaper—had offered large tracts of its land to birdwatchers and the Audubon Society, who leased the area for rights to "bird" the area. It was once a lima bean farm and for that reason is called "The Beanery". Foot-and tractor paths surrounded several fields and wooded areas. Like many American farms, old farming equipment lay rusting in its fields.

Tom slowed and pulled into the parking area near one of several trails. Two parallel rows of pines bordered the adjacent property. He grabbed his binoculars and jumped from the car to look around, appearing to be looking for birds, but really for birdwatchers or others in the area.

There was no one. He threaded his way through the trees to the barn and peered through the binoculars once again.

This structure was far from the nearest house and seemed old, yet still sturdy, unused but still capable of use. Once on this side of the wooded, tree covered area of the Rea Farm, Tom saw an old access road that led to this barn. With binoculars in hand he posed as a birdwatcher by scanning the tree line and the sky every few minutes. He followed the road and saw it exited to the distant house and turning left, also to a Rea Farm path leading along two lines of the trees separating the two properties.

Tom took the Rea Farm road back to where he had gone through the trees to the back of the barn.

Access to the barn is perfect, he thought. *I can go down this path and turn onto that property by car if I need to, or take the road by the house a quarter mile away, nearly hidden by a copse of evergreen trees.*

Keeping the barn between him and anyone who might see him, Tom came up to the barn from its rear and circled to its side. With his binoculars, he peered around the barn at the distant house, but still saw no one. No lights, no movement at all.

No cars, no one. Great! he thought. He sauntered around to the front of the barn ostensibly peering at distant 'birds'.

Again, there was no one in sight—just windswept frozen brown and gray landscape.

At the front of the barn was a large double door that could swing open for a tractor or other farm equipment. In the right side of the double door was the customary access door, allowing easy access.

Tom walked to that door and, after one final look into the sky and at the distant house, tried the knob on the access door. It opened with a creak that in the morning stillness sounded louder than what it was. He slipped inside and shut the door behind him.

It was dark, but with some diffused light through its few windows, Tom could make out the interior. Inside were supplies and farm implements: two rusted plows and a tiller attached to an old tractor. To his surprise a dust-covered, rusting Dodge he estimated to be mid-70s.

Tom looked around and saw there was a small loft that covered a third of the back of the barn. The loft was accessed by two ladders on each side. Bales of hay aligning the loft provided cover and shelter from whatever was in the loft.

As Tom's eyes began to adjust to the lack of light, he began to look around for somewhere to hide the money for a few days or weeks. He was about to try the car door to see if he could spring the trunk from inside but remembered that cars of that vintage usually needed a key for entry. He went to the trunk to see if it could be opened without a key. It wouldn't open. He intended to see if it could be sprung from the inside.

Then he thought: *Wait a minute. A trunk of a car is an obvious place to look or discover by accident. Better to stash both bags in an less obvious and unlikely hiding place in the barn. The trunk of this car is too damned obvious.*

He looked around the barn for a better place to stash the bags. He looked to the loft where the hay bales were stored. They were as far away from the doors as one could find. The place would do.

Before Tom went to retrieve the bags he slipped carefully in the low light to the window of the barn and, with his binoculars, peered across the field at the house. Nothing.

Maybe there's no one living there, he hoped. *That would be a break.*

Tom exited the barn and, casually trying to appear as if he was looking for birds, walked around it and scooted through the woods. At the car, he peered around and saw no one, then opened the trunk and hoisted one of the duffle bags to his shoulder. He had already decided to make two quick runs rather than one slow one.

Inside the barn he headed for the ladder that led to the loft. He dropped the duffle bag to the ground, then slowly ascended its wooden steps. There was some creaking, but the ladder seemed sturdy enough to handle his weight and that of the money, which Tom estimated to be near forty pounds. He reached the top and looked around at wired hay bales, piled four high, with a narrow aisle between them.

He retrieved the second duffle bag, hauled it to the loft and removed the top bale of hay from a pile of three and stashed the bag behind it, then placed the bale back in place. To prevent anyone finding both bags, he cached them in two separate hiding places behind the bales.

Tom stood back to see if it was that obvious the bales had been moved. As he brushed himself off, he decided it looked good enough not to attract attention, unless of course someone moved the bales. He moved the hay on the loft's floor to erase any footprints, then descended the ladder to the barn's window. He carefully removed every tick of straw and slapped his coat free of dust. *If someone has seen me bring those bags in here and they find them,* he thought, *he will be one lucky motherfucker.* He then peered out the window one more time. Still no one in sight.

Tom exited the barn, shutting the door as quietly as he could, then scooted around the barn out of sight of the house. He cut through the woods to the car. Using the binoculars again simply for show, nonchalantly traced the skies for birds and then, with purpose, the perimeters of the woods and fields for anyone who might have seen him.

Lucky for me, this fucking weather has even the craziest birdwatcher indoors, he mused. *If this were summer, there'd be a hundred peering eyes with high-powered binoculars and scopes.* He knew he would never be able to pull this off without being seen.

Tom drove down Beach Drive along the seaside promenade. Nearing the hotel, he saw Vince and a young woman he assumed to be Nina's friend Sherry walking arm in arm toward him.

Cold winds from the ocean made them hunch their shoulders and huddle together as they walked. In spite of that, they were smiling, talking animatedly, oblivious to the cold and wind. Tom pulled over to the promenade. He looked at his watch. It was already after eleven, and he expected to get grief from Vince. He got out of the car, jumped up to the promenade and walked toward them.

"Hey," Tom greeted innocently.

"How ya doin'?" Vince smiled.

"Bit chilly for a stroll along the beach, isn't it?"

"Yeah, but we wanted to get some air," Vince said.

"Tom, this is Sherry. Sherry, this is my nephew, Tommy D'Arcangelo."

Tom nodded, while she stepped forward and offered her hand. "Nice to meet you, Tommy."

"You hungry?" Vince asked. "We were waiting for you to get some breakfast. Had some coffee at the hotel, but we thought we'd get Nina and you and get something to eat."

"Great. I'm starving," Tom lied. His stomach was a bucket of acid on a trampoline—food was the last thing with any appeal.

Sherry turned to Vince. "Vince, I'm freezing my ass off here. Can't we drive back to the hotel?"

"Sure, Baby. Why don't you get in the car and call Nina? Tell her to meet us at the hotel and we'll go out to get some breakfast, OK?"

The men waited until she was out of earshot in the car.

"Vince—," Tom began.

"I love that babe, Tommy."

"Uh sure, Vince. She seems nice. Real nice."

"No, Tommy. I mean it, I really *love* that girl."

"Yeah sure, sure, Vince—," Tom said, "But—."

He looked at his uncle's face trying to gain his full attention. Vince was beaming at the girl in the car. Sherry had pulled the sun visor mirror down and was straightening wind-blown hair.

"So where ya been?" Vince finally asked, still smiling at the woman in the car, now pouting her lips to apply lipstick.

Tom looked at him in disbelief. "Looking at boats in the marina."

"They are something. See anything you like?"

Vince held up his hand, wiggled his fingers in a tender salute, and beamed a big grin to the girl.

"Uh … no, Vince. Remember I was looking for the dentist who owes Mr. Cardinello?"

"Oh, yeah. You didn't find him, I'll bet—"

"In fact, I did. His boat was there and he was on it."

Vince turned to him and laughed. "No shit! Good. After we eat and get the girls on their way, we'll go talk to him."

"That's going to be difficult."

"Why's that?"

"He's dead."

"Dead?"

"Yeah, dead."

"*Dead?*"

"Yes, dead."

"What do you mean 'dead'?"

"I mean 'dead' as in having no pulse. As in never being able to breathe again. Like"—Tom mimicked a priestly sign of the cross—"*Requiescant in pace.* That kind of dead."

"Wait a minute. You went to his boat, found him there dead?"

"No, he was *alive* when I got there. I spoke to him."

Vince looked again at the young woman in the car then turned to his nephew. "Oh-h-h Tommy! What'd I tell you? I told you not to talk with the guy, much less *off* him. We might have been able to get that money without ya killin' the guy. Did he make a move on you?"

"I got the money, plus some extra. It's in a gym bag in the trunk of your car. Fifty grand."

"You got the bread? No shit! *Goddamn!* I didn't think you had it in you, kid."

Vince looked Tom in the face and hugged him. The uncle turned and smiled again at Sherry, who held up her hand next to her face and was wiggle-waving fingers at him.

Vince returned the gesture. "Isn't she cute?"

"Vince, she's a knockout—."

His uncle turned to him. "Did you clean up after yourself? I'm worried that you left shitloads of evidence around. That's why it's good to have a *paisano* along, you know what I mean? I think we need to go back there and check out the place. I'm an old hand at this sort of thing. Ya need a cool head around for this type of stuff."

Vince suddenly grabbed Tom by the back of his neck and pulled towards him in a hug. "My boy! *Killer!* And—deep down I must admit—I thought you were too soft for this work!"

Tom winced at the label. "But *I* didn't kill him, Vince."

Vince went silent, his eyes hardened, surprised. Then he whispered "Huh? Whaddya mean?"

"Somebody else showed up and iced Schonfeld. I was in the john taking a piss. This other guy plugged him three times—."

"Huh?"

"It gets better. I had to take out the other guy. I was sure glad I had that gun with me. You—and it—saved my life."

Vince's face suddenly wrinkled as if he felt a massive migraine coming on. "Whoa! This is getting complicated now. This is really ruining my buzz here. Tell you what—let's eat, get the girls on the road and then we'll deal with this fucking dentist."

They picked up Nina at the hotel. She slid in the back seat with Tom.

"Hi, Sweetie," she smiled and gave him an exaggerated smooch on his cheek. "Missed you. Where have you been?"

"Went for an early morning walk in the woods," Tom answered. He could see his uncle looking in the rear-view mirror at the two. For his uncle's sake Tom leaned over and returned her kiss.

"You two have a nice evening?" Vince probed. "The food in the hotel restaurant was pretty good. You ate there, didn't you?"

Vince was never one for domestic small talk, so this might ordinarily have been amusing. But Tom's thoughts kept flashing back to the bodies on the boat and his theft of what looked like a shipment from the Philly mint.

Before Tom could offer a reply, Nina spoke up: "We had a real nice dinner there, don't you think, Tom? We spent time there talking, getting to know each other better."

Tom grunted an assent. Carla wafted into his consciousness.

"Great!" Vince said. "Maybe you girls can come to Philly and pay us a visit sometime soon?"

Sherry turned to Nina. "Sounds like a great idea, huh, Nin'? Maybe right after Christmas?"

Nina agreed. "Sure, why not?"

"Man, I'm hungry! Let's find a place that does pancakes real good," Vince said, zooming down Beach Drive.

At the pancake house—Uncle Phil's known for its circular architecture and lumberjack breakfasts—was still open, its last week before closing until March when they joined the majority of shore establishments closed for winter.

The four ordered first coffee, then breakfast. Tom ordered scrambled eggs and wheat toast, the only breakfast he thought he could get down. His uncle ordered a massive stack of blueberry pancakes slathered with butter and syrup, sausage and bacon and a fruit cup. The women, watching their dancers' figures ordered healthy egg-white omelettes with dry toast and fruit cups and left their meals half-eaten.

They ate unhurriedly, all the while making small talk about their many experiences from their childhoods at the shore. Tom, for the most part, said nothing, eating slowly. He chimed into the conversation only when he felt Nina's glancing sideways at him. He smiled at her. She then leaned over to him and whispered into his ear: "Morose."

Vince picked up the tab by dropping a hundred dollars on the table. They dropped the ladies at Sherry's car and, after hugs and kisses, they separated.

VINCE AND TOM pulled up across from the marina where they could survey where the boat lay anchored. Though it was midday they saw only one well-bundled woman lugging some packages to a large boat at a slip at the far end.

"See anyone? Police? Other than that lady?" Vince asked.

Tom scanned the perimeter with the binoculars. "No, no one. But at this time of year there shouldn't be too many people around—the holidays and all."

"If we see any cops at all, we're fucking out of here," Vince ordered. "Let's look around for a bit, say a half-hour. If we don't see anyone, I think it's safe to check out the scene. I'll go in there first. If they have the place staked out and question me, I'll just say that someone told me there was a boat for sale and I was checking it out. I'll signal if it's okay to come down. If you don't see a signal, don't come, got it? I'll take the duffle bag of supplies with me. I will walk to the end of the pier and catch a smoke. Keep the car ready to beat it—but don't run. If we should both get caught, let me do the talking, then follow my lead. You know the drill: 'We want to speak to our attorneys.' These fuckin' yokels down here won't know what to do with that."

Tom cautioned his uncle about the slippery deck, and, after a few minutes, Vince took off for the boat. Once there, Sarzano slid the hatch open and lowered himself down the steps. Leaving the hatch slightly ajar, he disappeared into the hold of the boat. Tom took one more look around for any signs that someone was on to what had happened earlier. He turned the Lincoln around to make a quicker exit if needed.

Just seeing the boat again had Tom's heart pounding. He waited for twenty minutes, trying not to swivel his head like a fearful running back, but nonchalantly moving his eyes side to side like an owl.

Finally Vince returned to the car carrying the duffle bag. He dropped the bag, now fuller, in the trunk of the car and slid into the passenger seat.

Vince looked around then turned to Tom. "Looked like fuckin' Omaha Beach in there, for chrissakes. You did real good, kid. It was a piece of cake."

"I think I cleaned up everything I touched," Tom said. "I switched the guns, so it looks as if they shot it out. A good crime scene unit should figure that something doesn't look right." He paused a moment. "Did you look at that guy? Did you ever see him? Know who he is or might be?"

Tom started the Lincoln and pulled slowly away.

"Never saw him in my life," Vince said. "But I'd say he was in the wrong place at the wrong time. Time to check out of the hotel and head back to Philly."

They saw no police activity, so Tom drove out and they returned directly to the hotel.

"Who do you think he was?" Tom pressed.

Vince shrugged. "Somebody that didn't like the dentist. I didn't look for ID."

"You sure you never saw him before?" Tom asked. "It was pretty dark in there."

"Fuck no. Did you? What do I care who he was? Besides I didn't want to screw up the crime scene with any more evidence—you seen CSI and those investigation shows! I wiped down everything you said you touched. We'll ditch that stuff and the gun you took and get rid of our clothes and shoes as soon as we get home."

"Just wondered why that guy was there—."

Vince shrugged. "He was there to whack that dentist, I guess. Why? Maybe Schonfeld owed him money, too. Maybe that wife of his had him removed. Whoever he was did us a favor. And we got our money, too. Couldn't be better. Teach 'em to fuck with a Philly boy, eh?"

"I just wonder who he was with," Tom said. "He must be with *some* mob."

"Maybe. He might have got word that the dentist had that money and was trying to jack it—on his own, I mean. That happens to drug dealers a lot."

"Maybe."

"He looked pretty young and had a tattoo on the inside of his wrist."

"Yeah? A *tattoo of what?*" Tom asked.

"A cross. A religious, ornamental cross. Didn't help him all that much."

Tom sat thinking about the man he had shot and Schonfeld. He had killed someone. And although it was in self-defense, he was alarmed. The recurring image of blood flowing out of their bodies made him slightly sick.

D'Arcangelo thought about an interview he had seen on TV right after the Iraq War began. Because his brother was involved in the fighting, Tom was intensely interested. A soldier was asked about some vicious fire-fights in some town in where the Americans had killed several Iraqis. In a surprise slip of the censors, the soldier had said: "Killing people does something to your soul."

THEY CHECKED OUT of the hotel and put their luggage in the car. Vince took the keys from him. "Want to get a drink before we leave? The bar opened at noon. One for the road. It's on me."

Tom didn't feel like drinking at this hour. "Maybe we should just get out of here?"

"Why? What's the hurry? Let's not appear impulsive. One drink and then we'll head home. We'll take care of the you-know-what on the way," said Vince, heading back into the hotel and its bar. "Let's at least get lunch, Tommy. I don't want to drive on an empty stomach, know what I mean?"

Tom nodded. "Sure," he agreed. But he had no appetite. He still felt slightly nauseous. He regretted not following his instincts coming with his uncle. He should have insisted Vince take Lou or one of the Maranelli brothers.

After lunch the pair headed for Philly. Tom's uncle took the wheel, popped in a Dean Martin CD and drove out of Cape May by Beach Drive.

"We'll listen to some Christmas stuff by Sinatra and Company as we get near Philly. Got to get into the Christmas spirit—it's the only way I can handle all that fuckin' shopping."

The events of the weekends seemed the least on Vince's mind. He seemed almost upbeat and cheerful. Tom doubted he would be able to get into the spirit any time soon.

"Take the back route—west—not the way by the marina, OK? Stay off the main routes until we have to," he said. "Sometimes cops are checking for people who go by crime scenes. I'd rather not get our plates on video."

"Makes sense to me."

Vince drove with his customary sledge hammer leg. He started to sing along with Dino. *"Return to me, cara mia, I'm lonely. Hurry back, hurry back, hurry back ..."*

D'Arcangelo looked in the mirrors and down the road for a patrol car. He tried not to show nervousness at his uncle's jackrabbit driving. Tom thought he might distract him by asking about Sherry, his new-found love.

"Vince, slow down a little; you're going too fast. How long have you been seeing Sherry? She seems real nice."

"About four months now. Met her in August in AC. Great girl. Really like her. She's a notch above."

"She recommended that 'existential' movie to you? *Woman in the Dunes?"*

"Yeah. She's going to college, ya know. Real smart. So's Nina, isn't she?"

"Nina? Yeah, yeah. She's real smart."

"And those dancers have great fucking bodies."

Tom looked at Vince, noting his capacity to swerve from intellect to physical attributes.

"That's for sure. Nina has a body that doesn't qui—watch out!" Tom shouted pointing to the deer bolting onto the road twenty yards in front of them. He covered his face to brace for the collision and deer crashing through the windshield.

Too late. The gray Lincoln Town Car slammed into the deer. It smacked into and over the car and off to the side of the road. Vince jammed on the brakes and the Lincoln slid sixty feet to a stop. Tom took his arms down and looked around. Not one mark on an intact windshield. He exhaled deeply. *"Jeezus fuck!"*

They both leapt from the car. Vince knelt at the front grill looking for damage.

He scorched the air with profanity. "Cocksucker! Mother Fucker! Jesus fuckin' Christ! Goddamn deer are all over the fuckin' place!"

While Vince inspected the grill and the head lights for damage, Tom started back to look at the deer.

"Not too bad," Tom's uncle reported. "A few nicks. Nothing serious. I don't give a shit what *Consumer Reports* says—GM still makes a fuckin' good car."

Thirty yards back the deer lay, half on the shoulder of road and the other half in the wood. It was still moving, thrashing slowly trying but unable to get on its feet. Tom walked back to it, stopped, then inched nearer. The deer's eyes were clouded and rolled back in its head, its tongue licking, going in and out of its mouth. It was a young doe. She was twisted half around at its belly area.

"Oh fuck! Its back is broken," Tom said. He saw that it was alive and suffering. He loped back to the car.

"Pop the trunk," he commanded.

Vince looked at him, hesitating.

"Go on! Pop the fucking trunk!" Tom ordered.

Vince looked around up and down the empty road, then did as he told. Tom reached into the trunk and looked up and down before taking the dentist's automatic out of the bag. Seeing no cars, he removed the safety and chambered a round. He held the gun down at his side against his leg and looked again down the road. Tom looked around up and down the road one more time, then jogged back to the writhing animal.

Vince looked around nervously. "Are you sure you want to fire that off here?" he shouted.

Tom ignored his uncle's question. He surveyed the road first one way, then the other, There was still no traffic or anyone in sight. The doe lay there trembling and hemorrhaging from its mouth. Tom stood over it and fired twice quickly into its head and then once into its heart and lung area. The shots echoed over the crystal landscape, sending startled crows into flight to distant woodlands.

Tom leaned down to speak softly to it. "I'm sorry." He felt his eyes tearing.

D'Arcangelo walked back to the car and slid the gun back in the bag and slammed the trunk.

The two men got into the car and sat there for a moment, in an odd mix of adrenaline and tension. Vince turned the key in the ignition.

Tom felt slightly dizzy. "Let's get the fuck outta here. *Slow.* I'll keep my eyes open for more deer."

ON THE WAY they stopped at a state park off route 347 and tossed the gun in pieces into a three different sections of a large lake there. Back in Philly, Vince drove straight to Tom's house.

Once inside, Vince closed the house blinds and took out a large black plastic bag and commanded:

"Strip and I'll get rid of it all at Dom D.'s crematory. Shoes, everything, except your wallet and keys."

Tom obeyed and dropped all of his clothes into the bag until he was standing there naked.

Vince knotted the bag. "Later," he said. He turned to the door, then stopped at the door, turned to his nephew still standing there. "Tommy—"

"Yeah?"

"Don't worry about anything. Ya did good."

"Yeah, sure," Tom replied and waved to signal goodbye. Vince turned for the door.

Tom felt his scrotum tightening as he stood there waiting for Vince to leave. He locked the door behind his uncle and headed up to shower. After toweling off, he came downstairs in terry cloth robe and slippers. He made himself a tumbler of Scotch and a splash of water over ice, grabbed the TV remote, and pitched back in his leather lounge chair.

Tom switched on cable TV and, while sipping steadily, praying for the quick soporific effect of liquor. He clicked through the offerings of paid programming, news, infomercials, sports news, public awareness channels, sports events, fitness channels, history, science and what passes for history and science, miscellaneous rubbish, and movies.

The thought of the day's activities made him question if he would be able to sleep at all. After all, he *had* killed a man that day. And he stolen thousands of dollars. Tom was surprised that his pulse had returned to normal. His mother's words came to him; Carla's words followed. He felt the fear, the regret, the dread of the day's actions descending over him.

Tom knew he should call Carla but, in his heart, didn't want to. He knew she'd ask if he had spoken to his uncle, if he had gotten away from the family business 'activities'. He couldn't face her just now.

And there was that business of Nina. Despite the fact that he had not really touched her, Tom felt nevertheless unfaithful to Carla. He wondered about this: why did he feel that way? Was it that he felt more and more distant from Carla? That he was being untrue to her some time?

Tom stopped at a classic movies channel, immediately recognizing the banter of *Reservoir Dogs*. Mr. Pink ignites a debate about tipping. Lawrence Tierney, the boss gangster, returns to the table and sees that the pile of money for the tip was lacking:

"Wait minute. Who didn't throw in?" he growls
"Mr. Pink."
"Mr. Pink? Why not?"
"He don't tip."
"He don't tip?"
"He don't believe in it," another offers.
"Why not?"
"He doesn't believe in tipping."
"Shut up. What do you mean you don't believe in it? C'mon you! Cough up a buck, ya cheap bastard, I paid for your goddamn breakfast."

Tom groaned. *A fucking gangster movie!* He clicked through several channels and stopped at the classic movies channel where the captivating figure of the young Lauren Bacall was leaning over and kissing Bogart. After a few moments Tom recognized the scene from *To Have and Have Not*. But before arriving at Bacall's famous whistling scene, overwhelmed with exhaustion, he nodded into sleep.

Two hours later he woke to the sound of a lapping ocean.

The television still on, the remote lay in his lap. Tom sat up and slowly focused on the screen. A tall black cloaked figure stood on a rocky shore, its face unsettling and alight. Tom had awakened to the hooded figure of Death standing on the rocky shore with waves of the sea washing eerily in the background before the knight in *The Seventh Seal*.

Bergman? Jesus Christ! he thought. Tom clicked the TV off and climbed the stairs hoping to find sleep once again in bed.

At his bedside he saw the LSAT exam preparation book on the night table where he last left it. Without looking at it, he tossed it into the trash can, then turned out the light.

4

Tom lumbered to the bathroom for his morning piss, flicked the light on and two-stepped to the toilet. Connected to the bathroom light was a radio tuned to local news, and weather in counterpoint to the percussive stream of urine launching into the porcelain bowl. The station's announcer reported that an arctic blast that had swept in from Canada over the Great Lakes and on to the mid-Atlantic states was abating a bit:

"Temperatures for this time of year are fifteen degrees below the average and will stay that way for the next week to ten days, although there is not much chance of snow since precipitation is not predicted. This will make Christmas shopping and holiday events extremely frigid, but not covered with the white stuff. So dress accordingly ..."

Although exhausted last evening Tom had fallen asleep in front of the television. After crawling into bed upstairs he slept fitfully. The events of the day before were not far away. That he had stolen hundreds of thousands of dollars from someone and hidden it was one thing, although that took a distant back seat to murder. That he had killed a man twenty-four hours earlier was his first waking thought, the greatest weight when he awoke. In fact, the burden of those deeds swirled around him in his sleep throughout the entire night. A vivid dream had shocked him awake sweating.

Tom stood now in front of the mirror to see if he could face shaving. He leaned forward to examine his face. Its lines looked deeper, more pronounced. Weren't there new ones? Didn't his eyes appear puffy? His mind drifted to *The Picture of Dorian Gray*, a film Carla and he had seen at a late night cinema.

Soon, Tom thought, *I'll need that Egyptian cat god and a painting of myself hiding in the attic.*

Tom filled the sink with hot water and ran his hands over stubbled cheeks and jaw, then lathered with Noxzema. He stared at himself disguised with a white beard, unrecognizable. With the razor, he pointed to the image in the mirror.

"That's better." He scraped the whiskers from his face, then shoveled hot water over now smooth skin.

The radio spewed the past evening's sports results, rattling on about upcoming football games, facts about Eagles injuries followed by the overweight head coach's weekly wheezing drone about how good a team the Eagles' next opponent is, prior to the AM station's wisdom of buying gold, the savvy of advertising one's business, the excellence of one of several local medical schools and hospitals, and the high quality of one of the country's major health care providers.

In the shower he allowed the hot water to wash over him. He wanted its soothing cascade to deflect his memory of yesterday, if only for a few moments.

But that was not to be for long. Scenarios of his attorney pleading his case to the jury pulsed from Tom's unconscious: (*'My client—a man with no prior criminal record—found himself in a gangland execution and defended himself, ladies and gentlemen of the jury. Of course he pleads "not guilty" to the charge against him. The jury will find that any one of them would have acted the same way Mr. D'Arcangelo did—purely and reasonably in self defense! Reluctantly he had to fire his weapon, a weapon he is licensed to carry and with which he has never used in a commission of any felony, a weapon that he carried for the purposes of his Constitutional right to defend himself. He was fortunate to have his gun in his possession or he'd be dead now. Who here wouldn't have done what Mr. D'Arcangelo did to save his life?'*)

Tom's lawyer—speaking with convincing delivery and the *gravitas* of Denzel Washington in the movie *Philadelphia* or the attorney protagonist of a John Grisham novel—would mesmerize the jury. If there's one thing the citizens of the City of Brotherly Shove believe, it's the right to dispatch one's attackers. Philadelphians revel at seeing someone get their ass beat. If it's legally defensible and righteously deserved, then so much the better.

Then that Worm of Doubt, of Uncertainty, gnawed at Tom, slithering into his thoughts: *What if the attorney I'd have was not that good? Court-appointed DA's are poorly paid, overloaded with cases, maybe even rejects from good law schools. My lawyer could be the B or C Team. Maybe they'd be looking for a plea deal of some kind to expedite the court proceedings. Maybe I'll need the backing of Jimmy Cardinello and the family business to pay for a sharp mob attorney—someone who gave a shit about his retainer.*

Tom's mind raced to life in prison, to fear of fellow inmates, the exercise yard, dreading the prison shower.

How does *one shower in prison?* he wondered. The water would be cold, of course, the experience communal. *How does one stay alert for HIV-infected thugs about to butt-fuck me while not intimidating others with perceived hostile stares?*

Death's head tattoos on hefty biceps of evil-looking biker gang members and white supremacists welled up in his imagination. *What were those gang hand signs about anyway?*

Tom had read that some inmates felt compelled to convert to Islam to survive. He had tried to read the *Qu'ran* in a comparative religion course and found it at least, if not more, boring than *The Bible.*

His thoughts drifted and shifted to a chaotic overdrive of sheer and utter dread: years in prison.

Tom remembered how two years ago on one bright Saturday in October, Carla had surprised him at school after rehearsal. She said she had a treat and took him to the Philadelphia Zoo. Trees had begun to turn and their leaves were beginning to fall, their yellow, red, and orange and brown leaves were beginning to crackle under foot, and the blue sky with high racing white clouds made the day memorable. Tom found zoos depressing and said so to her. In her customary logical manner, she said she did, too, but that when she thought of the ecological and conservation ideas behind zoos, she gained an understanding, an appreciation of them.

"It's not like Siegfried and Roy in Vegas. Zoos have their place," Carla concluded with her optimistic Save-the-Planet finality. She knew Tom exulted when an animal trained to act human and stupid to entertain people went berserk and mauled or trampled its trainer. A bull or horse or elephant stomping on its rider delighted him. Carla was persuasive.

Perhaps, he thought, she had a point.

Despite that, when they got to the primate area and looked at the monkeys and chimpanzees and apes and gorillas in their settings and cages, Tom became disheartened. They possessed such immensely human qualities. Many seemed sad or bored at existence in captivity.

Carla could read his face. "Zoos have their place," she affirmed. "You saw *Gorillas in the Mist*—poachers kill these wonderful beasts for their hides, elephants and rhinos for their tusks, just so someone thinks it makes their dicks stiffer or likes the look of an animal skin in their den. These animals are here to be *protected*. Zoos have a purpose; their mission is to *preserve* the species. A zoo is not a circus."

Tom nodded in agreement. He knew she was right, but his equating the zoo with prison just wouldn't evaporate with logic.

He wondered: *if chimps could choose to be in the zoo—even if it was a quasi-natural environment funded by a large local utility—or be in the jungle where a leopard could snatch the life from them, which would they choose?*

He posed that question to Carla. Of course, Tom meant it rhetorically. He didn't expect her to reply.

She smiled and said, "You're anthropomorphizing, Sweetie. They don't understand the concept of choice—it's a human ability to apply reason. They are instinctual. In some cases, humans have to decide what's best for them. I agree with you that sometimes it might not always work out in ways that are intended, but …."

Carla took Tom's arm and she steered him toward the lions, tigers, leopards and jaguars of Carnivore Kingdom.

TOM HAD SCHEDULED a nine o'clock emergency appointment with Dr. Horowitz after he returned home yesterday afternoon. (He had not called it that, but since he asked to have his weekly appointment two days after the last, the doctor had perceived it as such.)

The day began with a cold bright blue cloudless sky. Now its sun shone in flashes through the barest of trees lining the drives on either side of the river. The spare beauty of winter calmed him as he drove the winding Kelly Drive along the Schuylkill River to Lincoln Drive and on to the doctor's home and office in Mt Airy in silence.

Fairmount Park is Philly's geographical resource crown, its River Drives the city's scenic jewels. East and West River Drives, later named for John B. Kelly, the Olympic gold oarsman, and Martin Luther King, were surveyed and planned after the Civil War by its first park commissioner, a Philadelphian, noted engineer of lighthouses along the eastern coast, and the victorious general who defeated Lee at Gettysburg. Carla and he had often walked or cycled along these meandering drives. In high school Tom had run Belmont Plateau's hills and cross-country trails and hundreds of conditioning miles around the river drives while high school and collegiate oarsmen preparing for regattas knifed through the river's brown-green shallow waters.

AFTER HIS CUSTOMARY CUPS of coffee were brewed, Horowitz handed one to Tom, sat down and said nothing. His gaze reminded Tom of an lion on the veldt surveying his lionesses and offspring while they foraged and tussled. His eyes were penetrating; they projected wisdom and knowledge and with it, a certain inexpressible power. Tom wanted his shrink to have thick glasses and beard; he expected a more professorial mien.

"Aren't we supposed to talk about my dreams?" Tom asked. "Do you do that type of thing?"

The psychologist put down his coffee and circled a wave of his hand to proceed. "Sure. If that's what you do, we can talk about your dreams. Do you have a dream or dreams you want to discuss?"

"I do. Dreams mean something, don't they?"

He shrugged. "They might. If you believe they're important, why not talk about them?"

"Well, I had this very vivid dream last night. It was frightening. I woke up sweating. My pulse was pounding a mile a minute."

"Go on then—tell me about it."

"In the dream I had to attend a funeral. It was far away and I drove all night to get wherever it was to be. I arrived in the early hours of the morning and checked into a motel where the funeral was to be held the next day. This thin, old Vietnamese clerk checked me in and I went to my room to get a few hours of sleep. The motel was long—very spread out—and old. I went down what seemed blocks of hallways to get to my room. The place was run-down and seemed to need lights or something. It had very little light. Real dark.

"I go to the bathroom to brush my teeth. One of the lights in the bathroom was out and it was pretty dim, too. I kept straining to see. I started to brush my teeth and was looking in the mirror. Behind me was the shower with its plastic curtain drawn. It was translucent, but in the mirror behind me, through the curtain, I saw an outline shadow of something or someone. It looked like it was standing right behind the curtain. I peered closer at the mirror to see better and then I saw two burning red coal-like objects behind the shower curtain, like eyes, animal-like, with some kind of cat's eyes. I leapt around to see if they were really there, or if it was some kind of weird reflection on the glass of the mirror. And they were there, two glowing lights behind the curtain. I reached across and pulled the curtain open. But my arm just couldn't grip the plastic to pull it. My hands were unable to grab it and jerk it open. I tried several times—each time I failed. Then I began to scream, louder and louder. And I awoke in a sweat …."

The psychologist nodded and sipped coffee. "It has all the elements of an anxiety dream. It was terrifying to you obviously. You remember it in some detail. Do you have dreams like this often?"

"No, not at all. Well, maybe once in a while. Doesn't everyone?"

"Has anything dramatic happened since we met last? Have you been able to tell your Uncle that you don't want to be working for his 'business'?"

Tom didn't know how to answer. He shook his head.

"Do you have particular reason to be anxious, I mean?" the doctor pursued.

"Yeah, I guess I do," Tom admitted. He suddenly had the strongest desire to confess to the shooting but knew he had to resist that urge.

Suppose this shrink turned me in to the police? Tom clenched his teeth and sat in silence for a good few minutes.

"I just haven't been able to talk to my uncle or my boss about getting away from the business, I guess. I know I have to do it, but just can't seem to …"

"Tell me about your uncle. He seems to have played a big part in your life after your father died."

"He's been like a father since mine died."

"And you were how old, twelve or thirteen years old?"

"A little older. I just turned fifteen."

"And so Vince has been like your father for how many years now? Twelve? Thirteen?"

"I'm twenty-six. So yeah, eleven or twelve years."

"That's a long time. Has he been there 'like a father' for all that time?"

Tom nodded, feeling suddenly as if the shrink was implying something. "He's my mother's *brother*—it's not like he's Hamlet's uncle who killed the king to fuck his mother—Vince is my mother's brother, for chrissakes. What the fuck are you getting at?"

The psychologist leaned back in his chair and smiled.

"Nothing as Freudian as *Hamlet*. I mean just that Vince—your *uncle*—has been *like* your father for so long that you see him *as* your father. I'm curious about *how* is he like your father?"

"He helped provide for the family," Tom answered. "He did things my father did for both Matt and me."

"Like what exactly? I mean were there other things than the money for food and clothing—the security of those things?"

"He came to our ball games. Took us down the shore. Took us on fishing trips, on vacations, bought us gifts, looked after us. Important stuff, other than money for food."

The psychologist nodded and said nothing for a moment. He waited for Tom to add something, but when he saw there was nothing to be added, asked "Is that what you think fathers do?"

"He was *there* for us after Dad died. Why do you make it sound so—I don't know—so fucking inappropriate—so *abnormal*. Just exactly what do you mean?"

Horowitz did not reply. After several moments Tom continued. "Uncle Vince is a good guy. Really."

The psychologist remained silent, just that piercing gaze. It was beginning to irritate Tom.

Man, this motherfucker can stare!

D'Arcangelo went on. "When I was in 10th grade I was going to try out for the baseball team at Roman. It was in early March—cold as shit, real windy, nasty—and I mentioned to him that I felt rusty not having caught any fly balls for several months. Uncle Vince told me not to worry, that he'd be over first thing in the morning, before school, and hit some balls to me. We were out at the field at daybreak and he must have hit fifty flies and grounders to me. That's what I mean—stuff a father would do."

The psychologist nodded in understanding. "I wasn't implying anything strange or pathological about your uncle. I am curious how you perceive your father, fatherhood, your uncle *as* your father—that's all."

Tom nodded. "How do *you* expect a father to act? Is there a prescribed behavior for a father? I mean, look around today ... kids are so fucked up ... does that mean they can blame their fathers?"

"You mean if they have a father?" The psychologist shrugged. "Kids are fucked up for many reasons. Blame is not the issue." The psychologist then pointed a finger at Tom. "How do *you* expect a father to act? What does the word 'father' mean to *you*?"

Though seldom at a loss for words, Tom couldn't say anything for several seconds, thinking. He began to speak, found himself mumbling a few incoherent syllables.

"Uh, uh ... er, umm ... fathers should ... uh ...."

He found himself suddenly unable to speak. His brain and tongue were numb, frozen, over the meaning of fatherhood.

Horowitz sat there, saying nothing, peering at him.

Finally, Tom spoke. "The things I mentioned—Uncle Vince helped support our family, took us to Eagles and Flyers and Phillies' games, made sure we had a place to stay for a vacation down the shore. Watched Matt and me play games in high school. He didn't *have* to do that."

The psychologist took his cup of coffee and sipped it. "So you're saying that he showed you the *love* of a father—like your father?"

Tom thought for a moment. "Yeah, yeah. That's what I mean."

"Did your father do those things, too? What you say your uncle did for you?"

He thought for a moment. "Yeah, pretty much. Dad disciplined us more, of course. Dad helped us with our homework when he could. Uncle Vince left discipline and homework to Mom."

"So Vince was more avuncular in that way...."

"Huh? What do you mean?"

"Uncles and aunts, grandparents, godparents ... they can spoil or indulge children and not have to do—or choose not to—the less pleasant aspects of parenting."

"Oh, sure. Yeah, I see what you mean."

"Did you like your Dad?"

"Sure. He was a good guy. Everybody liked him."

"I'm curious ... was your father ever involved with your—shall we say—uncle's means of making a living?"

"No way, at least not to my knowledge. My brother Matt would agree with me on this. Mom wouldn't hear of it. She hated that stuff. She thought those guys are all lazy. She used to say so, too. I heard her once say to my uncle: 'Why don't you get a *real* job? Something *respectable?* Something you can take pride in.' I can hear her say that to this day. Mom didn't take *any* shit. She would give Satan her opinion if she met him."

Tom paused a long moment, then added, "Dad taught me and Matt to swim."

The psychologist nodded. "Many parents do."

"Not the way my Dad did."

"Oh? How was that?"

"A lot of parents send you to a class at the Y or expect you to learn at some CYO summer camp. My Dad didn't. Some parents just throw you in and let you thrash around a bit or assume that you'll learn somewhere else somehow. My Dad didn't do that either."

Horowitz nodded, said nothing.

"Dad taught my brother and me separately, not together. He *asked* us each if we *wanted* to learn how to swim—he didn't force us when *he* wanted. He told us it was important to learn to handle oneself in the water, that fear of the water, of drowning was a smart thing. In fact, he *wanted* me to be afraid of the water—even if I could swim. 'Even swimmers have drowned,' he told us. 'Respect the water,' he told me. 'It's okay to be afraid of it. We learn to swim not to be unafraid of the water—just to be able to handle ourselves as best we can.' That's what made him different, I guess—he allowed us to be frightened but didn't make me feel bad about it. Dad was … masculine without being macho, if that makes any sense."

Tom paused a moment, then said: "Our Dad was kind."

Horowitz nodded and said nothing.

"So your father *loved* you and your brother." Horowitz leaned toward Tom. "It's okay to say that he loved you."

Tom said nothing, his eyes suddenly filling with tears. He leaned forward and hid his face in his hands.

How well does a son know his father? His family? Tom wondered. He thought that he knew his father Tony D'Arcangelo as well as a fifteen year-old could. Isn't there always a hint of mystery to parents? And they're people. They keep things to themselves. They don't spill everything to satisfy their kids' curiosity.

Matt and Tom realized that when they discovered a picture of their father in uniform. In one of the older photo albums, stashed deep in a closet, they discovered photos of him. Tucked among the many albums of the family on vacation and at holidays and occasions was one photo of their father. Hard, erect, unsmiling, in the dress blues and white hat with Marine Corps insignia. They stared at the photo as if they were deciphering an ancient language never before seen.

What made this so remarkable was their father never mentioned being a Marine. Never. They had no military bric-a-brac adorning the house. None. Never one word about the military. If it weren't for their mother's religious images and statues, the D'Arcangelos could have been Quakers. Memorial Day came and went, with never a mention of the military. Matt and Tom agreed that they had never heard Dad express any feelings about patriotism or his military history. In their house the only books on the war were a set by Sir Winston Churchill bought by their grandfather and passed on his son.

"Whoa! Look at those ribbons! He was a sharpshooter, too!" Matt was breathless, spellbound.

"Did you know Dad was in the Marines?" Tom asked.

Matt shook his head. "Nope. I never knew he was in the Corps. Dad sure looked badass!"

Matt took the photo from its holder for closer inspection. Hidden behind its cellophane cover were two photos. In one, their helmeted father, in a sweat-soaked green sleeveless tee shirt, dog tags hanging from his neck, gleamed with four other sweaty, dusty soldiers arising from what seemed to be an iridescent midday sun funneling on to a machine gun emplacement with sandbags piled high.

The second photo showed Dad posed with two other GIs in camouflage, their faces blackened, boonie caps obscuring their eyes, cradling M-16s on their hips, with and ammo belts and grenades. The trio looked distant, unsmiling, grim, forbidding.

When they next saw their father, Matt asked outright: "Dad, were you in the Marines? Tom and I saw a picture of you in one of the albums upstairs."

Their father smiled weakly. "Semper Fi! Fourth Marine Division."

"Did you enlist to fight in Viet Nam?" Tom asked.

Another smile. A little laugh. "Not exactly."

"But you did fight there, right?"

"Oh yeah, that I did."

"When were you there?" Matt asked.

They were both curious and wanted to ask the question most their age want to know about warfare: Did he kill anybody? But they were old enough and sensitive enough not to ask.

"'69 and '70."

"If you didn't enlist to fight there, how did you come to go to Viet Nam?" Tom asked.

Their father smiled once more. "I was about to be drafted, so I went to the Naval Recruiter to enlist. Really, I was hoping to avoid that jungle, boys. I wanted to avoid the army. And you know, I always did like boats."

"While we were getting physicals, some old school Marine sergeant came into this large area where we were lined up and announced that they needed some volunteers for the Marines. No one volunteered. This gunny went down the line, looked us over, picked ten guys—I was lucky number five—told us to line up on the other side of the wall.

Tony D'Arcangelo then stood ramrod straight and mimicked that man's basso voice. His choice of language made the boys stand there with mouths open. Their father never cursed in front of his children.

"'You ten are now all members of the United States Marine Corps! Marines are part of the proudest tradition since 1775! I am saving you from the fate of spending your war with these Navy pussies! The Corps is—so the motto goes—looking for a few good men! We will certainly be lowering standards with you. Let's hope you're not faggots!'"

"Then he marched us off to another staging area. That's how your father became a Marine. It wasn't exactly Audie Murphy stuff."

"Who's that?" Matt asked. Neither of the boys knew about the most decorated hero in World War II.

"I have some work to do." Dad headed for the shelter of his workshop in the basement. "Look him up at the public library."

That day Matt and Tom hiked over to the library and asked the librarian if she could find information on a guy named Murphy they thought was a Marine. She gave them three books. They saw Audie Murphy was this little guy from Texas who became the most decorated war hero in the army in World War Two.

"Look in the index," she instructed the boys. "He played himself in the movie about his war time experience. It was called *To Hell and Back*."

The boys stared wide-eyed. In one of Murphy's pictures he had so many medals they could barely see his green uniform!

"So what did Dad mean? Dad had medals and ribbons," Tom asked.

Matt thought a moment. "I guess Dad meant he wasn't the war hero this guy Murphy was."

"Oh."

"But you know what I find funny?" Matt noted. "When we went to Washington last year—when we went to the Smithsonian and all those museums—we never did go to the Viet Nam War Memorial."

TOM STOOD OUTSIDE the psychologist's office and took several deep breaths to clear his head. It looked to be a frozen, bright day. He buttoned his coat and pulled on his gloves. Three crows flew in wild disarray overhead in the bright frozen sky. He looked around at the bare oaks and maples and the dark green of large pine trees lining the street and yards, then headed for his car.

D'ARCANGELO SPENT THE REST of the morning and early afternoon downtown shopping for Christmas gifts, getting them wrapped, and picking up a tree from the Italian Market. He offered ten dollars to a young black kid with a wagon to cart the tree home. On arrival Tom handed him a twenty.

The boy looked at it. "Sir, I don't have change."

"Did I ask for change?" Tom said. "Merry Christmas."

Tom dragged it up to the front door. Mrs. Saraceni, his next door neighbor, waved to him through her curtained door window. He waved in reply and plopped the tree in a stand in the living room by the front window, where it would remain until mid-January. He considered asking Carla to come over to help him trim the tree.

Tom grabbed the phone and first called her to see if and when she'd come over to the house, but was only able to speak to Mrs. O'Keeffe and leave his message. Then he dialed his uncle to ask him if he'd be around in the evening.

"I thought maybe we could have a drink? I need to talk to you about something."

Vince was notoriously abrupt on the phone. "I'll be at *Lou's* for dinner, around seven. See ya there."

Later Carla called him back. She was babysitting for her sister Carolyn, then was hooking up with her for some last-minute shopping.

"How about tomorrow evening, Honey?" she asked.

Tom wasn't in any hurry to trim the tree, and, although he just wanted to see Carla for an evening, there was so much on his mind he agreed without regret.

"Sure, Sweetie," he said. "Tomorrow's fine. Call you in the morning."

TOM ENTERED *Iron Lou's Saloon*, another restaurant and bar owned by the Cardinello family. He knew Uncle Vince liked to eat there when he was alone. Barring any large party function meeting there, Tom would find him in the small upstairs back dining room with its doors locked and only staff Vince approved of attending him. Old habits died hard. Vince had become a man during the assassinations of the '80s.

Johnny Mathis was crooning an upbeat Christmas song. One of *Lou's Saloon's* two black bartenders, Charlie Morrow, was mixing two martinis at the bar.

"Hey, Charlie," Tom greeted the bartender with a wave and then scoped the bar and foyer area for known faces. "Nice decorations! Really nice, I mean it. You guys do a great job with this stuff. Merry Christmas to you and the family."

"Same to you, Tommy. How's your brother? Matt coming home for Christmas? That would be nice."

"Don't think he's going to make it this year, Charlie."

Charlie leaned over the bar and almost whispered: "Ya looking for anyone in particular? Lou and the others are—," he jerked his head toward the back.

Tom saw Lou Spagnolo and Joey Argento in a booth opposite two female heads. From the distance Lou noticed Tom and held up his hand to acknowledge him, while Joey chattered on with the women opposite him.

A waiter came and took the two martinis. Charlie wiped the bar and nodded to the stairs. "Vince is upstairs, Tommy. His usual place."

As TOM APPROACHED the door, Valerie, a comely young waitress with whom he at times worked, stood with an empty tray unlocking the door. She recognized him but blocked the door and looked in toward his uncle.

"Mr. Sarzano? Want to see your nephew?"

"Let him in, Valerie. Thanks. Tommy!"

Tom turned to her. "Thanks, Val. Got that tattoo yet?" He referred to a talk they had one night when they had worked together. She was about to get a sacral dimple "tramp stamp" to please her boyfriend.

She smiled. "No, I listened to you about that. I saved the money for this summer's vacation. You can be pretty persuasive, Tommy."

Tom's eyes widened and mouth dropped open in mock disbelief. "Amazing—someone who listens to my advice! I should marry you. Take it from a true sacral dimple lover. In the future you won't regret it, darling. Nobody does body art better than Mother Nature. If you really need a tattoo, get a tiny decorative one on your ankle."

Tom passed her in the doorway then removed his coat and folded and dropped it on the chair next to where he intended to sit.

"You eat yet?" he asked.

"Yeah, I had the shrimp *fra diavolo*, the best dish here. Just having a 'Buca and coffee. Want somethin'? Valerie, bring my godson whatever he wants."

"Yeah sure, thanks. Bring me a Glenlivet straight, a glass of water and a cappuccino, Val, please."

Vince was reading the Philadelphia self-anointed People's Paper, *The Daily News*, noted for its clever, weird, and sometimes tasteless headlines. "How about this one—'Get Out Your Wolfbane!—Werewolf in Fairmount Park' I gotta read this one."

He read the title again and began in his John Facenda voice of gravitas.

"*The body of a deceased male was discovered along the Martin Luther King, Jr. Drive side of the Schuylkill River in Fairmount Park yesterday. The cause of death is yet to be determined, but initial reports by police say the victim had sustained severe lacerations and puncture wounds on the face and neck.*

A bicyclist using the park for recreational purposes reported he saw a large wolf-like dog running along the river near where the body was found. A woman jogger says she saw a large bearded man wearing a winter parka running in that area as well.

The police are awaiting the results of the Crime Scene Unit and the Medical Examiner's Office."

"Was it a full moon last night?" Tom asked. "Where can I get silver bullets."

"Probably one of those fucking dogs those Spicks are raising over in Kensington. Escaped from their dog-fights. How about this one?" Vince continued:

"*Penguin Stolen from Zoo Found at Local Frat Party*'— *Campus security at a local university in the University City area was alerted by a female student that a local fraternity had stolen a penguin from the Philadelphia Zoo. She telephoned the police to say that an inebriated penguin was dancing at a fraternity party. The police raided the party, seized the penguin and returned it to the zoo, where it was examined and is currently under medical observation. Fraternity members say that they had gotten the penguin intoxicated by feeding it fish injected with vodka using a hypodermic syringe and that the penguin, named Licorice Stick by Zoo Staff, seemed to enjoy dancing with everyone. Charges are pending on the outcome of the medical examination of the animal by Zoo personnel.*"

"Fraternities! They're real jokers," Tom said. "You will read about PETA protesting tomorrow."

Valerie re-entered with a tray and placed the drinks and coffee down in front of them and started to leave.

"Thanks, Sweetheart," Vince nodded, lifted his Sambuca. "Saluto."

After she left, he turned to his nephew. "Tommy, what do you think of Valerie? Cute, isn't she?"

"Cute? She's more than cute," Tom snorted. "She's a babe."

Vince scrutinized Tom's face for hidden meaning. "Real cute. Ever—?" Vince gave his fist a salacious slow hammering toward the table. "Eh?"

"No, Uncle Vince. Working here, I was afraid she might have a boyfriend or brother in the"—Tom pointed into the air— "family business. Never made a move on her. *Saluto.*"

Then he took a biting mouthful of scotch and waited for the burning to stop. His need for some highlander courage didn't go unnoticed by his uncle.

"So, Nephew, what's up?" he asked.

It was best not to begin with small talk. Tom decided to get right to the heart of the matter.

"You remember when Mom died? On her deathbed, Mom made me promise not to get involved with the Cardinello 'business'."

Tom paused. "And I have. I mean … I promised her that I wouldn't." Tom emptied the rest of the whiskey and shot Vince a glance of determination and waited for his reply.

Vince folded the newspaper and placed it on the table beside him. "Yeah, I know."

"You *know*?"

"Sure. She told me so."

"She did? She never told me she'd said anything to you."

"Well, she told me, but not in so many words. This doesn't come as a surprise, ya know, son. We both know how she felt about the business."

"I see Mom's face all the time, Uncle Vince. The cancer—she was suffering—I promised her then and there. She made me promise. When I did, she broke down and cried."

Vince winced. "I'm sorry I wasn't there at the end, Tommy, with her … with you. I just couldn't get there in time. I shouldn't have gone on vacation just then. I should have been with my sister. I'm sorry you had to do that alone."

"I'm going to tell Jimmy Cardinello that I want out, Vince. I'm not sure how he'll take it. I heard how these things go. I know that people who work in the business don't just walk away. But I want to keep that promise to her. Come what may, I need to keep my word."

"I'll talk to Jimmy for you—"

Tom shook his head vigorously. "No. No way. But I need to do this before I get involved in the business even further."

"You sure? It might be easier for you if I say something first."

"No, Vince. I can handle this. I can't go on not keeping my promise to Mom. I want out."

"You do what you gotta do, Tommy. I think Jimmy will understand."

Vince said that, but didn't quite believe it. He really wasn't quite sure how Jimmy would take it. Of late, Vince thought his boss had been uncharacteristically moody. He was certainly less predictable and calm than he had been over the years. Vince had chalked it up to stress and getting older.

"If it was me, there'd be no problem. I know you'd keep your mouth shut. I think the boss will understand. But I can't vouch for it."

Vince made up his mind to prepare Jimmy for Tom's defection in spite of what he said to his nephew.

"Vince, I feel bad about this. When dad died, I know that Jimmy and you helped us out an awful lot. What would we have done without him and you? I mean, he got me and Matt all those jobs, gave the family money. We owe him—and you!—big time. I know that. I'll pay him and you back someday."

Vince picked up the newspaper again. "Son, fuhgeddaboutit."

VINCE AND TOM WALKED down the narrow side street outside *Lou's* that opened to a small half block of park nestled between three old South Philly streets. It was cold and they hunched shoulders in their coats.

Vince stopped suddenly and looked at him. "So that's what you wanted to tell me, kid?" he asked. "I understand, Tommy. Really, I do."

Tom stopped and faced his uncle, unsure if he was serious. Tom said nothing, but his eyes must have shown disbelief.

"What? I understand, I really do," Vince said giving him a brief manly hug, then he hunched his shoulders and walked on. "I'm going to miss you working for me. You know, we made a good bit of money out there." He pointed out toward City Avenue where Tom had gone to school.

From the darkness a tall man with long hair scraggling from under a black knit Flyers cap walked toward them holding an unlit cigarette in one hand.

"Yo!" He waved the cigarette in front of himself as he neared them. "Either of you guys got a light?"

"No, sorry, don't smoke," Tom said. Vince said nothing and just shrugged.

The man tucked the cigarette behind his ear, then from his back waistband twirled out a ball peen hammer from his coat. He waved it over his shoulder, like a cobra waiting to strike.

"*Fuck you!* Gimme me your money! Both a' yas or I'll bust your fuckin' skulls!"

Spittle flew from his lips. He began to bob and weave, bouncing on the balls of his feet like some demented boxer.

Vince looked at Tom in disbelief then back at the thief. "Say what?"

"You fuckin' heard me, asshole. Give me your fuckin' wallets!" He screamed, waving the hammer above his head so it could not be snatched away. "Hurry the fuck up!"

Vince calmly turned to Tom, pointing at the robber, completely ignoring the threatening hammer. "Do you believe this motherfucker?"

"Whoa, man. All right!" Tom held up his hands in surrender and self-defense to the man who bounced menacingly in front of them. Tom started to reach into his pocket with one hand and give over his wallet.

But Vince would have none of it.

"Fuck you, muthafucka!" Vince shouted, so loud it startled his nephew.

The robber suddenly brought the hammer down on Vince's head in one short, quick stroke that eluded Vince's last-second parry of the blow. Tom heard the crack of it on his uncle's skull. Vince grunted softly, fell to his knees, then pitched backwards.

Before the assailant could hit him again, Tom launched forward. He raised his left arm to block any follow-up blows and shot in close to avoid being hit. Anger and adrenaline took over for fear and better judgment.

With a shout Tom drove his arm out quickly, thrusting the palm of his hand under the jaw of the man, snapping his head backwards with an audible clap. The hammer flew over Tom, bouncing to the pavement with a dull bell-like ring.

With all the momentum he could summon, Tom drove the man's face, now off balance and tottering, into the brick front of this last house on the block. Tom slammed his head hard, then after the rebound, slammed him again, then again, each time with even louder crack of his skull against the bricks. The mugger slid, neck twisted, down the wall to the pavement.

"Motherfucker!" Tom turned and kicked the hammer out of the man's reach. For a second he thought to bash the man's head in retaliation.

A grey-haired woman was now peeking out of her curtained windows, and an old man in a flannel shirt opened the door and placed one foot cautiously on his top step.

"What's goin' on out here?" He coughed a breath of steam. The old man's eyes opened wide at the blood now seeping from Vince's skull onto the pavement.

Tom shouted to him. "Call an ambulance! Call 911! Call 911! Quick!"

The man nodded several times with head bobble and disappeared quickly inside.

Tom looked around at Vince. He lay splayed on his back, head turned to one side, and even in the dim light he could see blood running out of Vince's nose and mouth, his hair matted with dark blood.

"Oh, Jesus! Jeezus! Fuck!"

Tom felt for his cell phone, then cursed that he had left it charging at home. He leapt the stone stairs and through the curtain could see the old man on the telephone.

Tom banged on the window. "Call 911! Hurry. Get an ambulance!"

He returned and knelt with Vince. "You're gonna be all right, Vinnie. Help is on the way. We'll have you at a hospital right away. Just hang in there, man. You're gonna be okay."

Up the street Tom saw a car moving slowly toward him. It was Lou Spagnolo's silver Cadillac. The car came to a slow stop. Lou recognized Tom. Joey Argento and he sprang out.

The two ran and stood over Vince. "What the fuck happened?" Lou asked, bending over to see who Tom was kneeling over.

Seeing who it was and the blood running out of the matted hair, Joey groaned, "That Vince? Ohhh!"

Tom pointed at the prostrate attacker, his head against the wall. "That motherfucker tried to mug us. Hit Vince with that fucking hammer!"

Lou and Joey stood over Vince and began to curse. In unison they sprang to the mugger and began to kick his crumpled body.

Tom looked up to see the old woman peeking out of her curtains in horror. He knew what they were doing wasn't good. The police would show up at any minute.

"*Lou!* Lou! The cops are coming! Get outta here! I'll stay with Vince—we'll get that motherfucker later."

Lou and Joey each gave him a few more kicks to his ribs and groin.

"I'll kill this cocksucker!" Lou roared.

"Motherfucker!" Joey bellowed.

Tom corralled and pushed them away. Lou started to leave but turned to the mugger's head and gave him a short quick stomp to his teeth and jaw. "I want to kill this prick!"

"*Lou!* The cops are coming. They'll think *you* did this guy. Let me handle it!" Tom pointed to the people in the house as witnesses.

He pushed Lou and Joey toward the car. The sound of a police siren was growing louder. The pair jumped into Lou's Cadillac and screeched off.

As soon as they had turned the corner, Tom turned to his uncle, now groaning and breathing heavily, barely moving. He took his scarf off and, afraid of aggravating the injury, carefully staunched the blood on Vince's head.

"You're gonna be all right, Vince! You're gonna be all right, believe it! We're gonna get you to a hospital real soon."

On cue a police squad car, lights flashing to the shriek of its siren, turned the corner and raced up the narrow street. An officer jumped out, his hand resting on his holstered Glock.

He surveyed the scene quickly. "What happened?"

Tom pointed to the assailant and his weapon. "That crazy motherfucker attacked us with that hammer! Get an ambulance here ASAP. He's smashed my uncle's skull open!"

The officer first looked at Vince's head wrapped in Tom's ever-reddening scarf. He spoke into a radio on his vest. "An ambulance is on the way," he told Tom.

Then the officer stepped over to look at the smashed and bruised face of the assailant.

"Did you do this?" He looked at Tom.

"After he hit my uncle, I snatched that hammer away and slammed him into the wall a few times."

"This guy looks bad, too."

Dark blood, visible even in dim street and yellow house lights, was flowing from shattered teeth puncturing his mouth on to the sidewalk.

"*Fuck him*! My uncle got hit first—he gets the first ride to the hospital. Those are just bruises from my hands and the wall. They're superficial. He'll be fine. I want that motherfucker drug tested, too. He's high on crystal meth or something. Fuckin' junkie!"

"I'm going to call for another ambulance." He took the police radio and rang for more assistance.

"You guys been drinking?" he then asked.

Tom glared at him. "Get that ambulance here—my uncle's dying!"

"Have you been drinking, sir?"

"It's fucking Christmas! Of course we've been drinking. I had *one* fucking drink! Go ahead and test me if you want. But get that ambulance here before my uncle's brains freeze to the fucking pavement!"

Tom realized anger or hysteria would get nowhere. He took a deep breath to calm myself. "Look, I'll answer any questions you want, but please, I'm upset about my uncle!"

Their conversation was interrupted by a call to the officer's phone.

Tom knelt at Vince's side. "Vin, they're coming. Hold on. Hang in there."

As he said that an ambulance turned the corner and pulled up. Its EMTs jumped from the car and ran to Vince to stabilize him.

A second ambulance rounded the corner. Police cars now lit the street from one end to the other.

"What hospital are they taking him to?"

"Jefferson. It's real close by."

Tom knew it was a top quality hospital—and nearby—and that reassured him. "Okay, okay. That's good."

He then gave the officer all the information for his report.

"Detectives will prob'ly want to talk to you, so don't leave town, okay?"

Tom nodded. "I'll be at the hospital tonight with my uncle. You have my name and cell phone number."

D'Arcangelo looked up at the elderly couple staring silently through the curtains in the window of their house. Tom waved his hand to acknowledge their assistance. The elderly couple waved a meek reply and disappeared behind the closing curtain.

Tom stopped back at his house to get his cell phone. He called Carla and told her what had happened, then raced off for the hospital. He thought of taking a cab—driving there made little sense—but decided he needed to walk there to unwind and clear his head.

Once at the hospital he went to the admissions desk where he learned Vince was heading for emergency surgery.

"We're getting his room ready for him. Are you his family?"

"Yes, I'm as close as anyone. I'm his nephew. We were together when this happened."

The nurse took Tom's phone number and address.

"Does he have a DNR order?"

"A what?"

"A 'Do Not Resuscitate Order' in case he should stop breathing?"

Tom didn't know but made up what he thought she would want to hear. "Uh, yeah. He has one. It's with his will. I can get it for you if you need it. For now, let's say 'no'."

"If there is a choice of a single room, would the family want that?"

"Yeah, sure, sure. A single room would be great."

The nurse said she'd call him when Vince was out of surgery and in recovery.

"When can I see him?" Tom asked.

"Mr. D'Arcangelo, we can't really say right now. When we know, we'll let you know. There's a cafeteria in the basement where you can get a beverage or a bite to eat if you want to wait." She handed him a map of the hospital.

Tom stood at the elevators and pulled out his phone to make a call. An olive-skinned nurse in blue scrubs turned to him after a sideways glance. "I'm sorry. This is a no cell-phone area. You'll need to take your call outside."

He nodded and headed for the doors. Tom stood just outside where cars circled under a turnaround overhang and dialed Lou Spagnolo.

"Lou, it's Tom. I'm at the hospital. Vince is in surgery."

"Yeah, I found out a a few minutes ago. I called Jimmy and told him what happened. We're coming over to be there when he gets out of the OR. I'll see you then."

Tom told Lou to call when they arrived.

AN HOUR LATER Lou Spagnola, Joey Argento, and Phil Maranelli arrived and met Tom in the cafeteria.

"Heard anything?" Lou asked.

"No. You know how time moves more slowly when you're waiting for someone? It's five times slower when they're in the hospital."

Lou looked around at the people in the cafeteria. "We need to find a place to talk. Is there a visitors' room around here somewhere we can take over?"

"My mother died here two years ago," Joey said. "She was here for two months. I know this place like the back of my hand. Follow me." He led the way and the four started off for the elevator.

They got off on the third floor and went to a small chapel and meditation room. Joey stuck his head in the door.

"No one here," Joey announced. "I thought so. I took my mother here several times. She liked it. Place gives me the fuckin' creeps! We can talk here."

Despite the privacy they huddled, heads together.

Phil spoke up. "We gonna take care of this guy? He's here, isn't he?"

"I just got finished with the Boss," Lou said. "Told him about what happened. He let it up to us as to what to do with the joker who hit Vince."

"We can find out what room he's in and I'll fix that motherfucker *tonight*," Joey said. "I mean he's not getting outta here."

Tom couldn't believe what he was hearing. He thought immediate retaliation was utterly stupid.

"I don't think Jimmy—or Vince—would think it's smart to do it here in the hospital. The cops are all around this mess."

Lou held up his hands to caution Joey. "Let's find out his name, where he lives, whatever, first—."

Phil agreed. "Okay, he won't get away, you can believe that. When he gets out of the hospital, he might need a little 'vacation'—some sun and sand in Jersey. Lots of sand. This place is too risky. There's a lot of room for error. We're under a microscope."

A few years back Frankie the Hammer Cannizarro had turned the Maranellis on to South Jersey.

"I like the Pine Barrens," Frankie had told them nonchalantly, as if selling real estate. "It's a longer ride, but fewer people. And those Pineys mind their own business. Avoid that fuckin' Tinicum Marsh—too many fuckin' people around. I was dumping somethin' there once and a fuckin' troop of boy scouts came through."

Lou gestured the three into a huddle and gave orders like a schoolyard quarterback. "Nothing's gonna happen here tonight." Lou looked at Phil. "Find out who this guy is, where he lives. Joey, you and Phil will settle accounts later. That's the plan."

Phil and Joey grunted assent.

"Look, they're gonna call us when Vince is outta surgery," Lou added. "I don't think he's going to be in any shape to talk to us anytime soon. As soon as we find out more, we'll convene back here. Keep in touch."

Tom looked around his small street in South Philly, saw no one nor anything unfamiliar or unusual, and quickly entered his home.

The lamp on the table under the front picture window had come on by timer. The rest of the house was dark.

He picked up the mail that had spilled from the mail slot onto the floor and walked through the dining room to the kitchen. He flicked the wall switch to turn on its light.

A light-haired man was sitting at his kitchen table flanked by two large granite-faced men standing motionless, their arms at their sides. Tom almost jumped out of his shoes.

"What the f—?"

"Tommy D'Arcangelo, I believe? How do you do?"

A seated man, with wavy, light brown hair, slender and wiry, gestured to the chair in front of him at the table.

"Have a seat. Let me introduce ourselves. I'm Liam Finneran. These are my colleagues, Nick and Brian." Without looking he pointed left and right, hands crossing like a pharaoh holding his crook and flail, pausing for theatrical effect.

D'Arcangelo detected an Irish brogue in the greeting. He sensed someone behind him and glanced over his shoulder. A fourth, rather large man had come up behind him. Tom's alarm was obvious. He had a sudden flash of Luca Brasi's last moments.

The man seated at the table nodded toward the tall, large man, "That's Billy."

Tom needed time to think. His acting training came to the fore. He slipped into *sangfroid*, hoping not to stammer.

"Nice to meet you you, Billy. Excellent stealth. Very quiet for a big man," he said over his shoulder to the man who looked like a former rugby player, his nose resembling a boiled potato. "These are squeaky old floors. Ninja Training 101?"

Billy scowled. Finneran continued. "Sorry to startle you. Have a seat. Please."

Tense despite his feigned coolness, Tom hesitated. Finneran shrugged, holding his hands out in a peace offering. "Relax. *Relax*. If we were going to hurt you, it would have happened already. You know that."

Tom realized that was true. His mind raced to plan an escape. He considered pulling out a pen and notepad and scribbling the house was being bugged by the Feds. That might slow them down. With that as ruse, while they considered what to do next, he'd bolt for the living room and dive out the window onto the street screaming bloody murder and perhaps not be sliced to bloodied shreds.

"Why did you break into my house?"

Finneran shook his head. "We didn't break in."

He slid a key across the table. Attached to it was a Phillies key fob, a spare he had given Mrs. Saraceni next door several years ago. "I apologize. We just let ourselves in. We didn't know when you were coming back, and it's bloody cold outside. We thought you wouldn't mind. I don't like breaking things, Tom. I'm not keen on violence, not on things, not on people. Not one bit. That's not our intention. It's Christmas time."

The man with the Irish brogue smiled.

"So Mrs. Saraceni gave you the key? You probably scared her to death. You didn't ... *hurt* her, did you?" Tom asked.

Finneran sighed for effect. He slowly shook his head in disbelief. "You're insulting us, Tom. She fell for the good old Irish blarney. Why would we beat up an old lady when we could just force your back door open? Do we *look* like we're from the fucking ghetto?"

Tom acknowledged his logic and sat down. He had resigned himself he wouldn't get out of there alive if they didn't allow it. He knew that they might be gathering information first, then taking him for his last ride.

"Well, Mr. Finneran, how can I help you?"

"Call me Liam, would you? I just have a few questions to ask. I thought maybe you could help me. I guess I can tell you that we're looking for some information. And some money."

"What do I know you'd want to know? And what money would that be?"

"Do you know a man named Schonfeld, a dentist with a gambling habit?"

"Sure, I know him. He owes Jimmy Cardinello. He's a guy that has recently taken to not paying his bills. He's into the Philly operation for thirty-two grand. He's disappeared from town. We haven't been able to find him."

"This dentist owes Mr. O'Connell—our employer—a bit of money as well. It's nothing to get one's knickers in a twist, as they say, but there's the principle of the thing. You understand that, I'm sure. But it's what happened *after* he failed to pay up that has us rather upset."

"Oh, and what's that?"

"One of our lads went to collect Mr. O'Connell's money and has since disappeared. We think our money was nicked from him, and our man might not be with us any longer."

Tom thought for a brief moment. He had to be careful to not disclose too much. "So maybe Schonfeld has offed your man? Maybe your guy got the money and took off for Brazil or Bangkok. Or County Sligo? Other than that, I don't know anything about your man or *your* money. Can't help you there. And you can believe I'd like to help you out. Find Schonfeld and the money and you'll find out about your man, I suppose."

Finneran shook his head. "I don't think our lad *would* do that, Tom. We don't think he took off with our money. We think he may have come to some harm. Weren't you and another of Mr. Cardinello's business associates in Cape May earlier this week?"

Tom nodded. "Yeah. We were. My uncle, Vince Sarzano, and I went to Cape May to see if the dentist was at his shore home."

"Sarzano? I know him—met him a few times at some business meetings between Mr. O'Connell and Mr. Cardinello. Did you ever find the dentist?"

"No. He never showed up. We staked out his house for two days, and it looked like no one had been there for some time. Lots of mail on the floor and stuff, so we headed back to Philly the next day."

"What did you guys do that evening, may I ask?"

Tom knew he was in rough waters here. He opted for partial truth. "Vince picked up some girls in AC and brought them to our hotel to party."

"Did you gentlemen have a good time?"

"Vince did." Tom decided to be frank here. "But I wasn't into it. I have a girlfriend. You know how it goes."

"A one-woman man. Admirable. And then what did you guys do?"

"The next morning we sent the ladies on their way, checked again for Schonfeld at his house—he still wasn't there—and came back to Philly. It's near Christmas, ya know. We needed to do some shopping."

Finneran nodded, then sat silent, thinking.

Tom spoke up. "May I ask you a question?"

"Shoot."

"How much does the dentist owe *you*?"

"Fifty K. He bet big on football and basketball. He's bet often in the past. He won big and he lost big, but he always paid off his debts. This last time he lost, he didn't pay up, and it seems that he doesn't intend to."

"Makes me wonder," Tom offered, "if he has other outstanding debts."

"Good point," said Finneran. "Now we know he owes Philly money and South Jersey money. Have you told Mr. Cardinello that you didn't find the dentist?"

"Yeah sure, of course, as soon as we returned from the shore."

"Did Mr. Cardinello say what he was going to do next?"

Tom laughed. "You better ask him. He doesn't talk about those things with me. I'm a small fish in a big pond. Personally, I think if Dr.

Schonfeld is smart, he'd not show his face around here any time soon, at least not without that money."

"Your uncle Vince is, shall we say, a big fish, if I remember correctly?"

"That might be 'was'—past tense," Tom replied.

"What do you mean?"

"Some motherfucker slammed him in the head with a hammer tonight and busted his skull. I just got back from the hospital. He's in surgery, in the intensive care unit, in critical condition."

Liam Finneran frowned, puzzled. "Who? Why?" He looked at his henchmen, who returned perplexed looks.

Tom shrugged. "Some fucking junkie—a nobody really. It looks like it was just bad luck."

"We're sorry to hear about this. You sure of that—just random?"

Tom nodded. "Seems to be."

Finneran stood up and reached across the table to shake hands.

"Thanks for your help. Sorry to hear about Vince Sarzano. I think I can speak for the O'Connell family in saying we wish him well. They have a good working relationship with the Cardinello enterprise," Finneran said.

Tom stood up and shook hands. "Sure." *Thank you for not killing me.*

Finneran gestured with his head to the others to leave.

"Let us know if you find this Schonfeld, would you? When you get your money from him, we'd like to talk to him about ours. You know what I mean?"

"I'll tell Jimmy Cardinello right away that the dentist owes Mr. O'Connell, too. If we see him first, I think Mr. Cardinello will hold him for you."

Finneran turned to leave. Tom stepped carefully from behind the kitchen table. He thought his legs might be quavering, and so made sure he wasn't leaning against the table.

"You guys like a drink before you go? There's whiskey over there."

"Thanks. None for me. We need to move along."

"Just curious about your man that disappeared ... Do you *know* that he located Schonfeld? Did your guy just disappear?"

Finneran shrugged. "Last we heard from him was that he had a tip the dentist was in Cape May and he was going to look into it. Next, our man called and said that he'd located him and was going to talk to him."

"So Schonfeld *was* in Cape May? We were at his house and we didn't see anyone there."

"We think he was in Cape May, but Brian didn't say where. He said he was going to just have a friendly chat with him and that we'd come back to deal with him if we had to. Merry Christmas. I hope Mr. Sarzano is going to be okay."

"Nice to meet you, Liam ... guys. Merry Christmas."

The four members of the Irish gang exited Tom's home with mumbles of holiday good wishes in Irish brogue.

After the door shut, Tom took a deep breath and exhaled heavily and broke out into a shiver. He went over to the spirits on the dining room sideboard, opened a bottle of whiskey and took a long pull straight from the bottle.

The liquor mixed with adrenaline that rushed into his bloodstream and nervous system. He was surprised he was still alive. He took several long, slow deep breaths, while trying to calm his pounding heart. D'Arcangelo knew that those guys didn't visit people without a purpose. They usually got what they wanted. Tom poured a full-size tumbler of whiskey and walked to the kitchen for a few ice cubes. His legs still felt shaky and weak. But Tom exulted that he wasn't dead with a plastic bag over his head.

After his adrenaline had dissipated and his heart returned to normal rhythm, Tom went to the basement where his father had his workshop. In a cabinet he had built for storage, Tom opened it and on the right side was the medium-sized gun safe.

In it were his father's hunting rifles, a Remington .30-06, two Remington double barreled shotguns and a 12-gauge Winchester pump; his grandfather's M-1 carbine and, hanging in a leather shoulder holster, his army-issue Colt automatic. His grandfather had carried the latter weapons in World War II. He had them sent home at some trouble and expense and intended them for his son.

Once home from what he always called "the Great WW Two"—his son sometimes thought he detected a tone of irony in his father's voice—he took his boy shooting in the mountains of central Pennsylvania. He said to him: "They're yours. Get locks or a safe for them. I'll never touch them again. But if I don't see you handling them properly, I'll take them to a gun dealer and sell 'em."

Anthony D'Arcangelo had likewise taken both of his sons hunting a few times. Matt had enjoyed shooting deer and ducks; Tom tolerated it once before summoning up the courage to say that he liked tramping about in the woods and camping, but didn't really enjoy killing animals.

D'ARCANGELO PULLED THE OLD .45 from an old army shoulder holster and inspected it. As with all of his father's tools, it had been cleaned and oiled regularly. The consummate craftsman, their father had taught Matt and Tom how to care for equipment. Tom removed the magazine; it was empty. He worked the chamber; it was empty as well. He slid the magazine in and chambered an empty round and squeezed the trigger. It clicked loudly. He did it once again, testing its spring, then looked in the safe for a box of .45 rounds and, when found, opened it and loaded seven rounds into the clip and slipped the Colt's safety on.

Tom jammed the weapon in its holster and slipped the holster over his head. He then went upstairs, donned a zip up sweater to hide the weapon, grabbed his coat and headed to the hospital.

5

TOM PICKED UP THREE RED POINSETTIAS—a lucky number for Italians, the symbol of the Trinity—at Ferrara's, the local florist, and headed for Carla's. This was his third year bringing them to the O'Keeffe household—Carla's mother loved red poinsettias—making it now a "family" tradition. He carried another shopping bag with gifts for the house, Carla's mother, father, sister and husband, as well as his girlfriend.

Tom peeked in the window of the row house two blocks from his family's home. He saw, not to any surprise, Carla's father, Charlie, sitting in his favorite lounge chair. The week's *Inquirer* and *Daily News* lay folded in a magazine rack at arm's reach. Next to him was his large mug with a CSX logo holding his first of several pints of coffee—decaffeinated now that his hypertension had reached medication threshold—and the *Daily News* on deck.

Charlie O'Keeffe had retired from his job two years ago after forty years "running" trains for CSX and Amtrak. He now suffered without complaining after losing his identity as a railroad engineer. He spent the first year getting his house ship-shape by completing several home projects, piloting three-times weekly shopping carts for his wife, bowling in a local seniors league, then confessed to his wife that he was going to seek psychological help if he wasn't around locomotives more.

Emily O'Keeffe rolled her eyes and snapped in exasperation: "Spare Medicare, will you? Take some train trips. Please!"

Tom tapped on the window. Charlie saw him and waved him in the unlocked door and greeted the man he regarded in all likelihood as his future son-in-law. "Merry Christmas, Tom. Merry Christmas, happy New Year and all that crap," he stated matter-of-factly but so low that his wife wouldn't hear him.

Tom smiled, put the shopping bags down and shut the door. "Same to you, Mr. O'Keeffe. Carla home? I know the missus is in the kitchen. I can smell her goodies."

"You can only smell Carla's goodies, not my wife's. I mean, of course, after you do right by my daughter."

Tom really liked Mr. O'Keeffe's off-color sense of humor. "Uh, of course, Mr. O'Keeffe. Not sure if she'll have me yet though. You know she's got high standards."

Tom didn't really know what to say about their relationship. So many things become understood between fiancées and future in-laws. Often what was thought to be understood was misunderstood and he now felt guilty that he was getting cold feet about his relationship with Carla.

Once a year Mrs. O'Keeffe commandeered the family stereo for appropriate holiday music and her favorite Handel's *Messiah,* the 1959 recording of the Philadelphia Orchestra and the Mormon Tabernacle Choir with Ormandy conducting. It was now blaring so she could hear it in the kitchen.

Mr. O'Keeffe sat in his easy chair that faced away from the kitchen and dining room. On the TV facing him, against the wall nearest the door, *Saving Private Ryan* was playing, its sound turned down low, so Mrs. O'Keeffe wouldn't hear it.

Tom nodded toward the falling, hemorrhaging, flying dismembered bodies, with the explosions and machine gun fire of D-Day on Normandy muted to a whisper. "I see you're in the holiday spirit."

Tom reached into the bag and took out a wrapped package and handed it to Mr. O'Keeffe.

"Thank you, Tom. This should help me." He held up the obvious boxed bottle of spirits and squeezed it. "Jameson's? Bushmills? Irish whiskey?"

"With a name like O'Keeffe? What else? Irish! Merry Christmas."

"Emily, Tom's here! Tom, why not place the gifts under the tree, if you don't mind."

Mrs. O'Keeffe first peeked around the kitchen's entry, then burst forth in befloured apron decorated with holiday symbols trailing the aroma of baking cookies and cakes with her. Tom headed for the kitchen and met her halfway in the dining room. She was wiping her hands with a towel.

"Hello, Tommy dear! Merry Chistmas! Carla is upstairs in her bedroom—wrapping gifts, I think. Better announce yourself on the way up."

Tom removed the poinsettias from the shopping bag and placed them on the dining room table that held decorative tins of cookies. "Here you go ... red only, as you like them. I put the other gifts under the tree, except for this ..." He handed her a wrapped sampling of cheeses and fruits. "Merry Christmas!"

"Oh, thank you so very much!" she gushed and leaned forward to peck him on the cheek. "Merry Christmas to you, Tom!"

He thought he detected a look of anticipation and excitement in her eyes, but since she was an avowed lover of all things festive and Christmas, he thought it might be her usual diamond-eyed gleam for the season.

"Carla is upstairs," she smiled. "Say hello and come back down for some tea or coffee and cookies when you're done."

Tom feigned the holiday spirit. "Ooh! I can't wait. See you in a few minutes."

He trudged up the stairs and went to Carla's room. It was unoccupied. Newly-wrapped presents piled on her bed and chair. Tom leaned out the door and shouted to the other rooms.

"Carla?"

"I'm in Carolyn's room," she called out, "down the hall."

AT THE DOORWAY Tom saw Carla wrapping more presents and piling them on her sister's bed. Carolyn had moved out five years ago. She had finished two years of accounting at Wharton and, although doing quite well, dropped out of college and announced that she was getting married to George Castellucci, whose father was about to turn over his garage and auto repair business to his son and to attempt retirement.

To spare her family the expense of a big wedding Carolyn and George were married at City Hall—Carla's sister was maniacal about money and financial matters. ("Weddings are a tremendous waste of resources!" was her only comment on not having a traditional wedding. "We're both Catholics, so what's the big deal? We'll have the priest for a quick service and have him bless the rings; we'll go to Church for christenings. I don't need a video of the wedding!" Carolyn took over the business end of the auto shop and literally got down on its floor to learn the business. Her father-in-law admired her ruthless efficiency and worshipped her business acumen. (He secretly doubted his son, although an ambitious and skilled mechanic, had any real business sense, and wondered if George could handle the business without Dad.)

D'Arcangelo entered the room and kissed Carla on her cheek. He looked at her closely for signs of relevant body language. "Merry Christmas, Sweetie."

"Hi, how are things? Haven't heard much from you lately. Been busy? I know it's Christmas and all—"

"Shopping and all that stuff. I got a tree today. Then there's Uncle Vince in the hospital ..."

"Yeah, I know. It's so terrible, so terrible. Is he going to be okay? I'm sorry. I don't mean to sound like a bitch ... I guess this Christmas will be a bit different than what I expected. How are you doing? I know Uncle Vince and you are so close."

Did she say that with a tinge of regret? Tom wondered.

Carla decided to change the subject. "I hope you didn't get my father any more railroad or train books or videos! He needs to develop some other interests."

"Right. That's why I got him an illustrated history of the Civil War. He seemed to like that Ken Burns documentary you got him for his birthday."

"Thank God! I don't want to feed his obsession for locomotives any longer."

With Carla Tom always felt he had to advocate her father's cause. "It's *not* an obsession. It's his passion, and he was so-o-o lucky that he could make a living at it all these years. You should be glad he had that. Most people hate their jobs and can't wait to forget them. Why do you think there was a taproom on every corner when our parents were kids? Now he doesn't have that reason for being. Don't you feel sorry for him just a little bit?"

Carla held her hands up in prayer. "Please, Tom. Don't feed into his 'passion'. Mom and I are trying to present a united front here to get him to develop another hobby. The Civil War is a good idea. Dad likes history. Maybe he could spend some time getting dressed up like those people do at all those battlefields. You've been to Gettysburg. Dad just needs to get away from railroads and trains!"

Tom had looked through the book he just bought and noted how many of the battles revolved around railheads and trains and bridges; there were scads of photos and illustrations of trains in the book. He thought of this somewhat devilishly, smiled at her and nodded. "Yeah, okay. Look, Carla, can I talk to you? It's important."

She put down the wrapping paper she was measuring. He put his arms around her waist and hugged her for a few moments.

Tom pulled a chair from a desk up to a reading chair in the room that had a few gifts on it. He removed them and placed them on the floor. "Sit down."

Carla looked at him, puzzled, then sat down. He sat on the bed opposite her.

"Look, there's a lot going on right now. I might need to leave town for a while. Maybe for some time. I need to confide in someone—and not a shrink."

There was a tiny flash of fire in her eyes. "I like to think I'm more than just 'someone to confide in'—but let's put that aside for now. Tom, are you in trouble? What's wrong?"

She paused a moment, then continued in her hard-nosed logic: "It can't be a medical thing if you need to leave town—it's not an illness."

Tom shook his head. He didn't know if—or how or how much to reveal—to her, so he sat silently for a moment.

"What do you mean by 'leave town'? Where? For how long?"

"Some place far away from Philly. I can't say how long. Maybe forever. But I think I need to get the hell out of Philly real quick."

Carla took his hands in hers. "You said that already. I *need* to know why?"

"Carla, I don't want to get you involved with all this. But I would love for you to come with me."

Her face whitened. Her hands slid from his and balled into fists of self-restraint. She leaned forward, her shoulder length hair fell around and covered her face. She took a moment to compose herself, then looked up and pushed the straight dark hair behind her ears.

"Tom, tell me why. I suppose you haven't broken away from Vince and his gang. Now you're in trouble from what they've been doing? Are you in trouble with Vince's guys? in something illegal? What? Tell me. Please, please don't tell me it's with the police—"

"Carla, I can't say right now. I'm not in any *real* trouble. Well, maybe some … but nothing I can't handle, okay? But I think the best way is for me to get out of Philly—right away. I want you to think about coming with me. If not right away, then soon."

Carla's face flushed with alarm. "Tom, look at me. I understand what you want. But now listen to me, okay? I am going to give it to you straight. I have good reasons why I can't do that: one, my family; two, my job; and three, my education. Okay? I have my *family* here. You *know* we're a close-knit family. I have a job—one that I admit I moan and groan about a lot—but one that I enjoy, that challenges me and that is helping to pay for my education. This brings me to item number three, my doctorate—my education, something I love. I finally found something I'm really interested in, that engages me, and you're asking me to give it up? Tom, I can't do that."

D'Arcangelo looked into her eyes. He knew that was what she'd say.

And she had said it. Carla's rationality would rule. She was emotional, but only after using logic. He believed Carla loved him. If she were to marry him and he came down with an awful disease or suffered some dreadful disability, she'd stay with him and see it to the end. But she had warned him about his involvement with the Cardinello 'business'. It was not something she would tolerate. Crime was not in her blood.

She took his hands in hers again and stared into his eyes. "Tom, I can't say yes. I can't leave with you. Not now. You need to face up to the situation."

Carla stood up, while he sat, looking at the floor. She reached to him and caressed his hair, then slid her cupped hands to his cheeks and pulled him to her. She put her arms around and hugged him, and he returned her embrace.

"Tell me what happened," she said. "Please. Didn't we agree never to have secrets?"

It was as simple as that. Tom told her about the two of them going down the shore to find the dentist, how he had found him and then someone else had killed him while he was pissing. He didn't mention the money. Or his self-defense shooting of Schonfeld's killer.

"Jesus, Tom. You could've been killed! So far though, you haven't done anything illegal. Did you report it to the police? Failure to report a crime like that has to be illegal."

"Are you crazy? No, I didn't."

"You just left? What about the guy who killed the dentist?"

Tom paused, at a loss for words, his mind racing for what to say. He said the obvious. "When I came out of the head, he had left the boat. He was gone."

"Just like that? Gone. So he was just there to kill the dentist?"

"I guess so. I don't know."

Carla paused to think for seconds. "This is worse than it sounds."

Fear that she could no longer trust her lover crept over her, slowly, emphatically.

"I'm sorry, Carla. I should have listened to you earlier."

"Do what you have to do, Tom. But get away from Cardinello and Vince and Lou—all those guys."

Tom went to the door and began to slip out, then turned to her. "Carla, it wasn't like some kind of Kafka story. I didn't wake up one day to discover I was transformed into a gangster. I got myself gradually involved—over years—with my uncle and then the rest of them."

"Get away from them. Now. For *you* and *your* future—not for us or me," she said picking up a roll of wrapping paper. "For *you*. *Our* future is over."

D'Arcangelo shut the door and took a deep breath to prepare to face her parents. He tilted his head to the door and strained to hear if Carla was crying, relieved not to hear sobbing. Like many men he hated to make women cry. When it happened, it usually meant the men were somehow behaving cruelly; it was the men who were at fault.

Tom slipped into his best performance mode. He sketched two rapid, neither intellectually precise nor courageous scenarios: the first, go downstairs and excuse himself until a later time, saying he had other holiday errands—fill in the best excuse—that needed doing. The second, to go downstairs, pretend nothing had happened and schmooze over tea and cookies with the O'Keeffes for fifteen or twenty minutes, fearing an enraged Carla would descend from above and decide to brain him with one of her mother's cast iron skillets.

And, although Tom thought he knew his girlfriend extremely well—he doubted Carla would come to the kitchen if she heard he were there—he took the least daring path.

Tom descended the stairs and noted the TV's offering. Mr. O'Keeffe was caught up with Tom Hanks' platoon about to take out a Nazi sniper in a bell tower.

"Mr. O'Keeffe, tell the missus that I can't stay and chat right now. She's busy anyhow. I need to check in on my uncle Vince at the hospital. He's still in the ICU and I want to talk to the doctor."

"Oh sure, Tom. We'll see you later. Thanks for the bottle. Hope your uncle is okay—"

"Mr. O'Keeffe, one of the cable channels is running the entire *Band of Brothers* the day before Christmas," he said smiling.

"Yeah yeah, I saw that. It might be hard at Christmas-time. Know what I mean?" He tilted his head, two men in that traditional male conspiracy, toward the kitchen. "See you for Christmas?"

"Sure." Tom smiled then let himself out. "Merry Christmas!" he said in his best improvisation of jollity, over a surprising lump in his throat. He knew he wouldn't be back.

TOM WAS UPSTAIRS AT HOME when he heard the doorbell. At the window he looked out and down to the street using the 'busybody', a contraption of mirrors invented by Philadelphia's most illustrious personality, Benjamin Franklin. Old Ben invented it to allow people to see the streets from upper floor windows in inclement weather, and many are still affixed to row homes in the neighborhoods of Philadelphia.

It was Nina.

Tom wasn't in the best frame of mind to see anyone. He debated not answering the door and just letting her leave. What would that do? Nothing, he reasoned. But he was curious. *What was she doing here in Philly?*

D'Arcangelo lifted the window and looked up and down the street and saw no one unexpected, just the dancer from Jersey standing below.

"Yo!" he shouted down. He tried to sound somewhat pleased to see her and offer a smile. "Hold on, be right down."

She smiled and waved a reply.

Tom pulled the .45 from under his pillow and tucked it in his waistband at his back. He pulled his sweater down to conceal the weapon and descended the stairs to open the door. *Maybe this babe is like that* Fatal Attraction *whacko.*

"Come in," Tom said. "What brings you here?"

"I was in the neighborhood and thought I'd stop by to say hi," she said with a slight smirk.

Tom snorted. "Sure. Really, why are you here?"

"Sherry wanted to come to Philly to see Vince. She asked me to keep her company on the drive up. I thought I'd stop by to see if you were in. Can I come in? Or are you busy?"

"No, no. Sure, come in."

She entered the house and, after taking a look down both ends of the street, Tom shut the door behind her.

"Did she go to the hospital?"

"Hospital? Why?"

"Vince is in the hospital. You haven't heard—"

"No, she doesn't know anything about it. Sherry said she wanted to come up to see him and asked if I wanted to come along. She was wondering why he never called her back—"

"Where is she now?" I asked. "Did she go to his house?"

"Yeah, he gave her a key to his place. That's why she was puzzled. What guy gives you a key to his house and then doesn't call you back?"

Tom pulled his cell phone out and dialed Vince's home phone first. "Nina, if I had your number I would have called you—," he told her.

The phone rang for several rings, then to his surprise he heard Sherry's tentative voice: "Hello, Vince Sarzano's residence. Who is this?"

"Sherry, this is Tom. Nina's here at my place," he said. D'Arcangelo then explained what had happened to Vince.

"I wondered what was up! I'm going to the hospital," she said. "Which hospital again?"

"He's out of surgery and resting. Just a word of warning—Vince doesn't look real good. He might not be able to speak to you. Visiting hours are over at 8:00 PM, so go before then. You're welcome to stay here with me and Nina, if you'd like."

"I'll probably just stay at Vince's tonight after I get back from the hospital. Sometimes they let you stay after visiting hours if you're family. I'll tell them we're engaged—"

Tom gave her his cell phone and home number. "Call us if you need us," he finished. "You're welcome to stay here the night."

"Thanks, but I think I might be in late. I'll stay at Vince's. Can I talk to Nina for a moment?"

"Sure." he handed Nina the phone. "Sherry is going to stay at Vince's after seeing him at the hospital. She wants to talk to you."

TOM LEFT NINA ON THE PHONE with her friend and went to the kitchen. It was late in the afternoon and he wanted to make coffee. He looked at his watch. *Was it too early to uncork a bottle of whiskey?*

He ground the coffee and set up the coffee maker. Nina appeared in the doorway.

"Want some coffee or tea?" he asked.

"It's kinda late for caffeine for me. Actually a drink with a nod toward dinner might be in order."

She stepped into the kitchen and looked around. "You cook? You seem to have all the right stuff."

"A little … yeah, I cook. My Mom was a terrific cook. She taught my brother and me some dishes. Italian stuff, mostly. I mean I'm not Mario Batali or anything…."

"What's your signature dish? The one you'd cook for friends?"

"Clams marinara with pasta. My sausage and meatballs is good, too. But that takes longer."

"Do we need to get anything?" she asked. "Salad stuff, I mean? Tomatoes? Bread?"

Tom shook his head. "No, I think we're okay. I went to the Italian market the other day and got stuff for the holidays."

"So let's do it," she urged. "Let's pour some glasses of wine. I'll set the table and you can get the pasta going. I'll make the salad and we're on for dinner."

She saw aprons on a nearby hook and slipped one on. "Red or white wine?" she asked.

"Red for me."

Tom thought that some other woman making herself at home this quickly should irritate him, but for some reason Nina didn't. She appeared in the door way with two glasses of wine and put one down on the table for him. "Can I make a salad?"

"Nah. I got it under control. Set the dining room table. The dishes are in that cupboard. Just relax."

D'Arcangelo turned on the kitchen radio, put water on to boil and got out the necessary ingredients. He changed from the local jazz station and looked for one playing Christmas music, then busied himself getting the dinner together.

A Philly radio personality noted for his lifelong obsession with Frank Sinatra announced a special "Christmas with Frank" program.

Vince would like this, he thought, and turned up the volume while peling and chopping garlic cloves.

NINA HAD JUST FINISHED SETTING the dining room table when she heard a faint tap on the front door. She went to it and peeked through its thin curtain and saw a woman wearing an overcoat and a ski cap, her dark hair framing her face, standing on the top step.

Nina opened the door. "Hi, you looking for Tom D'Arcangelo? He's in the kitchen making dinner. Hold on a minute, I'll get him."

"Wait." Carla halted her, looking at Nina and the apron. Carla paused for a long moment, then handed a small jeweller's envelope to her. "No, that's all right. Just give him this. I don't need to see him now. Thanks."

"You sure? I don't think he heard the bell or he would have answered. You wanna come in? I'll get him—it'll only take a second."

"No, no. That's okay," she said appraising Nina. Carla turned and quickly walked away, her breath streaming into the twilight.

Nina watched her, slightly puzzled at their exchange and the haste of her exit. Nina shut the door and headed to the kitchen.

IN THE KITCHEN Tom was chopping tomatoes while singing along with Sinatra. Nina came to the doorway.

"You didn't hear the person knock at the door, so I answered it." She held out the envelope.

"Who was it? My neighbor? Mrs. Saraceni? Elderly woman?"

"I don't think so. Not old—young and pretty. She left. I told her I would get you, but she just gave me this envelope and dashed off."

Tom dried his hands, threw the towel over his shoulder, then took the envelope and opened it. He removed a gold crucifix with a gold wedding band around the chain and dangled it from his hand.

Nina saw the pained expression on his face but said nothing. "Who was she?" she asked finally.

"Carla O'Keeffe. She *was* my girlfriend."

"Oh."

"We just broke up."

"Oh. What's that necklace?"

"My mother's crucifix and my father's wedding ring, which Mom attached to it after he died. Carla's giving it back to me."

"This doesn't have anything to do with me, does it? I mean, I can talk to her and explain that nothing has gone on between us really—."

"No, no, it's not you … though I can imagine that her knocking on the door and seeing a foxy blond making herself at home here didn't exactly mend fences."

Tom slid the necklace into his shirt pocket and exhaled deeply. He massaged his forehead and face. He thought he could feel a headache blooming.

Nina picked up her glass of wine and sipped it, watching the expression on D'Arcangelo's face.

"Look, don't overreact. It's Christmas, a time of lots of stress. Give her a call in a day or two and mend the fence."

"Ordinarily that would be sound advice. But in this case I don't think that will work."

Nina put her wineglass down on the kitchen table. "Maybe I should go and stay with Sherry …."

Tom knew that wouldn't make him feel better or heal the rupture between Carla and him.

"What for? Let's forget about it. Enjoy dinner. Relax. What's worse than eating alone at Christmas?"

"You sure?"

"Yeah. *Qué será será* and all that."

Tom turned to the task of getting dinner together, while Nina leaned against the doorway sipping wine. Sinatra from the radio cut into their silence with "Have Yourself a Merry Little Christmas."

The kitchen filled with aromas of garlic, tomatoes, and onions of marinara gravy. After a duet of Sinatra and King Cole on "The Christmas Song" and Frank's solo of "I'll Be Home for Christmas", Nina broke the silence.

"Let me know if I can do anything, okay?"

Tom picked up his wine glass and turned to Nina. "We're almost there. Salad needs dressing. The gravy is almost done. I'll pop the pasta in and mix the clams and we're ready to *mangia*."

"Smells great," Nina said. "Nice tree in there. Are you going to decorate it? It looks like a homeless person."

"Yeah, I know. I'll get to it later."

He thought of Carla and that she and he had decorated the tree for the past two years early on Christmas Eve, before going to Mass. "My girlfriend and I usually decorate it on Christmas Eve. But not this year."

NINA POURED two more glasses of zinfandel and they sat down to dinner in the dining room.

"Mind if I put on some jazz, some mellow Coltrane or Miles?" Tom asked her. "Christmas music is making me depressed."

They ate dinner in silence, she not sure what to say nor exactly how to say it; he thinking about Carla and the O'Keeffes. And those ever present bodies in the boat.

Try as he might to remain off the events of the past week, his thoughts slipped back to his shooting of the unknown man on the boat, stealing the very large sum of money, his uncle's injury, and today, his breakup with Carla. The Irish gang invading his house had unnerved him as well. He vowed never to leave the house without the .45 again. Having lived in Philly all these years where some of the gangland killings that ended up on the front pages of the newspapers crawled to the fore of his memory.

Nina studied him as they ate. She complimented the meal and tried some small talk, but Tom was reluctant to talk, distant.

"Maybe I was a bit harsh earlier this week—," she offered.

"What do you mean?"

"Remember that I called you 'morose'?"

"Yeah? Maybe you're right about that."

"I was being too judgmental."

"Let's just say that I'm a bit pre-occupied this week, okay? Lots on my mind."

"All right."

"Say, how's your mother doing?"

"No change there. She has her days when one hardly knows she has the disease. Other days …. My aunt is staying with her and Jimmy for a few days. She helps me out a lot. Thanks for asking."

"I read that they're making some strides with that type of disease." As soon as Tom said that, he winced at his worthless sympathy clichés.

"I never thought that my mother would get something like this," she continued. "After my uncle and all that … one sort of thinks that one's family has had its share of sorrows of that type."

"You had an uncle with Alzheimer's?"

"No, not Alzheimer's, but mental illness of some sort."

"Oh."

"He wasn't really my uncle; we just called him Uncle Friedrich. He was some distant relative of my mother. Came over here from Europe after Communism imploded and the wall fell. He was a college professor somewhere in central Europe. Once he was here in the States, he went bonkers. Ended up in an asylum. My mother took my brother and me to see him in the mental institution a few times a month—."

"Was that a good idea? How old were you then?"

"I was thirteen; my brother was fifteen. My mother thought it helped him to see and talk to us."

"Did it help him? Those places are not usually fun to visit, especially for kids."

"Not sure really. Who knows? He was completely delusional. He seemed to become people he read about in the hospital library. So he might be different any time we visited."

D'Arcangelo thought for a moment and joked: "So he was like some actors I've met. They're stopping off on stage before checking into the looney bin."

She laughed. "One month he was Diego Rivera. He rambled on and on about art, his wife and mistresses."

"The artist wife—the one with the eyebrows?"

"Yeah, it freaked my mother out. He'd blurt out outrageous things about making love to all of them, their physical attributes and sexual prowess, then rant about his art. How he hated the critics and that he was owed money on his commissions."

Tom laughed. "Did he do this in Spanish?"

Nina nodded and smiled. "And English. He used a mix of Spanish and English. No shit. Another time he thought he was Carl Jung—the psychologist?—and had us draw mandalas with crayons on paper while he lectured on mythology and read from Frazer's *Golden Bough*. There was one period when he would just play Baroque organ music on a CD player and 'perform' it for us on this organ keyboard he had drawn on a table."

"Christ, you should have gotten him a real organ. Maybe he *was* a genius—the next Bach."

"He had an incredible encyclopedic memory—his doctors were amazed at him. He would answer their questions with literary quotations from great writers—Shakespeare was his favorite. But the worst for us was when he thought he was some Austrian mathematician—he did nothing but work on equations on a felt board. He went on for the entire time we were there spouting formulas and expounding on mathematical logic—in German! At least we could listen to the Bach music!"

"Did they ever cure him? Give him drugs, psychotherapy?"

"No, he died—suddenly, of a brain aneurysm."

"Oh, that's too bad."

Nina smiled. "I'm not so sure of that. Is that a way to live? I spent a lot of time in my adolescence at what my mother called 'The Uncle Friedrich Show'. But I learned something from it all."

"Yeah? What's that?"

"A lesson in family loyalty."

Tom looked away, his silence hoping to signal a change of topic.

"Coffee?" Nina asked after they finished. "Dessert?"

"None for me. You can have some if you want. Just flip on the coffee maker—it's ready to go. I have some canolis and profiteroles in the fridge, and Italian cookies in the breadbox."

"No, I'm good," she said. "I might like an after dinner drink. Maybe a White Russian, if you have the ingredients."

"I'll make you one. I'll have a Sambuca."

Nina cleared the table and took the dishes to the kitchen.

D'Arcangelo snagged the necessary spirits from the sideboard and took them into the kitchen. Nina had the glasses, cream, and was cracking ice for her drink.

"Aren't you supposed to put coffee beans in Sambuca?" she asked.

"Very good. Three beans. They're in the freezer."

She poured what were double portions of her drink. He noted it, this after their three glasses of wine.

"Whoa. That's a powerful drink. Don't belt that down," he advised. "Those things made my head spin at a party once."

"No, Dad, I won't. I don't usually drink this much."

"I didn't think so. Lots of calories."

"I know, but I want to loosen up a bit," she said. "I need to relax."

On the few occasions when a woman had made a statement about loosening up, Tom knew it usually meant she wanted to get laid. In the past he would have routinely thought that if he played the proverbial cards right, he'd get lucky. Tonight, after all that had gone on, he was too exhausted even to think about it. Tom was not in a card-playing mood.

"How does that work? Does the alcohol lower one's inhibitions? Or does one use the excuse of alcohol to act crazy?"

"Actually both might apply. But I don't need an *excuse* to shed my inhibitions. The booze just makes the behavior easier. I had an old boyfriend who could never dance unless he had several drinks in him. I'm sort of like that."

"But you're a dancer, for chrissake. Don't tell me you need to drink every time you dance!"

"Oh no, certainly not for dancing. Most professional dancers are dancing fools—they hear three notes and start to move. I don't need to drink to dance."

They went to the living room with their drinks. Tom turned out all but one light, then went to the record player and put on an old, mellow Sonny Rollins album.

"Still with vinyl?" she asked. "I like it."

He shrugged. "These are classic jazz albums; I just can't ditch them. Some say that there's a big difference between the modern re-done versions and the vinyl. I can't hear that much. I must have a tin ear."

"Too bad you don't have your tree decorated yet. We could turn out the lights and look at the tree ornaments."

Tom pointed his fingers at her and, in an awful impersonation, struck an appropriate pose and lame imitation of Elvis, said, "Watch this, young lady."

He cut out all the lights and opened the blinds on the front windows. From the street one could see the reflections of all the houses' lights and holiday decorations shining from house and reflected from car windows.

"One of the advantages to living in South Philly."

She cooed approval. "Ooh-h-h! Very pretty."

They sat in music-filled darkness for a while, sipping the drinks in silence. She sat on the sofa, Tom in a small comfortable easy chair facing her. Sonny Rollins' mellow tenor sax drifted off at the end of the album.

"I'm going to turn in," he said. "I want to get to the hospital tomorrow early, before the doctors take off for Christmas shopping. I need to talk to them about Vince."

Nina stood up and took the glasses to the kitchen. Tom remained in the chair looking at the lights from the street.

She came up behind him, placed her hands on his shoulders at the base of his neck and began to massage. At first startled, Tom began to relax under her firm touch.

"Jesus, you're jumpy. You need this, for sure." After several minutes she moved her hands to his neck and around his ears, circling them slowly. She knifed her fingers through his hair, massaging his scalp, before sliding to his forehead over his eyes and cheeks. Slow and unhurried, her hands came back to his neck and shoulders.

D'Arcangelo began to melt into the chair. Her hands rolled to kneading the upper pectoral muscles, then she unbuttoned the top two buttons of his shirt and slid her hands to his chest working the muscles of his upper chest and neck. She slid her fingers gently to his nipples and circled them slowly until her fingertips touched them ever so delicately.

Tom felt the two goddesses of the human body, relaxation and intense sexual excitement, suddenly in the wonderful summit of sexual desire.

In the darkness, lit by the multicolor Christmas lights from the surrounding houses and their reflections from car and house windows, Nina massaged his nipples and leaned toward and pressed her face against his. Her hair with its fragrance, a delicate scent of—what was it? lemon or lime, something citrussy—grazed his cheek. She kissed and nibbled his ear lobe and then his neck.

Tom turned to her and said hoarsely. "You know you don't owe my Uncle Vince anything—right?"

"Correct. Escort Nina is off the clock."

"Does this mean I'm getting a freebie?"

"Ooohhh! You're insulting me. Keep it up and you'll ruin the mood. Why not think of it as you're giving me a freebie?"

"Now you're putting pressure on me—"

"Tom, what did I say? You need to relax. A lot."

She went back to massaging his neck and shoulders. After a few moments, she again let her hands slide under his shirt to his bare chest and nipples.

"Tom?" she whispered. "This doesn't happen often for me. Are you going to take advantage or not?"

"Let's go upstairs," Tom whispered.

He led her up the stairs and into the bedroom. Now, in near complete darkness, he stripped off her sweater. Nina removed his shirt in turn. He reached for the buttons of her blouse, found her bra and unfastened it, while she undid his belt and jeans.

Once undressed, he pulled her to him and they fell onto the bed, arms and legs entwined. Finally, their bodies interlaced, heaving and swaying, in that loss of their selves in the fervor of lovemaking.

6

TOM WOKE from deep, deep and dreamless sleep—the sleep of lusty, edgy sex. A sleep that was most welcome from the stress of the past few days. The warmth of Nina's body dragged him to a half-conscious edge of existence. She felt him squeezing her and she returned snuggled with cat-like purring.

They had made love in darkness and fallen asleep cuddled together. He slipped naked to the bathroom and, on returning, in the light from the bedroom windows, saw her lying on her stomach, the sheet covering her flanks, one leg extended from under the blanket and sheets, her hands under the pillow and her blond hair covering most of her face.

On seeing her he thought of last night. Her massage and the glorious love-making.

Tom stood over her and wondered if he could entice her for an encore before breakfast. In the morning male hormones are rocketing, but he knew that women were not always receptive at the morning hour.

Why were men and women's endocrinology so out of synch? he wondered. In last night's darkness Tom was unable to see tattoos and felt—miracle of miracles for exotic dancers—natural breasts. Now he saw her physique was unmarked, except for a small mole on her shoulder, porcelain white skin, a classical sculptor's model. He thought one trite but accurate accolade: she had the body of a goddess. Nina Cahill had been born beautiful and kept herself in first-rate physical condition. He regretted now he hadn't lit a candle last night to soak in her sheer physical beauty while they made love; there were only their shadows in the mirror across from the bed and the touch of the warm smoothness of her hard body.

Tom began to slide the cover from where her foot extended from the blanket up along her leg slowly, sure that a rapid whisking off of blankets would awaken her. Once the gluteal muscles of her right hip were exposed—gloriously no tattoos!—he exposed her lower back and peered at pronounced sacral dimples. He slid the blanket further off her body and saw muscular yet still shapely back. Her blond hair spilled over her neck onto the pillow and over her face.

"Jeezus!" Tom stood there holding the cover, staring with obvious desire and admiration. Disbelief that anyone that looked like Greek sculpture had made love with him was now arising. He wanted to believe he was studly-looking enough to appeal to her, but her curious remark that she wanted to drink to lose her inhibitions returned.

He inspected himself in the mirror. *Did she have to get drunk to fuck me? I don't look that bad.* In this moment of insecurity his mind visualized a brief collage of Nina's previous lovers: sun-blond Olympic gymnasts with demigod-like bodies and Raphaelesque faces.

He looked back at Nina. She leaned up on one elbow, pushed her hair from her face and turned to him, firm champagne glass-size breasts, pink nipples at attention.

"You're making me cold," she whispered. "Are you going to stand there watching … like some freak? Put the blanket back. Or get back in here and warm me up."

Tom leaned over the bed to her mouth and descended kissing her sacrum and back, then shoulders, neck and ears, to finally slide over her body and kissed and nibbled her neck. Her perfume had, with the warmth of their love-making, made the sheets and pillows awash with the scent of their bodies. Tom took her wrists and held them against the pillow.

"Ohhh-h! I like that blanket—ummm-h-h," she moaned.

THEY DOZED AGAIN for a time. Tom awoke with Nina's head resting on his chest, her leg thrown over his legs. He embraced her back and kneaded her shoulders and kissed her softly. She placed her chin on his chest and looked into his face. "Hey," she whispered.

"Umm."

"That was nice. *Real* nice."

Tom resisted his standard quip at times like this: "You know, you almost made me come!" He gave her an assenting moan. They lay in silence for some time, until Nina spoke.

"The other night I told you what my future plans were. Remember? What are *you* planning to do ... now that you're out of college?"

Tom was too relaxed to think about her question, to even shrug. "Is this your usual *après l'amour* conversation? 'What are you doing with the rest of your life?'"

"Uh-huh."

He groaned. "Don't know, really. Please. I'm savoring the afterglow."

"Sherry told me that you were interested in acting. Your uncle said you're fantastic."

"He would. Ignore him. He's the proud uncle. He doesn't even know who Kenneth Branagh is, for chrissakes."

"Neither do I, for that matter. Seriously, how'd you get interested in acting?"

He pulled his arm from around her waist and placed it behind his head. "In seventh grade in an Easter pageant I was a Roman centurion in charge of the crucifixion. I got to spear Jesus and laugh diabolically. The audience gasped at my performance. They loved me. I got a bigger hand than Jesus. Someone even hissed at my curtain call. Since then I have been involved in theater at some time—high school, college."

"Is that true? Really?"

"I'm exaggerating a little ..."

"Be serious. Why not see how far you can go?—you like it so much. Follow your dream and all that ...."

"Acting's a tough gig. You got to be talented, lucky, driven, and being good-looking helps. Did I say that talent helps a bit? You have to be able to bang your head against a wall ... well, possibly for nothing. I've been thinking about going to law school. There's a boat-load of acting there."

"But you're good-looking enough. You look like an actor my mother likes…Tyrone Power, I think his name is …"

"He starred in *The Razor's Edge*, one of my favorite movies."

Nina ignored him. "Or was it that Granger guy she liked? If you went into acting, what kind would it be? Stage, movies?"

"Stewart or Farley? Which one? Did she say what film she liked? Movies? Never. Film directors are too fuckin' obsessive. They're usually either neurotic or psychotic. I couldn't imagine shooting something over again and again until some director is happy. It would drive me over the edge. I think Clint Eastwood has the right idea: why re-shoot unless it's out of focus or someone's forgotten the lines? He said he often couldn't see any difference between take one and take twenty."

"Clint Eastwood's a shit."

"As an actor or director?"

"As a man," she said. "He treats women like rubbish."

Tom defended The Man With No Name. "His actors like him. He won an NAACP award for employing black actors."

"Ask Sondra Locke what he's like. He's got more illegitimate kids than a fuckin' NBA star. Eastwood's just a Hollywood big dick with lots of money."

"Oh, Jesus!" Tom said. It was all he could muster. "I don't want to debate Eastwood's private life—just his directorial style. Glad I didn't mention Woody Allen.

Nina pressed him. "How about writing? Plays? Screenwriting? Ever thought of that?"

"You think I should write a screenplay where Clint Eastwood dies and is confronted in purgatory by all the women in his life?"

"Can we drop Clint Eastwood?"

"I once thought Edgar Allan Poe deserved a play or movie. Poe had such a tragic, fucked up life; he'd make a great subject for something dramatic. You know he lived here in Philly for some years? Wrote some of his best stuff here, too. I'll take you to his house sometime. You interested?"

"That really stiffens my nipples, Tom."

"You don't like Poe then?"

"If you want to know, I think Poe's stories and especially his poetry were over-rated."

"How about Walt Whitman? He was one interesting character."

"Wasn't he gay?"

"Maybe bi-. He was a bit batty for his times."

"Better Walt than Poe."

Nina put her head back down on his chest and heard his heart drumming slowly. They drifted off again for fifteen minutes before awaking again. Nina rose to use the bathroom.

Tom's eyes followed her lithe body.

"You Irish?" Tom called to her as she vanished into the bathroom. The water ran for a moment, then she returned with her bouncy dancer's grace and stood naked in front of him.

"Half Irish. Mick on my father's side. Mother's family came from what was Czechoslovakia. Now it's the Republic of Something, I think. Petrazak was my mother's family name."

"After the Cold War ended Czechoslovakia split into two countries," Tom began to expound. "Now it's the Czech Republic and the Slovak Republic, I think. But if your family came here from a while back, it would have been called something else other than even Czechoslovakia. Some empire or other."

"I look like my mother. I inherited her skin. Saw a picture of her when she was young. She was a beauty. My brothers took after my father: fair-hair and freckles, big ears and thin lips. Hey, I'm going to take a shower to wash off our love liquids, okay? Can I get some breakfast?"

"Sure. I'll make some coffee. See you downstairs in the kitchen." Tom slipped on underwear, a sweatsuit, pulled on running shoes and headed downstairs. He knew he'd miss his daily run this morning. And he didn't really care.

IN THE KITCHEN Tom poured the water into the brew machine and measured out the coffee. As he flipped the switch on, in the coffee pot he glimpsed a moving shadow over his shoulder. He turned, expecting to see Nina had followed him downstairs.

A short, hulking man had emerged from behind the refrigerator next to the basement's door.

"*What the*—*?*" Tom's eyes widened in surprise, as the man launched himself.

The man howled like a bear behind a right hook directed at crushing Tom's head.

He had turned just in time to duck the massive man. Tom slid to his left to evade a devastating punch. His assailant slammed him into the cabinet, his fist splintering the wooden door. Wood and chinaware inside shattered and flew. The attacker's growl turned to a howl of pain from his fist's laceration. Tom turned to face the man, now enraged, shaking a mangled, bloodied fist.

Tom danced back across the narrow kitchen. He sized up his opponent and saw a great weight difference. The man was squat and powerfully built. Tom stepped forward and drove a side-thrust kick into the man's torso, who grunted as he was thrown back against the cabinet.

Tom turned to the counter top and grabbed his mother's solid wood rolling pin from a utensil holder. He turned and slammed the man across the head with the pin. The assailant's momentum coming forward, he avoided the full force of Tom's bludgeoning. He rammed him into the counter behind him with all the man's weight and they grappled, the man searching for leverage and to use his superior weight and strength. Tom flailed with the pin at his head again, but with no leverage. He dropped it to have better use of his hands as their bodies slammed each other across and around the small kitchen, sending spatulas, wooden spoons, the dish drainer and toaster flying.

D'Arcangelo's assailant tried to hold him at arm's length so as to head-butt him in the face. Tom tried to knee him in the groin several times with little effect. They spun around and slammed sideways against the refrigerator, then unleashed each other for another tactic. Tom snatched the freezer door and rammed it open into his opponent's face with a crunch of nose cartilage. He tried to pull the door back and slam him again, but the man had hurled himself with renewed fury. At close quarters once again, Tom kneed him once, then again, missing both times.

The assailant's large hands reached for Tom's throat, who responded by trying to insert his arms between the arms to blunt the leverage on his throat. Tom knew that once the stronger man had that control over him, he'd black out in seconds. It would all be over. Tom rammed his fingers into the man's face, looking for his eyes. The thug grunted and hissed and threw him to the floor, now using more of his weight to gain leverage in gripping his throat. Tom felt his windpipe being cut off and gagged at the strength of his fingers. Tom grabbed the man's wrists and tried to hold him from exerting any more force. He was losing consciousness with a fatalistic suffering of final seconds of life.

BONK!

As Tom drifted into darkness, he heard a bass drum "thunk" and could suddenly breathe again, ever more slightly.

BONK! Again he heard that sound, distant but pressing into his consciousness. His breath was coming more easily! He wavered at the edge of twilight and then began to feel a nauseating return to consciousness. Tom could feel the smothering heaviness of the man's body across him.

BONK! BONK! BONK! Slowly Tom came to consciousness—the world spinning and fuzzy red and blue. He saw the man's skull bleeding, with bloody hair matting from his head. Blood was seeping onto areas of the floor and smeared Tom's warm up suit.

He rubbed his neck to assess the damage, to determine that his larynx was not crushed—already it ached from bruising. But he exulted in just being able to breathe again!

Through whirling fogginess and arising nausea Tom saw Nina standing over him in panties and bra. She brandished an aluminum softball bat as if she were a Victoria's Secret model doing a spot for athletic underwear.

Tom tried to speak but was able to choke out a few gurgling sounds.

"*Jesus Christ!* You okay?" she asked. "I'll call 911!"

Tom slid from under the large unconscious man, coughing and laboring to move, as if returning from anesthesia, holding his neck, which was stiffening quickly.

"I thought all that commotion couldn't be from making coffee!" Nina exclaimed.

She gingerly reached down and felt the pulse on the man's neck, holding the bat away from him poised to slam him once more. "Be careful! That goon's still alive. At least I didn't kill him. Christ, look at all this blood."

Tom attempted once again to speak. He pulled himself from under the weight of the man, shoved him aside and staggered upright.

"If he moves," Tom croaked, "hit him again … harder this time. Motherfucker might have crushed my larynx."

He wobbled to the sink and tried to spit to inspect for blood.

Nina looked around the smashed kitchen. "You're going to need some re-modeling here. Are you handy?"

"Fuck the kitchen!" He pulled himself to his feet and tried to overcome dizziness and nausea. "Do all women worry about kitchens? Get dressed, will you? We need to get out of here."

"Wait a minute—who is this guy? Aren't you going to call the police? We can't just leave him here. We need to get our story straight for the cops."

"I'll take care of this guy. Just give me a minute to see if I'm all here in one piece."

Nina noticed the shattered glass carafe. "Goddammit! He broke your coffee pot! I should bash him again just for that. I need morning coffee."

Tom wasn't in the mood for humor. "Just get dressed. I'll take you out for some. Coffee's on me. I need to make a call and get this bastard removed from the premises. Give me that bat in case this ape comes to."

"Calling 911—the police?"

"Something like that."

Tom took the bat from her. "Go ahead. Get yourself dressed."

She started upstairs. "You owe me breakfast with that coffee, Mr. D'Arcangelo. You owe me big time."

As soon as she was out of earshot, Tom called Lou's cell phone and rasped out with difficulty what had happened in his kitchen.

"Be right there." Lou clicked off, no questions asked, no explanation needed.

Tom stood looking around the busted up kitchen and again at the man in the pool of blood on the floor. He took a glass of tap water, in part because he was thirsty, but just to see if he could still swallow.

Nina dressed and returned in ten minutes. Tom was leaning against the counter holding the bat on his shoulder and sipping water gingerly from a glass.

"What happened, Tiger?" she asked. There was a humorous gleam in her eye. "He get the drop on you?"

Tom shook his head. To show he had recovered from his throttling, he joked: "Not exactly. He missed me first, then I had my shot. Should have gone for the *mae geri keage* not the *yoko geri kikomi*—"

"Is that Japanese? Whatever, I think you need to work on those karate moves a bit more. Next time kick him in the nuts—real fucking hard."

"That's what I just said … in Japanese. Really, I think I need to work more on my grappling technique—." Tom thought of his brother Matt and his devotion to wrestling.

"Why don't you shower and get rid of that bloody sweatsuit?" Nina said. "I'll make sure he doesn't wake up and kill us."

The man on the floor moaned and stirred. Tom took the bat one-handed and thumped him over the head with another "BONK!" Tom handed the bat back to Nina, then headed unsteadily upstairs.

IN TWENTY MINUTES Tom heard a knock at the door. Nina went to the front door, peering through the shade. Outside was a small van marked 'Robertson's Carpets' ("You Pay a Little – We Lay a Lot") and a man in workman's gray coveralls stood on his stoop. Two other men in coveralls, carrying a large carpet rolled up in a large cardboard tube, stood on the pavement looking up at the door. All wore dark sunglasses and large moustaches.

Nina yelled upstairs. "Hey Tom, there's some carpet guys here! Shall I tell them to come back later?"

He heard her laughing. He yelled down, "No, I'll take care of it. Hey, keep an eye on that goon, would you?"

She frowned and went back to the kitchen with the bat.

Tom let Lou Spagnolo and his 'carpet men' in and briefly whispered to them what had happened.

"Don't worry," Lou assured him. "We'll take care of this guy. Then we need to have a meeting, okay? Call me later. We'll find out who this guy is and what's goin' on."

D'Arcangelo nodded. He tilted his head toward the kitchen. "I'm taking Nina out for breakfast, then I'll get back to you."

Lou gave him that fellow male half-smile, half-leer nod of approval of Tom's taste in women.

"Enjoy your breakfast, Tommy." He gestured with his head. "She's a real looker."

Tom nodded in agreement as he stretched his neck sideways to relieve the quickening stiffness. "Yeah, in this case a real life-saver."

AFTER TOM LET LOU AND HIS CARPET CREW in to dispose of the man now lying unconscious on the kitchen floor, and Nina and he walked to a nearby café on Fitzwater Street for breakfast.

Nina noted that, despite the stiff neck, his head seemed to swivel more than she had seen before, more than was even necessary for busy Philly streets and its menacing or distracted drivers, where right turn on red and a 'Stop' sign meant get ready to launch unless someone on cane, crutches or walker was crossing.

"Nervous?" she asked. "You sure look nervous."

"Me? Uh, not really. Just trying to stretch out my neck some. By tomorrow I'll be as stiff as a gargoyle."

"What *was* that about back there?"

"I was having carpet laid today, until that guy showed up, so they need to remove him before they start."

She snorted. "Right. I mean the thug, not the carpet guys. What was he up to?"

"Not really clear about that. I'd say he wanted to render me unconscious, either for a short time or permanently."

"Obviously. It looked as if he were going to kill you, for chrissakes!"

"—until you saved my life I'm sure you're going to add."

"Uh, yeah—sure looked like it. I like that—the ingratitude! And after last night, too! You men! After they get into your knickers, they're looking to the next pair of tits and ass."

"'After last night'? Why do women always do that? Sleep with you and act like they gave you the world. They get nothing out of it? Women are always doing us a favor? Come on!"

"Jesus Christ, the arrogance? Did I hear that right?"

"I'm serious about this. Hear me out. There I was sitting in my house, with my cup out—figuratively speaking of course—waiting for someone to give me a handout, and the beautiful Nina comes along and shows her blessed mercy and bestows upon this poor mendicant a sympathy humping. Is that it? Is that why you had to get tanked?"

"If that were just a sympathy fuck, you'd be dead now. I wouldn't have been there for the morning action—you know, the one where I saved your life. There's no need to stay over for sympathy cases."

Tom smiled at her reply, said nothing.

"I don't just mean for batting practice. I meant *none* of the morning action," she added, a salacious gleam in her eyes.

He nodded approval. "I'm glad you stayed. It was nice. And that's an understatement."

She took his arm. "Yes, it was," she agreed. "And not a mercy fuck. You know, Tom, I don't want to make love that often. When I do, I think the stars and planets must be in some kind of harmonic alignment."

"I'm glad of that. But whatever your motive, it was exquisite."

She hugged Tom's arm tighter. "Ooh, keep that up—I like it."

He then added: "—and I must confess I'm glad you saved my bacon today, of course."

"Well, we're back to where we started. That goon—why was he in your house?"

Tom shrugged. They stopped and he pointed to the diner's sign. "This is the place."

Once inside, the hostess seated them and they ordered. After coffee arrived, Nina started again.

"Look," Nina said. "We need to clear the air here, don't you think? Unless of course, this is the last time you're going to see me. In which case, then we can just enjoy our breakfast and part ways. How about we start by telling each other something that we're keeping hidden, that is, we give each other something, the way they do in hostage negotiation? To show good faith, I mean."

"I've never taken a hostage," Tom said, surprised at her new strategy to uncover secrets.

"Neither have I, but this is how it works: I tell you some secret about myself, and you tell me something about yourself. For example—let me start, okay? My name is not Nina Murray. Nina's my middle name; Murray is my stage name. My real name is Leslie Nina Cahill. That's how it works. I gave you something that I like to keep secret—not many people know my real name. It shows that I trust you. Now you give me something."

"My lucky number is fifteen—my mother was born on the fifteenth of June. I wore it when I played baseball in high school, I wear it now on my softball uniform." She tapped the table several times with her left hand and glared at me. "Unh-uhh. Not good enough. That's not a secret. Who was the guy in your house today? What was he doing there? Stuff like that!"

"Nina … er, Leslie, I don't know who he is or what he was doing there today. Can I still call you Nina?"

"You have no idea? None whatever?"

"Unless he was looking for someone like you to rape, I'd guess he was a burglar looking for Christmas cash … thought there'd be some around. That's the only thing I can come up with really…."

She eyed him suspiciously.

D'Arcangelo shrugged. "Look, check out my blog and you can learn everything about me you want! Okay, your turn," he said.

Tom leaned closer to her so the other diners wouldn't hear. "Tell me you just had the best sex of your life in the last twenty-four hours."

Their waitress arrived at the exact time to overhear that last sentence. She was on the downward slope of middle-age, with bleached blond hair bleeding into frosted white ends, large dollops of rouge and crimson lipstick, like a lemon meringue pie adorned with tomato slices. She placed a tray with their orders of omelettes and home fries, toast and orange juice on a serving stand.

Nina frowned at Tom and waited his answer

"Waitresses sometimes hear what is being said at their tables and it's usually boring," their server said. "We almost never comment unless spoken to directly"—she unloaded the plates and glasses onto the table and leaned over to them and confided softly—"but I have to hear the answer to this one!"

She smiled first at Nina, then at Tom, and leaned in a conspiratorial pose closer to listen.

"Tom, I don't keep a list and rank them in order of quality!" Nina said, then looked at the waitress for approval and agreement.

The waitress' eyes bulged in an expression of disbelief. "Honey, you better start," she advised, tucking the tray under her arm. "Some day you might want to go back and look that list over, for old-times' sake, know what I'm talking about? Let me give you another tip, dear. You always tell the guy who asks that kind of question *he's* the best." She pointed an index finger toward Tom from behind the cover of her tray.

Tom scowled at the waitress, then transformed it into a mock theatrical smile. "Thanks for your advice, Oprah." He pointed to other tables. "Doesn't someone need a warm-up on their coffee?"

The waitress shrugged and sped off to wait on others.

Nina brushed her hair away from her face. "I thought all you guys think you're the guy who can give a girl the best orgasm in her life. Have I found someone with an inferiority complex?"

Nina then continued in her confession mode. "Tom, my brother is in the mob in South Jersey. Now you—and don't tell me that your favorite color is blue either. How about why you have a .45 under your bed? In your slipper to be exact."

"It was my grandfather's—from the war. I keep it for protection."

She laughed. "Here's a suggestion for you—it won't help if you don't carry it."

"You're right about that. Your brother is in a South Jersey mob?" Now Tom was curious. "So your father *and* your brother—?"

"Yep, both of them. That's how I got the job at the Puss in Boots Club. My brother Brian got it for me. He also protects me from any nonsense going on. People know I'm Brian Cahill's sister and they keep their hands off."

"After this morning, I'd say you can take care of yourself."

"I told you I was a jock. Soccer, volleyball, softball all through high school. Volleyball and modern dance in college. I've also taken self-defense classes."

"Don't rub it in. Hey, that prick got me by surprise."

"Balls, throat, eyes—those are the vital areas. I'll show you some time. Shins are vulnerable, too. A good sharp kick can snap a shin bone easily."

"Throat? Did you see a neck on that guy? I don't think he had one—his head came out of his shoulders."

"Maybe those"—she held her fingers up and made quotation marks in the air and grinned— "'carpet layers' will be able to find out who he is, huh? They take him to the police?"

"No, I don't think they did. They might find out who he is though. In fact, I'd give fifty-to-one on it."

"Hmm. Now I'm getting the picture."

"What picture is that?"

"It's not for no reason they're called 'crime families' ".

"So you figured out that my uncle is in the mob. You're right."

"And so are you," she said. "You fooled me. I didn't take you for a mob guy."

"Uh no, I'm not really. Let's say I was on the periphery but am not now. It's a long story, as they say. Someday—maybe—I'll tell you. We better eat—our eggs are getting cold."

She looked skeptically at him and picked up her fork. "I'm famished. Violence makes me hungry—and I will be horny for days, too." She winked.

"It had just the opposite effect on me, Sweetheart. My John Thomas doesn't groove on near death experience."

Tom massaged his throat and flexed his neck. "First, let me see if I can swallow this omelet. I might be on a liquid diet for a few days."

They ate, paid the bill and left the diner. Outside the door they stepped on to the sidewalk. Nina observed him looking painfully around left and right and down the street in front of him. Tom's cell phone rang and he opened it to see that Lou was calling.

"Excuse me," he said to Nina. "I gotta take this call."

Tom stepped away and turned his back. "Hey."

"Hey, Tommy …"

"Did you find out anything about that guy? Did he have a wallet on him? Did he tell you anything?"

Lou hesitated. "No, no wallet. No ID. Tom—"

"Didn't he tell you anything?"

"No, Tom. We … uh … screwed up … sort of."

"What do you mean 'screwed up, sort of'?"

"The guy's not with us any longer. When we wrapped him in the plastic and carpet we used to take him out, we must have wrapped him too tight. I think he suffocated. Whatever, he was no longer with us when we got to the warehouse."

D'Arcangelo had heard the 'warehouse' mentioned before, usually in low whispers. He himself had never been there. He was becoming so involved with the gang that Lou assumed he knew where and what it was. Tom hadn't the vaguest idea of its location. This was not good news.

D'Arcangelo looked at Nina. He thought at first she may have killed the thug with her life-saving at-bat and didn't want to upset her. Maybe that last whack Tom took at him had finished the job. He would've asked Lou if they knew for sure that he was smothered, but Nina was at his arm. He'd ask later.

"Okay, Lou. Maybe next time. No big deal. Look, I'll call you. I got to talk to Mr. Cardinello later. I'm heading for the hospital to see Vince."

"I'll be there later. I got to talk to the Boss, too. Give you a call later."

Tom flipped off the phone and turned back to Nina.

"Everything all right?" Nina inquired.

"Yeah, yeah. Everything is just peachy."

NINA AND HE WALKED to the hospital. Tom fought the urge to crane his neck to survey the area for suspicious characters as he walked with her. Its ever-growing stiffness hindered him. Once in the hospital he felt more secure and relaxed his guard a bit.

At the elevators they pushed the buttons to ascend to the eighth floor. After three people exited Nina and he slid on, joining a female doctor and a nurse. The doctor was short and round with short curly hair. On her white jacket was the hospital's emblem, a caduceus and associated clinical department, "pathology", embroidered in red. She wore a badge that gave her name followed by MD and PhD. In her crossed arms she carried a laptop computer and a textbook thick as a tombstone. Tom noted the title, *Statistics for Epidemiology*. She turned and saw him looking over her shoulder at the book, then smiled.

"Interesting reading?" Tom asked, making conversation as the elevator poked along to the seventh-floor stop. Nina looked at him and then the doctor, who she imagined was rolling her eyes mentally. Tom hated the gravely serious atmosphere of hospitals.

"I was a math major as an undergraduate and I'm finding it tough going," the doctor said.

"Where did you do your undergrad work?" Tom asked.

"MIT," she replied.

"Oh." Tom nodded. "That's a good school."

She smiled weakly, giving the smallest of acknowledgment.

"I went there with some senior high kids … classmates, I mean," he continued. "My science teacher took us to Boston and then to MIT for a lecture. I think he was hoping, you know, to inspire us to go into engineering and science. Stuff like that. The atmosphere there made me feel thirty IQ points smarter."

The doctor smiled again at Tom and then at Nina and then back at him.

"And did it work?" she asked. He sensed she was eagerly looking for her stop to come.

"Well, not for me. Maybe some of the others … My math is terrible. I'm more the verbal type."

The elevator stopped at the seventh floor and the doctor smiled at the pair. "Nice talking to you."

The pathologist and the nurse exited the elevator compartment and its doors closed.

Nina stared at him. "Hospitals make you nervous?" she asked.

"Sure. They don't you? How old did you think she was?"

"The doctor? Maybe thirty-five. Why?"

"MD and Ph.D. at thirty five," Tom said. "I fucking hate under-achievers."

"She's bright and she works hard. It's probably her whole life."

The elevator stopped with a bing. Nina looked to see if it was the floor they needed. "Ten, isn't it?"

"Yeah."

"It seems," she remarked, "that they put you higher the worse off you are. It's symbolic, I guess. Like you're closer to heaven."

"Oh, we're philosophical now? The morgue is in the basement," Tom noted. "That shoots that theory."

"Not at all," Nina disagreed. "Heaven can't help you after you're dead."

They found the nurses' station and stopped to see if they were able to see their patient. A nurse was rapt in examining a computer screen. Tom and Nina stood in front of her for several moments. Finally, she looked up.

"Could we see Vince Sarzano? Is he doing okay?" Tom finally asked.

"I think someone's in there attending to Mr. Sarzano right now. Give them five minutes."

"How is he doing?" Nina asked again.

The nurse called up his record. "He's better. Much better than when he came in. Of course, you'll need to talk to one of the doctors …"

IN THE ROOM NINA AND TOM sidled softly up to Vince's bedside. He was hooked up to four monitors and three intravenous drips, his head heavily bandaged, oxygen tubes inserted into his nose.

Before they entered Tom called Lou Spagnolo and reported that Vince was doing better, but that he would be in the hospital for several more days and would need careful observation by the trained neuro-people.

"That's good to hear, Tommy," he said. "Jimmy and I are coming to visit him tomorrow."

"Great. But he is still pretty much out of it." Tom paused a moment. "Lou, I need to speak to Mr. Cardinello. Could you call him and see if he can talk to me?"

Tom expected Lou to put him off, and he expected to have to assert himself—as much as one could with a man like Lou Spagnola.

"Here's his number. He's there now. Call him and set up a time to see him." Lou gave him the number. "He's at his office at *Catania*."

Tom thanked Lou, took a deep breath, exhaled, and dialed Cardinello immediately.

After three rings, Jimmy Cardinello answered the phone. "Yeah."

Then a silence with an expectation of rapid reply but without the petulant edge Tom expected.

"Mr. Cardinello?"

"Speaking."

Tom took pains not to clear his throat.

"This is Tom D'Arcangelo …" He waited to see if Jimmy would possibly not remember him immediately.

"Hey, Tommy. How's your uncle? Lou and I are going to see him tomorrow."

Tom reported on Vince's status, being careful to stop short of giving more than the boss wanted to hear. He paused, then added: "Mr. Cardinello, could I stop by the restaurant and talk to you sometime?"

"I'll be here for a while. Do you want to see me today?"

"Uh … yeah."

"See you when you get here." There was a click on the other end.

Tom entered the employees entrance at the rear of *Catania* and headed to Cardinello's office casually, slowly. He had thought about what he would say, even practiced his lines in front of a mirror as he did in any theatrical production. Tom had even thought about the strategy to adopt with a South Philadelphia crime boss, acknowledging that this wasn't nearly like taking control of an audience at a college drama production. Hadn't his uncle Vince said that Jimmy was not in a good mood of late? That Cardinello had become more unpredictable than was customary?

Tom ascended the stairs slowly, deliberately, unlike his usual trips as a waiter requiring him to bound up the stairs with trays of plates. He wore leather shoes that made a heavy thudding on the steps.

When he passed the second floor, Tom turned to find the third floor flight to the boss's office with Joey Argento standing guard outside.

Joey recognized Tom immediately.

"Hey," Joey said.

"How's it goin'?"

"You here to see Jimmy?"

"Yeah."

"He expect you?

"Yeah, I called about an hour ago. He told me to come over and see him."

Joey nodded. He hacked a few times into a handkerchief.

"Still got that cold, huh?"

"Yeah, fuckin' bug just won't go away. I think it's goin' down into my chest. It's fuckin' ruinin' my Christmas. I think I'm getting' pneumonia." He coughed several times more.

"That's rough, man. Maybe you need to see a doctor or just get in bed with some whiskey and hot lemonade and sweat it out—"

"That's what I'm thinkin' of doin'—bed," Joey said.

Tom started to the door but Joey slid in front of him.

"Hey, Tommy. I gotta pat you down, y'know?"

"Sure," he said. "But I can tell you now I'm packing." Tom leant forward and opened his coat and sweater to expose the .45 in its holster for Joey to see.

Joey looked at him and repeated the policy. "No guns in Jimmy's presence. Not sure if you know that, but them's the rules."

Tom nodded. "Sure." He lifted his sweater and removed the automatic and held it grip toward Joey.

Joey took it, looked at it as a gun lover would, and jammed it in his belt. "I still gotta pat you down, Tommy. That's the rules."

"Sure, Joey, sure."

Tom held out his arms and waited for Argento to pat each arm, his chest and waist and back and travel down his legs for ankle holsters. When finished, he stood up. "Wait here a minute," he said.

The sentry tapped three times, then two, then four.

"Yeah?" came from the other side of the door. Joey entered and shut the door behind him. Tom leaned forward a bit to hear if he could discern anything.

Joey opened the door to face him standing casually. "Jimmy wants to see you," Argento said, then coughed.

Tom slid past him with a thanks and stood facing the Crime Boss of South Philadelphia.

Soft Christmas music came from speakers around the office. Jimmy sat at a rather large businessman's desk, meticulously kept, with files and in-basket on one side.

His uncle Vince had once said Cardinello's desk had one-inch steel plate around it, but Tom was never sure if he was joking or not. Requisite stapler and pen and pencil holder with other desk accessories were arranged neatly in appropriate places. Jimmy sat facing Tom with his hands folded over the desk blotter and a closed book. Next to the book was the .45 Argento had taken. It lay with the grip toward Jimmy, the barrel pointing toward the young man.

Tom looked at his gun on the desk and the book, but was unable to discern the title of the book. On the wall were pictures of Jimmy's family, his nephews in baseball uniforms and team pictures of them from football and soccer. Several civic and diocesan awards given to

Cardinello for sponsoring teams and functions and holidays adorned the wall in a haphazard manner. Mounted on a display rack in the middle of the wall was an old double-barrel shotgun.

The last time Tom had seen Cardinello he thought he looked like an accountant. Tonight he thought the head of the Philly crime syndicate looked more like Martin Scorsese, but on Quaaludes rather than amphetamines. Tom was determined to show no fear, not even to clear his throat showing nervousness, to act casual and at ease.

Tom soon found the silence uncomfortable without a greeting. "Hello, Mr. Cardinello. Merry Christmas."

Jimmy looked at him, raised his eyebrows and peered directly into Tom's eyes.

"Same to you, son. How's your uncle?"

"The doctors say it's still too soon to know anything definitively. Vince did *say* a few things. A few more days and they should know more. They said they have seen some positive signs."

Tom paused for a few moments to see if he wanted to reply. Cardinello said nothing.

"Who knows though? They could be blowing sunshine up our asses," Tom said. "They don't like to give bad news until they have to. What do you think?"

Jimmy looked down at the automatic and nodded. "It's been my experience that the White Coats play their cards close to their chest— in case they're sued. The less they say, the better. They all have fuckin' lawyers, ya know. Lou and I will be stopping over tomorrow. Maybe Vince'll be awake."

Tom did not reply then added: "If he's awake, he'd like to see you and Lou." As soon as Tom heard what he'd said, he thought it sounded lame, insincere, nonsense.

He waited to see if Cardinello was going to reply. Jimmy just stared at him, then reached to his dark horn-rimmed glasses, removed them and placed them upended on the desk in front of him next to the automatic.

"Opus Dei," Cardinello said.

"Pardon?"

Cardinello tapped the book. "The book—it's about Opus Dei."

"Oh right. Opus Dei. Yeah."

"I remember you were once interested in what I was reading? I know you're a college kid … educated … interested in books, I assume."

Tom nodded, not sure if he wanted to engage Cardinello on church doctrine or history. To change the subject he pointed to the air. "Yeah. What's the music? I don't recognize it."

Jimmy smiled. "It's called *Lauda per la Nativita del Signore*. It's a cantata. By Ottorino Respighi. I love it. You get tired of the same old Christmas shit, ya know?"

Tom grunted assent. "I'll say."

"You know Respighi?"

"Uh, yeah. *Pines of Rome*, *Roman Festivals*, *Fountains of Rome*, that composer?"

"That's right. Brilliant pieces, by one of the greatest modern composers. I think he's underrated."

Cardinello picked up the .45 and began to examine it like an archaeologist cradling an artifact. He looked up from his inspection. "Old school, this. Vintage."

"It's my grandfather's service pistol. Colt made a good gun back then. 1911 model. Saw action in Africa and Italy. My father took good care of it. Had to have a spring or two replaced. Dad took us kids shooting with it a few times. Said grampop killed four Germans with it. It's really my brother Matt's, but I borrowed it while he's away in the Marines."

Tom stopped himself. He was beginning to ramble. Nothing says nervousness more than talking too much.

"My father gave me a gun, too," confided Cardinello. He lay the automatic down on the desk, its barrel still facing Tom and still within easy reach. "Papa must have known something."

Cardinello pointed over his shoulder at a double-barrelled shotgun mounted on the wall. "See that? Sicilians call that a *lupara*. My father used it—for hunting. You a hunter?"

Tom shook his head. "My Dad and brother liked to hunt. Hunting doesn't do anything for me."

"Me neither. That's why they invented agriculture and cities. Cutting up an animal is a mess. I let someone else dress the meat. Not for me. I'd rather grow grapes and olives and tomatoes and peppers."

Jimmy suddenly raised his finger to his lips, then pointed to the ceiling and waved it around to the four corners of the room. He shrugged his shoulders in a questioning gesture. Cardinello picked up a remote control from the desk and pointed it at a sound unit on the table behind him. The decibel levels of the cantata tripled and covered the room with its orchestration and voices. He walked around the desk and stood in front of Tom, beckoning him closer. He placed his arm on Tom's shoulder and pulled him close, like a father giving his son confidential advice.

"In case the walls have ears, y'know what I mean?" he whispered into Tom's ear, who leaned closer to hear above the music. Being this close to Cardinello made him apprehensive, and he fought to relax. Jimmy had had garlic with his eggs that morning. He laid his hand on Tom's chest.

It occurred that maybe Jimmy was trying to see if Tom was wearing a wire. Vince had told him that Cardinello was becoming more and more paranoid.

"I think," Jimmy said, "I know why you're carrying that piece. Lou told me about some Irish guys at your house. Be careful. Gun laws are getting stiffer here in Pennsylvania. Especially if used in a crime. Don't go waving it around, like some dumb fuckin' monkey. They get cut out in traffic and next thing they want to do is shoot somebody. They're always whining 'He disrespected me', ya know what I'm sayin'? But I understand you think you need to protect yourself."

Tom nodded agreement, saying nothing. He was about to speak when Jimmy went on: "About those Irish guys … *mea culpa*. I think they showed up here because I didn't talk to old man O'Connell in South Jersey before you guys went there. They may have been thinking we were stepping on their turf when Vince and you went to check out that dentist."

Hearing this, Tom nodded again, stone-faced, hiding his anger. His mind flashed back to his bowel-loosening fear at their visit. *Mea culpa? They could have killed me!*

"Technically, we were," Tom said. "I think the dentist had a dance card that was full. There seems to be a line to collect debts from him."

"Yeah, Vince told me about it. Well, I spoke to Mr. O'Connell and explained what was going on. That should settle things down a bit."

"Let's hope so. I'm glad they didn't have a short fuse before finding out what was up. They were pissed off about one of their boys."

Jimmy waved his hand to cut him off. "Yeah, I heard about it. One of their guys had some problem. O'Connell thought it was us. I explained that it wasn't. I mean, we had no reason to do something like that. I didn't have to tell him that it was probably someone in his own back yard. I *think* he believed me. But," he added, "who the fuck knows?"

Cardinello looked at Tom and peered into his eyes. Tom thought, that without his eyeglasses, the man had depthless black eyes, like a shark. For an instant Tom thought he detected that Jimmy was wearing a touch of mascara.

Jimmy circled back behind the desk, sat down and leaned back in the swivel chair. "So what brings you here? You called and asked to see me, so I assume it's more immediate than just telling me how Vince is doing."

Tom spoke up, calmly and with a measure that he was not sure he could summon. He took a silent deep breath and began. "Mr. Cardinello, I appreciate everything you've done for me, my brother and my mother. When my father died we were in bad financial shape. Without your help—giving Matt and me jobs and all—I don't know what we would have done. Thank you ever so much."

Cardinello stared at him for a moment. "Ah-h-h, you would have got a job somewhere else. You're smart boys. But you're welcome, Tommaso. You know I love your uncle and his family. It was the least I could do."

Tom continued. "My mother never wanted to take any money from you or Vince. She didn't approve of the 'family business'—thought it was against the Church, ya know."

"Smart woman." Jimmy agreed, but without smiling. "The Church, eh?"

"She was always wary of Vince getting my dad into the business," Tom continued. "So he didn't … as least as far as I know. Vince said that he was giving her the money, but I know a lot of it was from you."

"Your father was a very smart man. I liked him. He played the mandolin at my daughter's wedding, y'know? That would have been a present enough, but he made two beautiful wooden end tables for my daughter and my son-in-law. You father was a real craftsman, an artist."

Then out it came: "Mom made me promise not to get involved with the family business, Mr. Cardinello. I'm not exactly keeping my promise to her."

Cardinello leaned forward and placed his elbows on the desk and with his hands folded over the book and gun. "So what are you saying? You're quitting the restaurant business?"

Tom tried not to appear defiant and to remain business-like and soft-spoken, sincerely grateful for all he had been given. "I can only work part-time in the restaurant … bussing, waiting, whatever, a few hours a week, when needed, but that's about it. I'm going back to grad school and I'm going to need more time to study."

Jimmy leaned back again and swiveled from side to side in his chair for several moments. Then he began nodding his head deliberately. His eyes seemed to narrow and his voice deepened an octave.

"You know, when you came in here, I thought you were going to ask permission to take care of the guy who fucked up your uncle or that you wanted more 'work'—outside of the restaurants, I mean. Every fuckin' time I turn around one of these guys"—he waved his index finger several times at imaginary men who worked for him—"is telling me he deserves more work, needs more money, is not getting his due for some reason or other, ya know what I mean? I feel like a fuckin' psychiatrist sometimes."

Cardinello lapsed into silence. Tom didn't know what to say next, so he said nothing and waited for Jimmy's next sentence.

"You know, Tommy, there are certain rules we operate by around here," Cardinello explained. "I'm sure you've heard that saying 'what happens here, what is seen here, what is said here, stays here'?"

"Sure, Mr. Cardinello."

Jimmy placed his elbows on the desk in front of him, laced his fingers together and examined Tom over them.

"That applies with all aspects of the family business. Understand? Keep your mouth shut. This is a bit of an unusual place you've put me in, Tommy. Your uncle swears you're a smart kid."

He waved his right hand around in the air in two small circles then locked them together again. "You won't say anything about the business." His last sentence was not a question, but a declarative statement. Cardinello sat upright and placed both hands on the desk. His face seemed to darken.

"Of course, Mr. Cardinello," Tom said. "Like I said, my family owes you and your family all the gratitude for what you've done for us after my father died. You're like family to me. You have my—our, my brother and I both,—loyalty."

Cardinello stood up. He blinked his eyes several times as if to peer more clearly into the D'Arcangelo's soul. "I think you understand that not everyone involved in the business is allowed to leave ... shall we say, so graciously?"

Suddenly Tom began to feel a bit of adrenalin. This exit interview was beginning to take longer than he hoped or intended.

"Yes, I do know that, Mr. Cardinello. And I appreciate it."

Cardinello leaned forward and said softly: "Do you know why that is, Tommy? Do you?"

Tom tried to look cool. "I think I do."

"And why is that, son?"

Tom stood there at a loss for the correct words and a quick reply. Fortunately, Jimmy didn't wait for his reply. His question had been rhetorical.

Cardinello held up his hand with his index finger skyward. "Because when one is part of a family, Tommy, one doesn't *leave* a family. A *real* man doesn't leave his children, his mother, his sister, brother. It's not like going on a date with a girl, fucking her and then deciding you don't like her tits. Understand what I mean? There's *familial* loyalty. *Capische?*"

Tom nodded vigorously. "Of course, Mr. Cardinello."

He picked up Tom's gun from the desk and cradled it in two hands. "A guy who forgets—or betrays—his family is a bad man."

He held the .45 out to Tom, grip first. Tom took it from him, all the while trying to maintain solid eye contact. He nodded at this last statement and holstered the gun. As soon as he grabbed it he noticed the clip was missing.

"Joey has your clip. I put the one that was in the chamber in the clip. Remember what I said about the gun laws."

"Sure, Mr. Cardinello. Thanks."

"Merry Christmas, Tommy."

"Same to you … and your family," Tom said and turned to the door. He took two steps and as he was reaching out for the doorknob, Cardinello interrupted: "Oh, Tommy—"

Tom turned and saw him at his desk. Jimmy held his black horn-rimmed spectacles in one hand.

"Remember." He raised his index finger to his lips in a hush motion but said nothing. Cardinello's eyes seemed blacker than before.

Tom nodded, then turned, opened the door and departed.

Outside Joey stood sniffling, with a handkerchief to his nose. He handed Tom the clip for the automatic.

"Take care of that cold, Joey. Merry Christmas, and if I don't see you before then, happy New Year," Tom said taking off down the stairs.

D'Arcangelo stopped in the men's room at the bottom of the stairs. He washed his hands and splashed warm water in his face, then took several deep breaths while he toweled his face and looked at his reflection in the mirror. He looked under the stalls for feet, but saw no one. At the door, he placed his foot against the door so no one could enter. He unholstered the Colt, removed the clip from his pocket, loaded it, chambered a round, placed the safety on and slid the gun back into the holster.

Outside *Ristorante Catania*, Tom again took several deep breaths and let the cold December air wash about him, then raised his scarf around his neck before buttoning his coat.

Did I just agree that we're family? Tom mused.

He looked up and down the street for anyone suspicious, then headed for home seven blocks away. What was cold blue sky had turned leaden. Snow felt imminent.

As Tom turned onto his street in the distance he saw a large man in his early thirties with a full but trim mustache walking toward him. Hatless with thick hair combed back, he wore a short black overcoat and charcoal scarf, with leather gloves.

As Tom neared the house, they were within thirty feet of each other. The man seemed to be looking at him with some purpose. When they converged at Tom's house, the man reached into his coat pocket and held out a leather ID holder. He flipped it open and held it toward Tom to display a badge and ID.

"Mr. D'Arcangelo?"

Tom ignored the ID, looked cautiously at the man, then became aware of another presence behind him. He leaned forward to see the ID, then twisted to see who was coming up behind him. Another man, a goateed African-American, dressed in a camel hair overcoat, white silk scarf, wearing a dark brown fedora had come up on Tom's right. His overcoat was unbuttoned and he carried his hand inside it.

"Thomas D'Arcangelo?" the hatless man asked, still holding the ID out.

"Why do you want to know?" Tom asked, stalling. While they didn't look like mob guys ...

"I'm Special Agent Edward McMillan and this is Special Agent Edwin Dyson. We're from the Federal Bureau of Investigation. We'd like to take a few minutes to talk to you, if that's okay. We have some questions you might be able to help us with."

Tom turned again to look at the man on his flank. "May I see your ID, too?"

The man frowned, took out his identification and flipped it open. Tom leaned forward to study it closely, looking for any hint of forgery. Since he had his own stash of fake identification, he was alert for tell-tale signs.

"Suppose I tell you that I can't talk right now? Then what?"

McMillan placed his ID in his pocket and smiled. "Mr. D'Arcangelo, this can be a difficult procedure or an easy one—difficult if we have to take you into custody and question you at headquarters. Or we can just take time to talk right here. Much simpler. For you, for us. It's up to you."

The FBI! And they wanted to talk to Tom. His stomach tightened, adrenaline shot into his system, and he suddenly needed to piss. He shifted the bag of groceries to his left arm and searched for his keys.

"Okay, but I'm not talking out here. It's freezing. This is my place."

Tom didn't want anyone seeing him talking to these suits, so he thought it best to let them in. He certainly didn't want the anxiety of going to their station. He opened the door and entered, the two men following. They stepped from the foyer into the living room. Tom didn't want to remove his coat, although he had a bulky sweater over the .45 and didn't think they could see he was carrying a concealed weapon. He decided to remove his coat and hung it up on a hook near the door. He was glad Philly had relaxed its concealed weapon permit process and he had taken the time to get one.

Once inside the agents peered around the house like children with grandparents in a Fischer Price store.

Tom set the groceries down on the dining room table. "What were your names again?"

"I'm Edward McMillan; he's Edwin Dyson." He accentuated the pronunciation of their names. "We're from—"

Tom cut him off. "Special agents from the FBI. Yeah, I got that," he said. "Did anyone ever call you the Fed Eds?"

They looked at each other. McMillan smiled; Dyson frowned.

"No, Mr. D'Arcangelo, no one has ever called us that," McMillan replied. "You're the first."

"I'm gonna have a shot of whiskey to warm up. Been out shopping. It's cold as hell out there. Would you like a scotch? A beer? Coffee? Water? Anything?"

"Nothing for us, thanks."

McMillan glanced at his partner. Dyson, who was in all likelihood was a former college fullback or linebacker, eyed D'Arcangelo like a panther looking at its next meal. He had opened his overcoat and the jacket for access to his firearm. Tom was making *them* nervous. McMillan took two steps toward the dining room to keep Tom within his sight as he went to the dining room, uncorked the bottle, poured two shots into a glass and stepped back into the living room, swirling the liquid in the tumbler.

"Now, how can I help you?" Tom asked. "I think I'm supposed to tell law enforcement if I'm ever stopped for anything that I'm carrying a gun. I have a permit to carry it, of course."

Dyson's eyes became slits. The two agents riveted on Tom.

"You are? May we see it? The permit, I mean, not the gun."

"Sure." Tom stood and riffled through his wallet for it and handed it to McMillan, who examined it closely. Dyson took an obvious step away from his partner to widen the line of fire as targets. He took a wider stance as if he were expecting a gun battle to erupt.

McMillan returned the permit. "Seems to be in order. Thank you for alerting us."

"I don't usually carry a gun. But my uncle and I were mugged a few days ago. He is in ICU in the hospital and it's made me nervous. There seems to be more of that stuff around the holidays."

"No need to give us a reason to legally exercise your second amendment rights. Thanks for agreeing to talk to us, Mr. D'Arcangelo."

"Sure," Tom said as he sat down in his easy chair. "Shoot. Have a seat, why don't you?"

His heart rate had jumped forty beats when these agents announced themselves. Tom needed some time to relax, to gather his thoughts, to take a few deep breaths and center himself. He pointed to the sofa and the other chair.

"Call me Tom or Tommy. Mr. D'Arcangelo makes me think my father's in the room." Tom smiled, waiting for the alcohol to reach his stomach. He wanted a moment to get used to being questioned about murdering someone and then stealing one point two million. He needed a moment to face the dread of imprisonment for a good portion of his life. His uncle's words came to mind: 'Don't say anything. Lawyer Up.'

Tom knew to stonewall anything by a simple shake of my head and a heartfelt "no" and not to volunteer anything. Anything. He thought it ironic that he had just come from talking to Jimmy Cardinello about keeping his mouth shut. *Did Jimmy know something was going on with the Feds?*

"Do you know a Mr. Lawrence Banks?"

This came out of left field. For two long seconds the name rang a blank. "Lawrence Banks?"

"He usually went by his middle name, Malik. His full name is Lawrence Malik Banks. Do you know him?"

"Malik! Sure! Sure, I know him. He and I were in a few plays together in college. We took some classes together, acting workshops, screenwriting, drama-related stuff."

"Are you friends with Mr. Banks?" McMillan asked.

"Yeah, I'd say we're friends. We worked closely together on those plays. It builds a bond. Malik's a fantastic actor."

Agent Dyson leaned forward. "How close a friend are you?"

"Well, it depends." Tom laughed. "We don't jack each other off."

Dyson scowled. When he next spoke his voice had lowered two octaves. "I mean, have you *seen* him recently?"

Tom thought back to when Malik and he last got together.

"No, I haven't seen him since early this year ... about nine months ago. March, I think. I saw him in the school production of *Hamlet*. We got together for the cast party after the performance. And once after that. I met him on campus for lunch. Just him and me. Wait a minute! I did bump in to him a few weeks after that lunch down on South Street, in a club down there. But I haven't seen him since."

"Any other contact? Phone, email?"

"I called Malik to set up our last lunch, but not since then. No email that I'm aware of."

McMillan scribbled furiously in a notepad. Dyson asked: "What plays were you in? With Malik?"

"He was the lead in *Othello*, MacDuff in *Macbeth*. Like I said he's a hell of an actor. I'm a little curious here. Has Malik done something wrong?"

McMillan looked up from his note-taking. "Mr. Banks is missing. We're investigating his whereabouts. You wouldn't know where he might be, would you?"

"No, not at all. Haven't a clue." Tom suddenly felt twenty pounds lighter and needed to muffle any jubilation. These guys were *not* looking for *him*!

"Do you know a Teresa Colston?"

"Sure. She acted in some of the same plays in the theater group with Malik and me. I saw her play Ophelia in *Hamlet* the year after I graduated. Why?"

McMillan looked at D'Arcangelo intently. "She's missing, too."

"Oh."

"How well do you know Teresa Colston?" McMillan asked.

"I dated her when we were doing *Macbeth*. Went out a few times, dinner, breakfast a few times. She was Lady Macbeth, I was Banquo."

Dyson leaned forward again, unblinking. "You dated her. Then what happened?"

"Terry and I went out for about three months, then we broke up. She's bit intense. It was one of those drama production romances."

Dyson repeated what Tom said. "So you dated her for three months? How long ago was that?"

D'Arcangelo thought for a moment. "Three years ago now."

"Had any contact with her recently, since then?" McMillan asked.

"None. I saw her as Ophelia in *Hamlet* and gave her some kudos. But no, I haven't seen or heard from her since."

Tom paused and eyed the two. "You guys are welcome to look in my basement," Tom laughed. "Search the house to your hearts' content. No warrant needed. Nothing to hide. Go ahead."

At that remark they exchanged glances.

"No need for that, Mr. D'Arcangelo. Were Malik Banks and Teresa Colston seeing each other?" MacMillan asked. "I mean, do you link them together in any way?"

Tom shrugged. "Not to my knowledge. It wouldn't surprise me, but I can't say they were or weren't."

The FBI agent read from his notepad. "Do you know a Tamara Jones-Wills or a Stephanie Anne Roberts?" He repeated their names slowly.

Tom didn't recognize their names. "Nope."

Dyson spoke up. "Why do you say that Banks and Colston together wouldn't surprise you?"

"Malik liked the company of women."

Tom knew Malik was a cooze hound *par excellence*, and Terry Colston was noted for her freewheeling libido. Tom once speculated she had a scorecard for the entire drama crew. He would be stunned if Lady Macbeth *hadn't* banged Othello. "Malik liked women. Teresa's a good-looking woman."

McMillan scribbled on to the notepad. Then he took four pictures out of the portmanteau and handed them to Tom. "Sure you don't know these two women?"

Tom looked carefully at some high school graduation and college age pictures. "No, never saw them. I can tell you that they were *not* in the drama club while I was there. That's for sure. I don't think I've ever seen them in any of my classes either."

McMillan took the photos back, tucked them into the folder and thanked him.

"Were those two women involved with Malik, too?" Tom asked.

"It was reported that they were." McMillan looked at D'Arcangelo intently for his reaction. "They're missing, too."

The FBI agent took a card from his jacket pocket and handed it to Tom.

"This has my number. Could you call me if you hear from Malik Banks or Teresa Colston? Or, if you think of something you forgot that might help us find him or her ... them?"

"Sure," Tom said. He pocketed the card. "Exactly what makes an agent a *special* agent, may I ask? Just curious."

"Special agents work on dedicated task forces."

"Oh. Like what?"

"Terrorism, human trafficking, drugs, subversive groups, organized crime, white collar crime, child abductions—that sort of thing," Dyson said.

McMillan smiled. "We're on a special task force to investigate serial murders. The local police have asked for our cooperation, since they believe these missing persons crossed state lines."

Dyson stood up from the chair and, like an NBA power forward over the team's equipment manager, loomed over Tom. "Do you know anything about Malik or Ms. Colston and their *religious* beliefs? Did they ever mention them to you?"

Tom thought he didn't hear him correctly. "Say again? Religious beliefs?"

"Were either of them into cults, odd religions, gurus, New Age shit, paranormal stuff—anything like that?"

Tom was amused. "Does yoga count? Teresa was into Pilates and Zumba. Seriously, I can't say what Malik or Terry did or didn't believe. Neither of them had so much as mentioned *The X-Files* to me. I think all that paranormal stuff is crap—alien abduction, ghosts, spirits, the Jersey Devil, Sasquatch. It's all horseshit to me."

Dyson smiled. "Well, the four of them reportedly expressed some interest in this New Age guy known as an inspirational speaker. They were all four seen at a book-signing by him after he lectured at the school."

Tom shrugged. "I'm afraid I can't help you there. Cults and their leaders are a mystery to me. How can anyone be that fucking naïve? Charles Manson, guys who cut their balls off because of a comet—those Heaven's Gate wackos. Scientology. Mormonism. I can't understand how people are so fucking stupid."

Why the fuck are you asking me and not that guy? Maybe these FBI guys are not as sharp as I think!

"Ever heard of a guy named Robert Hadley? He was the author at the book-signing." The agent pulled a photo from inside his coat and held it out. It was from a professional portfolio, arms folded across his chest, expensive suit and tie, teeth of white armor.

D'Arcangelo looked then shook his head. "Never heard of him. Is he like Tony Robbins, Joel Osteen, or that Dollar guy? You know, smooth-talking motherfuckers with big shiny teeth? Using religion and positive psychology to fill their wallets with money from people with low IQs?"

Neither answered. McMillan finished his scribbling. The pair stood up and thanked Tom. McMillan handed him a business card. "If you should hear from either of them or remember anything regarding this, give me a call, would you?"

Tom nodded. "Sure."

They shook hands, he showed them to the door, then watched them disappear down the street.

After pouring another scotch, he returned to his lounge chair, collapsed onto it and took a large and slow swallow of warming whiskey.

Four people are missing. If the FBI was looking into it, odds were better than even that, if they were not in drug-induced stupor or at some orgiastic rite in a commune somewhere, they were no longer among the living. Two of them Tom knew fairly well, two people he liked. It was all bad. And very curious.

But he was elated that the Feds weren't looking for Tom D'Arcangelo. *Malik and Teresa were both missing. Two other women missing? Joined a cult? Serial murders? What's that about?* he wondered.

"Merry fucking Christmas," Tom said, then raised his glass for the last swallow of whiskey.

7

I N 1911 THE SICILIAN MAFIA dispatched Salvatore Sabella to America. He demonstrated superior leadership qualities in New York City, then was sent ninety miles south to organize racketeering in the City of Brotherly Love. Sabella was the Black Hand's *capo* there for the next sixteen years. He then passed the *lupara*—the sawed-off shotgun popular in Sicily vendettas—to his successor in what turned out to be a contentious reign of mobsters.

Criminal gangs in Philadelphia go back before the Revolution, when for a time they assisted King George's men rule the city. The Doan Gang, the Moyamensing Killers, the Chockers, the Blood Tubs, the Schuylkill Rangers, the Tongs in Chinatown gainfully enjoyed criminal enterprise in the 18th and 19th centuries. These gangs were often joined by the city's firemen in shows of force and criminal mayhem.

Industrial development aided the growing population of the city. In the 1840s, after several deadly riots that the local constabulary had difficulty controlling, and with a growing numbers of criminals thwarting city police by escaping into any of twenty-eight neighboring townships and boroughs, the politicians were determined to rein in the rougher element. At that time the Philadelphia's borders stretched from the Delaware and Schuylkill Rivers and Vine Street and South Street, a mere slice of its modern territory.

In the mid-1800's Pennsylvania's governor signed a bill the state legislature had passed, and the Consolidation Act of 1854 brought the boundaries of the city together into the area it is now. Policing and fire-fighting became more centralized and, to the dismay of gangs, and more efficient.

When the Eighteenth Amendment to the Constitution passed in 1920, it fueled the rise of crime and an alcohol black market in cities all across America. Philadelphia was no different. The spoils of Prohibition grew ever greater, and with it the struggle between the police and the criminal enterprise. The gangs involved were often entangled in their own battles for the control of the street scene, in blood-spattering contests for control of the street scene.

In the 1980s and '90s the Philly mob scene was a constant struggle for supremacy. The city gained national reputation for its gruesome front-page mob hits that sold thousands of papers on the newsstands and fueled national television networks. After Angelo Bruno was gunned down the city erupted into a war for the control of turf. Bullets and bombs eliminated pretenders to the throne. Little Nicky Scarfo reputedly had over twenty potential rivals murdered.

The violence drew the attention of the feds and resulted in prison for many of the cast of characters. In two rounds of gang wars and federal incarcerations the scepter for Boss was passed to Jimmy Cardinello, who brokered a peace by urging more cooperation and communication by the families. He argued it was bad—as in unprofitable—business to do it any other way.

So Philadelphia, Quaker William Penn City of Brotherly Love, whose spotlight usually shown on its governmental corruption, became known as a battle ground for organized crime.

Philly had become known as the town that pelted Santa Claus with snowballs at Eagles' games and where visiting teams feared being hit by flying flashlight batteries. The city even convened a judge to hold court during games to rule on fans' unruly and violent behavior in the stands, where drunken brawls had escalated to pitched battles and flare guns were shot out over the field.

More recently, in a contest to add zest to the city's tourism—and perhaps distract from the growing crime rate—one enterprising mayor solicited slogans for a public relations campaign. Branding was, after all, the rage in business schools around the country. He wanted to augment

Philly's focus on 1776, Ben Franklin and Liberty Bell and shed its staid Quaker heritage. In addition, the stigma of W.C. Fields' condemnation of the town and the handling of Jackie Robinson still stung.

The citizenry had replied with homespun wit: "Philadelphia – Lock and Load", "Philadelphia, the City of Brotherly Shove", "Philadelphia – Watch Your Back!", "Philadelphia – Only the Strong Survive", and "Philadelphia – Hey! Where's My Car?" rolled off wry tongues.

JIMMY CARDINELLO SAT in his office in the rear of the third floor of *Ristorante Catania* reading *The Wall Street Journal*. He had finished Christmas shopping early, completed by the first week in December in his prompt and fastidious manner. He began the morning examining accounting reports—his legitimate businesses—while listening to an old recording of the Philadelphia Orchestra brass section playing traditional Christmas carols.

On the other side of the door Cardinello could hear Joey Argento, on bodyguard duty for today, coughing and sneezing, emitting an occasional curse at the fates for giving him a bad cold just in time for the holidays. After two hours Jimmy finally had had enough. Tired of listening to his bodyguard's hacking, Cardinello shook his head.

"Better not give that fucking cold to me, goddammit!" Cardinello exclaimed, then got up and opened the door.

Argento stood there, handkerchief to nose, and sneezed twice.

"Jesus Joey, whyn'cha go home? You sound like shit. I don't want you to give that fuckin' bug to me. *Capische*? Take off."

"Boss, who am I going to get to fill in at Christmas time?"

Cardinello scowled. "Fuck it. I'll be okay. Lou's coming here in an hour. I'll get him to get someone. Go on, get the fuck outta here!"

"You sure? I can wait until he gets here."

"No, by that time you'll have infected half the restaurant. Go on, get outta here. Go home. Take something for your throat. Make a hot drink with some lemon juice and honey and whiskey and get to bed. Get some sleep."

"Thanks, Boss," Lou said, wiping his sniffling nose and turning to Cardinello.

"—and don't hug me!" warned Jimmy gruffly. "And merry Christmas, if I don't see you before then."

Joey stomped off down the stairs as Jimmy went back into the office, locking the door. He sat at his desk and pulled out the book from a low drawer.

Joey Argento on his way to exit going past the bar, stopped to talk to the bartender, Dom Ianelli. The rotund man, never without a smile, was tending bar farthest from the door.

"Dom! Give Spags a call and tell him Jimmy told me to go home, okay?"

"Ho! Ho! Ho!" A large Santa Claus burst into the foyer and bar area of the restaurant. "Ho! Ho! Ho! Merry Christmas!" Santa began to pull small boxes of Ghirardelli chocolates out of a sack and hand them out to people in booths and at tables. "Ho! Ho! Merry Christmas!"

Joey pushed a handkerchief to his nose, too miserable to pay any attention to the invading Spirit of Christmas.

"Did you hear me, Dom?"

Dom nodded. "Yep, sure Joey. Consider it done." He headed for the phone on the wall behind the bar.

Santa swept through the bar dispensing candy and Christmas cheer, taking the occasional photo for a couple in a booth or with Santa.

Upstairs, Jimmy Cardinello sat down at his desk, realized the carols had stopped and played the Philadelphia Orchestra brass section recording again, then went back to reading the Wall Street Journal.

After fifteen minutes Cardinello called downstairs to the bar and spoke to Dom.

"Did ya see Joey leave? Call Lou Spagnolo and find out if he's on the way here. Tell him to bring someone for security, too, okay?"

"Sure Jimmy, I already called Lou. He'll be here in a half-hour."

After he hung up, Cardinello needed to use the bathroom. He customarily used the bathroom on the second floor, but as he left his office, he heard the gaiety of the Santa Claus downstairs melding with the music of carols and songs. He walked downstairs and saw Old Saint Nick schmoozing with an elderly couple at a table then he headed toward the first floor men's room.

As usual, the ever fastidious Cardinello washed his hands before relieving himself, then unzipped at the urinal. No longer young, he noted he urinated more frequently and not nearly as forceful as it once was.

A week earlier Jimmy Cardinello had mentioned his urinary problems at his annual physical. His doctor explained this was very common to aging men.

"But if you want to see a specialist in urology, I can refer you to one of the best. But your prostate feels normal for a man your age. If it felt abnormal, I'd recommend additional testing. Your PSA is well within normal range."

The doctor then went on at length about enlarged prostates, higher blood pressure, the need for more exercise, fewer lipoproteins and trigylcerides.

Cardinello cut him off: "Can you give me some good fuckin' news, Doc? You're depressing me!"

"Mr. Cardinello, medicine can't make you young again." The doctor sat down in front of his desk. "From this chair, I'd say you're in fairly good health for 72. Not great, but pretty damned good. Let me tell you what I see every week."

The doctor slipped off a rubber glove. "One of my patients has an unknown neurological disease. His hospital team is trying to find out what exactly is going on, while the man is rapidly slipping away. He can't stand up, his blood pressure varies greatly. No answer yet."

He slipped off a second glove and dropped them into the waste can. "I have another patient. Cancer of a salivary gland. Half his face has been removed. He frightens children. If you're feeling sorry for yourself, why not accompany me on my rounds to the hospital? Ever see the cancer ward at Children's Hospital? A visit there can make the archbishop doubt there's a god."

Cardinello just stared at him for a moment, then looked away.

"Do you want me to go on?" asked the doctor.

"No, I get it," Cardinello said. "Don't be a pussy, right?"

"Correct. Don't be a pussy. Man up. Have a good Christmas, Mr. Cardinello."

Just then the restroom door opened.

"Ho! Ho! Ho!" In came Santa clumsily carrying his satchel over his shoulder, banging into the sink and trash receptacle. His voice reverberated around the tiled walls in descending "Ho! Ho! Ho!'s"

Jimmy looked over his shoulder as Santa slung the satchel to the floor.

"Even Kris Kringle has to pee, eh?" Cardinello said over his shoulder.

"Oh, that's for sure," Santa replied. "It's a damned sight easier here than at the North Pole. If I can just get this old candy cane out of this costume—."

He set the bag down on the floor.

TOM HAD PARKED HIS CAR around the corner from the house. It was a large street—for South Philly, that is—with parking on both sides and a single one-way street. He found a spot at the corner and parked close to a hydrant, and now was leaving his house was retracing his steps past his car on the way to the hospital to visit his uncle.

Down the street a black, 700-series black BMW turned the corner and slowed to a stop. Two thick men in black leather coats exited from the passenger and right rear doors. They wore wrap-around sunglasses, and they tucked in scarves and buttoned their coats and, without a wave to their driver, hunched their shoulders against the cold and began down the street in my direction. One stopped a moment to light a cigarette with a gold lighter. The Beemer drove down the street and slowly passed him on the way to the corner stop sign. Tom looked nonchalantly at the car, but saw nothing through its dark tinted windows.

While not seeing that their behavior was especially threatening, he decided to cross before encountering the two men on a South Philly narrow sidewalk. He passed between two cars and headed on a diagonal across the street. The leather-coated men watched him cross, then one nearest the curb stepped between cars and walked diagonally across the street.

Tom estimated how close to allow him before he bolted. He felt adrenaline that was becoming all too familiar shooting in. The size of the two husky guys made fighting out of the question. Flight was his best tactic. At his age and fitness—twenty-six years old, running ten to fifteen miles a week and working out at the gym and dojo—and, although no longer the number two cross country man in the Catholic League, Tom believed he could easily outdistance them in a footrace. Outrunning bullets of course was another matter.

The man crossing the street looked right at him as they approached where they would intersect. Tom opened the top buttons and slid his hand inside his coat. He tried to look casually back across the street to judge what the other man was up to, but knew he failed miserably. He felt his movements to be that of a man with a neurological disease. The man now almost alongside him had decided to cross the street and would soon be joining again with his friend. Both were now on a path to close on Tom.

Suddenly, a loud banging—the clattering clip-clop of metal hooves on the street—and a horse's frightened scream ripped the air. An enormous white and grey workhorse, built like a Budweiser Clydesdale, came careening around the corner, tackless except for flying bridle, its eyes wide, its nostrils flaring, its spittle launching into the air. The equine was now galloping right toward the three of them about to converge in the middle of the narrow street. The larger man froze, the other threw himself back against a car. Tom vaulted with a crunch onto the crumpling hood of a small car.

The horse huffed and gasped, sputtered and snorted as it pounded by them. Right behind it, rounding the corner, came six feral, wild-eyed pitbulls of varied colors, snarling and barking, froth flying from their muzzles right on the heels of the horse. The man closest to Tom, who had frozen at first, stepped aside just as the horse was about to run him down. It narrowly missed him, then he saw the dogs and suddenly bolted into action to escape a possible mauling. He leapt for the nearest space between cars and jumped up on one's bumper and then climbed-slid-stumbled clumsily to that car's now-crackling hood.

Bullet-headed and fierce, blurs of brown, black, gray and white fur, the dogs snarled and bayed as they ignored the men in pursuit of the frantic horse. Blood-gorged tongues and spittle and clouds of steam flew from their mouths. The man on the car scrambled to the roof of the car in case the dogs were to jump after him.

Tom leapt to the ground and sprinted up the opposite side of the street, away from the pursuing animals as fast as he could go. He didn't break his stride to look to see if the men—or wild dogs—were following. But above the slamming of his shoes on the sidewalk and his increased breathing Tom heard police sirens. A police cruiser came to the intersection where the horse and dogs had come, then with tires screeching, the car turned down the street Tom had left. D'Arcangelo turned to look at his possible pursuers and saw the two men wildly bewildered at the sights of a huge, frantic racing horse being chased by pit bulls. One stood on the hood of the car, the other behind a car on the opposite side of the street peering over its hood. The man on the roof pointed to the police car that the dogs and horse had just passed by, and the car continued in pursuit with its siren wailing and lights flashing.

Tom rounded the corner and took off down a side street adorned with Christmas decorations. From a row home someone had outdoor speakers with holiday music playing, and as he sped by he could hear a rendition of "Dominick the Donkey", its singer braying the 'hee-haw, hee-haw' refrain. Tom swiveled his head around for any sign of the BMW, but neither saw it, nor the two men who—he had thought— were seconds from intercepting him.

He opened the top buttons of his coat and then his shawl collar sweater, to free the heavy .45 if needed. He cut through an alley that ran behind homes running north and south and headed north. He wanted to stay off the main streets in case the BMW was cruising for him.

Tom walked briskly, nervously, his head swiveling at intersections and, every few minutes, turning to look behind every several paces. When D'Arcangelo didn't see the BMW, he began to breathe more easily.

He had traveled several blocks south and decided to continue to the Italian Market to pick up some wine and cheese and olives and some other snack items in case he had company for the holidays. He began to think about what had just happened. Were those two men after him? Were those two men after him? And was he just saved by wild dogs and a runaway horse? D'Arcangelo wasn't sure. The men sure did look suspicious. But was he imagining it? He wasn't completely sure, but was thankful that the near surrealistic scene interrupted what might have happened.

It was just coming on twilight when Tom turned the corner of his street to begin the Great South Philly Quest for Parking. In South Philly only newly developed houses had garages or dedicated parking spaces, and the population density with iron chariots was greater than the geometrical locations for parking. This situation leads to all sorts of innovations to provide a resting place for the vehicles. His father once told his sons over the dinner table that a neighborhood friend of his had a mental breakdown at the constant struggle to insert his pickup truck into small parking spots and pledged to—and eventually did!—move to Alaska. At the family's look of amazement, Tom's old man had smiled and shook his head.

"Yeah, I know. Seemed a bit drastic. I woulda got a garage somewhere. There are plenty of cities and states with room to park without having to look out for moose on the roads."

On occasion, someone from another state other than permitted New Jersey or Delaware parked there—and unless their car had requisite, up-to-date, Eagles, Phillies, or Flyers emblems, bobble heads, or one of a hundred other local team or religious fetishes, mixed often with saints' medallions, crucifixes, crystal or plastic homage to Mary or lesser saints, garter belts, large dice, Mardi Gras beads ("Show us your tits!"), or the occasional dreamcatcher, hanging from their mirrors—suffered the consequences of wearing out their welcome after a few days and finding new scratches on their beloved vehicles.

But Tom always drove down his street just in case someone had just left a coveted landing zone. He scanned the small street with cars parked on one side and with trained South Philly eye saw no spots. The street was beginning to light up with Christmas decorations everyone had on and in their house. A few enterprising neighbors had strung lights, snowmen, and Santas across the street from their roofs, and they flew their sleighs overhead.

181

As he scanned for parking, he noticed a Santa Claus carrying a sack disappearing into a house.

"That's *my* house!" he said aloud. "Who the fuck is that?"

Tom drove by slowly, but the door had closed and he could see no one in the foyer. He drove around the corner and looked for a spot to park. He parked near the corner illegally in front of a hydrant and thought about what to do next.

Who the fuck was that? And how did he get into my house? Mrs. Saraceni?

His mind flew to Jimmy Cardinello, now the late reputed crime boss of one of the major South Philly gang families. The radio said that the police were looking for someone posing as Santa Claus because they believed someone in that holiday costume had murdered him.

Tom got out of the car looking around for anything unusual. He felt for the reassurance of the .45 under his armpit. He was damned glad that he decided to bring it. He walked quickly down the street to the small alley behind the houses and headed toward the house.

His father had built a high fence several years ago, but had left a small window in the gate door. He peeked through it, peering to see if anyone was in the kitchen. Seeing no one, Tom realized the lock was on the inside, and he needed to enter from Mrs. Saraceni's yard.

He leapt over her chain-link fence and hid behind his father's wooden fence. He looked to see if the old lady was in her kitchen, but saw no sign of her. Tom stood on a trashcan and vaulted over the fence and dashed to the cover of an overhanging awning over the basement's metal Bilco door.

D'Arcangelo opened one of the metal doors to the basement slowly to avoid any noise, then lowered the door to listen for any alarm or noise upstairs. Inside the basement he shut the door and listened. He pulled out his grandfather's automatic in the darkness and waited for his eyes to adjust to the darkness. He could hear someone speaking upstairs, but it seemed simply a conversation. Was that Nina's voice?

If they had seen me coming in, they'd be silent now, he thought. Tom moved across the floor slowly and went to the steps and stopped again for minutes to listen and plan his next step. He could hear muffled voices and, slowly walked up the steps, one step, pause, listen, another step, pause, listen, until he reached the floor level. The voices were louder but they seemed casual and conversational.

Tom determined to try to get the drop on them. He decided that if he saw weapons, he would start blasting, unless Nina was in the line of fire. If he succeeded in surprising them, he'd have them drop to their stomachs and put their hands over their heads.

He put his hand on the door and turned the knob slowly, then opened it swiftly—he heard voices in the kitchen— and jumped out crouched into the kitchen holding the .45 in two hands.

"FREEZE, MOTHERFU—!" he bellowed.

At the table sat a nearly skin-headed tanned and weathered Santa Claus with fake beard and hat on his knee sitting over a cup of coffee, with Nina cradling her mug across from him.

Santa looked at me, raised his hands in surrender, then turned to Nina: "Damn, he scares me. How about you?"

Santa turned back to Tom and laughed. "Did you just say 'Freeze, Motherfucker' to Santa?"

"Matt!"

"Yo, Bro. Glad to see your finger is on the trigger guard and not the trigger. Put that thing down before you shoot someone, would you? I came home to get a break from that shit."

Tom stood holding the old Colt two-handed in firing position, then lowered the gun. "Why didn't you call me to say you were coming home for Christmas? I could've fucking killed you."

"I did call. Check your messages, why don't you." He pointed to the gun. "Hey, isn't that Grampop's roscoe?"

"Yeah."

Tom carefully put the hammer down and slipped the safety on. He opened his coat and slid the gun into its holster. Matt shot an inquisitive frown at why his brother was carrying it.

"You remember Pop gave *me* that .45. You got the carbine," he said.

"I'll remember that, Matt. The next time I need to take out a machine gun nest full of Krauts, I'll break my M-1 out."

"You better let him keep that cannon," Nina advised. "Chuck Norris he ain't. Tommy's feeling vulnerable. He got his ass kicked a few days ago." She reported, grinning.

Tom returned her grin with a scowl.

"Is that why you look like shit? Is there a crime wave going on around here, or what?" He smiled at the irony.

"Things have been better," Tom said. "Did Nina tell you about Vince?"

"I just flew in on military transport. Landed in Dover and got a lift into Philly. The guy listened to country and western all the way. I went and got some gifts and this costume for Andy and Jennie's kids. Haven't seen a TV or heard a radio that wasn't playing *Little Drummer Boy* or warning about traffic jams since I got in early this morning. Thought I'd surprise you, and, if you don't mind, ask you to drive me to see the cousins and the kids. Now I hear Uncle Vince is in the hospital?"

Nina cut in. "How *is* Vince? I was just telling your brother about the speed freak that hit him over the head and that he was in the hospital—."

"Sherry hasn't called you?" Tom asked. "He's on the mend, sort of. Still no definitive prognosis."

"No," she replied. "I thought she'd call me on my cell, but she hasn't. Isn't she at the hospital? With Vince?"

"How is he? Any improvement?" asked Tom's brother.

Tom was silent. "Some improvement. But a long way to go. The worst is that there might be permanent damage."

Matt groaned. "Jesus!"

"Yeah, merry fucking Christmas!"

Nina stood up from the table. "Tom, would you want some coffee? Lunch or something? I was going to make your brother a bite when you came in."

"Yeah, yeah. That'd be nice." Tom took his coat off.

Matt stood up and hugged him for a long moment. "Where is the guy that did it?" asked Matt. "He still around? In the hospital?"

"He's in the same hospital as Vince. Don't worry. Lou assured me he's not going to get out of town. I would have killed that motherfucker myself if I wasn't trying to stop Vince's bleeding."

Nina had gotten some cold cuts and lettuce and tomatoes from the refrigerator and began toasting some bread.

"Why don't you two go into the living room and get caught up? I'll bring lunch to the dining room in a few minutes."

On the way from the kitchen Tom saw the envelope that Carla had returned sitting in a crystal cut-glass bowl on the sideboard. Matt opened it, slid its contents into his hand. He studied the ring and crucifix and chain for a moment. He knew that Tom had given it to Carla and immediately surmised what its return meant. He tucked it in his shirt pocket.

"Tom, why not go talk to her? These things happen. Christmas is a stressful time—you know that. Tempers are short."

Tom shook his head slowly and firmly. "That's not it. You don't know Carla. She doesn't get angry." Tom grabbed his brother around the back of his neck with his left hand and squeezed him. "Don't worry, Bro. I'll be okay. So will she. Sometimes things are not meant to be. This is probably one of those things. Give Mom's cross to the one you're going to marry."

Nina sat two plates with sandwiches down on the table. "I'm making a fresh pot of coffee."

Matt looked at Nina's familiarity with the house at then quizzically at his brother. Tom frowned and replied. "It's a long story, Matt."

"I'm on two weeks leave, Bro. I've got plenty of time."

LATER AFTER NINA AND SHERRY had hooked up to drive back to Jersey, Matt and Tom sat at the kitchen table over another cup of coffee.

"So tell me," Matt asked, "what's going on? What happened to Carla? Weren't you two engaged, for chrissakes? Who is this Nina? I thought you didn't like her type."

"Her *type*? What do you mean?"

"Isn't she a stripper? All tits and ass and makeup, no brains—that type."

"No, Nina's not a stripper."

"She told me she dances at a club in Jersey. Doesn't that mean she's a stripper? Have things changed that much since I joined the Corps? Gentlemen's clubs in Jersey don't host the fuckin' Royal Ballet."

"She's not like that, Bro."

"I spoke with her a bit. She seems nice and all. But I can't understand what you might possibly see in her…."

Matt paused a moment for effect, rolled his eyes and then effused: "Could it be she's a fucking knockout? But that shit never influenced you. You were never a pussy hound. Carla is no dog, mind you, but you always stayed away from dancers. Aren't they on your list of bimbos?"

"Are you kidding? Miles ahead of actresses. I can put up with a few neuroses."

"Well?"

"Matt, Carla and I broke up a few days ago. You know how that is—it just wasn't working out. It's better now that she and I both know. I need to find my own way. And, believe it or not, Nina has had nothing to do with it."

"That's too bad. I liked Carla a lot. She's smart and spunky and has class. She's got a great head on her shoulders. And she's great-looking, too. Her folks are real good people. Is this something you can work on? You might regret this in the future. Carla is sweet and has it all, dude."

"It's over. And Nina had nothing to do with it. Uncle Vince introduced us down the shore."

Matt looked at Tom with incredulity. "So she *is* a hooker? Man, that pussy must be fabulous if you're that fucking crazy over it. Tommy, tell me you're not ditching Carla for some dumb cooze. I *will* slap the shit out of you."

Tom shook his head. "She's *not* a hooker. Not at least like you say. Besides, we're not even an item, Matt. Nina's a friend with this girl that Uncle Vince is nuts over."

Matt held up his thick hands like a third base coach halting a runner. "All right. This is all your business, Brother. I said all I'm going to say about your love life. Tell me what is going on with Vince and the gang. It's like the '80s again. Shit, I came back from Afghanistan to get away from firefights."

"You have no idea, Bro. In addition to the guy who tuned me up the other day, I had an Irish gang from Jersey surprise me here—in *our* fucking house! I thought I was finished. Almost pissed myself. They thought I had knocked off one of their guys."

Matt's eyes widened in disbelief. "Here? You?"

"Yeah, me. I came home and found four fucking mick hoods here in the dining room."

"Here? In our house? No fuckin' way! How did they get to be *here*? They thought it was you? Why?"

"They thought Vince and I were Jimmy's crew and that we were poaching on their turf."

"Since when did *you* join Cardinello's crew? I thought you worked in the restaurants bussing and waiting tables. Mom would have a stroke if she were here, you know that."

"I'm not really in Jimmy's crew, Matt. When I was in school I did some work for Uncle Vince to make a little extra money."

"Like what? Catering alumni weekends?"

"Not exactly. More like … uh, providing some strippers and hookers for frat parties, selling weed and some X, mostly making book on football and basketball games. Shit like that."

Matt groaned, leaned his elbows on the table, and placed his head in his hands. "Jee-e-e-zus, Tommy! Fucking A!"

He massaged his face as if in pain. "Oh-h-h! You never told me about that." Matt glared at his brother in disbelief. "You must be outta your fuckin' mind. I thought we talked about this, and you were heading to law school. To a straight life. What… the… fuck … happened?" Matt emphasized each word.

Tom looked away then into his coffee cup, avoiding his brother's eyes.

"Yeah, yeah, yeah. I know. It started out simple. I took a few football bets to make some easy money. It snowballed. One of the frat leaders thought I had friends in low places and asked about some strippers and hookers. It went from there to some reefer. Then over a few semesters .... The money was *real* good. Real and easy good."

"Football bets! Jesus Christ, couldn't they just use the dad's credit card on the fucking internet? Bro, suppose they didn't have the cash? You'd have to tell Vince and then he'd tell some muscle. You know there's always some asshole that gets in over his head. Jesus Christ!"

"Yeah, I know. I only had one guy who couldn't pay."

Matt stood up, his thick thighs banging the table. "Stop! Just stop. I need a drink of something stronger."

He disappeared into the dining room and returned with a bottle of Jack Daniels. He poured two shots worth into his coffee and dropped the bottle down in front of Tom.

"What did you do then? About the deadbeat?"

"I paid Jimmy what was owed out of my pocket," Tom admitted.

"You finally did something right, you dumb fuck," Matt said. "Then what?"

"The kid was some dumb geek. I slapped him once and showed him an old picture of Frankie. I told him what he'd missed by my being a nice guy. I told him there'd be no more bets for him."

"Whoa! You strong-armed the kid *and* then paid for him? And you sold these college clowns *dope*? You can't be *my* brother! And you're supposed to be the smart one—the college guy."

Matt went on. "You are one dumb fuck, y'know that? Drugs are the worst. You could get into some real deep shit for that. Drug penalties are stiff these days. You'll do *serious* time. One of those kids could rat you out to the school, the police, even the feds. You're giving me *agita*, Tom. Do us a favor? I want you to put the house completely in my name. If the police find out you're a drug dealer, they could seize our house! Put it in my name if you're going to act like an asshole. Please. And there better not be any dope in this house or, brother or not, I'll break both your fuckin' arms.

"I didn't handle the dope at all. I hooked them up with someone in the crew. I never touched or carried the stuff itself. There's no dope in this house. You know that. I swear on our mother!"

Matt sipped his whiskey and sat for several moments mulling over what was unfolding. "So if you're not working with Jimmy's crew, why did the mick hoods show up here.

Tom sensed his brother was intent on ferreting out more than he wanted to tell.

"Matt, I am not doing *anything* illegal for the Cardinello family business any more. I wait tables. Period. I need that money, Bro."

"But those guys from Jersey *thought* you're Philly mob? Why's that? I'm trying to figure this out."

"This week Vince and I went to Jersey to collect a debt for Jimmy. The micks knew I was there and thought we whacked this guy of theirs."

"Oh, that explains everything, Tom," Matt said not trying to mask his tone of irony. "What about the guy who beat the crap out of you? Who was that? Was he one of the Irish hoods? Don't tell me that was a random robbery."

"We don't know who he was. It might have been a random burglary."

"Didn't Jimmy and his crew find out? Those guys must be slipping. It's only a matter of time until another crime family moves in and makes the Cardinello family extinct."

Tom shook his head. "Lou and his guys accidentally smothered him in a rug they wrapped him in. They never got to find out who he was working for."

Matt looked heavenward. "Ei-yi! See? That's just what I'm talking about. How fucking stupid can ya be!"

Tom uncapped the Jack Daniels and poured the whiskey into his cup and cradled it in his two hands.

"So who whacked their guy?" Matt asked.

"We don't know. They say they don't know. But it looks like South Philly is taking the heat for it."

Ever suspicious, Matt eyed Tom's every move, every eye blink, every speech inflection. To Matt, something was not right.

"Did you and Vince ever find the gambler who owed the money?"

"Yeah, we did find him—he was a dentist, by the way. He had been gambling with Jimmy for years. Then he stopped paying his debts and was hiding out on his boat in Cape May."

"And you found him and he gave you the money?"

"Yes and no."

"Whaddaya mean? You either got the money or not."

"We got the money, but he never gave it to us. We took it."

"You took it? How'd you do that?"

"The dentist couldn't *give* it to us—he was dead."

The elder brother stared in disbelief. He whispered as if there was someone in the room. "Fuck! Tom, you didn't! You and Vince offed this guy? Tell me that Vince did it, please! Tell me you weren't with him."

Tom shook his head vigorously. "Neither of us whacked him. Vince wasn't even there."

He poured another shot of whiskey and a swallowed a gulp.

"I was there ... by myself. I found the guy on his boat and before I could tell Vince I had found the dude, someone killed him. I was in the boat's can taking a piss. I know it sounds nuts."

Matt was incredulous. "You found this guy who owed Jimmy money, and while you were taking a piss, someone came along and killed him?"

"That's right," Tom said. He didn't want to say anymore. He knew the less he said, the better. Tom didn't want to implicate his brother in any way. The less Matt knew the better off he would be. Tom hoped his brother would drop his interrogation.

The elder brother started to laugh. He swallowed another mouthful from his coffee cup and thought for a moment, chuckling all the while.

"So you came out of the john, see the guy is dead, and you rip him off for the money to pay Jimmy? Is that it? What happened to the guy who whacked the dentist?"

"Matt—," Tom trailed off, reluctant to explain further. "I didn't come out of the john and find him dead. I hid in there because I saw the guy do the dentist. Then, after that guy left, I took off."

"Where was Vince in all this? He should have been with you, for chrissakes. That guy could've killed you, too."

"He was back at the hotel with Nina's girlfriend, Sherry."

Matt sat for several moments getting the entire picture. "So Vince is back in the hotel checking this girl's oil while his nephew is off on business—alone? Something's not kosher here. Who was the guy who took out the dentist? And why?"

"You got me. Maybe he was a private contractor of some sort. Some other mob guy. Who knows?"

"So how did you get the money? Was it on the boat?"

"Yeah. Before I left I searched the boat and found fifty grand hidden away. I gave it to Vince to give to Jimmy."

"Something isn't right about this. I can't put my finger on it. As soon as my uncle gets better, I'm going to ream his ass out for getting you into this. I know that's what happened, Tom. That is, unless you're a leopard that's changed its spots."

"I'm out of the mob thing, Matt. Really. Vince told Jimmy, and then I talked to him myself."

"What did Cardinello say when you told him you wanted out? You and I know that doesn't go over very well. Once you're in the family business, it's for good. It's a family thing."

"Yeah, I know. I thought he'd be pissed. Who knows how he'd take it? I might not be around now. But I thought that I had not gotten so far into the business that I couldn't get out. It was a chance I was taking."

"Cardinello has a real poker face, Tommy. I don't like this one bit. Guys just don't do business with him and walk away."

They sat there in silence, spinning and caressing glasses of whiskey, with an occasional sip.

Finally, Tom spoke up. "Have you ever killed anyone, Matt? In the service, I mean."

Matt looked at him for a long moment, then into his glass again. "Uh-huh. Yeah. I'm a Marine. In the front lines of a war zone. You can pretty much bank on being in a situation where you kill someone. Firefights are like that."

"I don't mean firing two hundred yards and taking someone down long range, where you don't even know if you did it."

"You mean... up close and personal?"

"Yeah ... where you can see their face, their eyes ... while they're dying?"

"Oh yeah. Yeah, I have. More than once."

Matt paused for a long moment.

"One time really sticks out in my mind. Our squad was cleaning out some buildings and suddenly it got pretty hot. Lots of small weapons fire. Everyone running around. Like some fucking live video game but with no re-set button—in that heat, with all that gear on, the fear of getting yourself or someone else killed, of fucking up ... the smell of grenades and gunpowder, the exploding rounds....I rounded a corner, jumped into an open doorway and *Damn!* There in front of me was this hajji stripping his AK of an empty clip. A woman was kneeling next to him handing him a new clip from under her robe. I fired a burst from my 15 and hit both of them. Most of my rounds hit him in the chest. One went right through her head. He was blown backwards; she just slumped over. Like she was praying the way Muslims do. Then suddenly it got real silent. The firing all around me had stopped. The only noise was in my ears ringing from gunfire and the radio attached to me crackling in my ear. In the corner of the room was a small crib. Suddenly I heard a baby crying. That got me."

Matt took a swallow of Jack Daniels. "Why do you ask?"

"Just wondering if that stuff got to you?"

"Sure. Oh yeah. Some guys are on a mission. It's why they joined up. 9/11— to kill the bad guys, the bastards that took down the Towers. Some actually enjoy it. At least they say they do. It's a rush for them, I guess. They seem to, from what I've seen. War can be like a big game. It's like a drug. Like football. Vengeance. Patriotism. Protecting their teammates. Maybe they're making reasons up, rationalizing. Maybe some are sick bastards."

"How do *you* feel about it? Once you get past the 'it's him or me' stuff?"

Matt poured another shot of whiskey into his glass and swallowed a large sip while considering his answer.

"How do I *feel*? Or what do I *think* about it?"

"I can't imagine you'd *enjoy* killing women and making orphans. What do you *think* about it?" Tom asked.

Matt took another slow swallow of whiskey.

"I think killing someone alters you in some way. I heard someone say it does something to your mind. Maybe that's the way to describe it. I don't know. Killing changes you."

Matt sat silent looking into his lap for a few moments, then finished his glass in one gulp and stood up. "Look, I'm tired. I'm gonna hit the rack."

He headed toward the stairs. "G'night."

8

TOM WRAPPED THE FEW remaining gifts he bought for friends and family: a fishing rod for his brother, a Bose sound system for Uncle Vince and a pin for Nina. He bought the pin at the last minute from a shop at the University of Pennsylvania Museum, a reproduction of an ancient Greek mask, and wrapped it, although it occurred to him that perhaps he shouldn't give it to her. Giving jewelry to a woman one hardly knew didn't strike him as particularly wise, either in practice or principle, but he wanted to give Nina something. What he chose seemed the most innocuous gift, less meaningful than a bracelet, certainly less than an anklet or necklace and emphatically less than a ring. He wasn't sure if she was a woman who even liked pins, but with masculine reasoning: *It's a gift. If she likes it, great. If not—well, it's the thought and all that.*

He placed them at the base of the light-less, ornament-less Christmas tree. Tom's brother had departed for his oldest friend's house in distant Bucks County to deliver gifts and play Santa Claus for the family. Matt would "Ho! Ho! Ho!" the evening and morning for Andy and Tara's little boy and girl. Tom urged him to stay the night there, rather than try to come home in the early morning. He knew if Matt stayed the night he wouldn't be home until later in the day after breakfast and the gifts were opened. Matt said he loved watching the kids open presents. The man was destined to be a father, Tom had always thought.

The early darkness of winter's afternoon had encroached, and Tom made his way to the kitchen to grab a bite for dinner. Once there, he found he had little appetite, so he poured some Irish whiskey and turned out the house lights. He found it unsettling to have them on. More than once he found himself peering through the window, scanning cars and people as they went by.

He put on a recording of sacred Christmas music of the Middle Ages and sat in the darkened house, lit only by the lights and reflections of the South Philly street decorations and streetlights. He chose a chair out of direct view of the front windows. He sipped his drink slowly, then poured another and sat down again and found himself lulled into a mellow early evening nod by the monks' intoning.

The doorbell startled him. From his vantage point from the chair in the darkness he couldn't see anyone at the door. His first impulse was to open the foyer door to see who was there, but since he was in the shadow, he decided to wait to see the ringer's insistence. There wasn't a second ring. Tom craned his neck to see if someone left the top step. He would only be able to spot them if they turned to pass the windows, and then only for the briefest time. No one. Silence.

Then he heard the lock on the outer door jiggling with a key's turn. Tom reached into his sweater and pulled the .45 from its holster, slipped the safety off but did not cock the hammer. Instead he placed it on his lap with his hand resting on the grip, finger over the guard and thumb on its hammer. While he waited for someone to appear through the foyer door he took two deep, long centering breaths.

The outer door opened, then shut slowly, deliberately, like someone unfamiliar with the lock. Then the inner door of the foyer opened and, by the Christmas lights from the street, he saw Nina.

She paused to adjust to the lack of light and to remember where the lamp on the table at the base of the stairs was. Then she reached under the shade, fumbled for the switch, turned it on and paused again to adjust to the light.

Tom said nothing. She turned and scanned the room to see him sitting silently.

"*Jeezus Christ!*" She leapt backwards gasping. "Jesus fuck! You scared me! Why didn't you say something—warn me for chrissakes?"

Tom slid the .45 back into its holster. "Sorry, I didn't mean to frighten you."

"Give me a few seconds to put my heart back into my chest, you bastard!"

"Nina, I'm really sorry."

"You were obviously expecting someone else—"

"I wasn't expecting you. That's why"—Tom pointed to the gun with his thumb—"Grandpop's shooting iron."

Nina dangled the key. He had given her the key in case she had come and he wasn't at home. Tom didn't want explain a new woman to Mrs. Saraceni.

"I rang the bell. I only let myself in because no one answered. I thought you might be with Vince or with your girlfriend."

"I saw him earlier today," Tom said. "He's doing better. And what girlfriend would that be? It's good to see you. I was going to make myself coffee—maybe add some Christmas Eve brandy. Want some?"

"Yeah, sure. Decaf, if you have it. Add a little brandy. Christ, I *need* a drink after that scare! Sherry and I drove up together. She wanted to see Vince right away. I came with her to keep her company and wanted to talk to you."

"I'm going over tomorrow morning to see him," Tom said. "I wanted to give him his gift, but I think I'll wait until he's out of the hospital."

He headed for the kitchen, stopping to turn off the light Nina had turned on. He grabbed the brandy from the sideboard along the way to the kitchen. She followed Tom to the kitchen and stood in the door.

"How is Vince?"

"Better, it seems. He's said a few things now. He's talking."

"Great," Nina said. "Sherry will be pleased. She really likes your uncle."

"He likes her. Or at least he did before that whacko re-arranged his brain. His doctor told me that there might be some behavioral or mood changes. I hope it doesn't affect his temper. He doesn't need that after all the work he's done to learn to control it."

Tom spooned out the coffee, flicked on the coffeemaker's switch, and poured a shot glass of brandy into his mug and a half for Nina.

"It's good to see you," he said. Tom turned to lean against the counter and looked at the blond woman still in her coat.

"Take off your coat—"

Then he saw a black snub-nose revolver pointed at him. He paused before finishing the sentence, his voice dropping, "—and stay a while."

She raised the gun toward his chest. He slowly raised his hands and stood up from his lean against the counter. "Well, maybe not—," he said.

"Don't try any fucking *kung fu*, Sensei. I'm warning you."

Her blue eyes glared steel-cold. He noticed she stood in the doorway and as far as possible from him.

"Take one step closer and you'll be under ground for the holidays. I know how to handle this." Her voice was convincing, hard and cold.

D'Arcangelo leaned back, lowered his hands and casually placed them against the counter. Like a cowboy leaning against a rail, he placed his right foot against the cabinet. He wanted to appear relaxed but be ready to dodge a shot or launch himself at her. He trained his eyes on her finger on the trigger. As an outfielder he knew getting a quick jump on the ball was often more important than sheer speed.

Tom thought to distract her. "Was I *that* bad in the sack? Wait! You're going to force me to marry you."

She pointed at the gun under his armpit. "Look, that cannon is making me nervous. Reach for it with two fingers—left hand, please— and remove it from the holster. Lay it down on the table. *Slowly ...* slowly."

He gave a mock laugh. "My holstered gun is making *you* nervous? How about that .38 you have pointed at me? Nina, you know I'm *not* going to hurt you."

Her voice was a growl. "Just do as I say."

Using his left hand and with thumb and forefinger, he lifted the gun from its holster with exaggerated deliberation laid it on the table, then slowly pushed it toward her with his index finger. She stood back so he couldn't reach her. Tom thought that now would be the time for her to shoot him, but he had already dismissed that likelihood.

If she were going to shoot me, she'd have done it already.

"Back up. Please."

He did as ordered. Nina reached over, slid the .45 from the table, keeping her eyes locked on him. She reached around and placed it on a sideboard in the dining room.

"I came here to get some answers, Tom."

"I guessed something like that. Otherwise you'd have shot me already. I'll give you all the answers I can without that gun in my face, you know. No coercion needed."

"I need to know if I have been fucking the guy who killed my brother."

Tom frowned and shook his head in denial. "Nina, I don't even *know* your brother," he said. "And I prefer to think of it as 'making love.'"

"You're a real fucking romantic."

Her ice-blue eyes flashed. "Not *knowing* my brother, Tommy, does that matter? I didn't know that guy I clobbered with that baseball bat. People kill people they don't know all the time. I need to know if you— or Vince—killed my brother. Tell me the truth."

"I don't know *what* you're talking about. Where did you get this idea?"

"Don't bullshit me, Tom," she said. "I think I've put together why the two of you were at a fucking shore resort during an arctic gale. You were there on Philly mob business."

Tom exhaled heavily and nodded. "Yeah ... yeah, we *were* there on business"—but added—"but neither Vince nor I killed your brother."

"My brother was looking for someone who owed the O'Connell family some gambling money," Nina said. "Then someone executed him. He was looking for the same guy you were. What a coincidence."

"So you spoke to Liam Finneran, I suppose?"

"Yeah, he told me you were there looking for the same guy."

"Did he tell you that we didn't find him? That's what I told Finneran. Remember when those Irish guys came to my house to talk to me? If they *really* thought I killed one of their crew, I'd be fertilizing shamrocks somewhere."

Nina said nothing, weighing what Tom had just said.

He went on. "Yes, we were looking for a dentist who owed some gambling money to Jimmy Cardinello. We didn't find him, so Vince and I came home."

The coffee machine beeped.

"And remember that Vince and I were with Sherry and you?"

He smiled. "Still want some coffee?"

"The police found my brother dead in his car at a marina in Cape May. Someone shot him twice in the head, Tom. In addition to making me ID him at the morgue, those bastards made me look at the crime scene photos of his head all over the car. Ever see the head of someone shot at close range with .40 caliber bullets?"

"Christ, that's awful," Tom said, his tone sincere but hiding a sudden exhilaration. That confirmed what he had heard from his uncle, and what he had hoped: he had not killed Nina's brother, but someone else.

"Nina, I'm telling you: I didn't kill your brother. Believe me. What marina exactly?"

"The one at the causeway."

"When?"

"The police said someone reported seeing the body in the car in the parking lot on Monday, and the police called me on Tuesday."

"Did the police offer any thoughts on who might have done it?"

"They think it was gang-related—some other mob maybe. Turf. Drugs. Retaliation for something. The cops tried to get me to pony up information about Brian's Irish gang. Said the feds are getting in on this. Tried to scare me."

That got D'Arcangelo's attention. "Oh. You didn't tell the Feds anything, did you? That wouldn't be smart at all." He took a sip of brandy from his cup before pouring in the coffee. "That would be a *real* bad idea."

"Hey, I'm not crazy. The feds did scare me, but not enough for me to rat on anybody. I know what happens to rats."

"And Vince? Was that a hit on him?" Nina asked.

Tom shook his head. "No, no, I think that was not mob-related. I think that was just random violence. Bad Philly luck. Shit-happens stuff. Some people hit the Powerball. Others get killed. Just chance."

"Who do *you* think killed my brother?" Nina asked.

Tom exhaled heavily, shrugged. "Round up the usual suspects. And there's a truckload around. Black gangs, Latinos, Russians—hey, we personally know Italian and Irish gangs. I'd bet the fucking Asians are into free market enterprise, too. Remember your much-needed baseball bat?" he said.

Tom jerked his thumb at the empty holster and looked into her eyes. "Why do you think I'm lugging this cannon around with me? If wiseguys around here were Crusaders, my street would be the fucking Holy Land."

Tom added extra brandy into his mug, poured coffee into the two mugs, placed hers on the table and nudged it toward her.

"You know, in the past two world wars, sometimes a truce was called for each of the sides to celebrate Christmas. I've even read they celebrated together sometimes. Can we have a truce and enjoy the coffee? That .38 is giving me a knot in my stomach."

Nina reached for the mug still holding the gun on him.

"I haven't told my mother or little brother about Brian. I don't know how to do it. I told my aunt, who's with Mom and him right now."

Tom shook his head and exhaled a long deep breath. "That *is* tough. I don't know what to tell you Really, I don't know what I'd do in your position."

"First my father, now my brother—." Her blue eyes began to ice over with tears. "This will kill my mother ... just kill her."

Tom reached toward her ever so slowly, deliberately, and squeezed the cylinder of the revolver tightly so it would not be able to rotate if she squeezed the trigger. He gently slid it from her hand. He held it at his side for a moment then returned it to her with the barrel still pointing at him.

"Truce," he said. "Sit down. Drink your coffee. You hungry?"

"Are you kidding? I'm starved. Been running on adrenaline since I heard about my brother and haven't eaten much. But my stomach is in knots."

"How about a sandwich? Is that okay? I can heat up some lasagna or stuffed shells?"

"A sandwich would be great."

Tom turned to the refrigerator and hunted out lunch meats, lettuce and tomato and condiments. "Wheat, rye or an Italian roll?"

"Wheat. Can you toast it?"

Tom dropped the bread in the toaster. He turned toward her. She was now nonchalantly, pointlessly holding the gun. He leaned against the counter. "Could I ask you a favor, Nina? A truce implies some trust—guns are usually put away. I don't want to be crapping in a plastic bag for the rest of my life as the result of sheer accident—."

She slid the gun into her pocket and gripped her coffee mug with two hands. "Sorry," she said. "Truce."

D'Arcangelo nodded. "Cheers." He held his cup up to her, then took a sip.

"Did you see Vince today? Sherry went to see him and took him her Christmas gift."

"I saw him today and he's looking better. Sounds a lot better, too. Actually he still *looks* like shit … lots of bruising and all those IVs and machines, but the most recent prognosis is better is what I mean."

"You know, I didn't really intend to shoot you."

"I figured that when you didn't do it right away. Still I'm always a bit nervous at the wrong end of a gun, I must admit. I thought you might feel the need to disable me because of my formidable karate skills."

She smiled in return. "I wouldn't shoot because I think that below the surface you're a pussycat."

"Does that mean I'm lousy in the sack?"

"My, aren't we insecure! What is it with you guys? Most of you think you're Don Juans. The others are Woody Allen. No, you're just the opposite. You're quite considerate in bed. Does that make you feel better? By pussycat, I mean your temperament. Men are either wolves, dogs or cats. Most mob guys are wolves. Some are dogs that think they are wolves—wannabe wolves— at least the ones I've met. You're not really like them."

"'Considerate'. I don't know whether I like that," Tom pondered the concept. "Do women like considerate? I thought they secretly liked the manly man, the bad boy—helps them get the big O."

"Trust me, you like considerate," Nina said. "Otherwise you might be dead right now. Besides, considerate gets me off."

"You'd have really shot me if you thought I was a wolf?"

"No, no, I don't think I would've," Nina smiled, then added, "I'd have my Celtic friends whack you. I think that Liam Finneran—how do they say it?—'fancies' me."

"You women, always using those feminine wiles! But that'd sure be a lot smarter than your doing it. They have more experience in these matters. And they have nothing to lose. I have been praying the fuckers don't come back to knee-cap me. A possible return visit by those guys has been giving me *agita*."

"Where's your brother?" Nina asked. "Still out shopping?"

"No, he's at a friend's house … out in the 'burbs. He plays Santa for Andy and Sara's kids. If he's lucky, they still believe—kids grow up wiser in the age of the internet. If they don't, he'll be disappointed. He should be back later tomorrow."

"That's sweet. Sherry wanted to give Vince her gift tonight. She needs to be home for Christmas and can't get back to Philly for two days—family stuff. As soon as she's done here, she'll pick me up and we'll head home. I figure I'll tell my Mom after Christmas. I'll try to keep a game face. I don't think there's any hurry, but I want to be there in case someone finds out and calls her."

Tom felt terrible for Nina and her family, but there was nothing he could say to lessen the pain of losing her brother. But he was relieved, even exhilarated he hadn't murdered her brother, in self-defense or for any reason. Tom wondered if the police had even found the bodies of Schonfeld and his killer yet. He had searched the local papers and online and had found nothing about two mysterious corpses on a boat in Cape May. He mused that perhaps they wouldn't be found for some time, maybe even months, when their odor overpowered that of the haul of the fishing and lobstering boats. *The longer the police took, the better*, he had thought again and again. *Less viable evidence for the medical examiner.*

"Telling your mother won't bring your brother back. But you'll need to deal with her sometime soon. Better that she find out from you and not the police or some neighbor or stranger."

Nina nodded. She sipped her coffee. Tom set the kitchen table, put the sandwiches on plates and got out condiments, coleslaw, and potato chips.

"I know, I know. I want to wait until the day after Christmas. She'll be surprised and upset when Brian doesn't show up tomorrow—"

"Not much of a Christmas Eve dinner, I admit," Tom noted. He went to the doorway of the kitchen and reached for the .45 Nina had placed on the sideboard and handed the butt-end of the gun to her. "I'm getting a candle for the table."

She shook her head at the offer, and he slid the gun into its holster.

He returned with a red candle, lit it, turned on the radio for some Christmas music. Lou Rawls was singing his smokey version of "White Christmas". He turned off the overhead light and sat down with Nina and they ate their sandwiches. Tom was finally hungry.

Later, they sat on the sofa in the house's darkness, lit by the street's house lights and ornaments, listening to music and holding each other.

They fell asleep lightly until awakened when Sherry rang the doorbell.

It was late afternoon and near twilight as Tom entered the hospital to visit his uncle. He checked in at the nursing station to get a progress report before going to Vince's room.

The nurse checked his file. "Oh, yes. Mr. Sarzano is doing much better today. He was almost chatty when I checked on him last. Still a ways to go, but he's alert and vital. Even mentioned getting out of the hospital."

She smiled. "He doesn't really like the food here. Wants more Italian. Just don't wear him out, okay? He still needs to rest."

Vince was awake and greeted Tom as he entered. He still looked bruised and not his usual self.

"Ey! Tommy! How ya doin'?"

Tom grabbed Vince's hand and squeezed it, noting his strong grip.

"You're looking better," Tom said. "Nurse says not to wear you out though. You gotta go easy at first."

"I am feelin' better. When Sherry was here last time, I got more than a little twinge from the big fella down there. I'm on the mend."

"Just take it easy, Vince. You're gonna be here for a few more days at least. Guess we'll see you home after Christmas."

"Yeah, Christmas here is gonna be a real fuckin' treat."

"This is a teaching hospital. I'll see if I can get some student nurses to come round to do some lower abdominal palpations."

"Not sure I know what that is, but it's got to be better than some of the shit they do to you here. And that fuckin' catheter is out, thank the Lord. This TV is pure crap."

"Not too long, uncle, and we'll spring you from this place."

"None too soon, Tommy. None too soon."

"Hey, how's your memory? Just tell me if this is not the right time, okay?"

"My memory? Fuzzy after that prick hit me, but test me out on the old stuff."

"Remember the boat, when you cleaned up after me?"

"Yeah."

"The guy had a tattoo. Was it a Celtic cross? Know what that is? An Irish cross?"

"Sure I know what a fuckin' Irish cross is. He didn't have one of them. It was a regular cross with a bar at the bottom. Isn't that a Russian thing?"

"You sure?"

"Fuck yeah. I'm sure. An Irish cross has a circle around the center of it, doesn't it? This was Greek or Russian or something."

Tom EXITED the hospital. He pulled on his gloves and tugged up his collar around his scarf as he looked up and down the street, now crowded with Christmas shoppers and people leaving work for home. The cold weather went almost unnoticed in his new found elation. His Uncle Vince's memory authenticated what he believed; it was confirmation that he had not killed Nina's brother.

D'Arcangelo set off for home toward South Philly, taking a meandering and unpredictable path. The air was numbing, made even more so by a strong wind. Half way home he found himself at the corner where Turk's Tavern glowed warm. Feeling content his uncle verified what he had hoped, Tom decided to stop for a drink to celebrate.

Inside, the tavern was moderately occupied, mostly with locals stopping off after a day at work for a quick beer. Some were ordering a bite from the appetizer menu. A few groups of young men and women laughed and talked at a few of the booths that lined the wall.

Tom surveyed the crowd and then went to the end of the bar. He slid off his coat and hung it on a post. Tom threw down a twenty on the bar.

The bartender, a broad, bald-headed, dark-skinned African American with a full black beard and horn-rimmed glasses, came up to him.

"Would you like something to drink? Something to eat?"

"Yeah. Give me a Jack Daniels, water on the side, would you?"

The bartender nodded. He returned with two glasses, set them down in front of D'Arcangelo and took the money. When he returned, he dropped the change on the bar and stood there. Tom took the shot and sipped it.

The bartender spoke up. "I can't believe it. You don't recognize me?"

D'Arcangelo peered at the man, then shook his head.

"Have I changed that much? Good Lord!"

Tom looked more closely for a clue. Still nothing. He shook his head again.

"Sorry—."

"Mr. You Lo Tengo Man! We shared an outfield that lost two consecutive Catholic League championships?"

Tom suddenly lurched up from his barstool: "Hobson! Damn! I didn't recognize you, Lynmore!"

"Well, I'm not Hector Casanova, our leftfielder obviously."

D'Arcangelo extended his forearm and clasped Hobson's outstretched arm. The pair reached over the bar and hugged.

"Do I look that different?" Hobson asked. "I guess I do, I guess I do.

Tom laughed in agreement. "Three inches in height, thirty pounds—."

"Make that forty," the bartender interjected. "Let's be honest."

Tom continued in his defense "—no hair, beard, and your voice has dropped several decibels. Man, you got that Isaac Hayes or Barry White shite goin'."

"Isaac Hayes? Really? Hey, my wife says she loves my voice. Maybe that's it."

"Shit, will you ever let me live down that 'You lo tengo' thing?"

During the summer between their senior year they both played in a hispanic baseball league. Tom thought that "yo lo tengo" was "you lo tengo" and meant for the other guy take the ball. When he and Hobson were converging on a fly ball Tom shortened the phrase to just "you". They collided and knocked each other out of the next three games. The leftfielder later told him that all they needed to say was "Lo tengo."

"Glad you weren't built the way you are now when we collided," Tom said. "I'd be a paraplegic."

"I heard you were going to college. Did you play ball there?"

"No, couldn't pull it off. Classes, work, and all. I got into drama. Even that sucked away time from schoolwork. The drama teachers are more appreciative of your time. Baseball coaches want you to worship at the altar of the team, ya know?"

"That's right. I remember you did some theater stuff in high school. You look to be in shape. Still working out?"

"Run, go to the gym a bit. Play a little softball in the summer. So what are you up to now? You own this place?"

"That's a joke. No, but I'm the senior man here. The owner is my wife's brother. Trusts me. He's a Roman guy. I completed community college, got married. My wife's a nurse in the intensive care unit right down the street at Jeff. She's encouraging me to go back to school for nursing. It's interesting stuff, really. I need some science courses, then I'm going to apply to Temple. What about you?"

"I'm thinking about going to law school. Studying for the LSAT. Gotta figure out how to pay for it."

"I hear ya, brother. I figure I need to go back to school now so my wife and I can have kids. It doesn't look like you're married. Girlfriend?"

"No, not married. Had a girlfriend but we just broke up. Things weren't working out, I suppose."

"It happens. Best to make sure before taking the leap."

"'Taking the leap'? I thought that was taking the plunge. Like in a lake. You make it sound like suicide.

"More like a leap of faith, man. Don't do it if doesn't feel right. You still working in that Italian restaurant you did in high school?

"Yep. Still there and at some others."

"You know all of us guys in high school were scared to death of you and your brother? We all thought you had mob connections. You notice you never got picked on?"

"My brother never got picked on because he was a badass. I never got picked on because everyone was afraid of Matt. All that mob stuff? Crap."

Hobson grinned. "Whatever you say, Tom."

"Lyn, not every Italian businessman is in the mob. People have seen *Goodfellas* too much."

Hobson looked at his watch. "Five o'clock. You might be interested in this then. Let me see if it's the lead story." He picked up the remote control, switched off a European soccer game and switched to the local news. He turned on the audio and raised its volume.

A red-haired female newscaster was standing in front of *Ristorante Catania*. Police milled about in the background. Crime scene tapes encircled the perimeters as investigating personnel roamed in and out of the building. The reporter spoke into the station-branded microphone:

"Philadelphia police are investigating the apparent murder of James Cardinello, reputed head of one of the city's crime families, at his restaurant today. In what appeared to be a mob-style execution, the alleged elder statesman of the South Philly mob syndicate was gunned down at *Ristorante Catania* around 3:30 this afternoon. Early reports on the possible murderer said he was a man in a Santa Claus costume who had socialized with the patrons earlier. In a statement from the city's police commissioner, announced that the FBI is joining in the investigation in coordination with the Philadelphia Police The Federal Bureau of Investigation had noted a marked uptick in gang-related violence and activity in the Delaware Valley region. This follows up that story earlier today from Atlantic City, reported by this station's New Jersey reporter Len Starr, about that running gun battle in a parking lot outside the Hotel Borgia that left three alleged members of crime families from Jersey and Philly dead and another struggling for his life. The Police are hoping that this isn't a return to the organized crime turf wars of the '80s. This is Molly O'Connell reporting from South Philadelphia."

Tom sat stunned. Jimmy was dead. A gang war going on?

He forced himself to finish his drink.

Hobson set off to tend to other customers.

D'Arcangelo wondered who the other casualties were. Then he thought about his uncle in the hospital.

TOM LEFT A LARGE TIP, gave felicitations for Christmas and the New Year with his farewell to his former teammate, grabbed his coat, and exited the tavern. He looked up and down the street for anyone looking suspicious, realized that he was being foolish and set off for the hospital.

At the hospital he entered the lobby and headed for crowded elevators. Most of the people had exited by the tenth floor. At the announced floor, the doors opened and he stepped out, walked around a corner to look immediately in the direction of his uncle's room near the nurse's station.

There were two uniformed policemen, heavily armed standing at the door. In one glance Tom saw a barrier with yellow tape around it. A nurse and doctor in a white coat were talking to a man in an overcoat, who was taking notes, standing near Vince's room.

Tom walked away in the opposite direction. He found a pass through to the other corridor on that floor that shielded him from any recognition by the nurses he had met or to whom he had spoken. He stood there for a moment to gather his thoughts.

If he went and inquired at this desk about the patient, he would be stopped for sure. He could phone later and find out more. They would be calling him, no doubt. He was the closest relative. If this were a police matter, they'd no doubt want to talk to him.

No way I want that, he said to himself. He walked around the corridor and turned to the elevators. He pressed the button and waited for the doors to open, hoping that the detectives didn't exit at the same time.

When it arrived, Tom stepped in with one elderly man and his son talking about their wife and mother's condition. Tom said nothing, looking down into his chest as the elevator picked up and discharged people on the descent.

On the first floor the doors opened. Two uniformed members of the crime scene unit stood carrying packs and suitcases of equipment.

Tom stepped out past them and headed for the hospital lobby.

9

D'ARCANGELO SET THE ALARM for 2:00 AM and fell asleep in his clothes with just a blanket pulled over him. He dreamt wildly and woke with that feeling of mild nausea and deep chill, of disjointedness when one is jerked suddenly from deep sleep. He sat up for a moment trying to gather his thoughts.

Tom had earlier that evening returned home from the hospital, sneaking into his house from the back yard into his cellar. He didn't turn on any lights. He made a sandwich in the dim light and had a ginger ale, and stole off to his bedroom early, then turned a radio on softly and sat in the darkness for some time. He expected to hear police knocking on his door and the phone to ring. But there was nothing. *It was odd that he received not one call. Almost ominous.*

Tom didn't turn on lights but found his way to the bathroom and splashed water on his face in darkness. He returned to the bedroom and grabbed the holstered .45 from under his pillow. He took the weapon out, checked the clip, chambered a round, and slid the safety on. As he hefted the sidearm and grabbed his sweater he thought of his uncle's words: 'Better to have it and not need it than to need it and not have it.' Indeed, those words had saved his life. It never occurred to him to go back to Cape May unarmed. In fact, he thought it best to have the gun with him at all times, given what had gone on in and around his house and neighborhood.

He slipped the sweater over the shoulder holster. But his father's words came to him: 'When you have a hammer as your only tool, everything looks like a nail.'

Tom considered that statement for a long moment, then removed the sweater, took the holster off and slid it under the bed. Carrying the gun *was* making him nervous. He immediately felt better without it, but that little voice inside him kept whispering: "You might regret this."

Tom went downstairs, first to the kitchen, turned on the dimmest light possible, the one over the stove, then flipped the coffee maker on. He had packed the night before and placed a satchel with an overnight travel kit. He gathered it and brought it into the kitchen, along with his hooded winter jacket. Tom took out a black knit watch cap from his jacket's pocket then, imagining he looked too furtive for a Christmas morning drive to the shore, put on a light gray Irish driver's cap for the trip to Cape May.

For a quick meal he had smeared peanut butter on an Italian roll, wrapped it in aluminum foil and placed an apple in a paper bag. When the coffee machine beeped, he filled a Thermos, placed the roll and coffee in the satchel, swung it over his shoulder and let himself out the back.

The early morning's frigid air shocked him fully awake. The sky sprinkled stars like crystals of ice.

D'Arcangelo allowed his eyes to adjust to the darkness for a moment, then left the yard and walked softly down the alley to the street around the corner. The car was parked right across the street from the alley's exit. He put the satchel in the trunk and slid into the driver's seat. Tom slipped the key in the ignition, then before turning it, felt an icicle of fear and an accompanying pulse of adrenalin.

What if—? he thought. He opened the glove compartment and took out a small flashlight, then looked under the steering column and dashboard for any disturbance. He decided to check the floor and under the seats for anything unusual. Then he looked once more, still more carefully. Tom sprung the hood then exited the car, opened it, shining the flashlight around the engine. Then he dropped to his knees to examine the underside of the car.

Nothing. *Jeezus, I'm getting real fucking paranoid.*

Back in the car, he turned the key. Although Tom had found nothing suspicious, he steeled himself, wincing and reflexively clenching his legs together as he turned the key. The Buick started with its customary purr. He realized that, despite the frigid temperature, he had begun to perspire. He took a long deep breath to calm himself. For a brief moment Tom thought of his brother in Iraq and Afghanistan expecting to get blown up at any time or any day. *How can he stand it?* Tom wondered.

"You can do this. C'mon!" he whispered to himself, flipping the car's heat control switch, then slowly driving from South Philly towards Jersey,

He headed for the Walt Whitman Bridge. Several times Tom looked in the rearview mirror to see if anyone was following, but saw nothing suspicious. Traffic was extremely light. He cautioned himself neither to drive too fast nor too slowly, nor to change lanes often. He didn't want to get stopped by a trooper in Jersey, but at least he wasn't carrying the gun. On Christmas Eve he knew there would be patrols primed for alcohol-fueled drivers, so he had not had a drink since the following day. "I need clarity," he told himself when thinking about drinking the night before.

Once over the bridge Tom took the expressway to route 55 and drove his usual route to Cape May: routes 47 to 9 at Rio Grande. Rather than take the causeway near the marina, he took the road to the western side of Cape May Island, closest to the farm where he'd hidden the money. He drove slowly down one of the back routes past the Rea farm, then turned around and passed the farm once again and slowed to the road next to the house and barn where he had stashed the money. He pulled onto the back road, extinguished the Buick's headlights, and parked in the frozen, rutted road that ran parallel to a group of trees and bushes that lined the farmhouse and barn where he had hidden the money. Tom turned off the engine so nothing illuminated him. He sat in silence, except the ticking of the engine cooling, and ate the peanut butter sandwich, then washed it down with coffee.

He swapped the gray plaid driver's cap for a black knit watch cap. Tom was glad that he decided not to pack that gun. If he were to be caught with it by police, he'd be in deeper legal waters.

And if the mobs were after him, it wouldn't do him much good. He slid from the car and, before shutting its door, looked around, first at the starlit sky and shadows of trees and a light distant on the highway.

Tom shut the door quietly and opened the trunk of the car. Earlier he had unscrewed the light bulb from the trunk and now, with difficulty in the darkness, grabbed the satchel and rooted in it to feel for the flashlight. He found it and closed the trunk but not entirely. He thought to leave it ajar to make for easier access when he returned.

He looked around and, as the cold air surrounded him, felt a shiver of cold and nervousness come over him as he contemplated what he was about to do. It was one thing to steal a million dollars and bury it somewhere; it was another to get that money and carry it around and spend it. D'Arcangelo realized his risks of being caught would increase astronomically.

He stood looking around for a good two minutes, planning how to begin, summoning hi nerve. *Breathe*, he heard his acting coach's usual advice, his admonition: *Breathe!*

His breath escaped into the darkness as vaporous ghosts under the sky full of stars. Tom started for the barn, holding the flashlight but not lighting it. He walked with purpose and tried to appear nonchalant and at ease. He entered the line of trees bordering the property and crossed through them to the side facing the barn, the field fronting the barn and its distant house.

Tom stopped and looked at the house for some light or sign of occupants but saw nothing. Although the night was just beginning to yield to dim twilight, he saw no sign of a car or truck.

He came to the side of the barn nearest the access door, skirted the wall, and stopped at the entrance to the barn. He looked again across the field, scanned the house for minutes, then behind him but saw nothing.

D'Arcangelo padded to the door and tried the handle. He had brought a crowbar, but left it in the trunk of the car. He reasoned that since the barn was unlocked last time, it would still be. The steel bar was just in case of an emergency. Tom turned the door knob and went in.

It was much darker though warmer in the barn, with only light from stars shining through the few windows. He held the flashlight down to the ground and flicked it on. The barn looked the same as when he had last been there.

Then the thought came to him that he ought to take the one bag, place it in the car first, then come back to get the second. *Suppose someone had seen him come in and had called the cops? Better to get some of the money out of here first,* he thought. Tom couldn't carry both bags and move quickly. This way he could spy around to see if anyone seemed alerted. Better to have half than get caught being greedy.

Tom slung the bag again to his shoulder and turned toward the door. He peered at the now barely discernible twilight from the door's window and saw nothing unusual and opened the door, shut it behind him, scuttling around and behind the barn to the tree-lined boundary of the property. He tried to follow the path taken to get to the barn, but realized that the brush and overgrowth made that impossible, so he crackled and crunched back to the Buick.

As soon as Tom got within sight of the car, he stopped and thought better about putting the duffle bag in the car until he was ready to leave. Suppose someone saw me put it there and took it before he got back. Unlikely, but he had been born and raised in Philly where cars were stolen while they were double-parked for a delivery, where SEPTA buses, ambulances and police cars had been hijacked. Tom dropped the bag under a pine tree, carefully noting the angle to car and took a branch that had cracked from the tree and obscured the bag.

He moved back through the trees and then stopped suddenly for a moment. Then he heard a distant sound.

Was that a car? What was it? D'Arcangelo strained to listen without the crackling of leaves and brush and wind, swiveling his head like an owl. *Did I hear something? Or did I just imagine it?* he thought. He took three deep breaths to still his heart. He remembered he had heard that one could hear the blood rushing through one's ears and think it was an outside sound. *Was that true?*

He listened again. Nothing.

Tom tramped through the trees and came to the field, once again skirting behind to the left of the barn. He hugged the barn to avoid being seen from the house as much and for as long as he could, then when he could do that no longer, hurried quickly to the barn access door. Tom looked across the field toward the house and toward the entrance driveway from the main road. He spied lights from a car approaching along the highway coming toward the east. It appeared following its shafts of light, and he could make it out as a pickup truck. It sped along the road and disappeared into the twilight—just someone on their way home.

Tom looked at the distant house for some sign of life but saw nothing. Casting one final glance for anyone, he grabbed the door knob and went quickly in.

Inside, he flicked on the flashlight and found the ladder to the loft. He put the flashlight in his jacket pocket and pulled himself up.

Tom went to the bales of hay where he had constructed a hiding place for the duffle bag and began to slide the bale at the top of the pyramid when a flash of light sliced wildly through the upstairs window and then the ground floor door window before disappearing. He stopped and slid to the sole window on the loft, expecting the light of another person commuting to Cape May past the Rea Farm.

Instead a car had entered the driveway to the house circled the field across from and was purposefully moving toward the barn. And him.

He peered at the car and even in the darkness of twilight could see it was not a police car. Then it turned its lights out. I waited for some moments to discern if it was indeed coming to the barn and if it was going to stop there.

Maybe it's just circling the property for an inspection and would head out to the road, he thought. His car was out of sight behind the trees and couldn't be seen from this property. *Don't panic just yet.*

The car pulled around in front of the barn, now out of sight. He listened for it to stop or continue on the road circling the field.

The car stopped. Then silence. Then the slamming of doors.

Fuck! Motherfucker! What the fu—?

He had to hide himself somehow in the loft. And quickly. Tom slid behind the hay bales that hid the duffel bag of money, between the bales and the barn wall, a space of roughly two feet and knelt on one knee. He knew he would be visible—and pinned against the wall—to anyone who came up to the loft and walked to the wall or window, to anyone who was searching with a flashlight for someone in the barn. He thought for a moment about hiding under the bales with the money and sized up how he could lie beneath a pyramid of bales and not be seen. But Tom dismissed the idea immediately. The claustrophobia would be too intense—he could imagine it like being in a coffin—and he would not be able to react quickly if by some chance they pulled the bales apart. His uncle's words about the gun came to mind. *Better to have it and not need it.*

Fuck, I sound like my uncle! Who knows, maybe waving a gun around could get me killed rather than save me. Suppose these guys are undercover cops! His mind sizzled with dire possibilities. Then his reasoning came back to him: *In Cape May? Don't I wish. On Christmas morning? No fucking way. Could they just be whacky birders? The owners investigating after someone reported a person on the property?*

Tom heard the door below open and some footfalls. He saw a flash or two of lights across the ceiling and listened through the six-inch space between the bales of hay. There seemed to be at least two flashlights.

Tom's mind darted as to what to do if they were armed. He began to wish he had brought the gun. How many were there? He would just stay hidden as long as possible. He reasoned he could wait them out. After all, they didn't know he was there. Did they? Who were they? Why were they here? Now?

Tom waited for seconds, then long, long minutes for more information from below. He dreaded hearing anyone climbing the creaky ladder to the loft. Then what should he do? He didn't want to—couldn't—think any further.

Then Tom heard someone exclaim: "I don't see nobody!"

Then a second voice: "Me neither. Didn't you say you saw someone come in here? Where is he?"

"I said I *thought* I saw someone come in that door, but he's not here. It's dark, man. Look, the lo-jack tracker took us here. Let's find the car. It's right around here close by. It has to be. Unless the prick found it and tossed it out the window—"

D'Arcangelo had heard it all. Now he understood how they found him. They hadn't followed the car; the car had led them to him.

"Let's find that car. Check that tracker agai—"

"Shh!"

"What?"

"Quiet!"

The noise of a car suddenly speeding to a stop outside took his attention away from the men below.

"Who the *fuck* is that?" asked one in lower, deeper tone. "Cops?"

Tom heard the answer: "It's not a fucking police car. Cops don't drive fuckin' Beemers!"

The men below scuttled around hurriedly. Tom thought that one of them would spring up the ladder to the loft, but he heard the click as they chambered rounds into weapons. *They must be taking cover*, he thought.

D'Arcangelo slid forward a foot or two to hear better and be able to better defend myself. With his left hand he felt for a plastic binding on the top bale and slid his fingers in it. Tom planned to pull it in front of him as a shield if someone showed a gun. He thought a bale might stop a round.

He heard the door slam open and many rapid footsteps sliding around below.

"Motherfucker!" someone yelled. "Behind the ca—!"

Before the sentence ended, there came the loud explosion of a gunshot. Then sustained rapid gunfire. It was loud, the shots echoed around the metal barn walls, although there were the muffled hisses of silencers from some weapons. He heard explosions as the shooters emptied clips hurriedly. Tom heard a curse and a groan as one was hit, and then another collapsed noisily, his gun clanging to the floor. He heard another groan and gasp and what he thought was a cry of despair. There were more curses and a pained scream.

The exchange of gunshots ended suddenly. Tom leant forward to hear as best he could. The silence seemed even greater after the loud explosions of the gun battle. He heard someone thrashing slowly and groaning. The smell of gunpowder reached his nose.

He realized he had to get away from there as quickly as he could. If anyone heard that commotion, they'd call the police. They'd be there within twenty minutes, with perhaps some extra time thrown in due to the Christmas holiday.

Tom slid forward. Still, he heard not one person walking around or moving. He listened for what seemed like an hour but in reality was minutes. Silence. He slipped forward to the end of the hay bales. Tom heard nothing. He crawled on his knees to the top of the loft to hear better. Still nothing.

D'Arcangelo made a snap decision. He would step back and grab the duffel bag of money and look over the loft to the carnage below. He slid the bale of hay aside and grabbed the remaining duffel bag, hoisted it to his shoulder and stepped to the top of the loft. Getting down the ladder to the ground carrying the bag would leave him vulnerable. He peeked over the loft. There was just enough light from the windows for him to see. Below he saw four prostrate bodies, in various positions, one in a seated position, folded like a scarecrow. In that dim light Tom saw the reflection of blood in rivulets and tar-like puddles around the bodies. One man lay on his back, his arms out and his legs spread eagled, looking oddly like someone making snow angels. From his head flowed a large black lake of blood. Another man curled into a fetal position and from his arms ran slow seepage of his blood to the dusty and hay strewn floor.

Tom looked down at the floor. He saw nothing moving and heard little, except a low moaning from what he believed was the man behind the tractor.

Tom turned toward the window and craned his neck to the front of the barn. He saw the BMW but no one moving near it. They might have been below his range of vision from where he stood. Tom needed to look out a window facing the field and the distant house. He wanted to get out of there—and quickly.

He decided to throw the duffel bag down to the floor, in order not to have to carry it, and to see if anyone would go for it or see if someone was up there. If they did he planned to jump to the hay bales for protection.

The bag landed with a *Whump*! and rising cloud of dust. Tom listened and heard nothing except a continued groaning. He came to the ladder and, for a moment thought about jumping to the floor himself, but the height was too great. He feared breaking an ankle or even worse. He rejected jumping as a certainty as soon as he saw the height again. He listened one final time and watched the cloud of dust settling on and around the bag. Tom swung to the ladder, looking around once more but saw no one. The smell of gunpowder and gun smoke was now clouding the air. He quickly climbed down halfway and spun and dropped the remaining five feet. He landed on the balls of his feet with one hand steadying the fall, hitting the floor in a three-point crouch like a football lineman. Scanning what seconds ago was a battlefield, Tom saw a gun to his right on the floor. He thought about grabbing it but dismissed the idea immediately. There was no way he wanted fingerprints on murder weapons!

The groaning had stopped suddenly and he heard only heavy, deathly silence, more emphatic after the gunfire. He stood up and stretched to see over the hood of the car and around the tractor and lawnmower. He glimpsed three bodies, none of them moving in the least, and blood slowly streaming from and pooling around two of the bodies.

How much time had gone by? To him it seemed like hours. Seconds slipped beyond mere measures of time. He focused his hearing to the outside of the barn, then shouldered the duffel bag and peered around the open door.

Outside, two cars sat with no one around, parked perpendicular to each other but with engines and lights off.

Tom listened intently but heard only a distant squawking of crows. He took one last look and leapt out of the door. With the duffel bag on one shoulder he twisted like a hunchback around the corner of the barn on the side away from the road and field, and hurried to the rear of the barn to get out of sight of the house.

Once there, he stopped to look for anyone and to lift his head to better hear cars—or worse—sirens. Tom was jubilant hearing nothing and set off at a quick jog into the small wood behind the barn toward his car and the other satchel. The ever-growing light and his familiarity with the brush made walking over it now easier than before. He slipped through the wood to the tree where he had stashed the other bag, then decided to take what he shouldered and load it into the trunk first. He dashed to the car and opened its trunk. Tom threw the duffel in, then looked quickly around in all directions. He saw no one, then leaving the trunk open, set off to get the remaining duffel bag. In the copse of trees he uncovered the second bag and slung it over his shoulder and ran to the car. He tossed it into the car and shut the trunk slowly and deliberately so as not to make a great deal of noise.

D'Arcangelo heard a crackle of brush under foot from the trees he'd just left, then the recognizable cocking of a pump shotgun. He halted, then heard some more crackling of sticks and brush.

"*Freeze! Freeze right there!* Raise your hands so I can see them."

Tom did as he was told, not moving his head but slowly putting arms in the air. He fought an adrenaline surge to run.

"Turn around so I can see you. Do it real slow."

He turned deliberately toward the sound of the approaching man. He knew this guy might fire as soon as he faced him, that for some there was often a reluctance to shoot someone in the back.

In front of him stood a man of medium height in a knit cap with longish hair splayed around a wide face wearing a black leather thigh-length coat. The man cradled a 12-gauge pump shotgun from his shoulder and slid carefully toward Tom, now less than twenty feet away.

A voice under a Fu Manchu mustache spoke with what Tom recognized as an Eastern European accent: "What's in de trunk? In dose bags?" His mouth displayed a large gap between his top front teeth, visible even in dim twilight.

Tom said nothing. He was at a loss for words. That this guy might shoot him at any minute and just look for himself circled and twirled through his mind, distracted him, making him unable to speak. He was facing immediate death.

"*What's…in…dose…fucking…bags?*" the man enunciated each word more slowly and loudly. He stepped a few feet closer, the twelve gauge looming larger and ever more lethal.

Tom found his voice at last. "Nothing. Clothes. Some books. Overnight shit. Wanna take a look?" He jerked his head toward the trunk. He knew the closer this guy got with a shotgun, the greater chance he had to close on him to grab it. Tom dangled the keys toward the man. He held onto the electronic button for keyless entry. He hadn't locked the car, not wanting to make any more noise than the gunfight in the barn had created and to alert people where he might be.

The man in the black hat gave D'Arcangelo a suspicious look. He eyed the keys, then gestured toward him. "Throw me dose keys. On the ground. Right at my feet. Slowly. Step away from the car and get down on your knees."

Tom tossed the keys on the ground in front of the man. He stood for a second then moved slowly, stepping sideways while keeping his eyes on the shotgun's muzzle. He stood there for a moment, not kneeling.

"On your fuckin' knees!" the man barked. "Lock hands behind head."

Tom obeyed, going to his right knee first, then his left to the frozen ground.

The gunman stepped forward and without taking his eyes from D'Arcangelo, lowered the shotgun from his shoulder to his side. Still pointing at the man on his knees, he picked up the keys. The gunman worked the electronic key to unlock the car and swung around in a six feet arc.

At the car's trunk he reached down and sprung it, then reached in and tugged the bag open, his head swiveling rapidly from Tom to the trunk. He saw packets of money and pulled the bag toward him to see the entire contents. "*Motherfucker!*" he said.

Tom looked across the wooded area, then upwards at the sky, now a solid light gray. Several crows were scooting high across the tree line. In his darker moments he had wondered what his last sight would be. He had conjectured that dying while looking at nature would be best. It would sure beat a nursing home or intensive care IV.

The gunman slammed the door shut and looked at the keys to see if the ignition key was there. Then he turned his full attention to Tom and walked carefully in an arc to face him.

"Whose money is that?" He leveled the shotgun at Tom.

D'Arcangelo had to give himself time. He had to give his opponent something to think about. "Not mine. Not yours either. It belongs to a Philly gang—a big one—and they're gonna want it, you can bet on it. They know I was getting it for them."

The man was silent for just a moment. "Yeah, right. Bullshit. I think it's payday for me."

"You—and anyone around you—will be sorry if they find out you took that bread," Tom said. "They'll skin you alive and your family, too. I'm doin' you a favor. Believe me."

"Shut the fuck up!" the moustached man shouted in warning.

Tom could think of nothing more to say. The barrel of the shotgun loomed ever larger.

"You a religious man?" the gunman asked.

Tom held his breath. He sensed his time was up. He knew if he said he wasn't, the man would execute him immediately. Staring at imminent death made him immediately devoutly religious.

"Yeah, I'm Catholic, I'm religious."

"Say your prayers then."

The man raised the shotgun to his shoulder and gathered Tom into its sights. He inched closer to assure his shot, but not so close that the kneeling man could leap at him.

Tom just looked directly at him as he approached and said nothing. He fought not to turn away from the approaching explosion.

"*What'd I say?* Pray, motherfucker!"

Tom took his hands from his head and pressed his hands together, bowing his head with his eyes on the gun. He began to say the "Hail Mary", still keeping his eyes on the man. Tom didn't want to see his end, but thought it might be easier for his murderer to pull the trigger if his victim didn't look directly at him.

Tom's legs seemed frozen to the ground, his knees buried in a block of ice.

"Hail Mary, full of grace—," he began.

"Unnnhhhh!"

The moustached man suddenly slumped and fell. Tom felt the light splash of a red, warm mist filtering in droplets onto his praying hands. It was followed by the sharp crack of a distant rifle and then its echo across the fields.

The man slumped noisily to his knees. The blood from the bullet as it passed through his skull turned to an aerosol cloud, the mist twisting in the air and filtering down to the ground. After seeming to pause for long seconds, he fell awkwardly forward and to his left side. The shotgun thudded to the frozen ground.

Tom turned toward the trees in the direction where he thought the shot had come. He dropped to the ground on his belly and reached for the shotgun, expecting another shot to come his way. Then he thought the better of getting the gun and scuttled like a crab for the car keys.

Tom pulled up in the driveway of the small ranch-style home and checked its number. The Cahill name was stenciled in Celtic script on the mailbox. He got out of the car and looked around. The sun was barely up, but he could see it was going to be a chilly, bright clear day. Down the street a lone man was outside with his young child on her bicycle with training wheels. The man was showing her how to put on the plastic helmet.

D'Arcangelo walked to the Cahill house, leaned toward the door to see if he could hear anyone stirring, and then rang the bell. The curtain parted and it was Nina. She opened the door. She had a terry cloth blue robe tied at the waist.

She seemed surprised to see him.

"Hi," he said.

"Hi."

Tom held out a sealed envelope. "Merry Christmas," he said. Puzzled, she looked at it.

"Tom, I didn't get you anything—I thought the pin was my gift," she said.

"This is not just for you. Think of it as ... a family gift."

She looked even more quizzical.

"Shall I open it? I mean come in, have a cup of coffee … I'll make some breakfast and I'll open it." She gestured to come in.

Tom shook his head. "Thanks, but I have something to do now … I would love to come in. No, don't open it for a while. Tuck it away somewhere. I wrote out instructions on how to use it. You'll see. Remember that you didn't get it from me. Okay?"

Nina's initial perplexed look became suspicious, startled.

She hefted the weight and the size of the envelope, felt the outline of packs of money.

"Tom, is this mob money? Illegal shit? You know I don't want to be part of any of that—"

"It's *not* mob money. Well, not exactly. My instructions explain it all …. Well, not all. Please, read what I wrote and then destroy the note. Burn it. Hide the money for your use. Forget you have it for a while."

"Tom—," she began to protest.

"Just read what I wrote … and do as I say, and everything will be fine. Trust me."

"Trust you?" she said. She folded the envelope and placed it in the pocket of her robe.

Tom leaned forward and kissed her lightly on the lips. He stroked her blond hair away from her face. She leaned against him, took his head in her hand and pulled him to her. She kissed Tom's cheek, saw a few droplets of dried red near his temple. She took a tissue from her robe's other pocket and moistened it with her mouth, then wiped the drops of blood away from his face.

She held the tissue for him to see. "Trust you?"

"Remember that lesson in family loyalty you told me about?" D'Arcangelo asked. "The crazy uncle?"

She nodded. "Yeah."

"Think of this not as loyalty to me—think of it as loyalty to Brian Cahill."

Tom pecked her once again on the cheek and headed for the Buick.

"Tom!" Nina called out.

"Merry Christmas!"

As he drove down the small back street of this South Jersey township he saw the man running next to the little girl on her unsteady first training wheels, ready to rescue her if needed.

Before Tom reached the bridge he pulled over at one of the refurbished new old diners along the turnpikes of New Jersey. He took out his cell phone and dialed his brother at their home phone in South Philly. Then, thinking better than using his cell phone, he used the pay phone outside the diner.

Matt didn't pick up and the voicemail came on.

"Matt, pick up the phone if you're there! Pick up the phone! It's Tommy!"

He waited but there was no pick up. The diner was piping Christmas music outside and Nat Cole's version of "Silent Night" was filtering into and over the taped message in his ear.

Tom took his cell phone and called his brother. Matt answered laughing. "Hello? Tommy! Merry Christmas! Where ya at?"

"Matt, my cell phone battery is dying. Call me at ..." Tom leaned to get the pay phone's number. "Try to call me there, okay?"

Tom hoped that the pay phone could receive calls. In Philly many couldn't receive calls to cut down on use by drug traffickers and prostitutes. But the phone rang and Tom snatched it up.

"Hey! What's up?" Matt asked.

"Matt, listen to what I say. Be a good soldier and follow orders. Okay?"

Matt laughed. "Well, maybe—it depends on what they are, man!"

Tom spoke calmly but emphatically. "Don't go home today. In fact, don't go to the house at all. Listen to me. I know what I'm talking about. Please, follow my orders: *do not go home.*"

Matt laughed again, then became serious. "Well, okay. But want to tell me why, Bro?"

"Someone might try to kill you. I'm serious. I think there's a gang war about to start, and they know where I—make that we!—live. I don't want you to get caught up in anything, okay? You might be safer in Afghanistan."

"Tommy, I thought you said you weren't involved in the family business," Matt whispered. "Now what's going on?"

"Matt, I'm not. I swear. I have been trying to get out. Uncle Vince knew about it and told the others that I was no longer to be involved. I spoke to Jimmy and he cut me loose. But both of them are no longer around. Lou knows. Hey, listen to me. There's an ocean of shit around here … and it's at high tide right now."

"Tommy, okay, I'm not going back to the house. What are *you* going to do?"

"Not sure. But I'll be in touch. Just be careful yourself. If you have to go back to the house, take several people with you, know what I mean?"

"If? You mean 'when', don't you? I need to go home before my leave is over …"

"Matt, just follow orders. If or when you go back to the house, be sure to call Lou and the crew. Take three or four of them with you. Tell them I said to do this, okay? *Be careful!*"

Matt said nothing for a long moment. "Okay, Tommy. I hear you. Look, take care of yourself."

Click!

D'ARCANGELO PARKED OUTSIDE and headed for the main door of the psychologist's house. He rang the bell and a dark-haired woman with page boy haircut opened the door.

He cleared his throat. "Is Dr. Horowitz there? I'm a patient of his and I'd like to talk to him for a few minutes, if I could.?"

"Sure. Wait a minute and I'll get him. Who shall I say it is?"

"Tom D'Arcangelo."

She eyed him up and down. "He's upstairs on the computer. Why not come in until I get him?"

"Thanks."

The woman disappeared upstairs and turned to the left, her footsteps falling away on old, worn Persian rugs. Tom looked around at the artwork on the walls of the entrance hall and into the living room.

Horowitz appeared at the top of the stairs and paused a moment. He descended the stairs slowly, dressed in his usual running shoes and pinstripe Oxford shirt.

"Hello."

Tom raised his hand weakly. "I know this is not a scheduled visit—"

The doctor nodded, holding out his hand, laughing. "Correct. I'm glad that you recognize that. Is everything all right?"

"Look, could I talk with you for a bit?"

He smiled and joked. "Is it because I'm Jewish? This *is* Christmas. Psychologists seldom have office practice on holidays."

"Yeah, I know. Sorry. I didn't have your number or I would have called first. Look, I can pay you cash, right now." Tom pulled out a few hundred-dollar bills and waved them. "It's real important."

Horowitz arched his eyebrow at the crass offer. He waved his hand at the outstretched Ben Franklins. "I have some time if you'd like, although it *is* Christmas and my wife does like the holiday."

"Thank you. Thank you, Doctor. I'm sorry, but this is a bit of an emergency."

The doctor showed him into the office from a side door at the bottom of the stairs. He observed the carriage and the heaviness this otherwise twenty-six year-old displayed on entering the office and had not seen this before; Tom was exhausted.

"Would you like some coffee?"

"That'd be great. Thanks."

Horowitz returned in a few minutes with two mugs of black coffee. He gave one to Tom, then sat and placed his on the marble-top desk next to his chair. He laced his fingers together in his lap and looked at Tom.

D'Arcangelo sipped the coffee and looked at the doctor. Horowitz raised his hands skyward in an invitation to speak.

"I need some advice. I don't have a lot of time," Tom said.

Horowitz cocked his head and looked at him with what Tom thought was a degree of sadness.

"Tom, this is the third time we've met. We are not even at the spot where I ask if you and I can even work together. This is therapy. Therapy takes time. It's a process—a process that sometimes takes years. It's not tax preparation or speed dating."

"My uncle Vince died in the hospital suddenly," Tom replied, "before he could get home. He had a stroke. He seemed to be recovering; I had just talked to him. Something happened."

"Oh, I'm sorry to hear that. You have my condolences. I know you and he were close. Is that what you want to talk about?"

Tom ignored the sentiment and question and spewed on.

"Today some people tried to kill me. They came as close to killing me as you and I are standing together here. I'm fucking lucky to be alive. It was like I hit the lottery actually. The city's becoming a fucking war zone."

"Yes, I read about it in the newspapers. The South Philly mob boss's death made the local television news."

"I'm afraid to return home."

"Oh dear. That *is* worrisome," Horowitz said. "What do you plan to do about that? Have you gone to the police? Asked for protection?"

"I can't do that. We don't go to the police. We can't."

" 'We?' " asked Horowitz. "What do you mean 'we'?"

"My family. We don't go to the police. Besides, if I did, it wouldn't help me."

"Go to the police." The psychologist shrugged. "That's my advice. That's what I would do. And what I think you should do as well."

Tom placed his face in his hands, then slid his fingers through his hair, massaging his scalp. Then he took up the mug of coffee and leaned back on the sofa, then let out a long sigh.

"Going to the police aside," Tom asked, "what would a *second* option be? If you *couldn't go* to the police? If they didn't exist?"

The psychologist took a long breath. "It's not a complicated decision chart, Tom. If you don't go to the police, you need to remove whatever is threatening you. If that's not possible, you need to remove yourself from the threat. Get far, far away. What seems best for you?"

D'Arcangelo cradled the mug of coffee in his hands, consumed in thought.

Horowitz took another deep breath and exhaled audibly. He leaned forward in his chair and fixed his gaze on his patient. "Tom, I'd take the money you were waving around in front of me and use it to get far, far away."

Tom sat, silent, staring through the psychologist. Horowitz shrugged with finality: "You asked for my advice? This is it: Get the fuck outta town."

10

Two years later …

MATT AND NINA WALKED slowly along Bremerton's
downtown district, window shopping despite a cold,
slight but steady drizzle. Though still twilight, the rain
and overcast sky made it seem like night. Bremerton is the largest city
on Washington's Olympic Peninsula, an hour's ferry ride from Seattle,
home to the Puget Sound Naval Shipyard and naval base.

Matt held an umbrella over his pregnant wife with one arm and
encircled her waist with the other. They looked in one art gallery,
boutique and craft shop after another until they had traced the entire
area. The Marine in Matt admired his wife's stoic attitude toward
fatigue and discomfort, but realized that she was approaching the limits
of what her sixth month of pregnancy would wisely allow.

"Hungry? Want to grab a bite here?" he asked. "Or just want to wait
to eat until after we take the ferry back?"

"Are you kidding? Sure. I thought you'd never ask. I'm starved. But
even more than eating I'd like to get off my feet for a while! They're
killing me, and wet feet make me miserable. I vote for eating here."

"Great. I'd like a drink and some dinner before we head back to
Seattle. It's later than I had planned."

"There was a place a few blocks back we passed that looked nice—not
too upscale—and since it's raining harder and the wind is picking up."

"I know the place you mean," Matt said. "I've been there a few times with some fellow jarheads."

The couple spun around and began to re-trace their steps with purpose while rain shrouded the sky and the street with near complete silvery blackness.

Along the way they passed a small shop with an old-fashioned hanging wooden sign, suspended by metal braces with lights shining on either side. Matt had not noticed the shop's sign when they first passed by, its light not yet visible in the twilight.

Above them the sign read: *Jos. Porter, Woodworker.*

Matt peered into the rain-streaked window as they passed. Two chairs, a cabinet, a large library table, an end table, a desk, and a mirror of natural wood that hung on a wall, all individually made, were visible for sale in a small display area. The name of the woodworker was painted on the outside of the large window in red letters, with a mandolin under the name and that entwined by roses that ran the width of the window and up the other side. Matt paused to look at the furniture.

"Matt, there's the place I meant—*Mike's Harbor Lights.* It's right across the street," Nina pointed to a small restaurant's lights, that seemed all the more inviting as the rain and a sudden wind squall grew to soak them. "I hope this dies down before we're finished eating!"

The pair slipped between the parked cars and splashed across to the other side and hurriedly ducked into *Mike's Harbor Lights Restaurant.* Inside, they shook the wet from their clothes and savored the warmth and dryness for a moment. A hostess came to seat them.

"Welcome to *Harbor Lights*!" she beamed. "Interested in dinner?"

"Dinner and shelter from the storm," Nina said. She surveyed the restaurant and spotted a glowing fire in the fireplace. She nodded toward a table near the fire. "That looks fantastic!"

"Do you have a reservation?" the hostess asked them.

Matt helped Nina slip her coat off, displaying her bulging abdomen. The hostess spied this and grabbed two menus.

"Forget about it. We're not that busy right now. This way."

Matt whispered in his wife's ear as they followed in the hostess's wake: "Perfect timing, hmm?"

The hostess seated them at a table near the fireplace and handed them the menus. "A waitress will be with you soon. Enjoy your dinner."

"A Marine uniform," Matt continued, "is sometimes good for quick seats—on occasion someone even buys me a drink—but the baby belly tops dress blues. Someone with reservations will miss out on these great seats," he said. "That fire sure feels great."

"You have no shame, Matt." Nina grinned as she turned to the flames. "I would never take advantage of my condition. But I will slip off these shoes and try to dry my feet!"

A waitress came to the table and introduced herself. "My name is Karen and I'll be taking care of you this evening. Would you like to hear the specials for tonight?"

Nina nodded at the waitress, menu in hand. Nina turned to Matt for his response, when the waitress first squinted at then smiled toward Matt.

"Hey, weren't you the Marine who was in here a few weeks ago? With some other service guys who were just back from Afghanistan? I waited on you at the bar." Her already smiling face took on a sudden glowing radiance.

Nina arched one eyebrow at her husband and flashed him a quizzical smile.

Waitress Karen smiled and folded her arms, shoving ample breasts a bit higher. "I thought I recognized you ... even out of uniform. I remember you."

"Yes, um-hmm. That's right, ma'am." Matt smiled back at her and nodded recognition. "I was in here with three Marines a few weeks back. We had a few drinks and decided to stay for dinner."

Nina raised one eyebrow at the waitress and then arched the other one at her husband. She turned to the waitress. "And was my husband well-behaved? Or was he angling to get your clothes off and into the nearest bed?"

Karen held her hands up to Nina. "No, no, oh no, that's not what I meant. I meant I remember 'you'—you plural. All four Marines."

"And were these Marines—?" Nina began.

"They were all gentlemen, I want to add!" Matt said.

Nina ignored him and continued, "—*all* of them angling to get your clothes off and into the nearest bed?"

Matt gave a mock harrumph. "Tell my wife how well-behaved we were," he urged. "Or at least how well-behaved I was!"

"You were, you were! They all were well-behaved," she said earnestly to Nina. "Really!"

"Well, why then did you remember *these* particular marines, may I ask? There must be platoons of them in here. Did you remember them for their extremely courteous and gentlemanly behavior?" Nina asked with a wry smile.

Matt interjected before the waitress could reply: "Four of the most well-behaved, courteous, handsome heartbreakers she's ever seen in here. And they tipped well—or as well as their meager salaries allow—for her excellent service."

Nina smiled at the waitress. "You recognized them for their extremely large hat sizes, I'd imagine?"

Karen pulled a coaster out of her top pocket. "One of them left me this." She turned it over and on the back was a caricature of her and a phone number. She handed it to Matt, who looked at it then handed it to Nina. "You'll note that's not my writing," he commented. "And you know I can't draw for shit."

Nina read aloud. " 'Please. Call me!'—real poetry there!—and there's a phone number. The drawing is cute. Are you thinking about calling him?"

The waitress took the coaster and pocketed it. "I wasn't sure which one had left it. One was wearing a wedding ring—besides you, I mean!" she said pointing to Matt and nodding her head to Nina. "I didn't want to call and get his wife."

Nina looked obviously at Matt to see if he was wearing his ring. "Married men are the worst. Trust me."

"That would be Frank Skillman," Matt said. "He's artistic; he can really draw. He's not married. Frank's a really nice guy. Actually a bit on the shy side—"

The waitress turned to Nina. "Should I call him? Would *you*?"

"Me? No, I wouldn't call him. Never. Not on your life. If he wants to meet you, he'll come in again. Then you can make your move. Calling him makes you look needy. Men secretly dislike that. They might take advantage of needy—in fact, they home in on it—but deep down they really hate it. Make *them* chase *you* until *you* determine if they are worth catching. That's the strategy."

The waitress looked at Matt for his opinion. With both index fingers he pointed at his wife.

Karen smiled. "Sounds like good advice," she said, then whipped out her receipt book.

Nina picked up her menu. "What were those specials? I'm so famished, I might order a full course."

AFTER DINNER and before coffee and dessert, Matt excused himself. "Order coffee and a Sambuca for me. No dessert. You can order two, if you'd like. I'll take a bite. You earned it after all the walking we did today. I will be a few minutes. I want to check on something I saw in one of the shops down the street. I'll only be ten minutes, okay? Entertain yourself by talking to the baby … and remember, *no* alcohol."

Nina eyed the desserts on the menu. "Sure," she said shooting a curious glance at his back in his departure.

Matt went to the entrance of the restaurant, grabbed his coat from the rack where he hung it and exited into a lighter but still insistent rain. Through the restaurant's door window he looked across the street to the woodworker's store front, exited into the rain and crossed the street.

He peered once again up at the painted wooden sign lit by a lamp on each side, and the window's markings. He stood under murky cones of light cast by the overhanging lights of the sign, the rain appearing in the light that tracing the drawing circling the window: a mandolin on the left entwined with red roses that curled around the bottom of the windows and upward on the right side.

Matt went to the window and peered in, then went to the door entrance. He thought he saw a light under a doorway far to the back and away from the showroom. He knocked on the door. No answer. He knocked again. Still no answer.

He was about to knock once more, this time more emphatically but decided against it. Instead Matt walked to the end of the block. He rounded the corner and found a back street that allowed for deliveries and other commerce and walked back behind the stores that fronted the street. Counting the establishments that he had passed, he stopped and looked at the woodworking shop's back windows that were curtained but still visibly lit. He went past a dumpster and some trash cans and peered into the nearest window.

Rain beat on his baseball cap and, by now, had soaked his Marine green raincoat to a deep jade green. Inside he saw a woodworker's workshop, with work benches, saws, miters, vises, and tools on a peg board mounted on one wall. Through a narrow slit in the curtain Matt saw a man with long black hair and beard seated on a stool. The man leaned over a red mandolin and was picking and fingering chords, his hair hanging and shading his face. Matt could only hear the percussion of the rain on the plastic covered dumpster and trash cans and nothing from within.

He went around to the front of the store and rapped once again, more insistently, on the window of the door, hard enough to rattle the frame of the door. He intended to knock so insistently to bring someone to the door.

Matt saw light under the door flicker with foot movement and then the interior door opened. In the doorway in backlit silhouette stood a tall man who was pulling on a coat as he turned out the light, vanishing into complete darkness. The man walked to the front door and stood for a moment there, a collage of the dimmest gray and black shadows in silhouette.

Matt stood back in the rain to allow the figure to open the door in order to see him and not feel threatened by a lone figure at that time of night.

The figure in the shadows opened the door. A small bell attached to its frame gave a tinny clang. He stood in the door frame and said nothing.

Matt stepped forward, trying to see the man more clearly.

"The shop's closed," the man in the shadows said.

He recognized his brother's voice. "My father played a red mandolin," Matt said.

The figure stood silent in the darkness for a moment, then stepped forward into dim light: "So did mine ... brother."

"Nice catch last week, Tommy. You always could play centerfield."

They embraced each other in the doorway, rocking like boxers that had gone twelve long rounds. They could never remember hugging each other that tightly.

TOM HAD NOT HEARD his brother's voice in two years; it sounded familiar yet strange, but more welcome than he had imagined. He had missed his brother.

"You saw me on the field last week? Why didn't you speak to me then?"

"I was in town and having lunch and a few beers with some jarheads. We sat on the hill overlooking those fields when your team won and there was all that celebration. I didn't want to ruin your high. I preferred to meet you alone. I admit I didn't recognize you right off in your mountain man disguise. But I spotted that stride of yours and that signature hotdog way you windmill your throwing arm after you made a catch. Oh yeah, and the number—your number fifteen."

Matt pulled back to examine his beard and long hair. "Damn, you look like shit!"

Tom laughed. "It's not easy living off the grid, man."

"'Joseph Porter' ... that's not you, is it?"

"Yeah, right. What? I became a master woodworker in two years? Joe, the owner of the store, is the master woodworker. I just work for him. Small jobs and help out, pick up supplies, whatever he needs done or when he needs four hands. Learning a bit here and there. He thinks I'm some kind of apprentice. I did learn some things from Dad after all. Don't tell Joe Porter I said this, but I think he sees me as the son he never had. Hey, he lets me live here upstairs in that small apartment. For *nothing*. He wants me to keep an eye on the place and stop anyone from breaking in and stealing his tools and equipment. He even left me a Remington shotgun upstairs. He's one of the more unusual old guys I've ever met, but a good guy really."

"You? Security? Does he know you came from a South Philly crime family? I'm gonna tell him to watch out for *you*, for chrissakes."

"Still the comedian, Matt. What the hell are you doing here in Bremerton? How did you find me? Don't tell me it was just dumb luck—"

"I'd like to say I am in Marine Recon and found you, but that'd be bullshit. Believe it or not, that's what it was: coincidence. Pure chance. A harmonic convergence. New Age synchronicity. It's in the Pacific Northwest air."

"I've been recruiting for the Corps in Seattle for the past two months—inspecting recruiters and evaluating recruiting in this area, stuff like that. Outreach programs to high schools and colleges. I'll be doing that for four more months. It's soft duty really. I lucked out."

Tom wagged his head in disbelief. "Coincidence. What a small fucking world, eh? I should have gone on up to Canada, I guess."

"Glad you didn't. Hey, thanks for that money."

"Oh well, easy come, easy go."

"That kind of money wasn't that easy coming, was it? I always thought you'd tell me if you hit the lottery."

Tom shrugged, not wanting to elaborate on the circumstance that allowed him to strike it rich. Then he realized that his brother might not see the gesture in the shadows.

"No. Well, maybe you'd call it that. It doesn't matter," Tom said finally.

Matt stood there in the dim light, suddenly silent.

"Before I ask you to get some manners and ask me in, I need to tell you something," Matt said. "I'm with Nina ... we got married."

Tom was not sure what Matt expected him to say. Or do. "Yeah, I know."

"How'd you find out? Did someone tell you?"

"Christ, Matt, this is the age of the fucking internet."

"Did you know that she's pregnant? That we're going to have a child?"

"Now that I didn't know. Congratulations! Great news! Hey, that means I'm gonna be an uncle."

"Tom, we're having dinner down the street over at *Mike's Harbor Lights*. Nina's probably wondering where I got to …. Come over and have dinner with us."

Tom hesitated. "I don't think so, Matt."

He could hear Matt exhale long and slowly. "Is it because of Nina?"

"No, Matt. It's not. Really, it's not."

"Why not then? It's been two years—I'd love to see my brother. For a while I was worried. I thought that you'd hung around Philly and ended up compost in Tinicum. I kept reading the papers on the internet looking for the bad news: 'Body Found in Swamp; Suspected Mob Hit'—and it would be you."

"That's why I'm in hiding, brother. Unlike you, I have an acute survival instinct. And besides those mob guys, there's the other thing you know about. You know, the guy at the shore? On the boat?"

Matt stood there for a moment. "I don't think you need to worry about that, bro."

"Oh? Why's that? Did Jersey get a statute of limitations on homicide?"

"Nope. The police got their man. Case closed. Guy confessed to the killing and gave self-defense as his motive."

"What? Who the fuck would do that? Let me understand this: they caught someone who confessed to killing that guy on the boat? That's crazy. Who—or why—would anyone do that?"

Matt shrugged. "Don't know. Why look a gift horse in the mouth and all that? I'd say it's safe to go back to Philly for a visit."

Tom said nothing.

"You remember Sherry? Vince left her his house and some money. She's going to nursing school. Keeps Nina out of trouble. She's still single, man."

"Are any of her family in the mob?"

Matt laughed. "Not that I know of. Nina's never said anything about it."

"Well, that's a plus. You know, I've gotten used to not being around criminal enterprise. Growing up like we did, I think I expected everyone to be a crook or related to someone who was. The rest of the world is not a Martin Scorsese movie."

Matt's reply was a grunt. They stood there, silent, for a long moment.

"I finally knew you were alive when you sent the money to me," he said. "Nina wants to thank you for what you gave her. She spent a lot of it on her Mom's nursing care. She died three months ago. Her mother did see her daughter pregnant though. That was a lot of cash you gave Nina."

"That's why I thought I'd end up dead if I didn't take off for distant places—that money. Someone's out a lot of dough. You know what those guys are like—they'll kill you on principle *and* because you took their dough."

Matt cut him off. "They're not anywhere around here. Come on, join us. Nina would love to see you."

The rain whipped in a sudden gust of wind on to the two of them standing in the doorway.

"Hey, come on in a minute," Tom urged.

"I gotta get back to the wife, man—she'll think I went AWOL."

Matt stepped into the dimly-lit foyer out of the rain and shut the door behind him.

"One minute—," Tom said. He thumped up a stairway and returned in a minute with an envelope. "Here."

Matt took it and in the dimness opened it. "Whoa! That's a chunk of change—"

Tom embraced his brother again, longer than was their custom. "Congratulations. It's a wedding gift."

"That's a real nice gift."

"Fifty grand. You deserve it. Save it for the kid's college. Buy a soccer mom van. Take a vacation to Italy. Do whatever."

Tom paused, then said: "Without you I wouldn't be here. Neither would that money."

"So you figured it out—"

"Took me a while. Who could make that shot except a Marine? And who the fuck would want to save me?"

"We D'Arcangelos are crazy bastards," said Matt. "You almost got yourself killed for that money and now you're giving it away? If the police had showed up and I had gotten caught … Well, I would have lost all I've ever worked for."

"Yeah, I know. Taking the money was insane. Really stupid, in retrospect. I realize you put yourself in great jeopardy for me. Why did you even follow me and get involved?"

"You're my brother, Tom. My younger, damned dumb, crazy fuckin' brother. You know, I wouldn't do it now that I'm married and a father …."

"Matt, go back to Nina. Don't say you saw me. Please. It's better that you guys know nothing about me or what happened when I took off—"

Matt cut Tom off. "A lot of shit hit the fan right after New Year's the year you disappeared. Gang wars like the '30s—but without the machine guns. Remember Vince told us about the '80s? Worse than that time. But the '00s were subtler. Fewer public executions. We lost several guys. Frankie Cannizarro's a fucking quadriplegic. He's like Stephen Hawking but fat and without the brain. Lou Spagnola, Joey Argento, Ray Malzone were all—"

Tom waved his hands to halt him. "I know. I lived in Seattle for six months when I first got out here and read about it at the public library."

"Russians, the Irish, the Italians all fighting it out for the better part of a year—it was like a fucking war," Matt continued. "The Asians even got into it. Lots of guys went missing. Philly was like South America. A few innocent people were killed as bystanders. The Feds got involved. They came down hard on everyone."

"It seems to have died down now," Tom said. "I haven't picked up anything on it for the past year or so. Is it over?"

"There's a truce, I'm told. Who knows? They might be going underground for a while. The less I know about it, the happier I am. I'm done with all that shit now. I have a career in the Marines and a wife and kid on the way. When I retire from the Corps, I'm not going to live in Philly. Jersey either. There are other cities. You know, maybe I'll become a cop in some small, peaceful New England town. I've always liked New England. Great hunting and fishing. But hey, I'll always be an Eagles, Phils and Flyers fan."

"Did you ever see or hear about Carla?" Tom asked. "Know how she's doing?"

Matt looked at him, silent for a long moment. "Yeah, yeah. I did hear roundabout from a friend of her sister. She met a guy, they've been going together ... I heard they're engaged. He's a lawyer for the city. An assistant D.A. or something."

Tom was silent for a moment. "That's pretty much what I thought ... She knows what she wants."

"It's best to move on down the line, man. Forget about the one that got away."

"Right, Bro. I know." Tom embraced his brother again. "Look, Matt. Take care of yourself. Know what I mean? Don't volunteer for more combat in Afghanistan or wherever the fuck they want to make safe for democracy. You've done your time. Let someone else do theirs."

"It's not that simple, Tom. Marines follow orders," Matt said. "When are we going to see you again?"

Tom shrugged and said, "Not for a while yet."

"You're going to be an uncle. Don't you want to see your niece?"

"I'll be back when she's starts playing softball ... or for her first dance recital. You know where I am. If I leave, I'll tell you where I'm going. But please, Matt, don't tell anyone back there or Nina. You didn't see me. No one back there. Okay? Those guys have real long memories—even out here, I find myself looking over my shoulder at times. It's not a way to live."

"Promise you'll sneak back? That you'll stay in touch?"

Tom nodded. "Yeah, sure. I promise."

He followed his brother from the front door, and, under the dim lights of the woodworker's sign, they turned to face each other and embrace a final time, saying nothing. Then Tom stepped back inside into its shadows. He flicked off the lights of the shop, then returned to the door to watch his brother disappearing down the rain-glazed street.

11

N THE FOLLOWING WEEKS and months Tom often thought
about going home to see Matt and Nina and his new niece.
Five months later he learned Matt didn't tell him that he
would be heading overseas on his next six month deployment.

Before leaving for Afghanistan Matt wrote a letter that was typical
of him:

> *Yo, stunad! I thought you'd said you'd stay in touch! I
> haven't gotten one word since we met in Washington. For
> all I know you might not even be there—gone off to Tibet
> or Patagonia.*
>
> *Why don't you come to Philly for a visit? See your niece
> and Nina. Things are clear around here. I think you'll be
> safe if you stay away from the usual places. Hell, I think
> you'd be safe anyhow. The Feds have the place strapped
> down, or so the papers say. It's not as if you testified in
> front of a grand jury and fingered anyone. (In fact, I'm not
> really sure what you're dodging. But that's another thing.)
> Besides, with your mountain man look no one here will
> recognize you.*
>
> *How do I know if you're still there? (See the first
> paragraph of this letter.) Write me and/or call Nina.
> Francesca's adorable and already showing how smart she's
> going to be. She already looks like Nina, and has her*

brains, thank God. Once she hits puberty I'll have to guard
her with a baseball bat.

Our home phone number is still the same we grew up
with.

-Matt

P.S. Francesca's going to need an uncle to teach her
how to play the outfield. And spoil her. *Come home.*

Tom noticed Matt had underlined his last sentence. He did not yet
realize that those were to be his brother's last words to him.

D'ARCANGELO PARKED JOE PORTER'S TRUCK around the back of
the shop after delivering a table and set of chairs to Mercer Island. He
entered the back door where Joe was once again sanding a cabinet. Joe
became aware he had returned and switched the sander off.

Tom took his gloves off, jammed them in his coat pockets and stood
there watching Joe as he rubbed his hands together. The last few days
had seen the arrival of a chilling gray winter in the Pacific Northwest.

Joe pulled his protective goggles down around his neck. "No
troubles with the delivery, I presume?"

Tom shook his head. "None whatever. Why? Did you expect some?"

"Only with their payment. I've grown wary of my fellow man since
I've started my own business—been stiffed so often," Porter said. "At
times I think I want to strike up a deal with the local mob enforcer for
some debt collection."

Tom laughed at the remark. Joe didn't realize to whom he was
talking.

"Not sure you want to get too involved with those guys," Tom
offered. "Small claims court might be the better way to go. But first,
let's try trusting our fellow man ... at least for a few weeks. Besides, I
wouldn't bet on this couple *not* paying up."

"Yeah, they sure look well off. Did you see the inside of that house?"

"Oh yeah. Real nice crib. Husband's a civil engineer or something—
builds skyscrapers around the world. I think they pay their bills."

Joe Porter pointed to a desk on the far wall.

"Say, Tom, the mail's on the table. Do me a favor and sort out the junk from the important things, would you? Hate doin' that shit," Joe said, then added: "Oh, yeah. Two guys came here to see you while you were out—about an hour ago. I told 'em you'd be back in an hour and a half."

Tom removed his peacoat and hung it up.

"Must be Johnny," he said offhand. "We're going out on a double date tonight. Dinner and a movie ... the usual stuff, I suppose."

John Lomanno, the first baseman on the softball team, had introduced his sister to Tom. Cecilia and he had gone out several times over the past months. Lomanno had a great sense of humor, an enormously handsome smile and a squad of women drooling over him. His teammates hung around him to get his rejected ladies. Lomanno was a muscular six-foot four, who trained in Gracie jiu-jitsu in his spare time. His teammates were reluctant to date his sister. Tom had always been reluctant to date anyone related to a friend or relative. Those arrangements often didn't work and friendships were ruined. When Lomanno said he wanted to introduce him to his sister, Tom told him what he thought about arranged dates.

"C'mon, Tommy. Everyone I know is afraid to date my sister. You've seen Cecilia. She's good-looking, she's smart. She told me she thinks you're interesting—says she thinks you're 'mysterious'. So there's some chemistry there. Just ask her out and see how it goes," John said. "Don't worry, buddy. I don't butt into my sister's life."

Lomanno thought for a moment. "Well, that's not completely true. Some fool she was dating smacked her once. I broke his arm. Knocked him out." Then Lomanno smiled, before his face turned to stone. He made two large fists and flexed enormous forearms, his knuckles cracking. "So if you hurt her, I will seriously fuck you up."

"That's certainly reassuring, John."

Lomanno grinned at the expression on Tom's face.

"It goes without saying I won't hit her," Tom said. "But you have to promise not to break my arm if it doesn't work out—if the mystery wears off. Okay?"

Cecilia and Tom had gone out several times and were beginning to feel comfortable around each other. John was right. His sister was kind, street savvy and book smart. She was also a great cook, who loved Italian food—always a plus for a South Philly Boy from the Boot. Cecilia had a great love of animals, with a cat named Fred and a huge Rottweiler named Patton she rescued. Tom felt it was time to move to the next step, from dating to a relationship. Just the previous week they talked about taking a week to go camping along the Olympic Peninsula or the Oregon coast.

If we can camp together on vacation, Tom reasoned, *we might have something going.*

Joe Porter looked up from his work. "John, the guy from your softball team? No. Don't think it was him. These guys were in uniform. Marines."

"Marines? Huh! That has to be my brother. He must be back on leave from his deployment. I'll introduce Matt to you, Joe."

Porter shook his head. "Don't think it was him, Tom."

"Did one look like a *paisano*? Italian. Dark, about six-one, muscles?"

"Nope. One was pretty fair. I think he had red hair and freckles, light-skinned. The other guy was black—African-American or whatever we're calling Negroes these days."

Joe slipped the goggles on and went back to sanding.

Tom went to the desk, sat in the large desk chair, and began sifting through the stack of mail, dropping the junk mail into the trash can, and piling up bills and mail that seemed worth a future look. When done, he took a letter opener from a mason jar that held pencils and pens, sliced the envelopes open, and began reading the mail. The doorbell rang and he stepped from the workshop to the showroom.

Two Marines were standing at the door.

Tom unlocked it. "Yeah? Can I help you?"

"Are you Matt D'Arcangelo's brother?"

"Yeah, Matt's my brother."

"May we come in?" the red-haired Marine asked.

Tom stood blocking the entry. "What's this about?"

The black soldier removed his garrison cap, reached forward and held out his hand to shake Tom's. "We're friends of Matt. We deployed with him a few times."

In the backroom workshop Joe Porter's sander whirred away, stopping intermittently for the old woodworker to blow away sawdust. When the sanding paused, the music from a local radio station could be heard filling in the sudden stillness.

The red-haired guy removed his hat and held out his hand as well.

"I'm Frank Skillman, this is Ty Randle," he said. "Could we come in and talk?"

"Uh, sure. Sorry. C'mon in," Tom said. He opened the door in invitation; they entered, and Tom shook the hands they had extended outside. Once inside the Marines stood nervously fingering their caps.

They looked at each other. Skillman took a folded envelope from his pocket and handed it to Tom. "Matt asked me to give this to you."

Tom took the envelope and saw his name was typed on the front. He started to open it.

"Wait," Randle interrupted. "We need to talk to you before you open that. It will explain some things, I guess. Don't open it just yet. Okay?"

The two looked at one another again to see who would speak first. Skillman finally turned to Tom.

"Your brother was killed a week ago in Afghanistan. Yesterday your family in Philadelphia was supposed to be officially notified."

"This is not an official Marine Corps death notification," Randle interjected. "We're probably breaking some Marine regulation somewhere, but it's been twenty-four hours since we believe his wife was notified. As his friends, Matt made us promise that we'd contact you immediately if …."

Skillman continued. "He told me you're estranged from the family and that you might not find out for some time. He knew we were still going to be stationed in Seattle for the next year. Matt made us swear never to tell anyone you were here in Washington."

"The Corps should have notified Matt's wife yesterday, to inform her about arrangements for his funeral and other things for the family,"

Randle said. "We wanted to alert you in case you wanted to contact them about the funeral. Needless to say, we're terribly sorry for your loss."

Tom's mind spun in a sudden cyclone of disbelief, of denial.

"Matt? Dead?"

Tears came to his eyes. "It's impossible to believe—"

The two Marines said nothing for several moments. Then both moved forward to surround him with an arm.

Then Randle said, "It's hard for us to believe, too. He was a great guy. A great soldier. Skills here and I are sure going to miss him."

Tom stood dazed, unable to say anything. Skillman looked at Randle, then turned to Tom. "Look, we're gonna leave you alone for a bit. Are you okay? If you want, we'll stay."

Tom shook his head. He wiped tears from his cheek. "Sure, sure. No, I'm okay. Thanks for bringing me this note and the news. I appreciate your coming."

Skillman took a card from his overcoat pocket. "Here's our phone number in Seattle at the station. My cell number is on the back. Call us, if you want to talk. If you have any questions. We'll come out again and see you if you'd like. Okay?"

Tom wiped his eyes. He stood there for a long moment. "Yeah, sure. Okay. I might do that ... after the dust settles."

Skillman reached out to shake Tom's hand. "Matt was a great guy. We're sorry for his wife's loss and yours. Both of us will miss him."

Randle took Tom's hand, cradling with both of his, and shook it. "Really sorry for your loss."

Tom let them out the front door watching them through tear-filled eyes as the two Marines disappeared down the street. He locked the door and reversed the 'open' sign in the window.

In the dim light he opened the envelope and read:

> *Tommy,*
> *I'm scheduled for a tour to Afghanistan for six months.*
> *If I'm unlucky, my time is up, or whatever, and I should*
> *come home in a body bag, you'll need to come to Philly or*

at least call Nina to straighten my will and our finances out. I left my half of the house to her and Francesca. You'll have to work all that out with Nina. I listened to what you said. She doesn't know where you are. I did tell two buddies, which technically doesn't violate my word to you not to tell Nina or anyone in Philly that you are (were?) in Washington.

Come home, Bro. You'll be safe. Semper Fi!
-Matt

It was scrawled in Matt's Catholic school cursive. Tom re-read the note again and again and again, savoring his voice and his signature. He folded it and placed it in his pocket and returned through the curtain to the workshop.

Joe stopped sanding and looked over at him, once again removing the protective glasses. Tom stood there, staring, his eyes glazed.

"You okay?" the old man asked. "Everything all right?"

Tom hesitated a few moments and steadied himself before answering. He didn't want to burst out in child-like sobbing.

"No, Joe. I'm far from okay. My brother was killed last week ... in Afghanistan."

"Oh, Jesus." Joe was silent for a long moment. "There's nothing I can say ...."

Tom turned to him, tears vanishing into his beard.

"That's right, Joe. There's nothing to say. Just *don't* tell me he was a hero or warrior, fighting for America, the flag, our freedom, or any of that crap. Most of all, don't tell me he's in a better place. Okay? None of that shit will make me feel better ... or his death any more or less meaningful. Matt was my only brother. I'll never see him again. What's far worse is that neither will his wife and child."

Porter laid the sander down and pulled off his gloves.

"Tom, take some time off. The week, a month, whatever you need to straighten things out. I'm sorry—for him and for you and his family. You might want to take some time to go home. I can lend you some cash for airfare if you need it."

Tom was about to thank his boss for the offer when the telephone in the shop rang. He held up his hand. "Let me get this, Joe."

Porter put down the sander and got up from his stool. "I'm gonna quit for the day. I'm done here. Take the call in the other room while I clean up a bit."

D'Arcangelo stepped into the showroom to get the phone. As he suspected it was Nina.

She paused for him to say something. "Tom, have you heard about your brother?"

"Yeah." He paused a long moment. "Two Marines came by here and told me. It was unofficial. They were friends."

Nina charged right ahead. "Your brother stipulated in his will that, if he were to be killed in service, he wanted to be buried at Arlington National Cemetery. I'd rather that he be buried nearby, but those are Matt's wishes and I intend to honor them. I'll be going to the burial ceremony."

"Nina—," Tom began, then stopped, unable to say anything.

"I'm not sure you're able to come back for his funeral. You do as you see fit. I'm not going to say anything as ridiculous as 'Matt would've wanted you to be there'. Tommy, I will not fault you if you don't come; I understand if you choose not be there. I sincerely mean that. I will need to talk or somehow get in touch with you in the future about your house, your family's belongings, things like that."

D'Arcangelo stood there, still, silent.

"I—," he began, but could find nothing to say. He wiped the beginning of tears.

"Yeah, I know how you feel. Look, I'll talk to you later," Nina said. "Call me when you can talk. When this all sinks in. You know that you're welcome to come here at any time."

Tom was silent. Nina continued.

"When Sherry was going through your uncle Vince's things, she found a letter he wrote confessing to killing that guy on the boat. He told her she should send it to the police if he didn't make it out of the hospital. She said Vince told her that he had a dream he'd never make it out of the hospital. He said he had a premonition or something. A priest came to see him when he was in the ICU. Vince gave Sherry the will and told her to put in his safe at home. To open it only if he didn't make it. She thought he was just being overly dramatic. He was on some medication that was pretty strong.

"After Vince died, she opened the will. With it was this added letter, explaining how Vince had killed someone on the boat in self-defense after that guy killed the dentist."

"She called the police and told them about the letter. They came to get it and spoke to her about it. Sometime later they called her to say they were closing the case."

TOM PUT DOWN the phone. Tom nodded, thanked Joe Porter and went outside onto the streets of the small Pacific Northwest city he had lived in for now nearly three years. He walked down its main street under a steel-like sky to the waterfront. It began to rain, a steady but light, cold drizzle. He stood there looking out over the lights of the harbor and the sound and the old gray warship that rested there now as a museum.

The day's light had faded and the temperature was dropping.

He headed back to the shop to call Nina, still not certain what to say to her. As he walked up from the harbor, passing the local library closed for the day, he saw its electronic message board. Its screen intermittently flashed its hours of service and future programs for the community, interspersed by quotations from literary figures.

He stopped to read what next appeared, a quotation from Flannery O'Connor:

> "Where you come from is gone, where you thought you were going to was never there, and where you are is no good unless you can get away from it. Where is there a place for you to be? No place... Nothing outside you can give you any place... In yourself right now is all the place you've got."

After a few moments the quotation dissolved into the library's offerings for the next month.

"Well, that's something to ponder." Tom smiled. "I wonder what that says about the idea of Family?"

He started up the street to the woodshop, thinking about what to say to Nina. He would tell her he would not be coming back for his brother's funeral.

The light drizzle had now begun to freeze. Tom D'Arcangelo looked into the pewter sky and felt the first flakes of icy snow on his cheeks. But this evening's snowfall brought him no memories of his father.

Tonight, the ghost of the old man failed to appear.

[K. W. Garson, Philadelphia 2017]

Printed in the United States
By Bookmasters